# Enchanted Fate

# Enchanted Fate

## THE FATES ALIGN DUOLOGY
### BOOK TWO

## ALYSSA ROSE

ALYSSA ROSE BOOKS

# Also by Alyssa Rose

**The Fates Align Duology:**
Binding Fate (Book 1)

**<u>Coming Soon (Spring/Summer 2025)</u>**
**DarkFlower Jungle Saga (serialized novellas):**
Lost and Lonely
Dark and Defiant
Found and Fated

# Content Warnings

This book has a death scene, some violence but it is not glorified, overcoming personal hardships, and some low to mild romance (fade-to-black scene).

First Edition November 2024

Cover Design: Artscandare Book Cover Design

Developmental Editing: Devon Atwood

Line Edits: Nikki Landerkin

Proofread: Roxana Coumans

ISBN (paperback) 979-8-9893613-3-5

ISBN (hardcover) 979-8-9893613-4-2

❀ Created with Vellum

*To all those who love reading magical tales of adventures that keep you flipping the pages, by a dim light, under a cozy blanket.*

# Contents

# CHAPTER 1

## A Cry for Help

With brows furrowed, Alzerion's muscular arms and legs pumped hard as he descended the last little hill, this side of the Dark-Flower Jungle. If he stopped, they might catch up to him. Those hooded sorcerers followed like a tail he couldn't shake. They muttered phrases he didn't recognize, and he swiped a hand at the sweat on his face as he kept running. He kept that pace and kept fighting against every ache that coursed through his body. Even his lungs yearned for a reprieve, but Alzerion didn't slow down as he angled his head to see behind. Only the tops of their hoods could be seen.

"Celeritas," he said between audible gasps.

Alzerion felt his legs advance harder than before as he ducked under a low-hanging branch. Once more, he turned and a faint smirk crept across his face and scanned the space ahead. *Any place to stop?* There was no way he could keep at that quickened pace for long. Alzerion's eyes whizzed around until he rested on a flimsy hideout just visible over the most beautiful flowers. He made his way to the shelter and attempted to catch his breath.

"Close," he muttered through large gasps of breath.

Each time his lungs filled, he felt them scream as they inflated with air, and he hurriedly bent over to help control his breathing. Once he felt his heartbeat slow to its usual hum, he glanced around. He saw only two windows, *probably for safety,* he reasoned. Each window was positioned at opposite sides of the shabby enclosure, one overlooking the east, and the other on the west side. He just came from the east, so he looked out to see if they continued after him. Nobody was there. At *least he was in the clear, for now. Maybe they tired of following him.*

He squinted. The sky grew darker. Out the west side window, the sun descended, which gave the sky this mix of a golden reddish-orange mixed with shades of light gray.

After he gained his composure, Alzerion walked out of the shelter and strolled to get a better understanding of the area. He felt sure that he wasn't in immediate danger. There was no discerning the magic of those sorcerers. As he walked, he came to a small clearing among all the trees, shrubs, and mosses. He closed his eyes, his hand clung to the top of his shirt, and he pulled a bit. Each smell brought with it delightful aromas, and he smiled. The sweet scents ensnared his senses. *Whatever it was, it was quite nice.*

Eyes closed as he breathed in the sweet-scented air, he felt the muscles of his face relax. Serenity wash all over him, like he was bathing in a sea of calm. Only deafening silence surrounded him. He opened his eyes, and all he could see were the pretty flowers. They had some sort of pull, like he was being called toward them, and there were so many colors that covered the expanse. The closest to him were the whitest flowers that kind of reminded him of liquid cream.

Next to them were these unusually shaped periwinkle flowers that drooped. The mixture of the two enchanted him. He knelt down near the flowers, and there was this low, quick sound. It was faint—but enough that Alzerion pulled his hand back and shook his head. He stood, feeling a bit dazed, but then he heard the sound again.

"What was that noise?" he muttered as he came reeling back out of what felt like a dream.

Now alert, he circled around, checking all around, until he heard it again. *It sounded like a faint whisper, but from where?* This time he froze. It sounded like Aironell.

"What is this?" he muttered aloud. "Hello?"

No answer. *Did he really think that somebody would reply? Had he finally lost his mind?* Alzerion shook his head as he decided he should leave and find his way back to the portal to Bachusa.

As he trod back to the portal in the jungle, he had full control over his thoughts. His mind no longer clouded, Alzerion surmised that the clearing must have been cursed or something. It was getting late and soon it would be night, and he definitely did not want to be stuck here until dawn. He was being as careful as he could, but then he heard a branch crack, and he spun around. He couldn't see anything, but that didn't mean that he was alone. Alzerion smelled the delicious scent again, but this time, another odor mingled.

Alzerion's nose wrinkled as his mouth pulled into a frown. *What was that smell?*

He crouched low to the ground as he crept forward, trying to see beyond the patch of jungle ahead of him, when he heard the voice again. His entire face scrunched as he continued.

The voice grew louder, and it said, "Alzerion, stop!"

He stopped and his eyebrows rose as he was sure his skin paled. The voice sounded like *hers. Aironell. How could that be?*

"Alzerion, turn around."

He moved in slow motion. *Why was her voice telling him to stay? Was this some sort of trick?*

He crouched once more, face close to another one of those flowers. The scent bathed the air before him as the slightly familiar voice whispered once more.

"Al-zer-i-on."

His eyes pinched as he focused in on the flowers. The voice came from *them. What kind of magic was this?* Alzerion felt this pressure in his chest—the same feeling he got right before those strangers chased him. Alzerion rose, and then he sprinted in the opposite direction. *He wanted to be far from those flowers.* He craned his neck around and then, as he brought his gaze back, he felt a hard whack and everything went black.

*Was it seconds, minutes, or days?* Alzerion thought as he finally came through. He peered around and saw a small fire crackling, but he didn't see anyone.

"Ah, ouch," Alzerion winced as he placed his hand on his head.

3

"Sorry about that. I have been told I wield a stiff blow with the butt of my sword."

Alzerion squinted to see who was speaking to him. *Were they friend or foe? They did not kill him yet, but that didn't mean they still couldn't.* Their sounds were distorted as he rubbed at his head.

He was calculating the best escape plan when the man came closer, and Alzerion felt a rush of relief.

"Quairken? Is that you?" Alzerion rubbed at his eyes until his vision cleared.

"It is, Your Majesty. You gave us all such a scare."

"How did you know where to find me?"

"Alzerion," Quairken sat down next to him, "you were never good at hiding. I had a feeling you would come here to the DarkFlower Jungle."

"How?" he asked.

"I know you," Quairken chuckled while handing Alzerion a vial.

Alzerion grabbed it and drank his fill. "I didn't know water could taste so delicious."

"I imagine not, when you were traveling with no provisions."

Alzerion could see the disapproving look on Quairken's face and replied, "I promise I had them. I just did not realize I would get bombarded with strange beings and foliage...that have their own agendas."

"Alzerion, you should have taken some soldiers, or at least have had me come along."

"Quairken, I thought I could handle it. Plus, if some trouble found me, I didn't want that weighing over me if you got hurt. Isabella would skin me alive!" His eyes bulged, and he gulped.

Quairken laughed heartily and said, "I suppose she would."

"I swear I didn't mean anything by it. I just, well I..."

"Needed to find some answers?"

Alzerion noticed Quairken didn't waver on his question. Quairken's head tilted toward him and his gaze fixed right on him. Much like a bug on display.

"Well, did you?"

"Quairken, I'm not sure what I found, other than trouble." Then he gently tapped the bump on his head.

Quairken chuckled and shrugged, "Sorry about that. I didn't realize it was you until after I knocked you out cold, and I didn't want to take chances if it was something less than friendly."

Alzerion's head lowered as he took in Quairken's words.

"Alzerion, I view you as my friend and not just my king, so please don't take this the wrong way. Stop looking for trouble. You have plenty to keep you busy in Bachusa. Things have changed and you can't just leave with no warning, especially when you have guards and trained soldiers that could go on these missions for you."

Alzerion stood up. "Can we just head to the portal to Bachusa? Quairken, I know you're right. But everyone can't expect me to change who I am. You know I love a good search and—"

"And you love being in control." Quairken folded his arms as his eyebrow rose.

"That too," Alzerion's voice lowered, his face still.

Quairken cleared his throat, "Let's find that portal, shall we?"

*Good*, Alzerion thought, *anything to change the subject.* He nodded.

There was nothing but silence for a few minutes as Quairken extinguished the fire and they started toward the portal.

"Quairken," Alzerion said, breaking the silence.

"Yes."

"Did you have to hit me over the head so hard?" he asked, while rubbing at the lump again.

"Sorry," Quairken laughed as he patted Alzerion on the back. "I thought you could've been a foe. I was well trained." Quairken winked at Alzerion.

"Flattery will get you nowhere," Alzerion smirked and he shook his head.

Alzerion felt at ease as they continued, and then finally, they reached the back of the portal. He placed the portal perfectly, hidden but not impossible to find...two weathered-looking boulders and there the doorway was, tucked away. Alzerion took a breath and reached forward.

It was silent for a moment, and then a sharp *click*. It resounded,

5

almost like an echo, until it displayed this colorful space between those two enormous boulders. Without warning, the ground trembled as the trees nearby moved. Initially, Alzerion could only see the branches swaying back and forth as the trembling continued. Alzerion braced himself to steady his feet on the ground.

He hollered as the wind picked up. "Quairken, don't fall!"

"Easier said than done!"

At that moment, Alzerion saw Quairken bend his knees, but a branch knocked him over and he fell backwards.

Alzerion took slow steps toward a stationary tree branch, grabbed it with one hand, and shouted, "Firma!"

Alzerion glanced down as the ground liquified and hardened around his feet. He tried to take a step but felt anchored. Satisfied, he peered through the howling wind to see where Quairken flew.

"Quairken? Can you hear me?" Alzerion bellowed.

His eyes darted left and right—ferociously looking for Quairken, until he heard his voice.

"Here."

Alzerion's gaze fixed on the words and he saw the wind thrust Quairken against the trunk of a taller stationary tree.

He took his free hand, pointed it at Quairken and said, "Amplio Visio."

Within seconds, Alzerion could see much sharper, like his eyes were a magnifying lens. *No blood, excellent, whew. How to get him back here?* Alzerion released the tree he was holding, which caused him to sway a bit. He just focused on Quairken and thought hard about what he needed. As he held out his hands, he closed his eyes. He felt the force of the wind shift. He kept focusing on the rush of the wind, the force of the magic, and his unyielding will. Then the wind was no longer rushing against his back, but it was blaring him straight in the face. Alzerion opened his eyes and channeled his gaze to see that it was working. The wind pushed against Quairken's back.

"Quairken, let go!"

"Are you insane? This is pummeling my back. I can't let go! I don't know what will happen if I do!"

"You must let go. I won't let anything happen to you! You can trust me, always!"

Quairken did as instructed. The force of the wind flung him straight toward Alzerion, who grabbed Quairken's arm before he flew past him. Alzerion held on to him as his other hand waved about in a circle, and then the wind slowed to nothing more than a slight breeze.

"What the hell was that?" Quairken asked as the ground fell still.

"Not sure," Alzerion admitted as he did a spell to move his feet once more. "But we need to move quickly."

"Why? You stopped that craziness."

"Not really," he explained as he strode back toward the two large boulders. "Quairken, stay close to me," he instructed as he looked back. "We don't have the luxury of taking a break."

Quairken glanced around at the stillness and asked, "What's the hurry?"

Alzerion rubbed at the back of his neck and continued, "Look, we just don't want to stick around. The calm, it won't last long. We have to move before it starts again. I couldn't get rid of the forces of nature. The best I could do was slow it down...whatever caused it is not gone. Whatever strange magic is at work here is *not* on our side."

Quairken nodded his head and walked beside Alzerion as they came back to the boulders.

"They look changed," Quairken pointed out as his brows furrowed.

Alzerion saw what he meant. He stepped forward a bit to touch the boulder closest to him. The two boulders stood before him, undamaged. Except now there were trees that twisted around them. The trees resembled that of pretzel twists. Alzerion just stared in wonder. *How did the trees contort like that? These feel like the tree's roots.* He walked around the whole of the boulders and saw that the trees didn't just twist, but their roots came above ground and somehow wove around the boulders.

"Alzerion, come here. See this? Something is happening."

Alzerion raced back around the other side and saw Quairken's mouth gaped open. So, he ran toward Quairken, who pointed in front of them. Alzerion quickly turned around and saw that the space between the two boulders had changed. This time there were no trembling grounds or high-speed winds, but the space looked like a shiny prism reflecting all the colors. The shifting colors sped up, and Alzerion just kept staring with brows furrowed down.

"Alzerion, is it starting again?" Quairken asked.

Alzerion glanced at him and said, "No, this is different. I can feel it."

Quairken slowly moved his hand and grabbed at the sword attached to his waist belt, but Alzerion placed his hand over Quairken's and shook his head. Quairken released his grip and then Alzerion moved closer to the reddish color. Finally, the kaleidoscope of reds stopped shifting and all Alzerion could see was a shimmering hue of cinnamon red. Alzerion motioned for Quairken to follow and the two walked toward the center of the light.

Within seconds, Alzerion could feel a lightness inside of his very soul and then with a flash of light he was standing in Gorgeous Garden by the water fountain.

"Well, we are home, safe," Quairken exclaimed. "Thank the Gods for that."

"The understatement of a lifetime, my friend," Alzerion said between a couple of slow breaths.

Quairken faced Alzerion and grinned as they gripped each other's forearms and nodded.

"A job well done, Quairken. Thank you for coming after me."

"Don't mention it." Quairken gave a playful jab at Alzerion's arm as they started past the fountain.

"You are sometimes too modest for praises, my friend."

"I'm not being modest here. *Really* don't mention the details; especially to Isabella."

Alzerion smirked, "Agreed. I don't want to get on her bad side."

Quairken nodded and continued, "Anyway, I know there is a palace of people waiting to see you."

Alzerion and Quairken kept strolling through the front of the garden when he stopped, with the grand entrance within sight.

"Wait," Alzerion demanded. "Quairken, I'm not ready yet."

"What's wrong?" Quairken asked as he looked back at Alzerion.

"Quairken, there was something I wanted to tell you. It didn't seem like a suitable moment with us almost getting killed by the wind and trees."

Quairken's eyes narrowed on Alzerion, "What is it?"

"I kept hearing this recurring voice."

"Voices? When we were back in the DarkFlower Jungle? Alzerion, are you sure you weren't just dehydrated or hearing things?"

"No. I'm serious. Quairken, it was a voice I heard before. It is the voice that I mentioned to you once before, but nobody else can hear it."

Alzerion saw Quairken frown, so he continued. "I swear I'm not making it up. It sounds just like Aironell's voice."

"Alzerion-"

"Don't dismiss this Quairken," Alzerion said, tone raised.

Quairken's hands rubbed at his mouth and then replied, "Well, what do you think it means?"

"I'm not sure. I know she's dead. A fact that I'm aware of, but still her voice keeps calling to me. The strange thing, though—."

"Oh? There's something even more weird than hearing voices?"

Alzerion gave him a sharp stare and then continued. "Quairken, I tried to find the source and I swear it was coming from the flowers."

Quairken's eyebrows furrowed.

"I swear that's what it sounded like, but I don't know. I've never heard of magical flowers acting like a beacon for sound."

"I think you should tell Fransisco and Evalyn. Alzerion, they would want—"

"No," Alzerion boomed. "That is why I wanted us to speak out here. I don't want to worry or alarm them and we don't know definitely what it could mean. It could be a nasty trick for all we know. I'll have to see if I can find anything in the ancient books."

Quairken bent his head, nodded and asked, "What do you think it means?"

"I think it's a cry for help. Unless I'm being played for a fool." Alzerion said as he strode up the marble stairs and into the palace.

Quairken followed behind Alzerion. It was silent as they headed into the hall and passed by the many paintings of the royal family as they continued toward the Great Hall. When Quairken opened the big amethyst doors, Alzerion could feel the joy just spill out. Alzerion's mind was a jumbled mess. *Could it be Aironell?* He smiled widely as he entered. *Look the part*, he told himself. It had been years since her sacrifice. The agony he felt came rushing back, but he didn't feel that same way now. A thought that pained him. Alzerion believed he would be sad forever, but his duties gave him something else to focus on.

Alzerion heard the bang of the door close as he looked out at the crowd before him. He heard footsteps from behind, and he knew Quairken entered. He kept his expression pleasant for them. At any rate, now he had a clue, something to go on. He may not grieve any longer, but he vowed he would find the answers and bring her back if he could; and that was exactly what he would do.

## CHAPTER 2
### An Answer in the Wind

Within a few short moments, Melinda and Evalyn were on him. "Alzerion."

He was no musician, but he swore their voices rose an octave. Melinda on his left and Evalyn on his right as their embrace tightened around him. A tight squeeze. He gasped.

"Evalyn. Melinda. Let him breathe." Francisco boomed as he stood in the center of the Great Hall. "We don't want to break him now that he is home."

Evalyn beamed at Alzerion, but then took a step back and smoothed down the bottom of her deep purple gown.

"We're just so glad to see you're alright," Melinda replied after letting go of Alzerion.

"I'm so sorry I worried you all. I was searching for something."

"Alzerion, next time you get the urge to search for something, please take some soldiers or guards with you," Francisco's gaze honed in on him, like a skilled blade smith about to strike.

"I understand."

Francisco still had that sharp, kingly tone. Alzerion strode toward Francisco. His hand didn't wobble as he grasped Francisco's hand in a firm grip.

"I hope you listen for once."

Alzerion's teeth dug into the soft flesh of his cheeks. He turned around to see who gave the stern words of caution. He bit down harder —Isabella. She had this knack for putting him in his place.

He swallowed.

Things changed between them after Aironell passed. Then, after the birth of her daughter, she wasn't shy in her opinions, especially where Quairken was concerned. However, these things couldn't be helped. Her husband's value was great—what with him being like an advisor and his right hand with the Royal Army. Alzerion's gaze fixed on the sour expression on her face. Next to her stood a little girl with the largest brown eyes and the widest grin.

"Daddy, you're back!" The little girl ran up to Quairken. Her squeal brought a broad smile to his face.

Alzerion couldn't help but stare. Quairken picked her up mid-jump and hugged her while he spun her around.

"Daddy missed you Audrina, my little lovebug," Quairken beamed.

Isabella withdrew her sharp gaze as she rounded on her husband.

She stood between the two of them. First, she pointed at Quairken. Better than him, he thought, but then she brought her frustrations back to him. Of course.

"How could you be so careless, so thoughtless, and so reckless?" Her arms flailed.

"Isabella, I'm sorry," Alzerion slid a foot back, "but I didn't take Quairken with me! He—"

"He came after you! I know that, but if you didn't leave in the first place, then he wouldn't have had to," she continued without stopping for air.

Her face was red as she spoke with such ferocity. Making her worry was not his goal. He had his reasons for going—just not any he could share or explain to her at the moment.

"All I can say is I'm sorry," he admitted as the corners of his lips curled downward.

"I know I worried you all, but honestly, I was only gone for a day," he spoke as his hands stretched in front of him, palms up.

"A day?" Isabella clenched her hands together.

He looked around to see the others nod or make a gesture to agree with Isabella.

"Uncle Alzerion," Audrina's little voice broke the heaviness. She ran to him as her arms wrapped around his leg.

Alzerion knelt down, embraced her, and replied, "My, how you've grown. I swear you look like a little lady."

A sweet little giggle escaped as her face scrunched up. Alzerion knelt down to her level.

"Thank you."

He squeezed her for one more hug. His hands ran through her head of hair, and as he pulled back, her little face did not look like that little baby that he remembered. Alzerion felt like it was yesterday when Quairken asked him to be his child's godfather. He blinked and then rose. Time was cruel. Almost four years had a way of creeping on them.

"Alzerion, you were gone longer than that," Melinda said.

Alzerion scooped Audrina up and held her in his arms.

"That's not possible." His eyebrow rose.

"It's true," Francisco replied.

Alzerion sauntered to Isabella and put Audrina in her arms. "I'm terribly sorry. I didn't realize that time moves differently over there in DarkFlower Jungle." Alzerion's mouth pulled tight.

Quairken patted him on the back, "Why don't you go clean up? I'm sure there are other things you should check on."

Alzerion bit his lower lip, but then he nodded as he turned and left.

Quairken watched as Alzerion closed the door behind him. Chatter echoed around him. He faced the rest of the group. His eyes lingered on them.

"I'm sorry. What did I miss?"

"Quairken, should we be concerned?" Evalyn sat in the seat to the right of the throne.

"No, of course not." His gaze lingered only as he saw Isabella and

Audrina move closer to him. He wrapped his arms around them as he stared back at Evalyn.

Francisco sat in the seat to the left of the King's seat and then added, "Did he say anything to you? Maybe why he went off on his own to that place?"

"He told me he was looking for answers." Quairken's gaze fixed on Francisco.

He had to keep things a secret. Alzerion confided in him, and he couldn't betray that. He felt this pressure in the back of his throat. He swallowed.

"That's it?" Melinda's foot tapped as her eyes bore into his.

It was like she was searching for some sign or inconsistency in him. No, he wouldn't give them that.

"I'm sorry, but he didn't say more," Quairken tensed as he didn't break contact.

Isabella cleared her throat. Quairken glanced at her, and her eyes narrowed as she looked at him. He felt the lump in his throat as he swallowed.

"Well, I guess we don't have to guess what that means," Isabella said. She gazed at Francisco and Evalyn. "We all know what he was probably looking for, don't we?"

"Not necessarily," Evalyn responded, "it has been four years since Aironell's death. Isabella, there's no way that Alzerion is still looking for answers to that."

Isabella put Audrina down and shrugged her shoulders and said, "Maybe, but we all know that nothing rivals Alzerion's determination to duty."

Isabella grabbed Audrina's hand, and she led her out of the Great Hall.

"Could she be right?" asked Francisco.

"Maybe...I-I'm not sure," Quairken's voice wavered. He coughed into his hand and then continued. "I guess we will have to find out when he's ready."

Evalyn's face had this vacant look. Her eyes resembled that of someone deep in thought.

"Sir," Quairken turned back to Francisco, "I think we should all remember that Alzerion puts duty above all."

"What does that have to do with this?" Francisco said.

Quairken said nothing as he took a quick breath. "Didn't he promise you and Evalyn that he would find out what became of Aironell?"

Quairken glanced at both of them and then started toward the door. "I'm going to head to my bedroom chambers and help settle Audrina into bed."

Francisco nodded his head and Quairken left. Quairken plodded down the hall and stepped past the kitchen until he reached the back staircase up to the servants' quarters. He reached his little suite and entered the room. Isabella was braiding Audrina's long, thick hair.

"Did I miss all the fun?" Quairken winked.

"If by fun you mean her hair being done, then yes, you did. She is also in her nightgown, too," Isabella said as she placed the small tie around the last braid.

"Come, give daddy a hug and kiss little lovebug," he hunched over, arms opened wide.

Audrina scooted off the bench and ran to him. The bottom of her braid bobbed on her shoulder. A tight squeeze and a kiss on her head.

"Night lovebug," Quairken called after her as Isabella then escorted her to the bedroom right off of their own room.

A few minutes after, Isabella came back and sat next to Quairken on the bed.

She said nothing. There was no need. Her face told him plenty as her eyes glared at him.

"What?" his voice rose.

Her eyes relaxed, only a bit—less cold and more of just a chill. Isabella leaned over and placed a kiss on his cheek. "I'm glad you're home and you are safe."

"Me too," he smiled. "Thankfully, it was easy to find Alzerion."

"Thankfully," Isabella's tone sounded edgy.

"Why do I feel like I'm on trial here?" He poked his nails into the calloused bits of skin around the tops of his palms.

"Quairken, you're not on trial; at least not if you are being honest with me."

"What makes you think I'm not?" Quairken swallowed.

"Did Alzerion really tell you nothing of that adventure he took?"

Quairken could feel the lump in his throat rise as he said, "What do you mean?"

"You know exactly what I mean," Isabella demanded as she stood up facing him, "I always know when you are not being truthful. I don't know why you are keeping secrets."

"Isabella, I can't tell you what you want to know. I will say that yes, Alzerion may have told me something. He doesn't want it to be public knowledge, not yet. He doesn't want to upset anyone."

His lips pressed together as he grimaced. "Isabella, it pains me to keep things from you, but just this once...I must."

She caressed his cheek and said, "I trust you know what you are doing."

"Thank you," His lips curled into a small smile. "We both know he cared for Aironell—more than he cared for anything. I will say that he does still grieve, but I'm not sure to what extent."

Isabella kissed Quairken's head and replied, "I can't blame him. I miss her too, but I have accepted what happened."

"Me too, but I don't think he has."

Quairken undressed for bed, pulling on a long beige nightshirt. He jumped into bed as Isabella laid next to him. He cradled his arms around her as he felt sleep creep upon him.

Meanwhile, Alzerion sat in his room poring over books. He sat at his desk in a loose fitted nightshirt and brown slacks while looking through The Ancienne Magica de Bachusae volumes. Each night since he first heard the faint whisper calling out to him, he leafed through the pages of the books. It must be here somewhere. He could have sworn there was a spell for it.

"Yes!" Alzerion exclaimed.

"The Whispered Ones," he read. "The spellcaster can communicate even if they are not there in body. It gives the impression of faint low musings, as if carried on the wings of the wind."

This must be a spell that Aironell used, but how? He could see the usefulness of it, but the spell wouldn't keep her alive. How could he still be hearing voices now, even after all this time?

Alzerion touched the page and muttered under his breath, "Tabio."

Within seconds, it engraved the page with deep red markings, as Alzerion continued to flip through the pages. He was going through them slower, so he could read each description. He needed to be sure that he missed nothing. Alzerion reached the end of the book and slammed the back cover shut.

"Dammit!" His fingers pressed into the wood as he forced himself up and paced around.

As he turned, he saw the picture that sat on his dresser. Him and Aironell. Seeing it didn't bring him to the brink, not like it did before. The pressure of his canines dug into his bottom lip. *I will find you, Aironell*—for your parents and for the kingdom. With his goal set, he focused on some sort of plan. He strolled toward the window and gazed out—back against the wooden beam. His search didn't make him foolish. He was still the best tracker in all of Bachusa. It was a bit more of a pride thing, and he knew it.

Alzerion was past the grieving stage and spent the last few years boosting the kingdom's morale as he worked to leave his own mark. He took a breath as he pushed back the memories of the past. *Never again.* His eyes narrowed. He vowed to find her. Her sacrifice was his fault and in that moment; he made another vow to himself. *Never again would I let someone else get that close to me.*

"Alzerion...Alzerion."

He froze. Face turned back. His eyes pinched in as he looked around for the source.

Alzerion's gaze rested on the book. He went back to the desk and looked at the book once more. He tilted his body forward as he touched the book.

"That's it. Don't give up."

"Aironell, is that you or a trick?"

"Yes."

"Yes, to which?" he spun around. He didn't know where the voice came.

Aware that he probably looked foolish talking to himself.

"It doesn't matter. Do you remember the last thing I asked you?"

"Do I trust you?" he replied.

"Well, do you?"

"I always have, but I don't see what that has to do with anything."

"Trust in the plan. Fate knows what it is doing."

"What plan?"

"It starts with the book."

Then the Ancienne Magica de Bachusae Volume I flung back open to the middle.

Alzerion darted toward the book. His eyebrow rose, "I don't understand."

"Look closer."

Alzerion grazed the pages, but nothing. Then he tilted his head to survey the book.

"What is that?" He asked as he slid his fingers down the slight opening in the spine.

He pulled out the world's tiniest vial and opened it up. With each flip, the scrap of paper revealed a much larger piece of paper. It was some sort of message.

*Dear Alzerion,*

*If you are reading this, I promise I didn't make an impulsive move. I have a plan. I used the ancient magic combined with the world's strongest desire; Love. If I am not home and safely in your arms within a month of my sacrifice, then please invite Jezzabell to the palace. She can help you navigate my safe return. Look at the book of ancient spells in*

*the rare section of the library. I left my mark on the page.*
*You'll know it when you see it.*
    *Love,*
    *Aironell*


Alzerion's mouth hung open. He read the paper again and again. His mouth twisted as it curved into a smirk. There we go—a clue.

# CHAPTER 3
## Royal Meeting

E valyn mulled over the sausage link until she stabbed it with the fork.

"Francisco, I'm still unsure that Alzerion is fine." Evalyn pursed her lips before taking a bite of her food.

"I have to say that I agree," Melinda leaned into the table. "He seems like something is haunting him."

Evalyn stared across the dark oak table, waiting. She knew it may take him a few moments, as he just took a bite out of a chocolate chip scone. The table was brimming with the most scrumptious treats, with such a delicious smell.

"I think he's overwhelmed. He lost his first love and started Crown duties," Francisco reminded as he wiped the crumbs from his mouth. "Evalyn, surely you haven't forgotten how much work it is to run the kingdom?"

"Of course not," her left eyebrow raised. "I don't like what you are implying."

"I'm just saying that you two need to give him some space," Francisco warned, as he placed his napkin on the table and stood up.

"Please promise you will let him be," Francisco headed for the door.

"Of course," Evalyn replied as Francisco left the room.

Evalyn walked to the door and poked her head out.

"What are you doing?"

"Making sure he wasn't dawdling," Evalyn said in hushed tones, then she quickly strolled back to the table and sat by Melinda.

"Why?" Melinda raised an eyebrow.

"I have an idea," Evalyn beamed, "We should throw a ball for Alzerion."

"We should plan for it and tell him about it last minute." Melinda clapped her hands together. "I know my son, and I don't think he will want the party, but I think it could be a nice way to distract him."

Evalyn nodded.

"Where should we start?" asked Melinda.

"Let's speak with Isabella. She knows how to cook and will get a menu organized."

"Alzerion. Alzerion."

The words rang loud in his ears. He rubbed his eyes and looked around.

"Well, it took you long enough. I was worried you'd never wake up."

Alzerion's vision was still a bit blurred from sleep, but he saw the shape of Francisco sitting across from him.

"How did I get here?" Alzerion asked as he was trying to remember the events leading up to him falling asleep.

"That's a wonderful question. I left breakfast and came here. I found you slumped over these old books."

Alzerion followed Francisco's finger to the mess of books that laid around him.

"I must have come here last night and fell asleep."

"I figured as much. That's not what I meant, Alzerion. What reason would you have to come here...and so late?"

"Nothing really. I was just looking for something to help me sleep."

Francisco's eyebrows furrowed as he rubbed his chin, and his eyes narrowed at Alzerion.

"Honest," Alzerion said, "I had so much pent-up energy last night. It must have been the adrenaline from the journey to the DarkFlower Jungle. I just couldn't sleep." He shook his head as his chin lowered.

Francisco reached forward and grabbed one book, looked at the cover, and then locked eyes with Alzerion.

"So, you mean to tell me you find The Ancienne Magica de Bachusae Volume II, as light reading for bed?"

"Well, I figured the old-style language, coupled with the fact that it is more or less a magical history book, would do the trick."

"Alzerion, please find better methods to fall asleep," he chastised as he stood up. "I believe we have had this conversation once before, when you were younger."

His eyebrows raised. Alzerion locked eyes with him.

"I'm sorry," Alzerion stacked the books.

"I hope you're not in any sort of trouble. Your mother and Evalyn are worried about you."

Alzerion smirked, "They always are."

"Yes, well, sometimes they get carried away. I am here if you ever need to talk or if something is going on."

"I know you are. I just like to figure out my thoughts on my own. Let me clean up my mess here. Then I will get ready for the day, and then I'll meet you in the Great Hall."

"That sounds reasonable. Don't take too long. We have that Kingdom Assessment this morning."

"Crap. I forgot. Alright, I'll be right there. Please get them seated and have the tea and treats until I arrive."

Francisco bowed his head and left the library. Alzerion grabbed the book Francisco had picked up and said, "Transportare."

Then, in a puff of red smoke, The Ancienne Magica de Bachusae Volume II disappeared. Alzerion grabbed the stack of books and put them away. He pushed in the mahogany chair and hurried out of the library. He took the back way to his room. When he entered his room, he quickly undressed and put on black tight slacks. Then he pulled on a white loose-fitted undershirt and placed a long black tunic that had gold trim that ran down the arms and down the middle of the tunic. He then grabbed the long gold necklace from the chest of royal jewels. The necklace had the crest of the Royal family; the fleur-de-lis in a crown.

It still didn't seem real. Alzerion thought as he placed the King's golden crown on his head.

He glanced in the mirror while he tied up his knee-length boots.

He remembered the day of his coronation. Alzerion adjusted the crown as he twisted one strand of his hair around the auburn and ruby jewels.

He took one more glance at his appearance in the mirror, looked at the book that he had conjured up here, waved his hand and said, "Indiscernible."

He smiled as the book was out of sight. Alzerion walked down the corridor and down the Grand Staircase, waved his hand, and the doors of the Great Hall opened. He plastered on the biggest grin he could as he approached the large meeting table that was set up in the middle of the room. He could see people seated on both sides.

"Your majesty," came the deep voices of the Nobles. He watched as they stood and bowed their heads. He knew they wouldn't sit again until he did as that was the custom.

Alzerion walked to his seat and a young maid pulled out the chair for him, and as he sat, she pushed in the chair. Then everyone else sat, too.

"Your Majesty," Francisco's voice boomed, "I was just telling them about how grateful we are to have their continued support."

Alzerion nodded, looked about the table and said, "That is absolutely true. We cannot express our gratitude enough."

"I know I speak for the House of Sorcery when I say that I'm pleased to hear that, Your Majesty."

"Thank you, Phoebus," Alzerion said with a smile. "It means a lot to have the help of the great Houses of Sorcery."

"Your Majesty, we will continue the support, but some of us are wondering how we should boost morale?" This voice was filled with charm as he spoke.

"That is an excellent question, Adrastus, but based on what I am hearing, we should be fine."

"It is not our morale that I was alluding to," Adrastus replied with his deep, amiable voice, "but the morale of all of Bachusa. Even your lesser subjects."

Alzerion didn't flinch. Adrastus was a first-rate prick, but he couldn't let his feelings show. Adrastus' words always felt like a subtle dig or threat, even when he was being as pleasant as could be. Alzerion's eyebrows furrowed and cocked his head to the side. He didn't trust him, but he needed him. He swallowed...his family was one of the oldest and strongest in the House of Sorcerers.

"King Alzerion, Adrastus is not wrong," Phoebus frowned. "We may have your back, but we are just one faction in Bachusa."

"There are plenty others, sire." Alzerion spoke to the oldest of the group.

"Adonicus?" He glanced at each of his higher ranked nobles. "Does that mean I have angered the people? Why would morale be down?"

A silence that spoke volumes—Alzerion looked back at everyone once again. He lingered on Phoebus, who brought this to his attention. There was something about Phoebus Ponticus, an honorable quality. Then he glanced over at Adrastus, whose lip had a smirk of arrogance. He felt a heat deep beneath his skin. Adrastus Acidinus was the complete opposite of Phoebus. Alzerion leaned back in his chair as his arms folded across his chest. Still nothing. Adonicus was the oldest there, and he was more of a yes man. He held tight to old traditions, and often just agreed with what the group decided as long as it didn't pull Bachusa away from its core values.

He could take the silence no longer, "Phoebus?"

Alzerion locked eyes with Phoebus, but still nothing.

Adrastus' brown eyes brightened.

"Since you brought this up, what do you have in mind, Phoebus?" Alzerion shifted in his chair. He relaxed his left elbow on the table as he positioned his left hand under his chin.

"Yes, what ideas do you have?" Adrastus' voice was cold, but maybe only he caught that tone. Alzerion caught his sneer out of the corner of his eye. Nobody else seemed to notice.

"Well," Phoebus gulped, "I think it should be some sort of gathering. Something a bit more fun, almost like a party of sorts."

"Like a ball?" asked Evalyn.

Alzerion turned his attention to her. She sat quietly until now. His eyes narrowed, unsure what she was getting up to.

"I doubt that's what he meant," Alzerion said. His tone was crisp at the thought of being forced to endure any party; especially when he had more pressing things on his mind.

"Actually, a ball would not be a terrible idea, Your Majesty," Phoebus bent his head low.

"That's an excellent idea, Phoebus." Adrastus straightened up. "Why not invite the entire kingdom and maybe even give it some kind of theme?"

Alzerion sat as he tapped his fingers on his chin. He weighed it in his mind, but by the looks of those gathered around, he knew they outnumbered him. Evalyn had the biggest smile on her face. It was nice to see her so eager about something. He couldn't shake the feeling that there was more to it, though. And why did Adrastus want this?

"If we have this...ball," the words stuck in his throat, "then who is going to plan it all?"

"Why don't I do that for you?" Evalyn clapped and then folded her hands on the table.

Alzerion held back a chuckle as he pressed his bottom teeth into his top lip.

"It will be fun and a way for the townspeople to feel the hospitality of the Royal Family."

"Why would you want the hassle of planning such an event? I know it's for the town, but you would take on such a tremendous amount of work."

"I will enlist the support of Isabella and Melinda. I'm sure they would love to help. It will be quite the affair!"

Alzerion scowled, but there was no use talking her out of it.

"Evalyn, that is a splendid idea," Adrastus grinned. "Also, why not make it a masquerade? Everyone can dress up and wear a mask, so as not to feel overwhelmed by all the pomp and circumstance." His hands flourished as he spoke. "It could be a fine way to skirt that line, you know, so nobody feels less welcome."

Finally, Alzerion spoke. "I think... yes... it could be a positive thing. I know we have had no balls or festivities since my coronation. Therefore, if you all think this is the best way to boost the morale and confidence by all means, let's do it."

Francisco's gaze narrowed on him. Alzerion didn't let that bother him right now. He saw him out of the corner of his eyes. Francisco scanned Alzerion's features, but he let nothing escape. He knew nobody would detect his true intentions.

"In fact, let's expand the guest list." Alzerion stood with arms pressed firmly on the table.

"Expand to more than just Bachusa?" Evalyn perked up her eyebrow.

"Who would you have in mind?" Adrastus sat with back so straight that a coin could roll down. His piercing brown eyes revealed nothing.

"I would like to invite the neighboring kingdom of Lyricao." Alzerion had a gleam in his cinnamon-red eyes. He surveyed the table to assess their reactions. He noticed the quick exchange of glances from Francisco and Evalyn. The others gave little away, other than low chatter, furrowed brows, and the occasional jaw open.

"Lyricao?" asked Francisco. "I don't mean to question you, but that seems like an odd choice."

"Um, why? I... um... don't understand," Evalyn grimaced.

"I thought it would be hospitable. It may even give us more allies, and I just want to be friendly." Alzerion smiled as he spoke.

"Well, I think it is a splendid idea," Adrastus said heartily. "It couldn't hurt. It's always nice to meet with even the eccentric."

"Then please make all the preparations," Alzerion declared as he ignored the last comment. "Evalyn, have someone dispatch a letter to the kingdom of Lyricao."

Evalyn bit her lip but nodded.

Alzerion smirked. Whether she wanted to or not, she had to obey his command. At least he would get what he wanted out of this damned charade.

"If that is all, why don't we end this gathering? We all have much to attend to. Please inform your individual houses about the upcoming ball. I need all the Houses of Sorcery to make this happen for the entire kingdom."

Adrastus, Phoebus, and Adonicus nodded in agreement. More mild chatter, but Alzerion gave his closing remarks, and then the noble families left.

# CHAPTER 4
## Ancienne Magica de Bachusae

**D**rip. Drop. Plop. That was all Alzerion could hear beating in his mind. He sat alone, finally, in his room. He wanted nothing more than to thumb through The Ancienne Magica de Bachusae Volume II. However, every time he had a moment to himself, someone would interrupt with some sort of pressing matter. Finally, there were no catastrophes and no royal emissaries to entertain.

He should be able to focus, but he couldn't. He could not stop the damn rain. Again, all he could think about was the drip, drop, plop - hitting against the stones of the castle. His eyes peeked above the top of the book and out the window. The drops hit almost rhythmically and then rolled down the walls and then sploshed into a puddle. He watched as they rippled out. That was how he felt. A ripple. Like his life had been a series of ripples that started with the princess saving him those years back. He tapped his hands on his head and then, and zoned in on the page in front of him, knowing he had to find something.

He was looking for the mark. She said it was her mark, but he wasn't sure what kind of mark she would have left. He was quick to check the spine of this book, but there was no secret compartment holding a note. Of course, he thought, that would be just too easy. As he flipped through the old crinkled pages that smelled of dust; he felt something different from one page. At the bottom right, he felt something smooth. Alzerion bent so low that his nose could touch the page if he were any closer. He felt it, but he couldn't see anything. He blinked, twice. Now was not the time for his eyes to play tricks on him. It appeared to be just like any other page.

He pointed his thumb and index finger toward the page and said, "Amplio Visio." He could see the sharpness of the colors and textures around him, but the page still looked just as it always looked. This time, Alzerion closed his hand tight as he caressed the spot with his fingers. He cleared his mind, and then a spell flooded the recesses of his consciousness. As if he should have known it all along, in seconds, Alzerion moved his fingers to his lips. He pressed a kiss to his fingertips, placed them on the bottom right corner, and said the incantation, "Rosa discerna."

What if it still didn't work? Maybe he should just give up? No, he had to keep trying. Alright. This time, Alzerion slowly opened his right eye and gasped. His left eye quickly opened to see the etching of what looked like a beautiful rose in full bloom. Someone delicately layered each petal around another petal. This time, when he felt that part of the page, he could feel each section, like a puzzle waiting for him to solve it.

"Well, who would've thought," Alzerion chuckled. A rose. Of course, that would be her mark. A mark of the love they shared, and all they had been through. He took a deep breath, steadying his nerves. Then, he scanned the page he had before him. He knew this page must be important. There was Aironell's mark, after all. It didn't seem all that spectacular. It appeared to be an ordinary spell for magically encasing others.

Keep looking, came the mysterious airy sounding voice.

He shook his head but then flipped through a few more pages until he felt another smoothness at the bottom of a page titled "Magic Mishaps". Again, Alzerion pressed his fingertips and muttered the same small incantation. It rewarded him with another etching of a rose in full bloom. He surveyed the page, using his finger to trace the words line by line.

Alzerion came to a small passage about spells that could overpower even the most talented of sorcerers. Interesting. There wasn't much stated except that a powerful sorcerer could take precautions by charming their body ahead of time to protect against permanent maladies like death. Alzerion's face flushed at what that might mean. He closed the book, opened his bottom desk drawer, and placed the book there. He waved his hand and pulled on the knob, but the drawer wouldn't budge. With a smirk, he walked away and out of the room.

In his mind, he was forming a thousand questions to ask Jezzabell. She would know about these strange occurrences. She could guide him in the proper direction. It was she who fated them, who knew more than any about ancient magic. He could feel it in his very core. Jezzabell was the answer to his many questions. He just had to wait until that ridiculous masquerade ball. He smirked. At least he was getting what he wanted out of it.

# CHAPTER 5
## The Letter

Alzerion watched as the maids busied themselves with an extra special round of tidying up. Today was the ball. He greeted everyone that he came in contact with as he stood in the middle of the Great Hall with a strong posture. Feet planted and spread apart, he watched the many maids dusting and servants bustling about. He couldn't believe how transformed the room looked to enhance the dark appearance.

The little light in the room mostly emanated from the silver wall sconces. Each lit candle flickered against the stones of the walls, with a light that could settle the most restless spirit. In the corners stood candle stands with fleur-de-lis that patterned the length of the metal stands, and a fat candle sat atop each of them. The lighting created a quaint ambiance in the Great Hall. It was really coming together. The banquet tables lined up against three of the walls—covered in glittery white tablecloths that draped so low they almost touched the ground. The fourth wall had the musicians setting up their instruments for the night's festivities. Elegant from top down, nothing matched its splendor.

As Alzerion scanned the room, he saw Isabella, followed by lesser maids, bring in marble platters filled with masks. These, he knew, were for any guest that didn't come with their own. They had similar themes, but he immediately glimpsed that some covered only half a face, some

31

covered only the top part of a face, and others covered the entire face. Glitter, sequins, feathers, and other tiny baubles covered the masks. They would highlight each person who entered the masked ball.

Alzerion kept moving about, taking in the sights, when he felt a tug at his pant leg. He turned to see little Audrina grinning up at him. He knelt down and gave her a hug, "What are you doing here?"

"I saw the ladies with the pretty masks. I wanted to see them."

"Ah, let me help with that," Alzerion scooped her up in his thick arms and stood up.

He carried her to the table by the entrance that housed the platters of masks. Audrina's big round eyes swelled, if that was even possible. They looked like perfect globes. Alzerion smiled as the muscles of his face tightened. Audrina had a sharp intake of breath as her syrup brown eyes scanned each mask. Tiny shoulders dropped as she reached forward toward the masks. Alzerion moved his hands around her as she almost leaped out of his arms, like he was juggling.

He rubbed her back, hoping it would calm her energies. "What do you like most about them?"

"The most?" Her mouth turned down as her eyes shifted up.

Her little finger rested against her chin. It was hard not to laugh at the sight, like she was weighing some life-or-death question.

"They are so shiny," Her hands held out as she shrugged.

"Is she keeping you busy, Alzerion?"

He spun around to see Quairken dressed in a loose charcoal gray shirt and black fitted slacks.

"Never," he chuckled. "Audrina and I are spending some quality time together. Isn't that right?"

She nodded. "Daddy, look at the sparkly masks."

Quairken reached to grab the emerald green sparkled mask and placed it on the bridge of her nose. Then he wrapped the ties around her ears to adjust the fit for her. They both watched as she beamed from ear to ear. She turned to Alzerion and then her father, and did this a few times. Alzerion put her down, and she skipped toward Isabella. Alzerion just shook his head.

"She's something," Quairken laughed.

"She's perfect, Quairken. Promise you'll never forget that," Alzerion's voice was light yet solemn.

Quairken nodded and placed a hand on Alzerion's shoulder. "Thank you for saying so; I count my blessings daily and thank my lucky stars that I have her and Isabella."

"I can only imagine," Alzerion faced Quairken. "You have a beautiful little family."

"Hehem. Well, I came to see if you needed me to do anything. For the masked ball or anything else?"

Alzerion combed his right hand through his hair as he looked around the room. "It looks like the servants have it all covered."

"Well, do you need anything? You seem distant, if you don't mind my saying so?"

Alzerion's expression shifted. "How do you mean?" Alzerion motioned for Quairken to come forward as Alzerion took a leisurely stroll. "Let's sit," Alzerion commanded as he pulled out a wooden chair that had a black sash draped along the back.

Quairken sat. "Alzerion, I didn't upset you, did I?"

"Of course not," Alzerion snapped his fingers, trying to attract the attention of a maid. "I have many thoughts occupying my mind, that's all."

Alzerion peered around as his eyes caught a peculiar-looking girl. The girl came over and bowed. She had almond-shaped eyes that looked like the color of fresh snow. Alzerion watched as she grabbed the edge of her black dress with one hand while clasping a silver tray toward her chest with the other. With her head hung low, she then curtsied but lost her footing.

Alzerion moved swiftly. With one hand, he grabbed the tray before it could clamber to the ground, and then he scooped his left arm around her waist. He could see an odd mark that glittered when the chandelier light hit it just so.

"Are you alright?" Alzerion asked as he slowly steadied her on her feet.

Her cheeks flushed as she took a step back. "I-I, um, I am so sorry, Your Majesty. I should have been more careful."

Alzerion bent his head to catch her gaze, but she kept looking away. "It's fine. There was no harm done," Alzerion's lips parted to smirk. With hand outstretched toward her, he continued, "What is your name? We haven't yet met, and I feel at a loss."

"I'm Calistra," she said in hushed tones as she stretched her arm out.

Alzerion grabbed her hand to shake it. As he slowly shook her hand, he spied the mark as her sleeve slid up a little. There were lines that looked engraved into her skin as they swirled. Her sleeve covered most of it, and he saw nothing like it.

"Is that permanent?"

Calistra looked at her hand and pulled it back. "What do you mean, Your Majesty?" she gulped.

Quairken craned his head low as his eyes honed in on her arm. Alzerion watched as his face pinched.

"Calistra, I'm sorry if I am making you uncomfortable. It's just that I have never seen such beautiful ink work as that." Calistra flipped her right hand over and tucked it underneath her left hand.

"I should get back to work. Again, I'm sorry for the little mishap." She bowed and then was off.

"What was that about?" Quairken turned to Alzerion.

Alzerion's narrowed gaze shifted back to Quairken when Calistra was out of view. "I'm not sure. I swear she had a unique tattoo of sorts on her hand. Did you see it?"

Quairken picked at the little bits of stubble on his chin. "I'm not sure what I saw. I saw some sort of lines, but that was it. Alzerion, er, Your Majesty," he corrected.

Alzerion tilted his head to the side, but then scanned the room. He realized that there were more people bustling about. Ah, that must be why he was using such a formal way of speaking to him. The wonderful aroma of food wafted over and filled his nostrils as the servants plated it on the long banquet tables.

Alzerion stepped toward Quairken and whispered, "Can we go outside? I wanted to discuss something, but I don't care to be overheard."

Quairken's eyes shifted back and forth and then he nodded. Alzerion led the way out of the Great Hall and through a side door that exited out to the right side of Gorgeous Garden.

"Let's talk here." Alzerion positioned himself on the horseshoe shaped wooden bench that overlooked the circular reflecting pool. It was a small pool of minty greenish blue water that filled the inside of a silver basin. Quairken stood, arms crossed, with his back propped against the silver basin.

"Alzerion, what is it? I know better than to assume anything."

Alzerion snickered at that. Yes, Quairken knew better. The last time proved quite hilarious when Quairken misread a situation and they ended up in the thick of a brawl between complete strangers.

Alzerion shook his head and bit his bottom lip. "Honestly, Quairken, my old friend, I'm unsure where to begin."

"The beginning is always best," Quairken grinned as he scratched the collar of his neck.

"There's someone I absolutely must speak with at this ball tonight."

"That doesn't seem too hard of a task. I'm sure everyone will want to speak with the King of Bachusa."

"Quairken, that's just it," Alzerion stood and strode closer to him. He waved for him to lean in, "I need help with finding the time to have a private conversation."

Quairken swallowed and shifted inward. "Alzerion, who is it you want to speak with? I mean, maybe I can do it for you, and—"

"No. No, I must be the one to speak to her."

He watched as Quairken's eyebrows furrowed.

"It isn't anything bad."

"Well, I stand by my question. Who do you want to speak with and why must it be secret?"

Alzerion whispered so low and so close to Quairken that he was sure his ear would tickle from the heat of his breath, "It's Jezzabell."

Quairken paled, and he stumbled back a step. Alzerion countered by walking to the other side of the pool basin.

"Quairken?"

"I just can't believe it. You know that they all think you're up to something, right? Isabella even asked if I knew what it was."

Alzerion's lips parted, casually. He stretched his arms out and placed his hands on the silver basin, "Why are they concerned?"

"I mean, we all worry."

"Quairken, there's no need to worry," he fixed his eyes down on the pool of water.

He made out his reflection in the minty blue water. Speaking with Jezzabell would be interesting. To get some proper answers to his many, many questions. His reflection—the years of stress. It all took a toll. Plop. The ripples emanated outward in the water that caused him to pull his thoughts back. Alzerion looked up at Quairken who stood with hands on hips.

"Alzerion, what do you mean by meeting with Jezzabell? I mean, well, is that why you wanted to invite the Kingdom of Lyricao?"

Alzerion's cheeks puffed out as he took a breath. Quairken stood still. His gaze was strong.

"I have my reasons."

"Come on Alzerion. You don't need to be so cryptic, not with me."

Alzerion placed a hand on Quairken's shoulder. "You are the only person in all of Bachusa that I can trust with this information."

Quairken's face flushed, "What is it, um, I mean, er, what is that you need?"

The slightest wave bounced in his stomach. Alzerion walked back to that wooden horseshoe shaped bench and sat down. As he sat, he pushed away one branch of leaves from the weeping willow that cascaded around the bench. He quickly puzzled together how to continue.

"Quairken, please come here. I'll tell you my plan, but please, I beg you not to share it with the others."

This time, Quairken picked his head up and stared at Alzerion. His eyes softened as he strode toward the bench and sat down.

Alzerion motioned for him to come closer. "I just really don't want us to be overheard."

Quairken nodded. He slid his large body closer until he was within mere inches from Alzerion. Good, Alzerion thought.

"Thank you, Quairken. I promise I'm not up to anything dangerous. I've been hearing these voices."

"I remember you mentioning that to me before. So, I guess it wasn't just a by-product of the stress from coming back from the DarkFlower Jungle."

"No. It appears not. I swear it feels like it calls out to me. I can feel it deep in my core. My sense of duty piqued by the torch it lit. It's a puzzle to solve ... I can sense it, Quairken. It wants something from me."

"Any ideas what?" Quairken's boot tapped against the ground.

Alzerion let a small, nervous smile part from his lips, and then he nodded, "I have been searching for clues about Aironell's disappearance."

Quairken's face tightened as he sighed deeply, "I thought that was what this has been about."

"I made a promise, Quairken. I intend to keep it."

"Alzerion, nobody expects you to succeed. Evalyn. Francisco, and the rest of us ...well, we grieved. Alzerion, I feel like this voice you hear is playing games."

Alzerion felt a heat over his face. He was not a fool. He knew there could be this chance that it was all some joke.

Alzerion bit the inside of his cheek. "It's more than just a mysterious voice. I found some proof. It may be thin, but we need to see Jezzabell."

Alzerion could see Quairken's eyes narrow, so he continued, "I'm not entirely sure what I need from her. I know she was the originator of the prophecy about Aironell. So, maybe, just maybe, she has some information to share."

Quairken shook his head slowly as he looked down.

Alzerion turned his head about and surveyed the area. He could see one servant tending to the rose bushes, but that was near the grand staircase. To the right, he saw some burly men carrying boxes and packages, but they, too, were not close enough to hear.

He leaned in once more and slid his left hand into his front pants pocket. Alzerion tapped Quairken's shoulder as he pulled out a piece of paper that was twirled about to look like a little scroll. He held it up to show Quairken.

"What's that?" Quairken took the tiny paper scroll and unfolded it.

His eyes roamed over the page. Once done, his eyes were so large. Alzerion fought back a chuckle, as this was not a laughing matter, but couldn't help it. He swore Quairken looked like a wide-eyed owl staring at the paper.

"I can't believe it! How did you find this? When did you find it? Is it really from Aironell?"

"I'm sure you know her handwriting better than I. I believe it to be hers."

Quairken scrutinized the writing. He rubbed his hands over the words again and again. "I agree. It is her style."

"I found it hidden in the spine of a book. As you can see, it clearly states that I need to find Jezzabell."

"Yes, but this was written years ago, probably when—"

"It's still a clue. I am refusing to be defeated. Jezzabell must know something."

Quairken sighed, "You're not still, you know, in love with her, are you?"

Quairken's gaze was strong. Alzerion opened his mouth to speak, but then closed it. He felt a tightness rise in his chest. He hadn't allowed himself to think about that.

"Quairken, you know I don't do that. Not since that day."

"So this is all about duty?" Quairken's mouth pinched in as he held onto the scrap of paper.

Alzerion shifted in his seat and said, "The best I can say is, well, you know I always put duty first."

Quairken placed a hand on Alzerion's arm and patted. A reassuring curl of his mouth. "Alzerion, take it for what it's worth, but there is more than duty. Duty is great, don't get me wrong. But, well, you've been—"

"I appreciate it, Quairken, but I'm fine. I am focused and busy," Alzerion's right hand gestured around. "There are plenty of things to do around here. Besides, what you're talking about, well, it was all too much for me. I can't—no, won't make those mistakes again," he said.

Alzerion saw Quairken's head draw back, eyes wide. Quairken's hand was unsteady as he held out the message. Alzerion folded the paper and put it back in his pockets as Quairken stood up.

"Alzerion," Quairken's voice was low, "wouldn't Jezzabell have told at least Evalyn if she knew something about Aironell?"

Alzerion pressed his eyelids closed. He let the beautiful scent of the flowers fill his nostrils. He opened up his eyes and stared at Quairken.

"I'm not sure. Whatever our theories or the reasons, I must speak with Jezzabell."

Quairken nodded. He followed Alzerion as they paced back toward the palace. "I will do whatever you need."

"Excellent!" Alzerion beamed.

Alzerion chattered about what they would do. Quairken's words rang in his mind, but he couldn't allow himself to think about it. Once they got toward the door, Alzerion went silent. Quairken glanced at the palace and went in. Nothing would stop him, not even Quairken's doubts. Alzerion knew Quairken would take care of what he needed. Their silence was like a silent agreement ... a pact shared between two friends. With that, Alzerion left to ready himself for the festivities.

## CHAPTER 6
# *The Unmasked Masquerade*

Alzerion tugged at the hem of his long black fitted shirt. Even longer in the back, as it billowed like a shirt and cloak in one. He kept reaching back to pull at the bottom. This must be what it was like for a cat trying to catch its tail. He angled his body to see behind him. He picked off a tiny piece of fuzz with his jeweled fingers. Then, he picked up a coarse comb and rubbed the teeth against the fibers of his fitted shirt. Alzerion checked himself in the tall chestnut mirror to be sure he was in good condition.

"Checking yourself out, eh? I wouldn't have taken you to be vain."

Grinning, Alzerion tilted his head toward the door. "Mother, you know better than that."

Alzerion tugged at the opening of the shirt as he took a quick breath.

"Of course," Melinda said, "I couldn't help myself. Are you alright?"

"I'm fine," he answered as he smoothed out the red feathers that embroidered the front of his top.

Her gaze lowered as her eyebrows rose.

"Okay, well, maybe a little nervous."

"Honesty, at last," she chuckled.

Then she stepped closer, grabbed the comb and brushed it against the red damask embroidery that outlined the back of his cloak shirt. He felt the bristled threading through the material. She worked the comb down to his lower back.

"Thank you, mother."

"Not a problem," she said cheerily as she placed the comb down. "Now turn and look at me."

He felt like a little boy as he turned and did as he was told.

She scanned him from top to bottom then nodded. "Now, why are you nervous?"

Alzerion took both his hands and ran them through his disheveled hair. He turned back to stare into the mirror as he placed the gold crown on his head.

"That came out lovely. Who added the red feathers and the wrapped vines around the crown?"

"Oh that was Audrina. She really wanted to help me prepare, so I thought that was something easy for her to do."

"Well, she did a marvelous job. Where is your mask?"

"It's on my desk," he motioned to the right.

She grabbed the mask and handed it to him. "You must explain this red feathered look you are sporting."

"Well, I was going for something powerful and mysterious," he smirked. "It resembles a Phoenix rising from the flames of fate." He held the mask, only for a moment, and then he placed it on his face and pulled the band behind his head.

"I'll pretend that I don't understand the hidden message there, Alzerion," she said as she pulled him away from the mirror.

He felt the hardness of her stare, like she was searching for something. "I want you to have fun tonight. Please promise that you will allow yourself to do that."

"Mother. I will. I will dance and be merry, I promise, but know I will have to mingle and fulfill my kingly duties, too."

"I can live with that," Melinda stated as she sat down on the chair beside his bed. "You are my son and I love you. I don't want to see you neglect life—shutting out all it offers. All the joy! Meeting new people is not a burden, my son. Please don't let your past consume you."

Alzerion swallowed as he fixed his gaze on his mother. He knew she was only trying to help. Still, he felt this twinge in his chest. He smiled as he sat down to fasten the buckles on the sides of his tall black boots.

"Well, how do I look?" He stood and slowly turned about.

"You look elegant. Absolutely a vision in black and Phoenix red. Shall we?"

Alzerion nodded and wrapped his arm around his mother's arm. They left his room, and he escorted Melinda through the hall and toward the grand staircase. Below them, Alzerion could see the many people. They dressed in a variety of outfits, some of finer material and others of simpler fabrics. Either way, everyone was wearing a mask. At the base of the stairs, he spotted Francisco and Evalyn, who both wore silver masks with fleur-de-lis embroidered on them. Across from them were Quairken and Isabella, who went for a simple mask. Theirs were beige, and it brought the attention more to the shiny material of Isabella and Audrina's gowns.

Alzerion took a deep breath as he gave his mother's hand a slight squeeze as he held her arm in his. "You can do this," she whispered.

He smiled.

"Welcome, one and all."

His voice was loud and firm. It did not give away all the knots he felt in his stomach.

"I am pleased that you all could attend our masked ball." He heard the cheerful chatter and clapping of those below. "Please enjoy the festivities and there is a surprise for you all. In the Great Hall, there are plenty of refreshments and chocolate covered red velvet crowns. Plus, there is another fun little surprise. Each of you received a token. If you have a token with a rose on one side and a crown on the other, then you have earned a one-on-one meeting later with me."

Applause rang out, and many people chatted and hurried around.

He clung to his mother's arm as they finally descended the stairs and joined the crowd. Quairken let go of Isabella's hand and whispered something in Alzerion's ear and he nodded.

"Mother, I must make my rounds. I promise I will also get in some dancing."

"Of course," she replied warmly. "Maybe the lucky winner of the special token will be a nice girl."

He could hear the hope in her voice and see her eyes gaze inward, smiling. He bit his lip.

He just smirked, "Maybe."

He breathed out and walked into the Great Hall. He knew who would be the lucky winner of that coin. Quairken was brilliant for coming up with the idea. No, mother, it would not be a lucky girl.

"Good evening, Your Majesty."

Alzerion turned. A group of men masked in deep red and green moved toward him, and they bowed. Alzerion bent his head to nod.

"We wanted to pay our respects."

Despite the mask, Alzerion knew who spoke to him. Adrastus had a distinct air to his voice. Insincerity.

"Thank you, I hope you all enjoy yourself. I have to walk about."

"Oh, well, at least share a quick drink with us, right?"

One lowered his mask, and Phoebus stared back at him. "Just one."

Alzerion nodded as Adrastus stalked away. As Alzerion chatted with the nobles, Adrastus returned with a tray of drinks. He handed out each one, then he picked up the last goblet and handed it to Alzerion. Alzerion noticed the twitch of Adrastus' lip quiver. He didn't have time to stay with them longer, so he ignored that nagging feeling and guzzled down his drink. The wine was a nice hint of some sort of berry mixed with something else. It was tasty.

"Thank you. Now, I really must be going."

Alzerion heard Adrastus's croon to the others. He rolled his eyes as he walked away.

~

Jezzabell stood outside, facing the enormous palace. It had been many years since she was last here. Her opal-colored eyes spied the splendor. The palace, all the way to the rooftops of the town. How lovely it looked, shining in the moonlight.

"Eirini, enjoy the festivities, but be sure not to reveal who you are."

A younger woman bowed her caramel-colored locks. "If you think that best."

"I do. We don't know why we were invited and it would be best to stay out of any trouble."

"Of course," her voice lilted.

As she walked up the stairs and into the main entrance, there was such warmth. People laughed, joked, and just enjoyed themselves. It reminded her of parties from her youth...when Lyricaoans attended often.

"I'll see you later?"

"Yes, have fun. This is your chance to have some of that free time you seem to want."

Eirini turned and disappeared among the mass of people. Jezzabell scanned the main hall, taking it all in. Curious why the Elders of Lyricao received an invitation, after all this time. She had to be sure that this was a friendly gathering and not something else.

Such excellent questions, she thought. A feeling stirred, so she craned her neck left and right as she searched the room. She was not sure what she was searching for, so each step was slow as she made her way through the sea of people. Jezzabell rummaged in her shimmery sea-foam green gown for a place to store her coin. It had a crown on one side and a rose on the other. Then she reeled around to see a maid holding a silver platter filled with masks.

"Do you need a mask?" The maid's own mask was plain.

Jezzabell reached out with her bony fingers and hovered over the tray until she found one she liked. It was smooth to touch and shiny. It kind of looked like iridescent fish scales. They seemed to shine more when the light flickered over it.

"Thank you."

The maid nodded and then moved away. Jezzabell placed the mask on her face. She was careful to wrap the string under her silver hair. It would hurt to get that caught in her braids, that tied into her bun, all neat.

She sauntered through the main corridor and made her way into the Great Hall. As she looked about the room, she felt a tingling sensation in her head. She narrowed her eyes at a woman who wore a long red, flowy satin gown. Her mask was silver with fleur-de-lis on it. A thin smile curled. Evalyn. Jezzabell snaked her way through the crowd. Behind her, Jezzabell tapped her shoulder.

"How can I help you?" Evalyn stared at her.

Jezzabell said nothing at first.

"What can I do for you?"

"Evalyn, you don't recognize me? I know we are in masks, but still."

Evalyn circled around her. Her dress flared around with each step. "Should I know you?"

"I guess I'm not as memorable as we both thought. Let's try something different." Jezzabell stepped closer and whispered, "Evie."

Evalyn's mouth twisted up into a grin. A slight squeal left her mouth as Evalyn grabbed her arm.

"Jezzabell, is that you? I almost forgot how whimsical your voice sounds. Of course, only one person has ever called me Evie."

Jezzabell opened her arms and embraced her. Evalyn hugged back. "I'm so delighted that you could come."

"Did you invite me?" Jezzabell spoke in hushed tones, so low it could almost be unheard among the clamor going on around them. Evalyn wrapped her arm around Jezzabell and they traipsed around the Great Hall.

"I wish I did, but no, it wasn't me. It was King Alzerion. He decided we needed to branch out and make more allies."

"This kingdom is not an enemy of Lyricao," Jezzabell countered. "Still, it was rather nice of him. It has been too long."

"Well, my dear friend, maybe that will change," Evalyn smiled.

Jezzabell stopped abruptly and turned her face toward Evalyn. "What is troubling you?"

"You always had a skill at knowing things before others even told you."

"It is part of my charm," Jezzabell adjusted her mask. Her eyes locked on Evalyn.

Evalyn leaned in and spoke in her right ear. "I fear that there's more than alliances at play. I have no proof, only the feeling in my gut, but I think our king has some sort of plan concocted."

"What kind of plan? Do you think he's up to something bad for the kingdom?"

"No," Evalyn shook her head, "he never would jeopardize the kingdom's well-being."

"Then what kind of plan could he have that has you doubting him?"

"He has been acting strange," Evalyn unwrapped arms and motioned for Jezzabell to follow.

Jezzabell followed her as they neared the musicians, who played such a lovely tune. Evalyn sat down on a chair and patted the one next to her. Jezzabell sat down and kept her gaze on Evalyn. She felt this pull tugging her mind, like she might split in two ... being called away to watch a tall man dancing. She darted her gaze over to him momentarily. The man was robust, with a chiseled jaw and had pleasing cinnamon-red eyes.

"Evalyn, who is that?" Jezzabell pointed at the man dancing with a young woman dressed in an elegant gown. This time, she noticed the feathers and vines that wrapped around his crown. "Is he part of the royal family?"

"That is King Alzerion. Many nobles have thrown their daughters at him. He is quite the eligible bachelor."

"You sound sad," Jezzabell focused back on Evalyn.

"I would love to see him happy and settled down. I must admit, it also makes me unnerved. He is king because my daughter loved him. Aironell wanted him to rule over the kingdom."

Jezzabell was thankful for the mask. Certainly, without it, Evalyn would have seen her go pale all over her alabaster skin. Jezzabell swallowed and felt another tingle in her head. She closed her eyes tight and followed the images through her mind. She saw what was about to unfold.

"Evalyn, it was so nice to speak with you. I hope things become happier for you. Well, I'm going to meander and mingle. Maybe speak to the other Elders of Lyricao."

"Of course. I've missed these chats. Hopefully, we can chat again soon."

Jezzabell nodded. Then, with that, she stood up and danced her way toward the banquet table. She grabbed a raspberry tart, took a bite, and then turned to see if Evalyn was watching or not. Evalyn was busy talking with whom she assumed was the wife of a nobleman, so she darted for the door and slid into the main hallway.

She kept glancing back until she almost ran into a burly looking man in a beige mask. He wore a soldier's ceremonial uniform.

"You seem like you're in a hurry. Can I help you? Sorry, my name's Quairken."

"No. I just need a moment," she grinned as her eyes slowly looked at the man.

"You should stay close. I'm about to make an announcement for the big winner. How amazing it will be for someone to have individual time with the king."

Jezzabell nodded. "I won't go far."

She watched as the man ambled into the Great Hall. Then she heard the commotion die down. There was a deep and charming voice that spoke, and she knew it must be the king.

"Thank you all for coming tonight. Now for the lucky winner. Please, everyone, take out your token. If you have a token with a crown on one side and a rose on the other, then you are the winner! Please, come forward to meet His Majesty."

She peeked through the opening at the doorway. People all around her looked at their coins. Some groaned their displeasure at not having the special one, yet Jezzabell didn't take out her token. She didn't need to do so because she knew she had that coin. Now she understood. This was some sort of ruse. She found it too coincidental that she was the winner of that coin. *Well, Your Majesty, a talk we shall have.*

Alzerion looked out all around, but nobody came up to him. He walked around and Quairken came over and whispered something in his ear. Alzerion shook his head then he strode toward the door that led out into the main corridor. "Did it work?" Alzerion mouthed toward Quairken.

Quairken nodded.

Alzerion headed into the corridor. He moved with a fast-paced stride.

He felt the muscles in his neck tighten as he strolled about. Not paying attention, he bumped into someone. He saw the billowy pattern of a gown the color of the ocean. The perfect swirl of azure and white speckled with glitter.

"You should be more careful," she said.

"I'm so sorry, but I could say the same about you," he folded his arms.

The young lady adjusted her berry-colored mask as she looked up. Her candy-red lips pulled tight into a scowl, and her eyes looked like liquid amber. They glared at him through the slits of the mask.

"Look, I didn't mean to knock into you, but I am searching for someone."

"Of course." Her voice shifted.

A stranger, yet he heard that tone of disbelief. He swallowed as he tilted his head. "You wouldn't by chance be the winner of the special token, would you?"

A laugh escaped her mouth, "Sorry, but no. If you ask me, it all seems very, well, strange."

Alzerion stepped to the side as she countered. It was like they were playing a match of chess with their bodies, each matching the other's position or a strategic retreat.

The woman bowed her head as her caramel-colored locks rippled down on her arms. "I mean no disrespect."

"Somehow, I find that hard to believe. Your tone says otherwise." Alzerion's eyes furrowed beneath his mask.

"Oh?" Her hand rushed to her mouth. "Well, I'm so very sorry, Your Majesty."

Then her hands gripped the sides of her dress as she bowed low. Other party-goers stared over at them. He had to do something because he didn't need all those eyes on him, not now.

"I feel at a disadvantage. You know who I am, but I don't know who you are."

The girl slowly rose as her eyes fixed on him. They scanned him as she strolled around him. A sweet scent followed her.

She stood there, a curled smile plastered across her face. Her hand stretched out. Alzerion grabbed it, and he waited. There was silence except for the people chatting and all the laughter of the surrounding party. His gaze focused on the young woman holding his hand. Her mouth parted as her eyes shifted and then she pulled her hand back.

Alzerion's mouth twisted as his lips pinched in. His boot tapped against the stone floor. He had a plan, and nothing was going to spoil that.

"I have to go," Alzerion said and stepped to the side, but he felt a quick hand grasp his forearm.

Alzerion angled his body to see her hand clutching his arm as her eyes bore into his. Before he could speak, she tugged at his arm. He let her escort him out of the middle of the hall and back to a little corner near the Great Hall. He opened his mouth, but she shook her head. His eyebrows pinched in, mouth closed.

"You don't have to explain, Your Majesty."

"No, I don't, but you should start. What do you mean by cornering me, literally?"

The serious look on her face relaxed as she beamed.

"I can't tell you my name, sorry."

He pursed his lips. "You're not a criminal or something, are you?"

She shook her caramel-colored locks.

"Then why not?" His arms folded across his chest. "I don't like not knowing things."

"I can sense that about you. More like not being in charge of things, am I right?"

"H-how?"

"Doesn't matter." She stepped to the side as she faced him. "For a king, you make questionable choices."

The muscles of his jaw went slack as his mouth dropped. "I don't understand what you mean?"

"Hmm. You deny it. There's no need. I see it as clearly as I see the couple over there." She pointed to the bench against the wall, off of the Great Hall. Alzerion blinked.

She strode forward, away, but then he followed her.

"Wait."

She stopped. Alzerion stood at her side, gaze down at hers. "Who are you?" He had to know.

She shook her head. "May I give some advice, Your Majesty? Don't waste your time on following those clues of yours."

His posture perked up as he tilted his head.

"Is it really worth it? The price you'll have to pay...for someone everyone believes to be dead."

"Who have you been speaking to?" His voice was sharp and confident.

"Nobody. Doesn't mean that I'm not right." Her eyes flashed from the crowd back to him.

"Look, you don't know anything about me. You have no right to question my choices. Choices that you cannot begin to understand."

"King Alzerion, I have a gift, a talent. There's no need to deny any of it," she replied as she swayed to the side.

He saw people staring, and he grabbed her hand and pulled her closer to him. "Shall we?" As his other hand motioned to the dance floor in the Great Hall.

She bowed her head. Alzerion placed his right hand on her hip while the other held onto her right hand. He spun them around to the classical beats from the musicians.

"I don't like your tone," Alzerion said.

"People rarely appreciate being told when they are being foolish, Your Majesty."

Alzerion's gaze focused in on her. She was different, of that he was sure. "You're from Lyricao, right?"

She dipped her head as she pulled back. Alzerion heard a noise from the surrounding dancers, so he looked away. When he turned back, the woman was gone. He searched the crowd, but nothing. Alzerion walked back to the hall corridor, and still nothing. Then he felt a tap on his arm, so he turned.

He saw a woman with a sea-foam green gown and what looked like a shiny scaled mask. His eyebrows furrowed as he saw the woman move toward the back corridor. She stopped and waved at him. He licked his lips and headed toward her. He followed the trail of her gown as she turned corner after corner until they stood outside the door to the library.

"Shall we enter?" She spoke with such ease. "I know we have much to discuss." He blinked, trying to get his mind straight. Her voice sounded so lyrical, like there was this sing-song quality about it. Alzerion pushed open the library door and waved her inside. He followed once she had fully entered the room. He examined the room to be sure that they were the only two there. Satisfied, he snapped his fingers, and he heard the click of the door locking. Then he turned to face her.

"It is an honor to meet you, Your Majesty," she bowed and then gazed at him. "Am I correct in thinking that you have some pressing matters to discuss?"

"Yes, how do you know that?" He bit the inside of his cheek as he stepped closer to her.

"I know many things. It is part of my talent. I can see things. I know things."

"Then you are Jezzabell?"

"I am, Your Majesty," Jezzabell moved in one fluid motion.

She sat down on the cushioned couch that was positioned by a semi-circle shelf of books. Alzerion strolled over and sat down on a seat across from her that was the color of wine. They exchanged glances, however, silence filled the room.

Alzerion swallowed. "Do you know what I want to discuss?"

"I have my guesses, but I don't know definitively. Why don't you start?" She spoke with this coolness to her voice.

"Well," he cleared his throat, "I wanted to know more about the prophecy. I was told that you foretold a prophecy about Francisco and Evalyn's daughter."

He watched Jezzabell's eyes close. Was she trying to ignore him? He wasn't sure, so he just continued. "I guess what I'm really wondering is if you can tell me if Aironell is really gone."

"I see," Jezzabell spoke with a stillness as her eyes remained closed. "You don't think she's really gone?"

"I don't know. My brain says don't be so foolish, of course she's gone. I mean, she died right in my arms."

"Then why do you doubt it? It has been some years."

He took off his mask and placed it on the table. "I keep hearing this voice. The first time I heard it, it was shortly after we won the battle. I blew it off, but I have been hearing it with more frequency." If anything, he wanted to be sure that he wasn't just losing his sanity.

Jezzabell opened her eyes, and they glowed like two opal orbs of a pale white light. She straightened her posture and flipped her hands palms up. He stared with jaw gaped open as he saw two unique markings on her wrists. They looked like some cloud or shroud, with something flecked in it. They sparkled as the lights danced across the room. His mind was racing as this was the second time he encountered this odd-looking symbol. That, he knew, must wait for another time. For now, he had to know about Aironell. It was his duty to protect her. He had to know if she was truly gone.

"King Alzerion," she sounded soulful and yet slightly robotic, "the answers you seek are out there. The one you wish to find will be found, but whether you should is another question altogether. You must be careful if you plan to mess with fate."

His posture straightened up. He scratched his nose as he watched the brightness of her eyes dim back to normal.

She blinked twice and then looked at him. "Was that any help?"

"A bit. So, you're telling me she is alive?"

"Your Majesty," she said as she leaned across the little table. "I believe she is alive, and there's more I'd like to tell you. Not here. If you truly want my help, then come to me." She stood up and sauntered to the door.

"Wait," he called after her. "What do you mean?"

She placed one hand on the doorknob and turned her head to Alzerion. "I'm saying, come to Lyricao, where I could talk more freely. I will say one more thing before I leave. Aironell was quite adept at magic. I received some letters from her leading up to that fateful battle. If you want to know what we spoke about or anything else, then you must leave Bachusa. Secrets are best revealed in Lyricao...but not here."

With that, Jezzabell waved her hand, unlocked the safety on the door, and disappeared down the hall. He ran to the doorway, but she was gone.

Did she actually mean for him to leave his kingdom and journey to Lyricao? He felt the tension rise within. He had never been to Lyricao. It could be good for Bachusa and also bring him what he wanted. Jezzabell admitted that there was a way to get Aironell back. He smiled as he went back to the party. He felt the weight of his burden lighten.

# CHAPTER 7
## Hidden Secrets

Alzerion placed a hand on his head with a dull ache that split his head as it replaced the fog.

"Ugh," he groaned.

He sat up in his bed, and his fingers massaged the headache that made his temples scream. Was this from staying up so late? Alzerion took a moment to rest his head against the pillow behind him. His eyes shifted as he tried to recall the night's events... but the night was a blank slate—a blur.

A heavy thud hit against the door. His nostrils flared as he sighed.

He pulled the covers over his whole body and said, "Come in."

He winced as he rubbed the top of his head. Even the sound of his voice brought a sharp pain.

Quairken stood there, arms held out. "Don't tell me you forgot we had a practice this morning? You wanted the soldiers to practice sword handling."

"I did? When did I decide to do that?"

"Well, you told me yesterday to send word to the soldiers. It was earlier in the day before the masked ball."

"Ah, well, that makes more sense. I'm sorry. I'm feeling a bit out of sorts. My memory seems fuzzy and my throat is parched."

"Here, take your drink," Quairken said as he grabbed the glass that was sitting on Alzerion's nightstand. "It appears you have a note with it. How about I lead practice today? Later, you can tell me all about your meeting."

Before he could ask about what meeting, Quairken was out of the room.

Alzerion took a sip of the liquid in the cup. It was not water, and it tasted different, like a mixture of minty coolness, some sweetness, and like he just swallowed something woody. He took his fingers from his other hand to massage his forehead. Wait, Quairken mentioned a note. He fumbled looking for the note until he found it. It fell off the side of the cup and stuck on his blanket. He put the cup back on his nightstand and unrolled the note.

*King Alzerion,*

*It was a pleasure meeting you last night. If you wish to meet again and learn more, don't forget to come to Lyricao. I will wait for your arrival. Only bring those whom you can trust. If you are serious about your quest, then come soon. Drink this liquid in the cup, for it will help to sharpen your senses and refresh your memory.*

*P.S. We should discuss some safety measures for you.*

*Sincerely,*

*Jezzabell, Magic Seer and Healer*

*Lyricao Council of Elders*

As Alzerion blinked the last bit of sleep from the corners of his eyes, his memory of the night before drifted in his brain like a muddled mess. Pieces came back into being, like a slow reminder of what was. His forehead scrunched up as his fingers grazed at his chin. Who would do this? Make him forget, and why? He closed his eyes as more fragments of memory fell into place. Each whirred in his mind with such swiftness. His eyes pinched as he wrinkled his nose until one random memory flashed in his mind.

Adrastus. His eyes shot open. The barrage from the memory storm ceased, and he had no proof, but he knew it was Adrastus. It had to be! Alzerion frowned. That prick! He had to plan his trip fast, before Adrastus could try something else. Alzerion shook his wearied head as he tossed the blanket to the side and stood up.

As he grabbed an outfit and started dressing, Alzerion couldn't get Adrastus out of his mind. He was going to deal with him, somehow. He smirked at the thought of finally putting an end to his condescending behind—whatever that might be. However, that would need to wait because Jezzabell was his focus. Planning the trip needed his attention. Thank the gods there were no meetings for him, not today. Dressed, he strolled to his desk and scrawled a note for Quairken. Alzerion stepped to the side and opened the window. He tapped the little message and watched as it sparkled and flew out the window and zoomed down toward the practice grounds. At least Quairken would know where to find him. He closed his window and then headed for the tactical room.

Alzerion dashed down the corridor and down the stairs. He kept looking around to be sure nobody followed. He came to the library and continued past it. Finally, he came to a narrow corner and turned. Alzerion placed his jeweled hand on the wall. Flecks of magic formed a circle around his hand, then he muttered the secret word. The sound of rushing wind whirled by as a circle opened in the wall to reveal the tactical room.

It was smaller compared to many of the palace rooms, but it did the job. He knew that there needed to be a place to organize operations that were more private. As he walked in, the wall behind him returned to normal, and he slid his hands against the cool marble walls that were twisted of dark grays and browns. He usually enjoyed being there in the room, but today was different. He knew he had a time crunch looming over him. Alzerion moved briskly to the hexagon-shaped stone table at the center. The only sounds heard were that of his boots clacking against the wooden floor. With eyes closed, he rubbed his hands over the smooth surface and thought long and hard about what he needed to do.

With a quick wave of his right hand, a large scroll wrapped in simple twine flew out of a closed wooden wardrobe that was tucked in the back of the room. Alzerion flung his hand up and grabbed it in his fist. Then he pulled on the twine and unfurled it out on the stone table. As he smoothed it out he saw the kingdom of Bachusa positioned on the bottom right side of the map. He traced each bumpy landmass on the map with his fingers. Alzerion reached below the table to the small opened space and pulled out the compass and pencil. As he used the compass to plot the quickest way to get to Lyricao, he heard the low click of the door unlock and he looked up to see Quairken emerge from the opening.

"I'm glad you made it. Come so we can get this moving."

With an eyebrow raised, Quairken ambled over toward Alzerion. He looked down at the stone table.

"Well, what do you think so far?"

Quairken rubbed his hand to his chin, gulped down his saliva, and said, "You plan to make a trip to Lyricao?"

Alzerion nodded.

"Why? What happened at that meeting?"

Alzerion cleared his throat and walked to the stools that were set up by in the back of the room. He sat down. "Well, not much. Jezzabell asked that I meet her in Lyricao."

Quairken joined Alzerion on the stools. "I don't understand. She was just here, and—"

"Quairken," Alzerion leaned closer, as if trying to avoid being over-heard, although nobody else was there, "she told me she thinks Aironell is still alive."

"What? How? Why does she think that?"

"All in time, Quairken."

"I know, but that is reassuring. I know it'll make everyone happy."

"Quairken, you can't tell anyone. There's more going on, and she spoke like I needed to be cautious. In fact, I know I do."

"Why?"

"She didn't say, but I'm sure someone tampered with my drink last night."

"What? Who would do that?"

"Doesn't matter. I have no proof, but I know who. I will deal with them. But right now, the focus is on Jezzabell and Lyricao."

Quairken nodded.

"Jezzabell said that if I wanted to know more, I needed to come to her, So that is exactly what we shall do," Alzerion swallowed quickly, and then continued. "I want to take this as an opportunity for Bachusa, too."

Quairken just stared at him.

"So, we will sit with the Council of Elders of Lyricao as well. It can show a sign of goodwill and strengthen ties between the two kingdoms."

"I think it sounds like a good plan," Quairken stated and gave a curt nod as he tapped his boot against the wooden rest of the stool.

Alzerion stood and said, "So we only want to take a few of our most trusted soldiers with us."

"I can pick them for us. Maybe only bring two with us?"

"Sounds good! Thank you Quairken."

Quairken stood up and followed Alzerion back toward the stone table. The two chatted back and forth about ways to get to Lyricao. After they mapped everything out and decided what would be best, Alzerion then jotted down the notes on a scrap of paper. Then, he placed it in his pants pocket.

"Now we just need to tell Francisco and Evalyn, and of course, Isabella."

Quairken nodded. "Yes, we do," he said, as his eyes bulged.

Alzerion stared at him, almost scrutinizing him. "Quairken, what's going on with your face?"

"Oh, well, I am NOT looking forward to having the conversation with them. Isabella can sense when I am being less than honest, like a blood-hound that one."

Alzerion laughed.

"Hehem. Well, I won't tell her you said that." Alzerion patted him on the shoulder. "Tell her if you must. I'm not looking to drive a wedge between the two of you. Just be sure she says nothing of our true intentions to anyone else."

He smiled and nodded. They walked to the door and exited the tactical room and headed to the family room. Quairken pushed open the heavy wooden doors of the family room. Inside, Alzerion saw that Francisco and Evalyn nestled on the cushioned seat by the bay window. They were chatting and looking out the window. Melinda sat in a chair by the fireplace, knitting what looked like a blanket. He turned to Quairken and whispered for him to get Isabella and Audrina.

He left.

Alzerion strolled in. "Hello my family."

They turned to him with a smile.

"Where have you been?" Francisco narrowed in on Alzerion.

"We were worried," Evalyn added.

"Well, some of us were," Francisco shifted his gaze from Melinda and his lovely wife. Alzerion chuckled as he strolled to the ruby red armchair near the door and sat down. He understood completely. Evalyn and Melinda spent much of their time mothering him, although he didn't need them to do it.

Melinda glanced up from her knitting, briefly and said, "I believe you didn't answer Francisco's question."

He locked eyes with his mother. "I spent a bit of time in the tactical room."

"What for?" Evalyn turned her body to face Alzerion.

"I had an amazing meeting with the Elders of Lyricao last night."

"Oh?" Francisco folded his arms in front of him.

"Actually, they made an interesting offer. I think we can strengthen our ties with them."

"Interesting," Evalyn replied. She narrowed her focus right on Alzerion.

He swallowed, but kept his gaze steady. He couldn't waver or make a misstep. At that moment, the door creaked open and Quairken strode through with Audrina on his back and Isabella standing next to him.

"Come and join us," Alzerion said cheerily. Isabella walked to the ruby red couch and sat down. Quairken stood right behind her with Audrina clinging to him with her arms wrapped around his chest and legs around his waist. Francisco and Evalyn strode over and also sat on the couch and the other armchair. Melinda continued knitting from her place by the fire.

Alzerion bit his lip. He knew he had to tell them, but he didn't want to. He had to walk a fine line, and he knew it. Alzerion cleared his throat. "Anyway, the offer from the Elders of Lyricao had only one request."

"What was the request?" Melinda asked without looking over at them.

He saw Evalyn had this hint of suspicion in her eyes, so he had to act now.

"They asked that I come to Lyricao. Isn't that amazing?"

"How is that amazing?" Francisco asked as he poured himself a cup of tea from the quaint teapot that sat on the fleur-de-lis shaped table.

"Well, I have never traveled that far," I thought. "What a treat to see Lyricao and do something good for Bachusa."

"When you put it that way, yes, it is exciting," Evalyn chimed in. "I haven't been in such a long time. It is lovely, I must admit." She looked like she was unraveling fond memories as she closed her eyes and smiled.

Melinda placed her knitting on her lap, "When do they expect you there?"

He could hear a slight quiver in her voice.

"Well, they asked that I make it a priority trip. That's why I was planning the trip in the tactical room, with Quairken's help."

Alzerion noticed Isabella's wrinkled brow. She shot a quick glance at Quairken and then Alzerion. He knew Quairken must have told her already, so she knew the real reason for their trip. "Isabella, I hope you don't my taking Quairken on this trip."

She shook her head, "I- um, sorry, of course I don't mind. I find it an honor that you would take my husband."

She raised her arm up and Quairken grabbed her hand and gave it a slight squeeze.

"All I ask is that you both be safe. Bring him home, Alzerion."

He understood all too well. "I will. I promise we have outlined the safest passage."

Evalyn picked at the skin that surrounded her perfectly manicured fingers. Alzerion wasn't sure why, but he could sense that she was holding back. It was probably for the best. He knew she must seem suspicious, and didn't want to draw any attention to that.

"Well, I may be able to help," Evalyn spoke with an air of uncertainty. Alzerion and Quairken both focused on her.

"How so? Do you remember something about the passage?"

"Not exactly, Quairken," She cleared her throat and spoke louder. She stared at him directly in the eye. "There is another way to get to Lyricao. In fact, it is a million times safer and faster."

Alzerion cocked his head to one side. "How? I have scoured those maps for ages."

"It is not on the maps," she quickly added. "This way is a secret. Certain magical families have passed it down."

Alzerion just stared with his jaw gaped open. He decided anger would not win him any points, so instead, he took a few deep breaths. "Evalyn, why haven't I heard about this before? I have been king for some time now."

She shifted in her seat, and all eyes were staring back at her. "I swore to keep its location a secret. Francisco never even knew about it." She looked to her husband and continued, "I promise if we needed it when we ruled over Bachusa, then I would've told you, but we never needed to."

"Dearest, I- I don't know what to say. Why all the secrecy?"

"There is an ancient portal that connects Bachusa to other kingdoms in the realm. Which means there is a special portal that can take anyone directly to Lyricao. My family is one of the oldest and ancient families of sorcerers and therefore, it was our task to keep its location hidden."

Alzerion shook his head. He couldn't believe what he was hearing. "You mean to tell me we can just magic ourselves anywhere we want, in the entire realm?"

"That about sums it up, yes."

"Well, that is great news! It will surely—"

"Wait," Evalyn said sharply as she held out her hand, "there is a catch, so to speak."

"What kind of catch?" Alzerion asked as he tapped his boot on the floor.

"There is a minor spell or enchantment, rather, that must be said. Plus, you have to be at the exact location of the portal."

"Oh, is that all?" Quairken joked.

Alzerion glared at Quairken, and he slowly lowered Audrina down and sat her next to Isabella on the couch.

"Evalyn, is it an easy enchantment?"

"It is. You should have no problems using it. The only true issue is finding the portal's location."

"You don't know it?" Alzerion had this pinched expression as he continued to tap his foot against the floor.

"I'm sorry, I don't, but I know where you can find the answer."

Alzerion perked up.

Evalyn took a small swig of her tea that Francisco had poured her. "It was a family secret, but they passed all family secrets in the family book of spells. When I married Francisco, we had my family's book added to his; The Ancienne Magica de Bachusae Volumes."

Alzerion smirked. Whew, at least he knew exactly where that was. That was the book that started all his searching.

"Wasn't that the book that you gifted Aironell, when she came back to Bachusa?" Isabella asked as she looked about.

Francisco nodded. "We gave it to her so she could learn more about the kingdom and harness the magic from it."

"So, does anyone actually know where it went?" Melinda chimed in. "I don't mean to open any old wounds, but it has been quite some time."

She didn't need to finish. He knew what she wanted to say.

"I know where it's kept," Alzerion replied. "Since becoming king, I have been reading through its contents."

He stood up and started pacing back and forth. He stopped abruptly and turned back to Evalyn. "Where is that in the book? I swear I have been through it cover to cover, many times; and I have seen nothing like that in there."

He watched as she wrinkled her nose and blew out her cheeks. She must have been weighing the pros and cons, but still didn't understand why. Surely she knew that this group of individuals could be trusted. Still, he stood, waiting. Finally, she licked her lips and nodded at him.

"It's the ring that has what you need."

"What ring?" Alzerion asked. He looked at his fingers, trying to figure it out.

Evalyn stood up and walked toward him. She grabbed his hands and gently tapped the ring on his left pointer finger. It was the ring. The ring that symbolized his position as king. His eyebrows furrowed.

"Every king has worn that ring going back for many centuries."

"I know... I mean, how can it do what you say?"

She smiled at him. "Alzerion, my family enchanted that ring. The ruler of Bachusa can only find the portal locations if you wave that ringed hand over the last spell of the book, it will show you."

Alzerion's cinnamon red eyes shone bright with intrigue, and he was pleased to be one step closer to getting all his answers.

He straightened his back. "Well, first I guess I will collect the location from the book. Quairken, why don't you inform Brentley and Calderon to get ready."

Quairken gave Isabella's hand a tight squeeze. Alzerion saw the look in his eyes at his wife. How he longed for that. His heart ached at the thought. Then Quairken gave Audrina a sweet peck on the cheek and he left the room. Alzerion looked around the room and knew that when he returned, things would be different. Good. Bad. He didn't know, but he knew things were about to change. He felt a hand pressed against his back and he spun around to see Melinda standing there. With a heaviness in her eyes. Alzerion reached out and hugged his mother.

"I'll be back as quick as I can," he whispered in her ear.

Francisco walked over and with a hand outstretched, shook Alzerion's hand, and gave him a firm nod. "Alzerion, we will look after Bachusa until you return. I promise you, nothing should go wrong in your absence."

"Thank you. I know you will," Alzerion strode toward the door, craned his neck and gave them all one last glance.

Then he was off to his room, and he knew where the book was— locked away in his desk, along with the Ancienne Magica de Bachusae Volume II. Quickly, he meandered down the hall and came to his room. He walked in, shut the door behind him, and waved his hand over his desk which caused a swirl of magical flecks to appear all around as the bottom drawer opened up.

Alzerion pulled out the book and sat down at the desk. He flipped to the last page of the book, just as Evalyn had instructed. He held his eyes shut firmly and took a few deep breaths as he held his hand over the book. Nothing. He did it again and again, and each time nothing happened. Could Evalyn have been mistaken? Alzerion's eager expression disappeared, only to reveal a grimace.

He wanted this to work. It had to work. He felt this need down to the depths of his bones. He felt it was like a burning desire deep in his core. Suddenly, the fleur-de-lis design of his kingly ring glowed. He felt a warming sensation from where the ring sat on his pointer finger. This time, he opened his eyes and saw it. There, on the last page, the spell was visible. Alzerion chanted:

"All that comes must attest to his deepest desire, lest he be wrong and not feel the burning fire.

Open minds and truest conviction can only open me without friction."

Alzerion opened one eye, almost like a squint, and he saw it and opened both eyes. He saw the enchantment dazzle and glow, and then there was a low rumble. He looked out the window and around the room, but saw nothing was amiss. Alzerion stared back at the page to see what seemed like a trench on the page. Like someone took a tiny shovel or dagger and dug a hole in the page. He picked up the book, but no, there was no hole beneath it. With narrowed eyes, he placed the book back down. He blinked two times and saw that snug in the opening was a tiny little parchment of paper. Alzerion pulled it out gingerly. He unfolded it to reveal it in a cursive scrawl. The locations of all portals. He scanned for the word Lyricao until he found what he wanted. A smirk escaped his lips. He knew where this was. He folded it back and placed it in the opening. With a wave of his jeweled hand and another muttering of the incantation, the secret was hidden, once again, within the book.

Alzerion stowed it back in his desk as he readied himself for the trip. Alzerion pulled on his boots over his black leather pants. Then he grabbed the black and dark gray top. He smoothed his hands over the dark gray print that spiraled around the tunic-top. His hands even reached the lower part as it draped mid-thigh. He hated wearing formal wear, but knew he wouldn't have a choice this time. Alzerion bit his lip as he fastened the ties from his neck to right above his belly. Meeting with the elders meant he had to dress the part. He stowed a small silver dagger in his boot and then attached his sword to the belt at his waist. He left without glancing back to meet Quairken.

# CHAPTER 8
## Lyricao

Alzerion stood tall and poised on the marble steps at the front of the palace. Soon Quairken was there with Brently and Calderon at his side. Brentley and Calderon knelt and bowed their heads, with swords scraping against the ground.

"Rise," Alzerion's voice boomed. "I trust Quairken has shared the weight of what we are about to do and where we are traveling."

"If I may, sire," Brentley bowed, "he did not tell us where we were going."

"I h-hope it isn't too far of a journey," Calderon lowered his head.

Alzerion stepped toward him and gave him a reassuring pat on the shoulder. "It is a bit of a distance. We will portal out of Bachusa."

Brentley remained rigid, and Calderon's eyes bulged.

"I promise I will keep you safe. The journey will not be a perilous one. We are headed to the kingdom of Lyricao, and we will use magic to get there."

Calderon's skin color was pale, like he might vomit. Eyes sunk as his lips pressed together and his cheeks puffed out.

"Is there something the matter?" Alzerion raised an eyebrow.

"No, sir!" Calderon straightened up and his arms stiffened at his sides.

"Are you sure?" Quairken's voice was firm. "If you have something to say, now would be the time. I'm sure King Alzerion would like to get moving."

Brentley shook his head and straightened up as Calderon gulped, "I-I-um—"

"Calderon, spit it out, will ya!" Quairken blurted.

"Yes, sir!" He took quick breaths. "Is, well, er, are the rumors true? Is Lyricao all about magic? Will we be able to return?"

Alzerion looked at him with a softness, "Why are you concerned? We have magic here in Bachusa."

"I'm not that familiar with magic. I am, well, uneasy about using it to travel, that's all. Will we arrive in one piece? Will it mess with my mind? I've heard many stories about magic-users and those of Lyricao."

Alzerion smiled as he patted him on the back. "Don't worry. You have nothing to fear. I'm sure Lyricao is not as bad as those rumors. I have never portaled out of Bachusa, but you will be fine."

Calderon nodded.

"Well, then. How do we get to this portal you mention?" Quairken asked as he stood at the ready.

"The woods behind the palace. Shall we?"

Alzerion led the way. He craned his neck to the side and took stolen glances back to be sure that the men were fine. He knew he was asking a lot. Sometimes he forgot what people without magic thought of it all, but Alzerion wanted to ease their worries. He thought of ways to do so as he meandered through. He pulled tree branches over their heads so as not to get struck in the head. After a short trek crossing the rocks, trees, and the various shrubs, they came to a spot near the Hazy River.

Quairken breathed out, "Why are we stopping here?"

Alzerion turned to the little group, "This is the spot."

"Here?" Brentley looked around, "Where?"

Alzerion pointed to the river. He saw them share quick glances.

"What? Where is your sense of adventure, guys?"

"Maybe we have different definitions of the word," Quairken chuckled. "Where exactly is this portal, Your Majesty?"

Alzerion strolled toward the river and motioned for them to follow.

Quairken and Brentley followed without delay, but Calderon hesitated before following suit.

Alzerion took Quairken's hand, then Quairken held Calderon's visibly shaky hands, Calderon then held Brentley's, who grasped Alzerion's other hand. Like a chain, they formed a circle, and Alzerion led his trusted group into the middle of the river. The water had this bite to it—cold seeped through to his legs.

"Alright. Close your eyes and just breathe. Believe in my power. Trust that I will guide us safely."

Alzerion kept his focus on them. Making sure that each did what he asked. Then he closed his eyes, too. Alzerion directed his mind on the task at hand. He concentrated on that incantation from the book—knew he was true of heart and intent. He would not, could not fail. At least, he hoped. Deep breath in and then a slow whistle out. Alzerion could feel the fire burn beneath his fleur-de-lis ring.

In an instant, he could feel the water rise around his legs. He forced his eyes open to be sure of what was going on. He watched as the river water flowed up and around them. Like a tunnel of water, it swirled about them like a vortex. Alzerion could smell the fresh water with a hint of algae and moss. He focused his mind on what needed to be done. Then, the water shrouded them until a watery encasement surrounded them. No turning back now.

Alzerion flooded his thoughts of Lyricao, and then nothing. No noises of water trickling around. He still felt the hands clutching his hands. This time, when he opened his eyes, he felt a slight quiver in his stomach as he wrinkled his nose.

Alzerion licked his lips, as his eyes couldn't believe what they saw. "Guys, we are here. You can open your eyes."

Calderon opened his eyes quickly, and then he turned and wretched into the first bush he found.

"Are you alright?" Quairken mustered between his breaths.

"Brentley, how about you?" Alzerion checked on them.

Brentley just gave two thumbs up while Calderon stood and nodded, but still looked pale.

"Are you sure?" Alzerion circled back to face Calderon...at a distance.

Calderon nodded. "Just the whizzing and, of course, that wet feeling. I thought for sure I was going to drown and then we didn't, so I guess I'm wrestling with a mix of emotions."

"That is completely understandable," Alzerion smirked. "Now, let's find out where we go from here. Our host is the delightful Jezzabell."

Quairken nodded as he led Brentley and Calderon to follow.

Alzerion looked around to see such magnificent sights. He rubbed his eyes. Twice. Could this be real? He never saw such amazing views. They walked on a hilltop that was sprawling of these tiny lime green flowers. Below, he could see the clear blue of the sea. It looked like it could swallow the kingdom whole. Water crashed into the shores on each side of Lyricao. Alzerion kept moving downhill, getting closer to the town. The immediate smells and sights smacked him right in the face. He continued to smirk because it was pleasant, and Alzerion turned to the side as he mouthed, wow.

"Look out!" Calderon hollered as he pulled Alzerion by the arm. At the last moment, Alzerion saw someone zoom by at hyper speed, followed by some sort of flying creature.

Alzerion gasped as his hand pressed against his chest. It had some sort of thick scaled tail that curled behind. Alzerion shook his head. Off to the other side, he watched as people loaded onto another one of those creatures. He held his breath for a second before he pressed his hands to his head. It looked like a large flying seahorse, but more dragon-like. The swirls of silver, sky blue, and rust that plumed around its head. Alzerion stepped in its direction. The creature's purple eyes locked on him and then it flew off with its passenger.

"What was that?" Brentley stood at the ready, hand on the hilt of his sword.

"Not sure," Quairken admitted. "Your Majesty, did Jezzabell say where exactly we should go?"

Alzerion heard his name and focused back on his men.

"No, she did not," he admitted. Alzerion ambled forward to see what looked like market stalls. Some were selling many things. Fine silks and linens. Decadent sweets and elegantly crafted jewelry and pendants.

"Damn it!" Calderon tripped on a barrel of fish and caught it just before it ruined the whole shipment.

"That was close," Brentley chuckled. "Walk much?"

"Shut it."

Alzerion couldn't help but smirk. Those two fought like brothers. Alzerion motioned for them to walk in front of him. This way he could monitor them, so as not to annoy the Lyricaoans as they roamed. The scenery was unlike anything he knew.

He smelled the aroma of delicious sweets and a mixture of sea salt. As they strolled, they came to the other side of town that had less food stalls and more hobby shops and small places. Seers, conjurors, palm readers, mind readers...that was just scratching the surface. Each shop's symbols distinctly marked what they dabbled in. Alzerion tugged at his collar as they kept moving. Beads of sweat pulled at his temples.

After what felt like an eternity in the sweltering heat, Quairken stopped. "Your Majesty, there must be a better way."

Brentley and Calderon fanned themselves with their hands.

"Alright, I guess you are right. It is unbelievably warm," Alzerion rubbed the back of his hand against his forehead, wiping away any sweat that was visible. Then he knocked on the wooden beam of the closest shop. It looked like a small hut with sturdy wooden beams that were covered in a thick, light blue canvas of sorts. A woman with bronze skin and long cobalt hair came forward.

"Hello, what can we do for you?" She spoke with a slight musical sound to her voice. He couldn't quite figure out what, but her voice was sweet sounding.

"My name is Alzerion, King of Bachusa."

The woman's bright blue eyes grew wide, and she bowed so low that her white skirt mixed with the dirt from the ground. "It is a pleasure, Your Majesty."

"Thank you," he said as he reached out and grabbed her hand and helped her back up.

She looked at the group and pursed her lips. "What can I do for you? Are you looking for your fortune?"

"Is that your specialty?" Quairken stepped closer.

"Why yes, it is. It has been my family's calling for many generations," she said with head held high and a grin plastered on her delicate face.

Brentley and Calderon just stood there, like two anxious guard dogs.

"What is your name, if you don't mind?" Alzerion asked with such focus.

"Oh yes...of course...my name is Tarella." She stepped closer to Alzerion with her hand out. Alzerion shook her hand, and as he was about to let go, he noticed an orb shaped tattooed on her wrist. Like some sort of magical orb.

"What is that mark?" Alzerion flipped her hand over and pointed at the mark.

"That is nothing...it is a birthmark, really."

Intrigue rising, Alzerion narrowed his gaze and lifted his chin. Then, he slowly walked around in a circle of sorts.

"Your Majesty?"

Alzerion ran his hands through his hair and ceased pacing. He stopped in front of Tarella. "I'm sorry. I, um, I've seen a mark like that before. Well, not exactly like that, but kind of. I just didn't understand it."

"Come," Tarella said smoothly as she escorted them into the small canvased hut. Brentley and Calderon stood, standing guard by the door. Quairken and Alzerion sat on the two chairs across from where Tarella sat.

"They are birthmarks. The markings symbolize our power. Our birthright." She flipped her arms over, wrists up. "See, the circles. If you look closer, they are a fortune teller's mystical orb."

Alzerion tapped at his chin and leaned forward. "So what does a shroud of some sort symbolize? I think it glows when light hits it and had some sort of dust flecked around it."

Tarella looked down as she rubbed at her earlobe. "I- um- sorry, what?" She said as she cleared her throat.

Alzerion's nose flared. "Please. I must know."

She nodded. "It's a special mark. That is a rare find."

"What does it mean?" Quairken asked sharply. "Our king wants to know."

Tarella stood up. She looked down at Alzerion. "It is the mark of a seer. Many of us have our gifts, but seers are the gems around here. Something like royalty."

Royalty, he thought. Well, that kind of made sense about Jezzabell, but wait, why did that maid have that same mark? Snap out of it. Answers for another day.

"Tarella, could you help us find someone?" Quairken asked as he looked from Alzerion and back at her.

"Whom are you searching for?" Her lips went flat and her voice had a change of pitch, like an off-key flute. Alzerion surveyed her closely, but she revealed little but a wrinkled brow. He knew he had to ask her. She seemed nice enough, and he needed the help.

"I am looking for where to find Jezzabell. I have a meeting with her, but she was rather vague about where to go once I got to Lyricao."

"The Jezzabell? From the Council of Elders?"

Alzerion nodded.

"Oh, why that changes everything." She chirped. She bounced toward the opening of the hut. "Follow, please."

"Should we," Quairken whispered to Alzerion.

He shrugged his shoulders. "What do we have to lose?"

They followed her, and Brentley and Calderon took the back of the ensemble. Boy, did she move fast. Alzerion felt like he was racing after her. Her skirt gave the impression that she was flowing in the breeze, like the how waves roll over each other in the sea. She escorted them past a few more shops and then made a quick turn. Suddenly, all Alzerion could see were buildings. They looked like a mix of marble and granite buildings that stood tall against the backdrop of the azure skies above, with the cedar walls popping out. Finally, Tarella stopped in front of the tallest building yet. It looked like it could have been the oldest building in town. Alzerion gulped as his eyes scanned the tall sea-foam green domes at the top.

It had this regal vibe about it as they paraded up the granite steps, passed the marbled columns, and into the main entrance. Once inside, a coolness washed over them. Alzerion could feel almost a chill, which was a pleasant alternative to the sweltering heat he felt before. He turned around to see that Brentley and Calderon were still behind him, but this time he saw other men carrying a sword and shield. They must have been soldiers of Lyricao, but with brows furrowed, Alzerion wondered why they were following. Was this a trick? A trap? He hoped he did not just lead them into a huge mistake by coming.

"You made it!" Alzerion tilted his head to the lyrical voice. "I'm so glad to see that you came after all." Alzerion nodded at Quairken as a small smile crept from his drying lips.

"I brought them as soon as they mentioned your name, oh wise one." Tarella bowed her head low and held her hand to her lips. Jezzabell smiled as she stroked Tarella's head gingerly. "Thank you, dear. You are free to return to your business."

Tarella nodded, bowed once more, and left.

"So, these are your trusted men, eh?"

"Yes." Alzerion replied. "I came as soon as I could. I didn't want to waste one moment."

"That's for the best," she said cooly. "First, I should show you to your rooms."

Alzerion saw the hardened faces of his men shift. He knew what they wanted to say, but didn't.

"Jezzabell, um, what do you mean, rooms?" Alzerion stood with legs apart and arms at his side. Jezzabell meandered between the men and came to Alzerion. "Why, you need to refresh. I'm sure that heat was more than you bargained for." She spoke as she walked around with arms moving about like she was the conductor of a sort of ensemble. "Surely, what kind of host would I be if I didn't allow you and your men to bathe, have a decent meal, and rest?"

"Oh, that is so, um, thoughtful."

"I hoped you would see that." Jezzabell wrapped herself arm in arm with Alzerion as she escorted him out toward one of the side doors.

She walked with such briskness and then stopped. She spun them around. "Well, my servants will show you to your rooms." She snapped one of her delicate fingers and sure enough, two servants dressed in short silver dresses escorted Quairken, Brentley, and Calderon off and through one of the cedar doors.

"Now, it is just us," Jezzabell spoke. She had this breathy air in her voice. Alzerion did not know what to make of this. He narrowed his eyes. Something in his being felt like he could trust her, despite his slight uncertainty.

"Where are we headed?" Alzerion focused in on her.

"I thought we could go to my sitting room and have a small chat. How does that sound?"

"That sounds fine." He leaned in as they walked across the granite floors and through a columned archway. "I wonder if—"

"Not yet," she whispered as she held one finger to her ruby lips. Jezzabell stopped leading him when they came to an opal door. It shone iridescent as the sun's rays radiated against it. She strode forward, passed a seahorse glass table and laid out on what looked like a white cushioned lounger. Alzerion took a few steps and followed her into the room. The door closed behind him. He stared at Jezzabell, who grinned.

"What?" His gaze narrowed. "Is this all some sort of ruse? I'm feeling like there is more going on than I bargained for."

"Alzerion, King of Bachusa, relax. Come. Sit." She tapped the lounger next to hers. "I promised you an answer and I intend to keep my word."

Alzerion moved with a spring in his step. He sat down and grabbed one of the cups. He was about to drink when he paused. "That liquid in my room. Was that from you?"

"Yes." She raised her hand up in protest. "No, I did not poison you. I helped you."

"It helped me to remember."

Jezzabell took a sip of the cool contents of her cup and then held it in her hand. "I did. I sensed that someone would try to alter your memories."

"Why? Who?"

"Well, I'm not too sure on who, but the why... has to do with forgetting me."

Alzerion took a quick sip from the cup and was relieved that it was a fruity tasting water. He took another couple sips. He licked his lips. "Why would someone want me to forget you?"

"Well, I assume it is someone that doesn't want you to speak with me, given my line of work."

Alzerion finished his drink and placed the cup back down on the seahorse table., "Jezzabell, I need to know."

"I know. All in good time. If you trust your men, then I can do it later, after you have all rested and had an enjoyable meal."

"Is there any way to persuade you to do it sooner?"

She shook her head and said, "I know you are anxious. I promise it will be tonight."

"Thank you," he bent his head.

"Of course, let me have a servant take you to your room," Jezzabell made her way to a small weathered, glittered desk.

She grabbed what looked like a glass or crystal seahorse figurine, and then she shook it. It made a beautiful sound. It must have been some sort of bell, but it sounded like the pleasant melodious tune of something so serene. Jezzabell strolled toward Alzerion, and then a medium-sized woman in a glowing white sheath stood at attention.

"Please take our guest to his room."

The girl nodded.

"Give the King of Bachusa whatever he would like. Oh, and please have his bath ready as soon as he gets to his room."

Again, the girl nodded.

"I'll see you tonight then."

The servant escorted him to his own room.

# CHAPTER 9
## Unique Encounters

Hot...misty...Ah. The steam crept around him like a comfortable blanket of warmth. Each tense muscle loosened as he slid deeper into the tub, and steam mingled with the scent of mint. He exhaled.

"Would you like more of the aromatic scents?"

The servant waited on the other side of the marble door. He couldn't believe that she didn't leave.

Alzerion needed a moment to think. He sat up, a bit, in the enormous tub. It had these decorative stones of pale blues, greens, and yellows. The entire room was bright in pale colors and, of course, with tons of natural lighting. If he didn't know any better, he swore it was magical—like magic therapy. He smirked.

"Sir?"

"I, oh, sorry. Yes, more scent would be perfect."

He heard the door open, and the sound of sandals gently rapped on the granite floor. He smelled the freshness of the aromatic mixture. It smelled like lavender, some mint, and maybe jasmine. Whatever it was, it was nice. He let his eyes close as he took another slow breath.

"Would you like anything else?"

"No, that is all. Thank you." Alzerion opened his eyes and watched her leave. He could make out her silhouette against the candle lights flickering against the draped curtains. He felt so content, like he could stay in the saltwater tub forever.

Alzerion opened his eyes at the sound of fists on the main door of his room.

"Sir, there are some men here to see you. They claim to be yours, and one is called Qu-Quair—"

"Quairken?" Alzerion straightened up.

"Yes. That's it."

"Tell them to get comfortable, and I'll be right out."

Alzerion took one more deep breath to soak in the scents with the steam from the heat. Then he stood, held onto the smooth stones as he clambered out. He grabbed the thick, soft towel that was draped off the cushioned bench. He dried his entire self, and then found his clothes. Folded—neatly on the glass shelf next to the bench. Once dressed, Alzerion opened the door and felt the breeze set in from the temperature difference.

"Your Majesty," Brentley and Calderon bowed immediately.

"Sit. Please." They moved closer, and each sat on the opposite side of him.

"We came to walk down to the dinner festivities with you," Quairken said as he sat across from Alzerion. "How did it go with Jezzabell earlier?"

Alzerion looked at all three of them. "Not bad, however, she won't tell me more of what I want to know until after our dinner, though. She wanted us rested and fed."

Alzerion looked to Brentley, who made a sort of cough. "What?"

"Nothing, sir," Brentley said and blushed a bit.

"Do you think she is lying to me?"

"Of course not, sir."

"She is being rather cryptic," Alzerion stood and paced around where they were sitting.

"Why do you think that is?" Quairken stretched his leg out.

"I don't know, Quairken. I hope she gets on with it soon."

Calderon and Brentley kept their gaze to the floor.

"Shall we?" Calderon stepped to the door and opened it.

Alzerion nodded and started for the door. Quairken was by his side within seconds, and then the small group left the room. They walked down the hall, and Alzerion saw many pictures and paintings as they headed back to the open space of the entryway. He touched the seashell frame of the tallest painting of what looked like a ship at sea. Alzerion stopped as he brushed his fingers against it—eyes closed, tight. The brush strokes felt lumpy, raised. Yet, even more, he heard a distant whoosh. Alzerion's eyes rushed open.

"Anything wrong?" Quairken nudged his side.

Alzerion shook his head. "Of course not." He rubbed his hand against his forehead as he looked to see Brentley and Calderon staring at him. "Let's continue."

He didn't want Brentley or Calderon to know about the noise. Quairken, well, he would tell him later. He already knew about his senses. It was like the painting came alive when he touched it. The sounds of the waves crashing filled his head. The smell of the salt and dread clustered together in his nose. He swallowed. He couldn't get around the dark sky in the painting. Could this have been just an artist's imaginings, or was this real, somehow? Alzerion led his men across the openness toward the closed door, where he heard music seeping through.

Alzerion went to grab the doorknob, but a hand shot out and grabbed it first. Alzerion craned his neck and Brentley pulled open the door. He stood—chest puffed out with his back against the door. Alzerion's mouth curved up as he nodded, then he strolled through. Suddenly, he felt overdressed and underdressed simultaneously. Once his men entered by his side, Alzerion turned to Quairken and he shrugged.

The room was fancy. Glass with silver and sea-foam green marble accents everywhere. Openings where windows should have been, instead, had this smooth looking glass. It was clear with some swirls that wound about the edges of the windows—like how the waves rolled up onto shore. Such brightness from the sun emitted through those windows—crisp but not golden. As the rays crept through the glass, the light looked to be more like a mild yellow-white hue as it made the marble glisten.

Alzerion pulled his gaze away from peering out at the sea beyond. Such beauty. He reeled around and felt this warmth across his face. He bit his lip as he observed the guests. Their garments left little to the imagination. This differed completely from how it was in Bachusa, and he felt his body freeze.

His gaze shifted to some of the young ladies chatting and dancing about. The dancing felt more sultry. Alzerion forced a quick breath, and he gazed at Quairken and the others, eyes widened. Brentley looked stiff as he kept his face glued to the floor, while Calderon stared with mouth gaped open. Quairken shrugged, and his mouth flattened as his body angled—hand pointed out.

Alzerion raised an eyebrow but followed Quairken's hand. There it was. That heat he felt on his face returned, like a burning vortex on his skin. It didn't end there, but moved to his gut. He crossed his arms and shifted his weight to his other leg. There were no words. A woman dressed in a shiny opal dress ambled over toward him. Her movements were precise, and her dress had a slit on one side that ran the length of most of her thigh. He gulped. Merely inches away, he realized that opal-colored dress had openings at her hips. With each swish of those curved hips, that slit in her dress rose, slid down, and rose again. Heart beat increased. Face—burned. He scanned the room. Most of the young ladies had on dresses similar in style. Alzerion brought his gaze back to the young lady before him. His eyes narrowed as he felt a bit like he had had this experience before. Eyebrows furrowed.

"Would you like to dance?" Her voice was soft and warm.

His eyes glanced from her rich olive-toned calf and up—up to her face. Her hips weren't the only bare skinned areas he could see. Her dress spiraled around the space between her shoulders, dipped down, leaving the top of her chest mostly open. He blushed.

"Your Majesty," Quairken bowed before him. "The lady is waiting."

He pulled the collar of his shirt as he held out a hand. Her head bent as she curtsied. Then, in seconds, her amber eyes stared up at him as she shook his hand. Her skin was so smooth, flawless. Again, the feeling like he experienced her touch once before. He wracked his mind but nothing. He couldn't take his eyes off of her as she slowly rose back up on her feet. She radiated like she glowed, and a sweet scent tickled his nostrils. He cleared his mind.

Alzerion swallowed. "I'm sorry for being rude. You wanted to dance, is that right?"

Her lips curved. He leaned closer, then her delicate hands grasped his arm. Suddenly, he found himself arm-in-arm with her as she used her free hand to toss her caramel-colored locks behind her. He had no words. The warm feeling inside of him was in overdrive.

"You don't look at all how I expected."

Alzerion tilted his head to her. Eyes pinched in. "What do you mean?" His voice was low. Alzerion went to pull his arm away.

"Don't be so rude, Alzerion King of Bachusa." She rubbed at his arm as she spoke until her fingers grazed against him like tiny strokes. She stopped as she held out her hand. His insides betrayed him, as it yearned for her touch once more. A delicate touch. Well, he hadn't had that in some time.

"Your Majesty, please take my hand," Her words sounded like a slow purr.

He realized she held her arm above her head, awaiting his hand. He grabbed it as she giggled. Next, she stepped closer, grabbed his other hand, and placed it on that curved hip of hers. Her bare skinned hip. Again, she stepped forward as they glided across the floor. Each movement had them whirling around. He couldn't really make anything out as they went around, so he kept his gaze on her.

"You act as if you know me," Alzerion said, "but how can that be?"

Her lips pressed together into a small smile. "You really don't remember me? Not sure if I should be annoyed or flattered."

They spun around others as they danced.

"Then again, I didn't use my talent on you, so maybe I shouldn't be surprised. You seemed preoccupied when last we met."

Her face moved closer as she spoke, "You know, with finding that girl who may or may not be alive."

His mouth fell open. She was the girl from the ball. The one that disappeared. He swallowed. That last spin, she slid her body right up against his, like she was inviting him into her world. This time, the scent was clear. Jasmine and honey smacked right into him. He pushed away the sweet spellbinding scent, and instead, he focused his gaze on hers. His mouth opened, but then he closed it. He had to be sure how to proceed. He lowered his face enough to study her expression. No hint of trickery. Only a smile on her lips.

"Why did you leave before?" He held her close, and his hand felt sweaty as it rested against the skin of her back.

She was so close. With each of her breaths, he could feel the rise and fall of her chest against his, crushing into him. He bit his lip as he focused on her face.

"You had other things that kept you preoccupied."

"But, how did you know?" His head tilted.

He felt her hand on his arm push up as he watched her stand on her toes. His gaze shifted back to her face, level with his.

She leaned in and whispered in this captivating tone, "Magic, what else?"

"How?"

The music slowed, as if to pause before a new one started. Alzerion pulled away but felt the grip of her smooth hand on his forearm tighten —like that of a python on its prey. He blinked, twice. She eased closer to his face, as if she were standing on the tips of her toes once more. He should move away, he thought. There was plenty she wasn't saying. He scowled.

Then his mind blanked as her one hand rested against his neck— caressing his cheek. His cinnamon-red eyes glanced down as her hand cupped his jaw and propped his face up.

"I'm a minder and let's say that I can entice people to give into their desires."

Alzerion felt a heat wash over his face.

"Don't worry, Your Majesty," she crooned. "I won't tell. Your secret is safe with me," she whispered against his cheek.

He gulped.

"Who are you?" He tried to remain calm.

"Who am I?" She took a half step back as her right hand rested below her neck. "I'm Eirini."

"Eirini. That's a unique name."

Her body angled as she leaned into her right hip. She laughed, "As if yours is much better."

He just blinked at her. Then he shook off the comment. "How does your magic work?"

"Curious, I see. Well, this isn't the place."

Alzerion's gaze shifted, and he scanned the room until he found a spot. He stepped toward her, grabbed her hand, and before she could say or do anything, he cruised across the floor. Alzerion didn't want to scurry too quickly, for fear of drawing attention. He moved, hands entwined with hers.

She grinned as her other hand gripped her dress, as her feet quickened with his pace. Alzerion looked ahead. There it was, the large marble column. With one hand on the silver and stone blue column, his other pulled her behind it.

He pressed her curvy body up against the marble. His head stooped —gazed down at her. He hovered over as his right hand pressed against the firm stone. With a quick glance to the side, nobody followed or was near the column. A secluded area.

"So, how does your magic work?" His tone was low.

"You don't let up, do you?"

"Never."

She leaned against the marble. Arms crossed as her hands burrowed under them. "It's simple. I sense things about people and can access a window into the mind."

"I'd say more than slightly."

"Your Majesty, you flatter me." Her eyelashes batted. "In truth, my magic is only a fraction of what it could be. I haven't come into the fullness of my strength yet."

His eyes narrowed.

"Eirini, but—"

"No, no, no," she wagged a finger at him, "it's my turn."

She shifted as her feet shuffled on the ground.

"I'm not a child. No one has spoken to me like that in, well, a long time."

She leaned forward as her eyes focused on him. "Then learn to take turns."

Her tone was not what he expected. Like she did not care that he was a king. He smirked. It was nice to be treated just like everyone else. He almost forgot what that was like. Alzerion stepped back and glanced out at the room. He had to be sure that nobody would find their way back here. It was clear. He turned around to face her once more. This time, she stood with her back straight.

A slight laugh caught in his throat, "Alright, well, I guess it is your turn."

She took one step closer. "What brings you to Lyricao, Your Majesty?"

The smirk faded as his expression flattened. He couldn't tell her. She caught his attention, but he couldn't trust her with the true reason for his trip.

"Aw, why are you so conflicted?" Her tone was playful. "Don't worry. I think I already know."

Silence once more.

Eirini tapped her finger against her chin. "You know, for being a king, you're not that good at sharing details."

"I make it a habit not to speak so openly with strangers."

She winced. "I didn't think that was our level. But I sense that about you."

"Well, if you're clever, why don't you tell me what I'm doing here?" Alzerion held his stance.

Eirini stepped toward him once more, "The elders are busy, you know. There is a celebration going on."

His mouth opened, but she continued, "You'll have to wait."

He pursed his lips.

She stared at him, "Just ask your question. I can feel it burning in your mind."

Alzerion took a breath as he gazed at her. "You say that you only possess a fraction of your power. That's hard to believe."

"What is your question?" Her gaze held firm.

"How much of my mind can you see?"

Eirini winked at him as she closed the last bit of space between them, "Enough to wonder why you're so curious about this former princess, when your mind seems to be elsewhere." Her lashes rose with the tempo of her words.

Alzerion was still.

Eirini reached out, grabbed his arm and prodded him back. His body followed as she pressed him against the marble column. Out of the sight of the party-goers.

He swallowed. "Even if what you say was true, I hardly know you."

Eirini pressed her finger to his lip, "Do you want to convince me of that once more?"

He felt a heat return to his cheeks.

She licked her lips.

He shook his head. "You say that you didn't use your persuasive talent on me?" He raised his eyebrow playfully as a smirk crept across his mouth.

"Believe what you want." Eirini's hands pressed into her hips. "But I didn't. This is all me and, well, you." She giggled.

"What does that mean? What's the difference?" His voice rose. Alzerion pulled his body back as his eyes scanned her.

He would be ready for anything.

She leaned her face in, "Well," she whispered, "the difference is that I like you. I find you fascinating." She winked.

"Why?" His deep voice was full of distrust.

Eirini placed her hand under his chin as she coaxed his face up, and his eyes met hers.

"I'm sure the fates only know, but I like what I see—all of what I see. Every rough edge, pricks and all," Her mouth curled into a wide smile, "and you're handsome."

His face hardened as he tilted his head to the side. "That is ridiculous. You say that now, but I can be quite thorny."

She placed a hand on his chest, and the other rested on his cheek. He felt his heart beat under the warmth of her touch.

"Alzerion. I can just call you by your name, right?"

He nodded. His mouth felt dry.

"A little something about me," Her words were airy as they crashed into his face.

Alzerion took a deep breath.

"I live for excitement, and I'm going to kiss you. If you have a problem with that, well, the choice is yours."

He bit his lip as the pressure of his sharpest teeth made him straighten up. Eirini's hands slid up to the sides of his face. Now was the time to stop it, but he couldn't. He couldn't fight the feeling of wonder. She pulled his face in. He licked his lips, and then he felt her mouth against his. The feeling was different. Her lips moved in quick succession. The sweetness masked by the feeling that his mouth was being devoured as her kiss deepened. Honey tasting kisses, like that of a pastry. She stopped only long enough for him to catch a breath as she pulled his head in once more. The stroke of her tongue sent chills. He felt a weakness. No.

Alzerion pushed until their lips pulled apart. He saw her eyes furrow.

"Maybe we should return." Alzerion said between breaths. "To the party, of course."

"We could, if you wish it." Her voice was just as smooth as ever.

Her lips pursed almost like a pout as her hand caressed the side of his face—twirling a piece of his hair around her fingers. "We could always stay here or I can take you someplace a bit more private."

His jaw gaped open.

"There are such beautiful places to go—places that would take your breath away." Each word sounded airy as she stepped toward him.

Don't do it, he told himself. You are here for a reason. Duty first, like always. He licked his lips—his body yearned for that touch. Instead, he took one step to the side. He focused on the sounds in the Hall. Laughing, cheering, and then a deep voice grew in volume. Eirini frowned for a moment. Then she held out her hand. He escorted her from behind the column and back to the gathering.

Alzerion scrunched his eyes as he observed the speakers ahead. Men and women draped in iridescent silver. He swore he saw Jezzabell amongst them. They must be the Council of Elders.

The last voice he heard grew louder. A male voice that sounded old and velvety. "I'm pleased to present my daughter on her eighteenth birthday. Eirini, darling, please come up here."

The chatter bounded across the whole hall. His posture straightened as he let go of her arm. He stared at her.

"Your father is an Elder?" Alzerion swallowed hard. He tried to get rid of the lump that rose in his throat.

"Alzerion, it's alright, don't be so shy," her words sounded mischievous as her lips pushed together.

Her amber eyes twinkled as she laughed, "You can't say it wasn't fun." She squeezed his hand and then started toward the front of the Hall.

He cleared his throat. How could he have been that foolish? Damn it.

With each stride she took, Alzerion felt naked—felt the weight of his actions. Crap. This was why he didn't give in to temptations. His cheeks puffed up as he blew out air. He made his way back to where Quairken stood at attention. Brentley and Calderon focused on the Council of Elders. It was like a maze moving around the crowd of people until he stood beside Quairken. He heard minimal voices, mostly clapping, as Eirini made her way down the aisle and up toward her father.

"Where have you been?" Quairken whispered.

Alzerion's eyes shifted to him, and then they stared back at the council.

"Alzerion?"

Alzerion heard him, but his eyes narrowed as he lowered his brows—gaze fixed on Eirini. She hugged her father and turned to face the crowd as he, too, clapped. He stepped back.

She glanced from each side of the room. Those deceptively innocent amber eyes locked onto his. Her mouth curved, and he swallowed.

"Sir?" Quairken said again.

"I'm sorry. Distracted." He never looked away.

"I can see that. Where were you? I sent Calderon around the dance floor to search for you."

"Oh, well, we went somewhere off the dance floor. You know... to ... talk." Alzerion finally looked over at Quairken. His arms folded across his chest. He had that look on his face with his eyebrows raised. Alzerion brushed his hand against his mouth, "What?"

Quairken shook his head. Alzerion looked at the other two. Both Brentley and Calderon were far enough away. Then he focused back on Quairken. "Well, I may have had a momentary lapse in judgement." Alzerion felt a flush creep across his cheeks.

He stared at Eirini, who shook the hands of the other members of the council. He snapped back to Quairken. Quairken gazed at him with rapt attention, so he leaned even closer.

"It's not something I wish to talk about. Let's just say that I am well-acquainted with the birthday girl."

Quairken's brows furrowed as his eyes narrowed. Then his face shifted—eyes wide. He opened his mouth, but then closed it again. After a couple minutes, Quairken burst out laughing. Alzerion crossed his arms and his eyes glared at him.

Quairken cleared his throat. "I'm sorry. Only something like that would happen to you."

Alzerion shook his head as he shuffled a bit. The Council of Elders formed a semi-circle around Eirini once the last one shook her hand. Jezzabell stood in the center next to Eirini's father. Jezzabell's head bolted up, and she stared at him, eyes light like she was seeing something. Her opal eyes were slits as she looked at him, and he gulped.

# CHAPTER 10
## *Visions*

J ezzabell's eyes did not waver—not once. The soft opal of her eyes appeared harsh. Alzerion felt the coldness of them down in his bones. He looked away, but when he focused back on her, her gaze was still as sharp as the blade of his dagger. He felt the bite from her piercing gaze. Jezzabell and the man next to her placed their arms up, and the chatter died down.

"Thank you for your generosity on this most wonderful day," her voice was as lyrical as ever. "Eros and I are pleased to present our only child, Eirini. On this day of her birth feast."

Alzerion blinked twice as his hand draped across his mouth—trying to hide. Damn it. If he could start tunneling out now, he would. Wow! Who knew Jezzabell had a child? So much clapping and cheering. The man—Eros, and Jezzabell, turned to face Eirini. They placed a hand on each of her arms. Jezzabell placed her free hand over Eirini's forehead. She muttered something, fast—over and over until this silver light emitted from Jezzabell's and Eros' hands. Silence—save for the sound of the waves crashing in the distance. Alzerion furrowed his brows. He couldn't figure out what was going on. A celebration—how naïve was he to think it was solely about them?

They just stood, watching…waiting. Somehow, he felt rooted to the spot.

There was no leaving, even if he wanted to depart. The other council members remained in their positions as they fanned out. Eirini's skin glowed with this opal hue. Jezzabell and Eros removed their hands, pressed against each other's hands, and then they knelt down. Alzerion's mouth fell open as he observed them, kneeling—reaching out right above her ankle. A few moments passed and then the glowing faded, and cheering, hollering, and general excitement followed. The Council of Elders nodded and clasped their hands together. Alzerion felt this lightness in his muscles. He could move. Huh, he thought.

"Let the festivities continue," Eros' voice boomed as he stood by the council.

Alzerion stumbled forward as Quairken grabbed his arm. Alzerion spun around and saw the crowd jumping around.

"This is nothing like ours," Quairken said as he moved, blocking Alzerion from that rowdy bunch. Brentley and Calderon closed ranks around them. Quairken nodded at them—like they made some silent agreement. Alzerion strolled forward and then meandered off to the side, getting out of the immediate chaos of merriment. His trio followed close behind.

"Where do you think you're going? Leaving so soon?"

From her tone, he could tell she was toying with him. He was not in the mood, and he felt foolish and a bit out of control. None of which made him happy.

Alzerion saw her, and her eyes weren't playful. Her lips twisted into a grimace. Was she sad he was leaving? Eirini was a puzzle. A challenge. Alzerion felt a dull pain. He bit his lip as he stepped toward her, and Alzerion pressed his hand to her chin and coaxed her face up.

"Smile, Eirini. It's your birthday, after all," Alzerion smirked. He focused his thoughts on what he was telling her.

"Not always so easy. I'm sure you understand, what with new acquaintances leaving without a word."

"I wasn't leaving. I had to get away from the—"

"The chaos?" Eirini's eyes locked in on him.

He took a breath as he kept his mind clear. Then he nodded. "These celebrations are, I'm sure, livelier than back in Bachusa."

Eirini laughed, "True. Though I had a wonderful time at that ball you held."

Alzerion tilted his head. "I think you enjoyed keeping me in suspense more than anything else."

"Maybe I did," Eirini's hands clutched her arms as she pursed her lips. Still, a faint smile lingered on her face.

Eirini licked her lips, tilted her head down as her eyes gazed up at him, "I would still be willing to stick to the plan I suggested earlier." Alzerion's lips parted.

He folded his arms. He glanced over at Quairken, who said nothing. Seriously. Instead, Quairken gave him a thumbs up and then snickered. There was no help. He had to make his own choice. He turned his head back toward her, but she was on the move. Each movement was just as precise as she glided toward him. She pressed her hands against his chest. He gulped. She adjusted the top of his shirt. His eyes met hers. There was such a powerful pull. Different from anything he ever felt. She swore she wasn't using her magic on him. So was this an attraction? He bit the inside of his cheek. It forced his thoughts back on Eirini and the situation before him. He had to regain some control.

"Eirini," he cleared his throat, "I will be right back, there is something I need to resolve."

Her eyebrows furrowed, but then relaxed. She took a half-step back. "Of course, Your Majesty."

Alzerion pointed at Brentley and Calderon and snapped his fingers. He heard their innermost thoughts. Alzerion did this once before, but he stayed only long enough to relay his message. Stay here, by her side. Understood? Calderon shuddered. Brentley nodded—grabbed Calderon and pulled him closer to Eirini. Alzerion snapped his fingers again and exited their subconscious. Alzerion grabbed Quairken by the shirt and strolled out of the Hall and into the entryway.

"What was that for?" Quairken said in a hushed, gruff voice.

"You're supposed to have my back."

"Alzerion, I do. I always have your best interest at heart."

"Yeah?" Alzerion's hands clung to his sides. "Could have fooled me!"

He brushed past Quairken as he paced back and forth. Each step of his boots against the marble helped to calm his inner predicament.

"Alzerion, I don't get it. How am I not protecting you?"

Alzerion scowled at Quairken as he continued his pacing—arms folded. "With...Eirini," his voice was low.

Quairken's face softened as a grin emerged. "Let me understand. You're angry because a beautiful woman wants something from you—not sure what, but I'm guessing you do."

Alzerion walked right up to Quairken. His lips were taut. "Let's just say I cannot be alone with her—trust me." He clenched and unclenched his hands—then rubbed them against his chin.

Quairken laughed, then coughed into his hand, and cleared his throat. Alzerion saw the look still on his face.

"It's not funny."

"Not for you, maybe, but it is for me. I'm sorry. You really have the worst luck."

"Thanks," Alzerion said between gritted teeth. "She is challenging at best and, well, she kissed me."

"Ah," Quairken mouthed.

Alzerion saw Quairken open his mouth to speak, but then closed it.

"Just say it, Quairken. I won't get mad."

Quairken took a breath as he placed a hand on Alzerion's shoulder. "It couldn't hurt to let someone else in. You push people away."

Alzerion opened his mouth, but Quairken held up a hand and continued. "I know how precious Aironell was to you, and that can't be erased. I also know that you've made it your duty to find her."

Alzerion's sharp gaze watched him. He craned his neck to the side.

"But that is duty...loyalty, not love."

Alzerion's head lowered as he listened.

Quairken patted him on the back. "If you still love Aironell and I mean truly love her, then I'm sorry for what I'm saying. However, if there's a chance that I'm right, then Alzerion, you need to face what is."

"And what is that?" Alzerion took a few slow, even breaths. He stepped around until he stared blankly at Quairken.

Quairken scratched the back of his head. "Look, the fact remains that what is real is that there's a young woman in there. She's real—flesh and bone. And she seems interested in your stubborn ass."

Alzerion smirked.

He let out a long breath as his arms folded in front of his chest. "Quairken, I hear you ... I do. I've come too far to give up on my search. Regardless of the reasons, I want to find Aironell. Duty first, remember? Nothing else matters. As far as Eirini, I don't have time for a distraction like that." He strolled toward the marble bench against the nearest wall and sat.

Quairken knelt down in front of him. "Then what is the problem?"

Alzerion sighed. His hands pressed against his forehead as his elbows rested on his knees. Alzerion breathed out his nose, "There is no problem."

Quairken raised an eyebrow.

Alzerion felt Quairken's stare in his core. Like an invisible lashing to beat some deeper truth. The truth was, he didn't know why he felt conflicted. A problem for another day, he thought.

Alzerion's hands lowered and rested on the marble bench. They squeezed the marble between fists, "I can't explain any of it."

Quairken stared at him as he remained on his knee.

"She seems like she's trying to get to know me but, Quairken, I have a hard time believing that this isn't a trap."

Quairken tilted his head. "What would be the purpose, though?"

"I don't know," Alzerion said as his head perked up. He scanned the room.

"She seems nice. Definitely a free spirit, that one."

He watched as Quairken moved from the ground as he sat next to him. Alzerion cocked his head toward Quairken as he raised an eyebrow.

"What?" Quairken shrugged.

"She seems like a handful, Quairken," Alzerion stood up and paced.

"In what way?"

Alzerion moved closer to the Hall. He angled sideways to face Quairken. "In every way possible." Alzerion ran his fingers through his hair. "It doesn't help who her parents are. Eirini is like royalty around here, what with her parents being on the council of Elders and being powerful," his arms fell to his side.

Quairken's mouth stretched apart. "Yeah, I don't envy you." He ambled closer and then patted Alzerion on the back.

"Oh, well, thanks for that."

Quairken chuckled.

A sound of clacking on marble reverberated around him, so Alzerion turned. Eirini.

"Did you finish your business?" Her eyes shone brightly.

"I did, but—"

"The other two are standing in the doorway. They were adamant about being near me. I assume that has something to do with you." She stared at him, but her eyes were soft, not harsh.

Good. They at least tried to follow his instructions.

Alzerion glanced at Quairken and said, "Please wait in the doorway with the other two."

"Of course." Quairken left.

"Eirini." Alzerion dropped his gaze to her amber eyes.

She grasped his hands and escorted them to the corner closest to the Hall. An ivory sofa nestled in that space. They sat, and Alzerion fiddled with the bottom of his shirt.

"Your Majesty? Sorry, Alzerion."

His name sounded airy—melodious even. He smirked as he looked back at her.

Alzerion's knee bounced as he tapped his foot on the ground.

"Nervous or bored?" Eirini pursed her lips.

"Those are my only options?"

"The only ones that make any sense," she commented as she folded her arms.

His bottom lip lowered as a slight smile appeared. He glanced around the room—empty. His gaze reeled back as he felt her soft hand on his knee. Her palm rested there. He stopped his leg from bouncing, and down.

He pushed off and slid closer to him on the corner sofa, hands folded in her lap.

"Well, which is it?"

"Now, who's the persistent one?"

She shook her head, "I guess I earned that."

"Why didn't you tell me who you were?"

"Do you mean back in Bachusa?" She tilted her head.

"Sure," Alzerion dug his nail into the skin around his thumb, "you didn't tell me who your parents were, either."

"Oh, I didn't know that we were at the sharing stage," she nudged into him as she grinned. "If that's the case, why don't you tell me why I make you nervous?"

Alzerion's words caught in his throat. He kept a straight face as his eyes narrowed.

"You know there's no use denying it, either."

His nostrils flared. "Maybe I don't like the idea of someone invading my personal boundaries, mental or physical."

He watched as her expression shifted, and her mouth curled low as her lips tightened into a pout. Alzerion bit his lip as he stared down. A glow radiated from just below the hem of her dress.

"What exactly is that? On your ankle." His eyes skimmed past her dress and to the spot where the mark was visible. "I noticed it earlier during your celebration."

"Just the mark of my talents. They will be stronger now that I have had the birth feast."

"Oh?"

"Don't sound so skeptical." Eirini stood and moved to the other side. She slid her back into the corner of the sofa. Alzerion straightened up.

"You should relax, Alzerion." Eirini's voice sounded fluttery. He peered down and her mark glowed a bit.

Alzerion's face scrunched up as he gazed at her, and she motioned for him with the crook of her finger.

"What kind of game is this?" He tilted his head.

"None."

Eirini leaned forward, grabbed his shirt, and tugged, and Alzerion felt his body arch forward. He resisted, but her eyes narrowed.

"Alzerion, now is not the time to be so stubborn."

She pulled once more, and he sighed. Alzerion scooted closer before she ripped his shirt.

"Happy? I'm here. What did you want?"

She blew at him, and he caught the scent of honey. Then she laid back into that corner as her eyes lowered into slits of amber, and her arms folded across her chest.

"You don't have to be a jerk about it. I only wanted for us to relax. It's nice getting to know the other sides of yours."

"My other sides?" His brow rose.

"Don't worry. If I wanted to know all your secrets, I could. I've never really had someone to have fun and joke around with."

"Why does that matter to you? You sound like a little kid, just experiencing things for the first time."

Eirini blushed.

Alzerion leaned forward as he slid up against her. Her eyes had this hint of pain. Then she rested her head on his chest.

"In many ways I am. Being an only child of two important people, well, let's just say that comes with certain expectations."

His voice filled with confidence as he said, "I'm sorry."

There was a moment of silence.

"Well, are you relaxed?" Alzerion glanced down at her.

He felt her head shift as her eyes stared back at him. "The better question, Alzerion, are you?" She grinned.

He sighed. "I am actually. Should I assume you had a hand in it?"

"Maybe a little," she purred.

"Eirini?" Alzerion said. There would be no mistaking his somber tone.

She bit her lip as she stared at him. With her head nuzzled into his chest, Alzerion traced her jaw with his fingers.

She giggled and then looked up. "Don't do that." Her long lashes moved up and down to the cadence of her words.

"If you wish," He smirked.

"Oh, anything I wish?"

"No," Alzerion said fast. "Somehow, that sounds like trouble."

"Huh. I didn't think the King of Bachusa scared so easily."

He watched her as his lips parted. "What is it you want?"

She tapped her chin and then a grin spread across her face.

"That doesn't look good."

She pressed her hands into his chest as she angled her head back. Her eyes fixed on him.

"Again, what is it?"

"Well, it is my birthday."

"So I have learned ... and?" His eyebrow rose.

"It is customary for someone to bring the birthday girl a present of sorts. Well, you came empty-handed."

Alzerion chuckled. "What is it you want? Be fair."

She said nothing. Instead, her eyes shimmered. They had this come and get me look about them.

He tucked a loose strand of hair behind her ear. "Eirini, you already took a kiss from me tonight. I think that was enough, don't you? That should count as your gift."

She shook her head.

He clenched his teeth.

She slid up just enough that her forehead pressed into his.

"What's going on here?" A deep male voice boomed.

Eirini pushed Alzerion to the side as she stood in front of him. "It's not what you think, father."

*Crap.*

Alzerion felt a tightness in his chest. There was no curbing the tidal wave of thoughts in his brain. He didn't want her to know what he was feeling. Maybe she would be distracted by her father. He felt the softness of Eirini's hand as she grasped his hand. He looked down, quick, and then stared back out.

"Oh? You weren't in a compromising position with a man? Doing the fates only knows what."

Alzerion gulped as he stared at Eros, her father. How did he let himself get into this situation? They weren't doing anything. But how to convince her father?

There was a commotion of voices from the doorway as four figures came out of the Hall and halted. Each gazed at them and back at Eros.

Brentley and Calderon exchanged glances as they stepped to the side with their backs to them. Quairken held his breath as he and Jezzabell moved closer. Quairken took a step closer toward the side where Alzerion stood.

"Eros, what seems to be the issue here?" Jezzabell's voice sounded strained. She crossed to the side of her husband.

"That is precisely what I want to know!" His arms remained firmly crossed.

Jezzabell's gaze pierced him. Her opal eyes glowed, and then her face was expressionless. "Let's move to my sitting room."

Alzerion opened his mouth, but Jezzabell and Eros already strode away. Alzerion let out a deep breath. He followed, too. Eirini glided ahead of him. He focused his eyes on the floor. When he reached the entry to the sitting room, He turned to his men.

"You can stay here."

Brentley nodded and stood at attention. Calderon's face wrinkled, but he did not creep forward.

"Alzerion," Quairken grabbed his arm. "I'm sorry, but I think you should have at least one of us in there." Alzerion studied him. He stared, unblinking, as his eyebrow drew together.

Alzerion nodded.

He took a breath and entered as Quairken trailed behind. Scanning the room, Alzerion noticed Jezzabell sat on her lounger, while Eros stood with his hand on her shoulder. Where was Eirini? She was ahead of him at one point. Maybe she was asked not to join them. Alzerion strolled over to the elongated lounge chair across from them. It had silver cushions with the most interesting arm rests—heads of what looked like those sea-dragons. Alzerion sat down—the smell of cedar tickled his senses. Quairken stood off to the side of him, his back draped against the wall.

As he was about to speak, the opal door opened. Eirini. She ran her hands through her caramel-colored locks as she glided into the room. Alzerion snapped his focus back on Eros and Jezzabell. He was already in some trouble, no need to make it worse. His eyes focused on them, but he could see Eirini strolling through the corners of his eye. His heart thudded as she stopped right next to him and sat down. Please don't make it worse. Now was not the time for Eirini's version of funny.

"Oh no," Eros said. "Young lady, you can sit over here." Alzerion turned to see his hands pointing to a single person chair near them...far from him.

"I want to sit by our guest." Her voice had such an innocent airiness.

Alzerion noticed her leg brush against his as she moved. He gazed over at her. She kept perfect focus, staring back at her father with those wide eyes. His jaw opened and then snapped shut. No gawking. She may be the reason your plans fall through. Alzerion rubbed at his mouth as he glanced at the little trio.

Eirini batted her long lashes. Oh, she was good—too good. Alzerion snapped his attention towards Jezzabell, who sat motionless. The muted calm of a predator before it went in for the kill. He bit his lower lip as her eyes followed each of his movements. It was like a delicate game of chess, but who would be victorious? Eros folded. His face hardened, but he did not argue with his daughter.

"Well, Your Majesty, do you have anything you would like to say?" Jezzabell spoke with this calculated tone.

Oh no, he thought. She was angling for something. "I'm not sure what you mean." He focused on his words. Short and to the point—free from misunderstanding.

"If nobody is going to say something, then I will," Eros annunciated each word with such harshness. He stood—legs apart, grip tightened on Jezzabell's shoulder.

Alzerion wasn't sure how that didn't hurt.

"You're a leader? I'd love to know from where." His features tightened. Finally, he moved his tough-looking hands and closed them into fists that hung down at his side.

Alzerion crossed his arms.

"I mean, what kind of alliance do you think you will make with us after...you know."

"Take a breath, Eros," Jezzabell spoke as she raised her hand. "We must be respectful of the King of Bachusa." She shifted her gaze to her husband. "We are above reproach in our actions."

Hard not to think that wasn't a dig at him.

Jezzabell stared back at him, still hints of some sort of scheme in her eyes.

Alzerion cleared his throat. "I'm sorry for any misunderstanding, truly. My goal wasn't to cause problems."

Alzerion's gaze lowered.

Eirini grasped his forearm and squeezed. It felt more like a comforting gesture, but he shot his eyes to her—eyebrows narrowed as he shook his head ever so slightly.

"Hehem," Eros croaked. "I appreciate that, but we have a problem. You were huddled up in that corner—quite close to my lovely daughter." His hands shook around as he spoke.

Alzerion bit his lip. "Truly, I'm—"

"No need to apologize again, Alzerion." Jezzabell shifted in her seat. "It begs the question, though."

Alzerion's eyebrow rose as he waited.

"Maybe this meeting is premature—your tastes seem to have changed."

He didn't miss the raised pitch of her voice.

Eros stroked at his chin. "What does that mean?"

Alzerion breathed out.

Eirini's eyes drew closer. "All of this just from some talking?"

"Eirini," Jezzabell snapped. Her eyes narrowed on her. "I know about the marble column. I saw that when we presented you at the celebration."

Alzerion bit his lip.

Eirini stared at Jezzabell for a moment. "Mother, what does that mean, his taste?"

Alzerion couldn't help but notice she did not deny it. The kiss from earlier.

Crap.

"Alzerion, King of Bachusa, is here seeking help."

"We will support him, won't we?" Eirini placed her hands in her lap.

Eros moved behind the lounger and stood. He propped himself up by pushing down on the back of the lounge chair. "Your Majesty, what kind of meeting is this?"

Alzerion opened his mouth, but his lips pulled taut. He glanced over at Eirini—blinked and turned back to Eros. "There's a vision that Jezzabell agreed to share with me." He gulped. "It has something to do with the true heir of the throne of Bachusa, Princess Aironell."

He didn't need to turn to know what Eirini thought. He could imagine the look on her face. She already guessed or saw his intentions for being here. Like a fool, he turned to her anyway. Her bottom lip dipped lower, as he saw a slight glow from the mark on her ankle. Eirini looked away; her face was rigid.

"Now you've done it," Eros boomed. "Jezzabell, my sweet, please give this fool what he needs so we may get rid of him."

Alzerion swallowed as Eros glared at him. He felt a force pulling his attention back to Eirini, and he saw something different about her. No smile or confident look, like all of her playfulness sapped out of her.

"Eirini?"

She didn't look at him. Alzerion weighed the pros and cons of his next choice, and took a deep breath. He knew this could get him into some trouble, but he reached toward Eirini, anyway. His fingers touched her cheek as he gently moved her face to look at him. Her eyes narrowed as she pushed his hand away.

"Leave my daughter alone," Eros' sharp voice boomed. "You really have some nerve."

Alzerion stood and faced Eros. "Sir. Eros—"

"No excuses. You come here about another woman, yet you...my daughter." His hands clenched into fists as he took a step toward Alzerion. Quairken strode closer, but Alzerion waved him down. There was truth in his words. Eros' words sliced worse than any blade. He may want to find Aironell to keep his promise, but Eirini was a person. Her family would have their own feelings about things.

"If you weren't a king, I swear I'd—"

"Enough," Jezzabell's voice had some bite to it.

Alzerion's eyes widened as he stared at her. She moved toward him in a way that seemed like she was floating. Eirini grabbed Eros' hand as she moved toward Alzerion. She pressed Eros' hand to her mouth—kissed his knuckles. They sat back in the lounge chair. Alzerion didn't move. He waited with his arms limp at his side.

"Alzerion, I gave you my word," Jezzabell gazed at him as she clung to Eros' hand. "Despite any other feelings, I always keep my word."

"Thank you." He flexed his fingers. Foot tapped against the ground.

Jezzabell motioned for him, and he strolled closer. He knelt down before her and Eros. Eros gave him a smug look, as Jezzabell placed her hands palms up. Eros picked up Alzerion's hands and laid them on top of Jezzabell's palms. Silence save for Jezzabell muttering. It was like a whisper—that grew louder, like her words soared around the room.

A breeze crept in through the window. There was a crispness in the air as Jezzabell's hair swayed. Her eyes glowed, just as before; white. Alzerion nibbled the inside of his cheek. Hopefully, it wouldn't be anything too difficult. His luck hadn't been great as of late. Suddenly, her hands shook and then gripped him—tighter with each chant. Their hands moved in a sort of pattern.

"Danger. Grief. Schemes. Order."

It was like she couldn't spit the words out fast enough. Jezzabell released his hands. Hers flitted about as she continued. "A friendship to mold, love's newfound ache to break one's dutiful hold. A fate of not two, but three unfold."

Eros tilted his head. A look of wonder on his hardened face.

*"One made anew for thee.*
*One purpose found. One soulmate abounds.*
*Fate woven tight. Nothing but night.*
*A cost so stark. Heart of a forest so dark."*

Jezzabell blinked, and her eyes no longer glowed as her arms dropped to her lap. She exchanged quick glances with Alzerion, then Eirini, and up to Eros.

# CHAPTER 11

## *Decisions*

Alzerion's head spun with her words, a swirl of confusion.

"What does any of it mean?" Eirini's sweet voice pierced the deafening silence. He heard her feet on the ground but didn't turn.

Eros rose. "Will he succeed?"

Jezzabell locked eyes with the pitcher of water on a nearby table. Alzerion saw Eirini from the corner of his eye. She poured some liquid into a cup and handed it to her mother. Jezzabell swirled it around in her mouth and then stared back at Alzerion.

"Yes. You will succeed, but I'm afraid there will be a cost. I fear it will be steep."

This time, Alzerion glanced at Eirini. Her shoulders shrugged as she looked away from him. Could, she have known about this? Was her talent as powerful as her mother? He took a deep breath as his face turned back to Jezzabell. He was sure Eirini mentioned some sort of cost.

Alzerion cleared his throat. "It doesn't matter." His voice was firm as he stared at Jezzabell.

Eirini's gasp was audible, and he moved closer as she stood at his side. "You're not serious, are you? You'd risk well, possibly everything for—for a memory?"

Alzerion's nostrils flared as his mouth squeezed together, tight.

"You don't know what she has been through all this time. No clue why she never even tried to return."

"Doesn't matter." Alzerion said, quite crisp and confident. He stared at her. "Unless you're telling me you have the answers to those questions. Well?"

Eirini's amber eyes darted away.

"I owe her that much at least." Alzerion turned back to Jezzabell. "I promised, no, vowed to find the truth. So, yes, Jezzabell, I will do it."

"Alzerion," Jezzabell's voice was but a whisper. She strode toward him and placed a hand over his heart. Alzerion looked down at her palm and, with eyebrows furrowed, he glanced back at her.

"There's one question I must ask." Alzerion nodded. "Are you willing to put yourself through danger for her? Is your devotion that strong?"

Alzerion glanced over at Quairken with a piercing look. Damn it. He asked him the same thing. As he slowly turned back, he spotted Eirini's glowering gaze. She leaned closer as her hands gripped the skin near her elbows.

"Well? Is it?" Jezzabell asked once more. "Is the bond so deep that you would risk whatever price awaits you?"

Alzerion bit his lip as he tapped his finger against the side of his jaw. He didn't really know what to say.

"Mother, don't let him go." Eirini strolled into view between Jezzabell and Alzerion.

Jezzabell raised a hand that stopped just in front of Eirini's face. "It must be his choice. I'm sure you see that as clear as I, it seems."

Eirini licked her lips and glanced back at Alzerion. He locked eyes with her. She knew something. Her hands tightened into fists as they pressed against her leg.

He didn't miss the silent moment between them. Jezzabell's gaze was harsh as her eyebrow rose. She turned back to Alzerion, mouth flat.

"Jezzabell, I've only had one goal—one motive. I want to bring Aironell back. I will save her. Nothing else matters...not my intentions or what obstacles may present themselves. Costs be damned."

Jezzabell flipped her hand over his heart and tapped twice. A slight of her eyes and then her mouth parted. "Do you love her? Is she the one? It matters more than you know."

Alzerion felt a warmth over his face. He bit the inside of his cheek. He could feel the eyes of everyone in the room on him. As if his answer could single-handedly change the course of history. He breathed out as he saw a quick glance between Eirini and Jezzabell. He sure wished he knew what they were thinking. Even Eros moved closer and stood behind Jezzabell. His mind sifted through what to say. He lowered his mouth but said nothing. A dryness filled his throat. He felt a tight grip on his chest as his breathing quickened.

A soft hand rested on his shoulder. Eirini. She nodded at him.

"Relax." Her words exuded serenity, like that of a stream flowing in the middle of a field of lavender and honeysuckle.

The fog inside lifted as her hand slid down to his and she squeezed. Her lips curled up into a thin smile.

"Better?" Her voice had a slight lilt to it.

He pulled his hand back and straightened up. Alzerion rubbed the back of his neck and dipped his chin as he let his eyes rest back to Jezzabell.

"I guess that tells me all I need to know," Jezzabell said. "King Alzerion, you're at an impasse. I'm not sure you truly know the answer to my question, at least not on the surface. I feel you've buried that deep inside."

"I'm sorry," Alzerion's voice was low. "I haven't let myself think about those answers. Success hinges on my willingness, and for now, that is all I'm able to give as an answer."

Jezzabell took a step back, and Eros placed his hand on her shoulder.

"Not to worry." Jezzabell tilted her head. "I have seen a piece of the puzzle that is hidden deep in your core. I guess time will be the actual test."

Alzerion tilted his head.

Eros stared at Alzerion, chin raised, and then he glanced at Jezzabell. His lips parted. "Where does that leave things?"

Eirini strolled around until she paced behind her parents. It looked as if she muttered something as she strolled around to the right side of Eros. Alzerion frowned as he waited.

"I think I have an idea," Eros continued.

"What might that be?" Jezzabell asked.

He clapped his hands together. "Why doesn't Eirini join him on this journey?" The moment the words came out, he shook his head. "Did I just suggest that?"

"Yes," Jezzabell said, as her eyes narrowed.

Alzerion's jaw clenched and then he blinked back at Eros and then stared at Eirini. This was her, but why? Why would she want to come on this quest? She knew something - whatever it was - that Jezzabell didn't want him to know.

Jezzabell pulled Eros by the hand until they sat back in their seats. Eirini stood between Alzerion and her father.

"Would she even want to go?" Jezzabell turned to Eirini.

Alzerion dug his fingers into his chin. "Surely, neither of you can think this is a wise plan?" Alzerion shifted his gaze to Jezzabell and Eros.

Jezzabell folded her hands together as she stared at Alzerion. Her focus fixed on him, until a half smile formed on her lips. Then she shifted her gaze to Eirini.

"Well?"

"I would love to," Eirini bowed her head.

"Why?" Alzerion spat out before he could stop himself. "You heard your mother. There's a cost to this quest. Surely, it means there's some level of danger. What's in it for you?" Alzerion took a few steps toward Eirini.

Eirini grinned. "Wouldn't you like to know, Your Majesty?"

Tension throbbed at his temples. Alzerion bit down on his lower lip as his hands held firm at his side.

Eirini moved closer to him, and her eyes sparkled. Alzerion studied her expression and mannerisms. This made no sense. She stared at him, eyes not letting up. Alzerion was still as his nostrils flared.

"There, there, Your Majesty." Eirini patted him on the shoulder. "It should be fun. All I will say is that an adventure sounds exciting."

His jaw gaped open then Eirini turned and moseyed back toward Eros.

"Plus, I get to see what the fuss is all about, that unhealthy obsession of yours." A smile flashed across her face.

She had to be out of her mind. His wide eyes blinked as he shook his head.

Jezzabell stood up and moved to Alzerion. She grasped his hand and held out her other to Eirini. Jezzabell held both hands together.

"Be strong and take care of one another out there. Trust will be key."

Alzerion could not believe his ears. Jezzabell was serious.

"Eirini, you should prepare for the journey," Eros said as he wrapped an arm around her as they exited.

Alzerion blinked twice and then motioned to Quairken. He shifted his weight and nodded.

"You and the other two should get some rest. We leave tomorrow."

Quairken bowed his head and left.

Only Jezzabell remained.

He cleared his throat. "Am I the only one with any reasoning skills?" His hands flew into the air as he pivoted around. "This is a horrible plan." Alzerion ran his hands through his hair.

"I disagree."

Jezzabell spoke with such an even tone. For someone sending her only child into harm's way, she seemed pretty calm.

"Alzerion, I've seen enough. Not every outcome or piece, but enough to know this is exactly what you need."

A knot twisted in the pit of his stomach.

"What I need!" Alzerion seethed. "No. Jezzabell, this is some scheme that either you or Eirini concocted, of that I'm sure." His voice wavered.

"Eirini? She has planned nothing. You're mistaken." Her voice was fierce.

"You're right, I was mistaken. I shouldn't have come here." Alzerion lifted his chin. Each word felt strained.

"Don't be foolish. There is no plot against you. None by my family, at least. You have no enemies here in Lyricao. If you fear enemies, well, you had that in Bachusa."

He took slow, cautious steps away from her. His eyes stung as he blinked.

"Don't forget that vile man who tampered with your memories."

"I'll deal with him later." Alzerion's hands clenched into fists.

"As you wish, Your Majesty." She bowed her head.

"How can you do this to me?"

Jezzabell's head rose. Alzerion stared at her without blinking.

"You're making me responsible for the safety of another person—you know how that turned out the last time." Alzerion gritted his teeth.

Jezzabell patted his shoulder. "You aren't to blame for the choices Aironell made." Jezzabell glided to a little desk and scrawled something onto a slip of paper. Then she handed it to him. "Don't open it until you are working on the preparations for the journey."

Alzerion tilted his head as he grasped the piece of paper. "What is it?"

"More details about the trip. It should help."

Alzerion nodded as he slipped it into his pocket. Jezzabell sauntered toward the opal door.

"Wait."

She turned halfway.

"You say I will be successful, right? Does that include keeping everyone safe?"

Jezzabell pursed her lips. "I have not seen the end result of what will pass. Fate has not willed it. From what I have seen, I guess that depends on how you look at it."

Alzerion opened his mouth. Before he could say anything, Jezzabell raised her hand up. He kept silent.

"You seem to have an unruly soul that you keep at bay. Those inner demons of yours will plague you." Jezzabell tilted her head.

A coldness crept through him.

"You're going to face many choices. We shall see what fate has in mind for us all. You are the architect of our futures—choose wisely, young king."

Then Jezzabell strode out of the room.

# CHAPTER 12
## *Morning Surprise*

Jezzabell had to know something more—some hidden truth. Alzerion sat up with two plump pillows against his back. He recounted the events of that bizarre meeting, like how Jezzabell glimpsed into his soul. He shook his head, leaned forward, as his arms held him up as he stared out the open window. The windows were some sort of beige colored cedarwood, with sand-colored curtains. They swayed side-to-side as a breeze blew in from the sea. The smell of salt water was strong.

Alzerion smirked. Beautiful yet different. Odd, but wonderful. He tugged at the linen of his nightshirt. A light tap on the door caught his attention. Alzerion pushed back and flung the thin blanket over him.

The door parted just a crack. "May I come in?"

He recognized the lilt, the enticing undertones of her voice. "Come in, Eirini."

A scowl awaited her.

Eirini closed the door and twirled around. She saw him. His cinnamon-red eyes felt like fiery flames ready to scorch her. His eyes trailed her as she sat on the bed, legs crossed.

"What are you doing here?" Alzerion's sharp words cut through the air.

She tilted her head as she smiled. "Now, that's not nice, Alzerion."

"After last night's events, you're lucky I'll even speak with you."

His face was still, but his tone was deep. He was cute, even with all of his prickles. She laughed.

Alzerion's lips parted.

Eirini rocked to her knees. Hands against the smooth linen sheets as she crawled across the bed. Moving closer to him.

Alzerion leaned forward and held his thick arms up, hands pressed out. He grabbed her arms.

"Eirini, what are you doing? You really shouldn't be in here."

She flipped her hands up and let her fingers graze against his lower arms. Alzerion quickly unleashed his grip and pulled back.

"You worry too much."

He shook his head. "No. You don't worry enough, and I'm not sure why."

Eirini's cheeks flushed as her grin widened. She just waved his comment away.

"Why are you so gloomy this morning? It's a beautiful day out." She pointed out his window and then turned back. "Plus, you return home so we can start this journey of yours." Her body bounced a little as she sat on her knees.

She watched him as she waited for his response. Alzerion sighed. Her left hand rested on her mouth as she nibbled at her bottom lip. Come on, Alzerion, loosen up already. He straightened up as he stared at her. Her eyes darted down for a moment. A slight heat in her cheeks as she realized he looked exquisite in his nightshirt. His hair and eyes were a pleasant contrast to the sandy colors. Then she brought her gaze back up to his eyes. They still held this wonder, but she sensed he had these guards up.

Eirini held a palm out to him. He looked at her hand and then back at her—his eyes pinched in. His arms folded across his chest.

Silence.

Each stared at the other and nobody caved. Much like a silent battle with Alzerion. He was stubborn. She felt the coolness spread on the mark she received yesterday from her celebration. She gazed down for a moment and saw the curly heart in a shroud sparkle. Eirini looked back at Alzerion. She blinked back her realization. Alzerion held tight to the bitterness of his past! How can I break that chain that bound him? Her head tilted as she gazed at him. A twinge gripped as her heart beat skipped faster. The sight was clear, but she had to keep a straight face. He couldn't know that she saw a flash of some of his darkest moments. She felt his pain. His self-defeat. His doubts. Even the ache that once gripped his heart tight. Alzerion must be a master of masks.

She took a deep breath. She wanted to learn more, to know him. Eirini scooted closer to him until she felt his calf under the blanket.

"Don't panic," Eirini said.

Alzerion remained stiff and his face didn't change, either. He held that puzzled look in his eye. Eirini sat next to him and positioned herself on her side as she propped her body up with her elbow against the pile of pillows.

"I just thought you know we will travel together. Maybe we should get to know each other a bit."

His gaze lowered to her like a predator. "Did you know about the cost from your mother's vision?"

Her cheeks puffed as she blew out. "I knew there would be a cost. I told you there would."

"But, did you know it would be a hefty price?" His eyebrows angled down.

She pushed herself up as she faced him straight on. "Alzerion, I didn't know that." She licked her lips. "I didn't see that level of detail."

He didn't trust her. She sensed that clearly.

"I know you don't know me all that well, but I want to help you. I may poke fun at your quest, because I think you could do better."

His gaze softened.

"I mean, she is alive. Then where has she been? Why hasn't she come back to her family or you? Did you think about that? Maybe she isn't worth risking everything you have."

"You wouldn't understand." Alzerion's head bent.

"Try me." Eirini placed her hand under his chin as she pressed his face back up. He bit his lip, and she pulled her hand back.

"I wouldn't know where to start. Why do you care? I believe you have some sort of angle, some kind of game you're playing. I just can't figure it out." He leaned back.

Her mouth curled, and slowly a smile formed. Eirini laughed.

"I'm sorry." She cleared her throat. "Alzerion, there is no game. I swear."

His eyebrow rose.

"I can see trust does not come easily to you." She slid a little closer to him. "Alright, so here's the deal. I believe I can be of help on this quest of yours."

He leaned forward as his hands lowered onto his lap. "You truly only want to help me?"

His eyes softened. Finally. The muscles of his neck relaxed.

"If that's the case, then tell me, Eirini, what do you get out of helping me?"

Eirini raised her chin. "Adventures, Alzerion." She beamed.

He frowned. 'Adventures,' he mouthed.

Her hands clasped together. "I want to help you but I also want to experience some excitement and maybe have an adventure."

"You're insane. You know that, right?"

"No," she chuckled. She shuffled closer to Alzerion, closing the space between them. This time, he did not pull away.

His face watched her with such wonder.

"I'm tired of being shut in because I'm ready to see other places. Experience all that life offers." Her hand pushed against his chest, and didn't move. She licked her lips as she breathed out, slowly. She let her nails trace each muscle as they slid across his chest. His gaze scanned her body and then rested on her face... just as the faint hint of a blush covered his cheeks.

Eirini placed a hand on his cheek. "Alzerion, you're different. Not like the stuffy men I am restricted to meet around here."

"Not sure if that is a compliment." Alzerion swallowed. He placed his hand over hers. She felt his fingers rub into the fleshy parts between her fingers.

She giggled. "That tickles."

"Eirini," his tone shifted.

He was serious.

"I'm sure it'll be an adventure, but we must be cautious. We have to be on guard. I'll need you to listen, though. Will you be able to do that?"

"Don't talk to me like a child," her voice rose a bit. "Alzerion, I'll be a team player, but I won't pacify you either."

His cinnamon eyes fascinated her. She sensed the unspoken challenge between them. His smirk clung to his face.

Alzerion's lips parted. "Maybe we should get ready for the day. We leave for our journey this afternoon."

She crossed her arms around her chest with her chin tucked in.

"What?" Alzerion tilted his head and smirked. "You were expecting something different?"

She leaned her face forward. Alzerion leaned forward. She whispered, "Maybe I did."

He swallowed. "What could you have—"

Eirini moved her left hand to trace the lines of his lips.

"No."

Her fingers felt the pulsing movement as he spoke.

Alzerion grabbed her finger and held them. "Eirini, I think I should be clear about something. I don't indulge in whims."

"Maybe you should," She wrapped her fingers around his as she lowered their hands, "it could be fun."

Alzerion shuddered as she knelt forward and plunged her hands into his hair, pulling it back. Eirini pulled, just enough that his face gazed up at her. She saw a pained expression.

"You really don't want me to kiss you, do you?" Her eyebrows pulled down.

Alzerion sighed. "A part of me does, but Eirini, I—"

Eirini swooped in and placed her lips on his. It was a sweet little peck. As she kissed him once more, she felt a hand to steady her back. She arched her head down as her nose grazed his. She smiled at him. Alzerion had no expression.

"I thought maybe once you relaxed, you would be fine."

Alzerion's other hand cupped under her chin and pulled her face in. This time, his lips did all the work. She felt his lips crush down on her. After each kiss, his mouth pulled at her bottom lip and he nipped her. Eirini felt at ease with him. Then he pulled back, shoved her to the side and darted out of the bed.

"Alzerion, wait."

He was already in the washroom.

Eirini bounced out of the bed and followed him.

"Alzerion?" She tried not to let her words waver.

He didn't turn. She grasped his arm, and then he pulled her into him. His expression was stony and the pressure against her arm tightened. It didn't hurt, but he was strong.

"Never do that again. Eirini, do you understand?" He gasped.

It made little sense. He kissed her that time. She felt the eagerness in that moment they shared, yet his face reflected something different. It was like he struggled with two different wants in one body. Almost like he was in constant conflict. She could sense his struggle.

A slight ache coursed through her veins. "I'm sorry. I didn't mean to anger you so much."

He took a more controlled breath as he bent his head down. His grip relaxed. "I'm not angry." He licked his lips and then pulled away. "I don't like losing control. I rarely put myself in a situation for that to happen."

He faced the marble wall with his hands against the stone. She went to say something, but then decided against it. Instead, she rested her head against his back as she wrapped her arms around his chest. "I'm sorry."

She felt him squeeze the back of her hand. He was a riddle; she thought. She loved puzzles. Slowly, she withdrew her hands and backed away. "I'm going to get dressed and be sure that I'm ready for our departure. I hope you will be in better spirits then." She glided across the floor, almost out of the bathroom.

"Eirini, wait." He was next to her faster than she could process his words. "You're not upset with me, are you?" He was adorable. His face wrinkled as he awaited her response.

"I'm not. I just thought—it sounded like you could use some time alone. Soon you will be stuck with me until the end of your quest."

His lips stretched into the widest grin she had seen from him, yet. "Well, not too much time. I get lonely." He winked.

Eirini's lips parted as she stared at him, stunned. She turned and left.

# CHAPTER 13
## Preparations

His mind still tried to make sense of it. How was he going to get by with her on this journey? She loved countering him every chance she got. Eirini was clever and quite fascinating, if he was being honest. He took a sip of water, gobbled up his breakfast, and headed to Jezzabell's sitting room. A safe, peaceful place to think—that's what he wanted. His hands pushed open the doors and Eros sat at the desk, in all his silver clothed glory. Ugh, great.

Eros didn't look over at him, not until he sat on the window seat.

"Do you like the view?"

Alzerion's eyes narrowed. "I do. We don't have the sea in Bachusa. It's so—"

"Pretty," Eros said.

Alzerion nodded and then stared back out the window. "I was going to say serene. There is something about it, kind of deceptive." Alzerion faced Eros. "You don't have to worry about me. I hope you know that."

Eros held the book he was reading—eyes flashed toward Alzerion. "I'm not following."

Alzerion scratched the back of his neck. "There's no deception, not on my part." He swallowed. "I will do what I can to keep her safe."

Eros blinked as his light green eyes stayed on him. "Which her do you mean?"

Alzerion felt a heat creep into his face. Eros closed the book and placed it on the table. He started toward Alzerion, but then the door opened.

"Sir, we are ready for the journey," Brentley bowed.

Alzerion stood and strolled over, but Eros held out a hand.

"Brentley, tell Quairken I will be right there."

"Sir?"

"What?"

Brentley didn't get the chance to speak. In waltzed Eirini, and his eyes blinked twice. She was a vision in her travel attire.

"What do you think?" She twirled around.

That outfit squeezed each curve of her body in perfect harmony. Alzerion clenched his teeth as he snapped his attention back to Eros.

He humphed.

Alzerion watched as Eros' jaw tightened. "I will give you...two minutes. Okay?" He looked to Alzerion and then Eirini. "Then I will be back with Jezzabell."

Eros shook his head as he left the room.

"Well?" Eirini's eyes dazzled as she gazed back at him. Her hands on her hips as she posed.

There weren't enough words that could do it justice. He took long breaths but kept his distance. Eirini strode over and closed the space between them. She placed an arm around his back. His hands held her hips, to keep her an arm's length away. The black, leathery material of her pants felt smooth against the curve of her body.

"You look nice." Alzerion cleared his throat.

Her dark boots covered most of her calves, but everything fit just right.

"Wait, how did you get this outfit?"

She grasped his forearm. "I have my ways." Her lashes rose as her candy-red lips smiled.

"Oh?" He smirked.

His hands slid up the loose sleeves of her tanned blouse—fingers trailed across the curved neckline. At least she was covered this time.

Eirini licked her lips and pulled back as she grasped his hands. He felt the softness. He stared at her as her eyes sparkled.

"If you wanted us to be alone, all you had to do was ask, remember?"

Alzerion tilted his head. "I don't know what you mean? My focus is on the trip back to Bachusa."

"Right." Eirini squeezed his hands. "Don't forget that I can sense the truth, Alzerion."

Alzerion bit his bottom lip as he breathed out. Her eyes fixed on him as she squinted and then paced around him.

Alzerion stepped back as his eyes narrowed on her. "Let's set some boundaries."

"What boundaries?" Eirini's arms folded.

Alzerion straightened up as he pointed at her. "You can't just pop into my mind whenever you want. I don't want to feel like I have to add extra guards up."

"That's because you're already so guarded." Eirini fired back.

"I'm not playing. If I have to bring you on this quest, then you have to respect my wishes. Do you understand?" His tone was deep and firm.

Arms still crossed, Eirini strolled toward him and stopped right in front of him. Her face twisted with irritation as her mouth scrunched up into an adorable pout. He smirked as he shook his head.

"Hey!" Her voice rose. "You don't get to be a world-class jerk and then laugh it off." Her arms swirled around her.

"Of course." Alzerion whispered as he leaned forward. "Would you rather that I kissed you off?"

Eirini's jaw dropped as she blinked back at him. She swallowed and then frowned.

"You're going to be a puzzle, Alzerion, but I swear I will figure you out."

Alzerion held out his hand. Her eyes pinched in as she grabbed his hand.

He smirked. "Best of luck." His grip was firm as he shook her hand.

"Fine." Eirini said through gritted teeth. She pulled her hand back as she tossed her hair behind her. "I'll stay out of your head, as best I can."

Alzerion nodded.

"But if you're in trouble, all bets are off. Do you understand?"

Alzerion chuckled. "I won't need saving."

Eirini was within his personal space. He saw her hands clench into tight little fists. If she wanted, she could swat him.

"Hmph. What, you think you're too good for my protection or help?"

Alzerion chose his words carefully. "No. It's just that—"

"Hehem." Alzerion's face turned to the noise. Quairken stood before them. At least it was a break from her. Somehow, he had a knack for making things worse with her.

Quairken looked to Eirini and then to Alzerion. "We're ready, Your Majesty. I believe that Eros and Jezzabell want to send us off before we can leave."

There was silence as Eirini's eyes glared at him. Quairken interrupted a bad moment. Quairken stared at him as his teeth shone through such an awkward smile.

"Send them in," Alzerion said. His gaze lingered on Eirini. She lifted her head, chin up. Still, she said nothing. Her silence was deafening. He heard Quairken speaking to the others.

Eirini's eyes flashed a light sparkling hue of amber as she grabbed his left arm and squeezed.

"What are you doing?" Alzerion spoke low, like he practically growled the words.

She said nothing.

Alzerion felt this twinge in his skin. He wriggled his arm, but the pain intensified as he felt like a flame was searing into his flesh. He bit down on his lip so as not to cry out from the pain.

He tugged, but she kept her grip around his wrists as she soared toward him. Alzerion held up his free hand, so she didn't collide against his chest. Her face was inches from his. Her eyes glimmered once more and then they returned to normal.

"Now, I won't have to worry if you're foolish enough to refuse my help."

Alzerion's mouth laid flat against his face as his eyes darted in. His nostrils flared.

"Tough," she snarled. "You may be brave, Alzerion, but even you're not above needing help." Eirini let go of his wrists as her folded hands hung against her stomach.

Alzerion glimpsed at his wrists as he heard the shuffling of feet. It would have to wait.

"Eirini, are you all set?" Jezzabell said.

Alzerion cleared his throat as he observed them. Jezzabell's eyes scrutinized Eirini as she gave her a once over.

Eirini grabbed a small leather satchel and draped it across her hips. "I believe so."

Jezzabell kissed her on the forehead. Eros kept a fixed expression. His eyes shut tight as he hugged Eirini.

"Be careful." Eros' tone was sharp.

She nodded.

Eros turned his attention to Alzerion. "Take care of her."

"I will." Alzerion held out his hand.

Eros strode toward him and shook his hand. His lips parted as his eyes rested on his wrist. Crap. Alzerion saw it for the first time. An odd shaped heart with flecks glittered over it etched into his skin. Damn it, Eirini.

"Is that what I think?" Jezzabell arched an eyebrow.

Alzerion pulled his hand back as he yanked the hem of his sleeve down a bit.

Eirini raised her right hand, and there, on her wrist, was a matching mark.

His eyes grew wide. "I don't understand."

"It's a fail-safe. That has tethered you to my daughter." Eros laughed heartily. "Like a magical tracker of sorts, but much better. It'll allow her to find you and you can find her. I guess I don't need to worry if you break your promise. This will ensure that you keep her safe."

"You did what?" He glanced down at his wrist, and then he glared back at Eirini.

"Doesn't matter," Eirini said as she raised her chin up. "Now I can keep tabs on you, in case you're not as invincible as you seem to think." Her eyes dated to him.

"You can't control me," Alzerion said through gritted teeth.

Eirini walked up to him once more. She stood very close to him. "I wouldn't dream of it."

Quairken snickered and then coughed. "Hehem. Sorry." He tapped his chest.

Jezzabell exchanged glances with him, and then Eirini, but her face softened.

He swore she knew something.

Instead, she said, "Travel safely. Be alert and be prepared for anything." Then she and Eros left.

Thank the stars they were out of there. Alzerion had already transported his little group back into Bachusa. They walked through the wooded area behind the palace and stood before it. Quairken cleared his throat. Alzerion motioned for him to go. He wouldn't deny him time with his family —not when they would have to leave so soon.

"Brentley. Calderon."

They both stood at attention. "Yes, sir."

"You may go to the barracks. Prepare yourselves."

"What do you think we will need?"

Alzerion shrugged. "Pack what you can and wear the rest."

They dashed off.

Eirini inched closer and wrapped her arm in his. "So, what do we do?"

Alzerion stared at her. "We won't be here long. Just enough time to let Francisco, Evalyn, and my mother know what I'm up to."

Eirini's turned to the palace. Her amber eyes scanned the stoney structure.

"Something wrong?" His tone lowered as he gazed at her.

"Nothing. It's just so—"

"Different?" He laughed.

She nudged him. "Well yes. I have never seen it in the daytime. Much different from what I'm used to."

He held out his arm to her. She studied him and then wrapped her arm around his. Alzerion escorted her up the grand staircase, and they stopped in front of the Great Hall.

"Why did we stop?"

Alzerion unwrapped their arm. "Listen, there's so much you don't know."

"I'm listening." Her eyes invited him in to share.

He sighed. "It's a long story. For now, just know that you are about to meet the previous king and queen. Their daughter is who we are journeying to save—and I haven't told them anything about it."

Eirini's mouth flattened as her eyes went wide. He opened the doors of the Great Hall and allowed her to walk in.

Alzerion held his breath as they strolled over to the long wooden table against the closest wall. They draped the table in a berry-colored cloth. As they neared, he caught Evalyn's gaze.

Her face lit up. "Francisco, he's back!"

Francisco placed his cloth napkin on the table and stood. Alzerion strolled to an empty chair and pulled it out. Eirini sat down as he pushed her in. Alzerion noticed their eyes watching, inspecting his every move.

"Alzerion, who is your new friend?" Evalyn's voice lacked the normal enthusiasm.

Francisco went to speak, but then closed his mouth as he sat back down.

"This is Eirini."

She waved and then rested her arm on the wood of the table. Alzerion sat down next to her.

"That's a pretty name." Evalyn grabbed a chocolate muffin and placed it on her dish. Her eyes darted between her and the food. "Would you like one?"

Eirini nodded and said her thanks as Evalyn handed her one.

Francisco's posture straightened as his eyes glanced at Alzerion. "I thought you went to Lyricao."

Alzerion added some fruit and sausage to Eirini's plate. "I did." He grabbed a scone for himself.

Francisco's gaze shifted between the two of them—eyebrow raised. "How was it?"

"Was it wonderful?" Evalyn's voice sounded forced. He sensed something between them.

"It was very nice." Alzerion's free hand pressed into the grooves of the wood. "The views were breathtaking," Alzerion said with a bite of his scone. "Oh, and there was a celebration."

He refrained from glancing at Eirini, not that he had to. Her presence was powerful. He took another bite of his scone. Mmmm, such buttery goodness.

"What kind of celebration?"

Evalyn and Francisco both stared back at him as he wiped his mouth.

"I've heard that their gatherings are quite the sight." Francisco tilted his head.

Alzerion swallowed. "It was memorable. I will say that."

Which part?

Alzerion's eyebrow arched up as he scanned the room.

Meeting the heads of the council or me?

He cleared his throat as he glanced over at Eirini. Didn't I ask you to stay out of my head?

Her mouth curled upward. Fine.

"So, Eirini, how did you come to meet our king?" Francisco crossed his arms as he glanced at them.

"We met at the celebration." She popped a tiny grape into her mouth.

Alzerion frowned as he stared at her. Eirini glanced at him but then back to Francisco.

Alzerion, stop distracting me.

Me...what about you?

You want me out of your head? Then you have to do your part. Keep intense feelings out of your mind, especially when I'm so close. We're bonded, don't forget. It makes it easier for me to enter your thoughts.

She swallowed and continued. "The gathering was for me. It was my birthday feast."

"Oh, how nice," Evalyn added. "Have we met your parents, maybe? Did you all attend our masked ball that we just had?"

Alzerion felt flushed as he refrained from his desire to whack her for this stupid mind meld.

Not helping, Alzerion.

"I'm the daughter of Eros and Jezzabell." Her voice had that song-like lilt to it.

Evalyn smiled. "Jezzabell? Oh, how wonderful." She stood up and hugged her. "I'm not sure if you know this, but your mother and I were the best of friends."

"I do." Eirini grinned. "She speaks highly of you both." Her eyes lingered on Francisco.

He still sat with his brows furrowed and arms crossed.

"Maybe you should tour our gardens?" Alzerion said. "How does that sound?"

Eirini wiped her hands and laid them on his arm. "Will you join me?"

Alzerion was silent for a moment. "Why don't I find you when I'm done here?"

Eirini's mouth curved down. Her eyes narrowed on him as she stood up. She turned away from him.

"It was nice meeting the both of you." She bowed her head to Francisco and Evalyn.

Eirini's head craned back to him and with a wrinkle of her nose, she sauntered away and out the doors.

Just know I found that annoying, Alzerion. I'll get you back for dismissing me.

Just great. He took a deep breath. Thankfully, she didn't interject again. Once the door closed, Alzerion turned to face them. Evalyn's smile faltered for a moment, but Francisco looked at him with a sharpness.

"What's going on?" Francisco's gaze fixed on him.

He bit his lip. "You both know me so well." He breathed out. "I went to Lyricao to speak with Jezzabell."

Evalyn grasped her cloth napkin as he spoke. Francisco remained silent as he leaned forward.

Alzerion pressed his hands onto the table as he stood. "I believed Aironell might be alive. I found something that made me think so.." He paused.

Francisco's eyes relaxed. His mouth flattened. Evalyn's grip on her napkin tightened.

"Jezzabell has foreseen it. Aironell is alive. I just have to find her and return her, just like I vowed I would."

"What?" they said in perfect unison.

Alzerion paced around the table as he explained. He told them of his meeting and the newest bit of prophecy, then turned to face them once more.

Francisco sighed.

"So you plan to leave in search of our daughter?" Evalyn narrowed her eyes.

"Yes, that is precisely my plan."

Francisco rose. "You have our support, Alzerion, always."

"Thank you." He smirked.

Evalyn strolled toward him and placed a hand on his shoulder. Her eyes filled with tears.

"One more thing." Francisco rubbed at his chin. "Why is Eirini here? What part does she play?"

Alzerion felt a warmth creep across his cheeks.

"Alzerion?" Evalyn's voice sounded strained.

"Well, she may be my punishment." He hesitated. Alzerion pulled at his ear. "Eros caught us talking. Next thing I know, I'm told she's joining me on this journey." He spoke quicker than he ever had before. "I'm not sure if it really was his idea or hers, to be honest. She has her own talents. She is her parents' daughter, after all."

Evalyn patted his hand. "It's okay Alzerion. She's lovely."

Francisco cleared his throat. "Be safe. We would hate to lose you too." Francisco walked toward the door and turned. "You're the son we never had." He left the room.

Alzerion felt a warmth wash over his heart.

"It's true," Evalyn said. She took a step away. "We want to see you happy—whomever that may be with at the end." She, too, left the room.

They were something. He shook his head. Alzerion stopped at the little desk in the hall and wrote on a piece of paper. He had to leave soon, but he wanted his mother to know where he was going. Satisfied, Alzerion folded it and wrote her name on it. He left it there—she would find it. It was their spot.

"Leaving again?"

The words were heavy and gave him a chill. Alzerion turned to meet Adrastus' icy stare.

Alzerion's chest puffed out as he straightened up. "What can I do for you? We didn't have a meeting today, did we?"

"Of course not, Your Majesty."

Alzerion felt the venom in his words. His eyes scrunched up as he stared at him. "I'm in a bit of a hurry. Did you need me for something?"

Adrastus ambled a step closer as his hand rested on the little desk. "I ran into the two fools on their way to the barracks. Where are you going? It's not wise that you leave with so few men for protection."

"I appreciate the concern, Adrastus. I will be fine."

Adrastus' eyes and mouth resembled a shadowy grin.

"It's more that I care about the kingdom. Something might happen in your absence."

Alzerion leaned forward. "Are you threatening me?"

Adrastus' hand flung back and rested over his chest. "I would never. I just don't think that it is wise for you to be leaving Bachusa with no protection."

"Francisco and Evalyn will watch things for me. Don't accuse me of not thinking about the well-being of the kingdom."

Alzerion's face was firm, like the stone that made up the palace. His eyes glared back at Adrastus. "Also, I cannot prove it, but I'm sure you tried to poison me at that ball of ours. Watch your back Adrastus. I'll deal with you when I return."

Alzerion strolled past, but Adrastus seized his arm. His grip was tight. Alzerion glanced down at his hand and then up to his face. He simply grinned.

"We shall see," His words hissed. "In the meantime, I will keep a watchful eye on Bachusa for you. You have nothing to worry about."

Adrastus let him go and then strode off to the Great Hall.

Alzerion's upper lip rose as his teeth flashed. He had to get rid of Adrastus before he caused irreparable damage. He was like a predator— biding his time these few years. But to what end? Alzerion didn't have the time to wonder. He took a breath and headed to Gorgeous Garden to find Eirini.

He hurried through the garden until he found Eirini sitting on the horseshoe shaped bench. Her eyes flickered on the reflecting pool as she fiddled with the petals of a flower in her hand. He stepped with care, but he stepped on a twig that snapped under his foot. She looked around until her eyes caught him standing there. Alzerion straightened up.

"How did the rest of the conversation go?" Her eyes looked him over as he sat down beside her.

"Fine." He stared down at the reflecting pool.

"Are you intentionally not looking at me? Maybe feel guilty about sending me away?"

Her tone was lighter, hopeful.

He sighed.

"Eirini, I don't regret my decision." He turned to her. "The whole mind thing was too much for me in that moment, if I'm being honest. And, well, I was already feeling so—"

"Conflicted," she said.

Alzerion rubbed a hand through his hair. "Yes, I needed you away. I'm sorry if that hurts your feelings."

Eirini stood and gazed down at him. Her eyes weren't upset or harsh. Instead, they were soft, understanding. She held out a hand. He grabbed it as he stood up. Eirini inched closer to him. "I will prove that I'm trust-worthy, Alzerion. In time, you will see my worth, my usefulness. That is my vow to you, but until then, take this."

Alzerion's jaw lowered as the muscles of his jaw tensed. Eirini placed her hands on his shoulder and pulled herself up a bit on her toes. The scent of jasmine and honey tickled his nose as her face came closer to him. Then she kissed his cheek.

As she pulled away, Eirini said, "That should seal the end of my promise."

He swallowed.

Eirini tilted her head. "What?"

Alzerion's hand touched his cheek. He felt a warmth from her kiss. "So, that's how you make a deal with someone?"

Eirini smiled. "Well, that's how I do it with someone I find interesting."

Alzerion's face froze.

"Don't give me that," Eirini wagged a finger at him, "you let me kiss your cheek after all."

Alzerion reached out and grabbed her finger. "I'm not some sort of domesticated animal. Don't wag your finger at me."

Eirini pulled her hand back and folded her arms. "Then don't act like one."

Her face and tone were like a sass-filled pain in the ass. He watched as her chin jutted out and her arms tightened like a barrier between him.

Alzerion stepped closer. "Eirini." He reached out to her.

She swatted his hand away—eyes narrowed, practically squinting. Then she turned on her heels and stormed off.

Alzerion jogged after her. "Eirini," he called out, "don't you think you're being a little overdramatic?"

No answer. Her pace quickened as they passed by the rose bushes, the pond, and stood in the field before the palace.

"Eirini, please stop. I'm not sure why you're angry. You insulted me, remember?"

He finally caught up to her. Alzerion positioned himself in front of her.

"I'm not an ass. I'm pretty sure you have that part covered right now."

Alzerion opened his mouth, but then closed it as he bit his lower lip. His nostrils flared. Damn it. His hands clenched as his nails dug into his palms.

Her weight rested on that back left foot of hers. Her lovely eyes looked sharper—almost like a fiery amber hue.

"Let's talk about this, please?" His voice dropped lower.

She shook her head.

"I know it wasn't right but, stop popping into my mind. How is it fair that you're upset with something you never should have known? I make no excuses for my thoughts, but at least I didn't actually say that to you."

Her body stood there as it stiffened.

"I'm...sorry. Okay?"

Her eyes stared back at him.

Alzerion heard footsteps not far away. He craned his neck to see Brentley and Calderon approaching. As if on cue, Quairken stepped down the stairs. He was fit for battle. Sword hung at his scabbard. Alzerion snapped his hands, and he was ready in his dark leather pants and loose shirt, covered with his vest.

"Here." Quairken handed him his sword. "I didn't think you'd want to forget that."

"Thank you." Alzerion finally turned away from Eirini.

He focused on Brentley and Calderon. "Did you get everything? Sacks for some food items, containers for water, and sleep sacks?"

"Yes, Sir," Calderon said.

Alzerion looked back at Eirini, but her face was unchanged. She was upset, and he knew it. "Well, I guess it's time."

He pulled out a small piece of paper and unraveled it.

"Is that what Jezzabell gave you?" Quairken took a step closer.

It reminded him of a child awaiting some exciting news or secret to be gleaned.

Alzerion nodded. Biting his lip, his eyes scanned each word of the creme-colored paper.

"What's it say?" Quairken's gaze focused on him and that paper.

Alzerion felt a heaviness creep within. This had to be some sort of joke. His cinnamon-red eyes widened as he looked up. "It has our location."

"What luck." Calderon said, with a lightness in his voice. "This may be easier than you thought, sir."

Alzerion's head turned in his direction. Brentley slapped him in the head.

"Ouch! What was that for?" He rubbed his head.

Brentley shook his head. "Don't be stupid."

Alzerion walked around them, patted them on the shoulder, and peered back at Eirini; then Quairken. "It's not good."

"Where is it?" Quairken straightened up. "We can tackle anything."

Alzerion folded it back up and returned it to his pocket. He rubbed the back of his neck. "The DarkFlower Jungle."

Quairken stood still, almost lifeless. He blinked and finally spoke. "How can she be there? You were already there."

Alzerion swallowed. "It says we must go to the heart of it."

Calderon's face looked like he was about to vomit.

"Well, we know where we are headed, so let's get to the pond in Gorgeous Garden."

Brentley nodded and grabbed Calderon's arm—pushing him as they walked first.

Success was possible. Jezzabell said it was. He focused on that as he followed Brentley and Calderon. After all this time. Could he actually be about to find her? He had this pitting in his stomach. He reached his hand above the water as the others circled around. As long as he could keep everyone safe and find her unharmed, then it would be a success.

Quairken stood on his left, followed by Brentley and Calderon. On his right stood Eirini. She placed her hand on his arm. He didn't look at her. He didn't have the time to wonder if she was still upset with him.

His left hand stretched out, seeing the silent, unmoving water pull and pitch.

"Alright hold on to each other!" Alzerion spoke as the bluish-green water bubbled and swayed. The air around, picked up like a storm was brewing. They did as instructed, with Quairken grabbing hold of Alzerion's shoulder.

"Brace yourself!"

Alzerion heard the whistling wind, and he squinted as he held firm. "Portalis magica introitus!"

The water curved side-to-side as a bright white light appeared in the middle of the pond. The white space mellowed as the water curled around it. It looked like a watery crown that frothed at the entrance. He could make out trees and darkness through it. He gulped.

Alzerion stepped forward. The others followed his lead as they stepped into the transparent, shining destination. Then they were through.

# CHAPTER 14
## Cavern

The last through, was Calderon. He turned and vomited. His face was ghost pale as he stood and joined them.

"You good?" Brentley patted him on the back.

He took a deep breath. "I'll never get used to this moving with magic." Calderon gripped the leather strap of a sack as he adjusted it over his back.

"No apologies, needed," Alzerion nodded.

"This doesn't look like the same spot we entered last time." Quairken ambled off to the side as he looked around them—like he was spinning.

"It's not." Alzerion said. He strolled forward, passed the first bulky tree, and nearly tripped over something. "What the—"

He couldn't make out what it was. "Did you see that?" He pointed left, then right and left again. The thing had speed.

Eirini was by his side without hesitation. Her hair whipped about as she, too, searched—gazed down at the twisted vines and wooden floor. The group trod slower as they gazed around. A darkness overshadowed the place. Not as dark as where he was last time. More of a grayness with some strokes of deep red—much like the colors at sunset except deeper. So many trees and bushes. At least he didn't smell that sweet aroma. He remembered how enticing it was.

"Be wary of sweet-smelling flowers," Alzerion warned.

131

Alzerion's head jerked to the right as he heard a snap. Calderon spun around and around until he almost fell over...but ... nothing. There it went again. He saw something that appeared to dash as it bounded around them, kicking up dirt and leaves from the ground.

"Is that a rabbit?" Eirini's voice quivered.

Alzerion grabbed her hand and drew her behind him. Finally, the thing bounced into view. It sat on top of a boulder with the gray and dark red sky behind it. It looked like a rabbit.

"It's huge!" Brentley gasped.

Quairken crossed toward it. It didn't move, but its head angled to them. Then it bounced up—Quairken threw his arms up, blocking his face. The creature landed on the ground next to him. Alzerion tilted his head. It was larger than a normal rabbit—it came up to Quairken's waist.

Stay close. Alzerion glanced at Eirini. She nodded, and he turned back to the creature. "Can you understand me?"

"Sir," Brentley said—brows raised. "It's an animal. They don't speak."

"Who says?" Quairken scolded. "The laws of magic go far above what we know, right?"

Brentley's gaze shifted down. Alzerion knelt down, eye-level with the animal that had long antlers sticking out of its head. They looked like branches with many offshoots.

"I'm Alzerion, King of Bachusa," he tried again. This time, it tilted its head as if it bowed.

Its circular brown eyes stared back at him. "Greetings."

Alzerion's mouth opened. He could hear audible gasps from Brentley. It wasn't their fault neither he nor Calderon had much experience with magic.

"What are you?" Quairken broke the silence as he picked up his leg and shifted his weight.

"It's a jackrabbit," Eirini's voice wavered, "am I right?"

Its big thumping foot came closer as it whispered. "Correct, but what are you doing here? The DarkFlower Jungle is not safe for visitors."

"We have come in search of someone, she—" Alzerion noticed it paw at the fur over its chest. Its ears twitched.

"What do you know?" Quairken grasped his sword and pulled it out. The gleam of the metal reflected in its eye.

The jackrabbit bounced back and turned.

"Wait," Alzerion called. "We don't mean you harm. We, well, need some guidance."

It turned around. "You shouldn't be here, Your Majesty."

Alzerion stepped, with such care, closer to it. "How do you know who I am?"

"The whispers of the flowers! They are horrible gossips. You need to leave before he comes for you. He won't be happy that you've trespassed twice now."

"Who do you speak about?" Eirini whispered back.

Alzerion nodded and then turned back to the jackrabbit. "Please. I can't leave... not without the young woman I came to find. I fear she has been stuck here somewhere for a few years."

"Then you're better off not wasting your time, for she is lost to you." It straightened up. "This is the calmer side of the DarkFlower Jungle." Its eyes darted around and then settled back on Alzerion. "Where you must go...is not a place you should."

"Please," Alzerion pleaded. His nails dug into the leather of his scabbard. His voice steadied as it grew lower. "How do we get to the heart of the jungle?"

The jackrabbit's gaze fixed on Alzerion.

Odd being sized up by an...oversized bunny. He knew that - without its help his group could wander aimlessly.

"It might not be all that you hoped" it spoke with this air of wisdom.

Alzerion didn't waver. He took a deep breath and straightened up. "I would make any bargain?"

"Oh?" Its eyes had this shiny twinkle in them. "The question is, what will you be willing to sacrifice for this deal?" Its head cocked to the side.

Quairken grabbed Alzerion's arm. Alzerion shot him an icy stare and shook his head, and Quairken withdrew his hand.

Alzerion focused his gazer back on the jackrabbit.

"Anything." Alzerion's mouth tightened as he spoke. "I have always been willing to pay the price."

"Hmmmm," its mouth quivered.

"Wait," Quairken darted between the two of them. "you will risk a lot, Your Majesty; but I'm unwilling to let you—not yet." He spun around to face the jackrabbit. "Do you have a name?"

"Wise indeed. Name's Gael." He lowered his body and appeared to be resting on his hind legs.

"Gael?" Eirini's lilting voice broke the staleness. "Why, that sounds so...human."

Gael nodded. "I was human once. You will find many of us creatures here were once human. Best to be cautious," Gael's brown eyes bulged, "you'll have to decipher the actual beasts from the prey." His front paws clung together. " I was human, at least that was before."

"Before what?" Calderon asked in his bumbling manner.

He shook his head—antlers swinging around. "It's not safe to speak of it ... not here. However, I will tell you where to go. In order to get to the heart of the jungle or, as we refer to it—the secluded soul. You'll head east. That will take you where you need to go." Gael's head pointed in the direction.

Brentley and Calderon shuffled away from Gael and stood in the eastern direction, at the ready.

Quairken nodded at Gael and then joined the other two.

"Thank you." Alzerion stretched out his hand and shook Gael's front paw. "I appreciate the help."

"Good luck." Gael turned and bounced away.

Alzerion turned. Eirini patted him on the shoulder. Alzerion pressed a hand to hers, squeezed, and then let his hand lay at his side. He motioned to Eirini as he started the trek. He glanced at his side, occasionally, to be sure that she remained close by.

There was a rustling of leaves, and he remembered his last encounter here. Strange creatures and people that chased him, wanting something. He couldn't risk that, not this time. Alzerion motioned for them to run. Brentley and Calderon were in front, with Quairken behind. Many times, he had to pull Eirini, keeping her at his pace.

"Let's stop." Alzerion took a slow breath. It was a stretch of time, and he didn't think Eirini could run much longer. She grasped her knees as she caught her breath.

Alzerion paced around, holding his hands to his hips. With each slow breath, he took in his surroundings. It was growing darker. Could it be late? Telling time was hard here. No sun to base it on, what with the grayness.

"Are we going to rest here?" Eirini spoke between gasps.

Alzerion wrinkled his nose as he looked at them. He didn't want to stop. They may be safe for now, but that couldn't last long. He glanced at the group as he rubbed his mouth. His eyes rested on Quairken, whose face looked drained. There was a soft touch on his shoulder, and Alzerion tilted his head. It was Eirini.

"Alzerion, let's rest," her words sounded tender. "I'm sure we could all use a bit of rest."

"Alright." Alzerion sagged against the closest tree with smooth bark. With his back propped up, he slid down until he sat on the dirt.

"Sir. Calderon and I will collect wood to start a fire." Brentley spoke quickly.

Alzerion nodded.

"Wh-what?" Calderon clung to the strap of the sack he was carrying.

Brentley dropped his sack and then grabbed Calderon's too, tossing them toward Quairken. "Let's go, Calderon. Wood and kindling, that's our mission."

Alzerion glanced up—at least the leaves and branches had a large overhang. They provided a fair amount of protection. It was the perfect spot to rest.

Quairken pulled out the thin sleep sacks. Alzerion walked over and helped.

"Eirini, why don't you sit here?" Alzerion patted to the sack he laid in front of the tree he was propped up against moments before.

"Are you sure? I can help." A heaviness trailed across her facial features. For the first time he noticed how warn she looked. He felt a small tug at his insides, but he shook it off. "I'm sure. We will take care of it this time. Rest."

She moved to the spot and then angled her head in his direction. "Wait, why are you being so nice?"

Quairken let a slight chuckle escape. Alzerion's head darted back to him. Quairken mouthed "sorry" and then went about picking up stones.

"I don't understand," Alzerion focused on her.

"Look, I'm not saying you're not a nice person, but why don't you want my help?"

Alzerion didn't know what to say to that. Why was it then when she spoke he either felt like she was insulting him or was really sweet? There was no middle-ground.

Eirini took a step forward. "I can always mind meld, but I prefer not to. I am trying to give you the privacy you requested, and we are not in danger so, please answer me."

"Ugh," Alzerion groaned. "Sometimes you can be infuriating. Eirini, I was just trying to be nice. But, if you want, you can help. I mean, you wanted to be here on this quest."

Alzerion handed her a small cotton sack. Eirini took it as she stood within slapping distance of him. "You can use it to put any fruit or small food items."

Just know I didn't like your tone.

Alzerion's lips pulled taut in a straight line. No matter what I say, you seem to think the worst about me or my motives.

Eirini gripped the sack as she stepped past him. She turned. "Then don't act like an insufferable jerk. I don't care that you're a king."

Eirini strolled away.

Alzerion clenched his jaw. "Hold on!" He stormed after her.

She made it beyond a few wide bushes. The sky was even darker here with the splotches of red and the eerie sounds of life he didn't see. When he twisted his hand and she stopped in her tracks.

"Hey, what in the world?"

Alzerion dashed in front of her.

"Of course," she muttered. "What was that for?"

"Since arriving in Bachusa, you've been very confrontational. Why?" Alzerion's hands splayed out with his palms up as he spoke.

She squinted. "Unspell me."

Alzerion's nostrils flared, but he twisted his hand.

Eirini stepped toward him. "You have this God complex in Bachusa. Maybe it is always there, but it wasn't as noticeable in Lyricao."

Alzerion smirked. "Eirini, it is who I am. I was clear. Hell, you sensed my need to—"

"To control. I know." Her lashes flitted up as she spoke. "That doesn't mean that you can speak to me like a nuisance. I'm here. Let me be a part of the group."

"I gave you a job, as you wanted."

She wagged a finger, but then clenched her hands and pressed her finger into his chest. "Alzerion, not as an afterthought. I have studied many books and my talents could prove useful. Don't think of me as a damsel that you need to save. I am not that girl. When I need help, I'll ask for it."

Alzerion's gaze softened. "I'm...sorry."

Eirini stopped prodding him with her finger. Alzerion grabbed her hand, and his fingers grazed against her skin. "I can't promise that it won't happen again. In my experience, well, I'm sure you know."

Eirini's eyes glistened. She turned her hand and then rested it over his heart. He felt the warmth of her touch. "Don't worry so much. If you're not rude to me, we will get along fine. If you're controlling or not."

He blinked—as the start of tears pulled in his eyes. Alzerion backed away, turned, and wiped at them. There was a slight warmth in his heart. He felt her hand on his back.

"Now, I will do as you asked. I will find some berries or whatever may be around."

Alzerion spun around. He felt a relaxed feeling wash over him. "Eirini, maybe you shouldn't go alone. I know you don't need saving from me, but we don't know what we may encounter. If I'm being honest, when I sent you away, I was just trying to keep you away from me." His face lowered to the ground.

"I suspected that."

Alzerion's eyes rose and met hers. He rotated a piece of her hair in his fingers and then tucked it behind her ear. "You can be so, well, stubborn, but I don't want something to happen to you."

Eirini beamed. "I'll take that as high praise coming from you."

Alzerion chuckled.

"I can do this, Alzerion. You have to make sure to set the fire and get back before they all panic and rush to find you."

He felt the weight of the choice as it hit him. She wanted him to trust her. He could sense that. Maybe he could trust her with this task since she seemed so sure of success. Alzerion rubbed at his chin as he bit his bottom lip. "Alright. But be back soon. I don't want to search for you."

Eirini nodded, then turned and left.

He stared out at the space of where she left, and then he jogged back to the others. Quairken finished the circle for the fire pit as Brentley and Calderon pointed to the pile of wood. "There's plenty."

"Ah, you're back," Quairken said. "Where is Eirini?"

"Oh, she went to search for berries and small things to eat."

"Was that a good idea?" Calderon stumbled over a large piece of wood on the ground. He caught himself before he fell.

Alzerion shook his head. "She seemed determined."

He waved his hands over some pieces of wood and they floated and swirled into a neat elongated structure, where each laid against the next.

"Ignis." Fiery flames erupted in his palm. He blew, faintly, to adjust the smolder. Then he tossed it on the pile. Ah, yes.

Quairken knelt near the fire first. The other two joined in. Alzerion watched as Calderon held his hands over the flames as one flame lapped up. Calderon's hand darted back so fast that he nearly fell over. Alzerion pressed his hand to his head. That one was the clumsiest person he had ever met.

Alzerion sat with his back against the smooth bark of one of the trees. He found this conical looking slug with little wisps. Alzerion picked it up with his thumb and index finger and tossed it. Then his mind drifted off to the conversations they had. His eyes honed in on the mark on his wrist. Eirini. Surely, she should have found something by now. His fingers traced the lines of his bonded mark. After the third time he traced the lines, he noticed a slight glow.

"Alzerion, come quickly!" Alzerion bolted to his feet.

"Something wrong?" Quairken asked.

"Did any of you hear a voice?"

"A voice?" Calderon shook his head. "None other than us."

He turned as he peered out. Could that be her calling to him? From the mark? He had to find out. He observed his mark, but nothing. Silence, save for the sound of the fire. His eyebrows drew closer as he bit down on his lip. He felt the muscles of his neck strain as he stared out. Alzerion closed his eyes as he cupped around his ear. He focused his mind, clear of regret and concern. No, he needed to focus on any slight noise. There it was.

"Was that a scream?" Brentley asked.

Alzerion's gaze looked at them, and without warning, he ran.

"No!" Quairken shouted.

It was all he heard. Alzerion didn't stop or look back. It was Eirini; he was sure of it. He moved with such quickness. She needed him. He didn't like always being the one to save everyone, but he promised to keep her safe. But it was more. He couldn't pinpoint what it was, but like a thorn in his side, she grew on him. He wanted to keep her safe and not just because he had to.

Each muscle of his well-toned legs flexed and pumped. He came to a clearing.

"Eirini!" He called out. His eyes furrowed as he gazed around. The space was more open than not. It would be hard to hide somewhere. He saw Eirini running toward him. Someone was chasing her. He could sense her dread.

"Alzerion?" Her voice splintered.

His gaze fixed on her. He jumped over a few branches in his way as he met her halfway. They collided, and her body crashed into him. He placed a hand on her lower back as he propelled her forward. She wasn't running as fast as he needed, so he scooped her up and then dashed. He saw a couple of people in dark, hooded cloaks that followed. One raised a staff and, from the corner of his eye, he heard the sizzle as the shot hit the bush next to where he moved. Alzerion scanned the space. There wasn't another spot for them both to hide, so he put her down in a cramped little space between two trees whose branches coiled around the other.

Stay. Then he turned and dashed forward as he ran in a sort of circle.

Finally, he moved until the two strangers followed him and were away from Eirini's hiding place. Then he stopped. He stared at them and muttered a spell under his breath, and his arms hung high as he opened his hands, palms facing them. He felt the heat in his hands as a reddish glow covered his hands. The strangers exchanged glances and the one with a staff pounded the end on the ground. Then they disappeared. Alzerion felt a rush of relief course through him as he lowered his hands. He flexed them until they returned to their normal color.

Alzerion strolled to where Eirini sat stuck between the tree branches.

"They're gone, whoever they were." He reached his arms in and grabbed hold of her. "Jump up and I'll pull you out."

She bounced up, and he pulled. Her body flung up as she crawled out and laid against him. His nose touched hers as he felt his heart beat faster in his chest.

"Hehem, well, at least you're safe." Alzerion slid her to the side as he returned to his feet. "Eirini, stay close, please."

He stayed alert as he searched around them. He waved to her. She nodded and stepped cautiously toward him. He held out his hand as she grabbed holding him. He felt her nails as they dug into his forearm. He glanced down at her.

"Not to stir up any debate, but I guess you needed some saving." Alzerion smirked.

She licked her lips and, with a gleam in her eye, she pressed her mouth together. "I also asked for help when I needed it."

His entire face glowed as his smirk turned into a hearty laugh.

"Wait until you need saving. And don't tell me you won't. You will, trust me."

Alzerion angled his body to face her, and he held both of her hands in his. "Is that a vision you had?"

"Wouldn't you like to know?" She winked at him.

She waltzed past him, but Alzerion grabbed onto her elbow and spun her around until she rested against him.

"You know, you're starting to make a habit out of this. Not that you'll hear me complain."

Alzerion placed a finger over her lips and let his hand rub against the softness.

"Eirini, don't get yourself into trouble again, or take someone with you so you're not alone. We're lucky the strangers were easily swayed." His voice was firm.

"Who should I have with me?" She pressed off his chest and stepped ahead of him.

"You can take whoever you want, as long as you're not alone." Alzerion kept pace with her as she strolled toward the middle of the clearing.

She paused and turned to him. Her hand rested under her chin as she beamed. Oh, this couldn't be good.

Eirini stepped toward him, grabbed onto the collar of his shirt. Alzerion stared back at her.

"What?"

"I can have anyone, I might want." She whispered as her face drew closer to his.

He gulped and she tilted her head toward his. Eirini rubbed her nose against his cheek. "I choose you, you know."

He didn't feel annoyed. Instead, there was a lightness that filled him. He ran his hands through her hair while his other hand laid against her cheek. Alzerion licked his lips and then pressed them to hers. It was a slow kiss. He pressed each kiss deeper as he sucked in air to breathe. Each kiss was exacting, and a frenzy filled in his mind. He heard the crack of something as he pulled his head back. Eirini gradually opened her eyes, and she looked as if she was dazed from a dream.

Alzerion rubbed his lips and then looked for the source of the noise. He squinted as his eyes fixed on someone near the bush with deep purple blooms at the other end of the clearing. He wore a mask made of leaves and had some sort of markings on the shoulder.

"Who are you?" Alzerion hollered.

The stranger made no movements. Alzerion took a few steps forward. A male figure locked eyes on him. A rustling of twigs snapped and then the figure muttered something and then stomped on the ground. Alzerion heard it like a loud thwack. It reverberated through him. The figure dashed away.

"There over here."

Alzerion turned to see Quairken, Brentley, and Calderon come into view.

Alzerion felt the ground shift.

"Don't come any closer," Alzerion said.

It was too late. The ground crumpled until it gave way. They already stepped into the crumbling pull. Alzerion grasped Eirini and held her close. "I'm sorry," he mouthed.

Then they fell down. Alzerion felt a pull trying to rip him from her, but he held on to her hands, tight, even as they fell. When he saw the ground, he pushed until he was lower than her. No time for him to do anything, Alzerion held his arms firm so that gravity didn't pull her beneath him. He fell to the ground and Eirini dropped against him. He felt the soreness crushing against his back. A throbbing coursed through his body. Eirini knelt down beside him as she helped prop him up. He grimaced.

"Alzerion, are you alright?" Quairken coughed.

"Aer," Alzerion whispered and then lightly blew out. A light breeze picked up and when it settled, he could see through the dust. "I'm alright. A little sore. How are you guys?" His voice echoed.

"Calderon has a sprained ankle, but that's the worst of it."

Eirini stood up and glanced around. "Alzerion, what is this place?"

He winced as he stood, but walked over anyway. "Not sure." He rubbed the back of his neck as he saw cages of different sizes. Some with bones and others opened. He gulped. "What in the world?"

"Alzerion, there's something in this one over here."

Alzerion grabbed Eirini's hand and pulled her with him. Lighting wasn't great in the dank space. He could barely see. There was a staleness that mingled with rot. He was unsure if it was remnants of old food or whatever was kept in the crates. In some of the nearby cages, he could see bones lying on the floor—that was all that was left, most times. His nose scrunched up as he looked around. There was no water source, and all he could see were craggy stones scattered on the ground. Alzerion zoomed to the wall. His hands grazed over the cold, wet rock. Cracks etched into them from years of wear. As he slid his hand down, he felt the bumpy roughness. Then the rock that protruded out stuck him. He felt a slight burning in his hand. Blood. Crap!

Alzerion couldn't heal himself—that was beyond what he learned to do. Instead, he ripped off a thin piece of material from the bottom of his shirt. Feet shuffled on the craggy ground near him as Eirini grabbed the tattered piece of shirt and wrapped it around his hand. Then she pulled tight as she knotted it up. He flexed his hand. It didn't hurt as much, but the feeling was still there.

As he neared Quairken and Brentley, his eyes darted to Calderon, who was sitting on the ground. Quairken pointed off to the side. There was a massive metal cage. This one was different. Alzerion placed his hands on the bars, which were a mixture of tough metals and something else. It felt like magic. He blinked into the cage—eyes widened. Instantly, he fumbled until he found the lock. He was right. There was no key. This was a magical lock. He pressed his hands against it and closed his eyes. A reddish glow emanated from his hands as it spread across the cage until it disappeared. Then there was an audible click—the door creaked open. The creature limped out, its large wings curled tight to its body.

"Is that a dr-dr-dragon?" Calderon mustered.

Brentley went to speak, but then closed his mouth.

Ha, he learned his lesson.

Eirini broke the silence. "No, it's a creature that looks similar but is different."

Alzerion cautiously stepped nearer. The beast laid there, with its face pressed against the ground. Alzerion put his hand on the creature's back and slowly glided his hands toward the back of its neck. Each scale tarnished, but still felt the strength beneath his hands.

*I'm not a dragon.*

Alzerion looked at the creature. *Then what are you?*

*A wyvern.*

"Alzerion, what's going on?" Quairken asked.

"It's a wyvern," Eirini answered. "They are majestic creatures, powerful and magical. I've never seen one in person before." Her eyes widened as she stared at the wyvern.

Alzerion turned to them and nodded. "He can somehow communicate with me."

*What can we do for you?* Alzerion lowered his face, gazing into the wyvern's navy-blue eyes.

*I need my strength back. I've been down here for ages, locked up like a common prisoner.*

Alzerion grabbed an old-looking bowl and placed it in front of the wyvern. He waved around and touched the base of the bowl. As they rose, a clear liquid filled up. The wyvern's nostrils sniffed. Alzerion brought it closer, and it gulped the water. Alzerion refilled it. Again and again, until it perked itself up.

"Thank you. It's a start. Now for us to leave this prison."

# CHAPTER 15
## The Tale

The wyvern moved about rather slowly. It looked like it hadn't had a decent meal in some time.

Alzerion swallowed. Starvation was torture. A heat rose in his stomach that churned around like lava in a volcano. Only Eirini stepped forward. She held that unlocked metal door open as they stepped out and onto the dirt floor. Alzerion placed his hand on its scales.

*Do you have a name?*

Alzerion felt choked up. He never saw one before. He thought them extinct or works of imaginings.

*Endrus the wise.*

He lowered his scaly, dragon-like head. His eyes looked like slits of navy. He had this imposing look, with its snakelike tail and wings, with claws that looked like hooks at the closest corner of its wide wings. Alzerion nodded at him, almost bowing his head.

*Thank you, young ruler. Your kindness won't soon be forgotten.*

Endrus walked with its spiked tail curled inward. As he walked, Alzerion noticed a barb of sorts on the tip of the tail. It craned its neck.

*I need food to add to my strength. Then I can help get us out of this cavern.*

Alzerion stared into his eyes. Silence. Alzerion felt a truth in Endrus' navy-colored eyes. He lowered his snout, like an unspoken agreement. Alzerion turned to Quairken and the others.

"We need to search the area."

Calderon still sat on a pile of rubble. "For what?"

Brentley smacked him upside the head.

"Ouch, what was that for? I'm already slightly injured. I don't need more issues." He rubbed the back of his head.

Alzerion pressed his lips together so that he wouldn't burst out laughing.

"Alzerion." Eirini's voice soothed like a nice cup of tea. "Did it say something to you? A way to get out of here, perhaps?"

Alzerion nodded. "Endrus." He pointed to the wyvern. "Has been mistreated. He needs food to gain strength—to help us escape this gloomy cavern."

"What does a wyv—"

"Wyvern," Eirini said.

"So what does something like that eat?" Brentley asked. Alzerion saw his nose wrinkle as he stared between Eirini and him.

Alzerion turned back around, and Endrus was closer to him. He pressed his cold, scaled snout against his forehead. Alzerion saw the briefest of images—rabbits and rats.

*Anything that is unfortunate to come into contact with me and looks tasty.*

Alzerion furrowed his eyes.

*Don't worry, young ruler. I'm not fond of humans, especially not those who have rescued me from certain death in that metal prison-trap.*

"Calderon, you stay and rest that ankle." Alzerion turned his head to the others. "Eirini, stay with him, please."

She opened her mouth, but then stopped. Instead, she clung to the bonded mark on her wrist.

"Thank you," Alzerion whispered. "I needed someone to stay with Calderon. "

"Plus, I'm not breaking any of your rules. I'm not alone."

Alzerion sighed. "For once, you didn't argue." Alzerion stood before her.

Eirini's amber eyes softened. "It didn't seem worth the spat. Not when the task is something is gross, as it sounds."

"At least be careful." Eirini's words were pure as she forced his face up at hers. She pressed her cheek to his and as her face pulled back, she kissed his cheek. The warmth of her lips stirred something in him. His skin felt alive as she pulled back. Alzerion locked eyes with hers.

"I'll be fine, remember."

Eirini rolled her eyes at him as she crossed her arms.

As he stepped away from her and toward Quairken, he felt a wave of feeling. It wasn't his. He angled his face to see Eirini. A slight blush stained her olive-toned cheek, and he felt the pull at the strings of his heart. It was her feelings. He took a deep breath as he pointed to the area where they fell down into the cavern and Brentley went to search for the critters for Endrus. Then he motioned for Quairken to follow him. Endrus circled his large forest green and black marbled body until it angled his back toward the stone wall. As Alzerion led them down the tunnel, he glanced back. Eirini sat on a stone near Calderon. They chatted. *Good*.

As they roamed, he realized the tunnel was quite narrow.

"What are we looking for, exactly?" Quairken asked.

Alzerion cleared his throat. "Any rat or creature we can find. Even if it's dead."

"Sounds good. That may be the only option. I have seen nothing alive down here except for that wyvern."

Alzerion nodded.

A few minutes passed, or maybe more.

"Quairken. Thank you for not saying anything about it, you know." Alzerion stopped as he glanced at him.

Quairken turned on his heels, facing Alzerion. "I'm not sure what you mean."

"I think you do." Alzerion pinched the back of his neck. "I appreciate you pretending that you don't."

Quairken nodded as his face lit up. "Oh, that." He cleared his throat. "Well, it was nothing. A little kiss on the cheek." Quairken chuckled.

"Unless you're saying that there's more going on. In which case, man, it's about time."

Alzerion took a few steps forward, still glancing over at Quairken occasionally. "You don't think it would be horrible?" Alzerion scratched the back of his neck. "I don't think it's more than her being sweet and all. I mean, I protected her."

Quairken's face shifted. "Nobody thinks you're terrible."

Alzerion glanced back over. Quairken's hands were at his hips.

"Not even those two?" Alzerion pointed behind them, back to where they came.

"Why would they? They know their place, Alzerion. Shy of you doing something like making love to her, I think they'd keep their mouths shut."

Alzerion bit his lip. He struggled to find the right words. "But, I have them here, on this mission with us. All of you really."

Quairken nodded.

"This is all about finding Aironell and bringing her safely back home, and I'm here with another woman in our ranks."

"Kissing another woman, maybe?" Quairken added.

Alzerion felt the heat of that creep across his face. Alzerion looked down at his hands.

Quairken moved toward him and patted his back. "Wait, have you kissed her?"

Alzerion cleared his throat as he looked up. "She has kissed me twice." He tried to play it off. *It was nothing. It wasn't like she was in love with him or something.*

Quairken tilted his head as his eyes bore into him.

"Okay, I may have kissed her, but it was only one time." Alzerion's hands moved about as he spoke.

Quairken snickered. "Look, you will have no judgement from me. You're overdue for some. Well, just getting some."

Alzerion shook his head.

Quairken cleared his throat. "You've already said that this trip is about fulfilling your promise, so well, maybe it couldn't hurt to get to know Eirini. I don't know her all that well, but she seems pretty straight-forward, and I have seen a glance or two your way."

Alzerion snapped his attention to him. "No," he said with a light little laugh.

Quairken patted him on the shoulder once more. "You really do not know people and their cues, do you? That or you're in denial, my friend."

"Well, maybe a little of both, if I'm being honest. Either way, I have no intentions of having a romantic tryst of any kind."

"Aha, well, I guess we shall see," Quairken chuckled as he went back to scouring the rock wall.

"See about what?" Alzerion stared at the back of him.

Quairken craned his head to him. "Well, a beautiful woman is here with us. One that challenges you in ways that, well, nobody else has. I'd say it's a matter of time. I don't need magic to see where this is going."

Alzerion shook his head. "Your wrong." He strolled down the path again. He stepped over larger boulders and any scrapes that lay before them.

Quairken's words struck something in him. *Was he oblivious? Has Eirini been putting out signals? It didn't matter. He had no time for that. Duty must come first. Especially when he dragged them all this way for a single goal. He didn't even know if he loved Aironell or in what capacity if he did. He hadn't let himself think about it. It was the only way he could move on from what happened to her.*

Alzerion ignored it all, pushed it out of his mind as he squinted his eyes back at that crack of light. Alzerion got on his knees as he crawled. The light seeped through the smallest fissure in the stone. Branches twisted around. *Thank the stars,* Alzerion thought. Something scurried farther behind the branches. He shot his hand out and grabbed it. It was a rodent of sorts. He grabbed it and handed it to Quairken so he could get out and back to his feet.

Alzerion stood and then grabbed it from Quairken.

"What is that?"

"Not sure," Alzerion eyed it, "all I know is it fits the criteria."

They headed back down the tunnel. When they emerged, Alzerion found Eirini helping Calderon to his feet. Brentley stood a bit off to the side as Endrus was munching on something.

"You found him some food?" Alzerion glanced over at Brentley.

*That would put it kindly.* Endrus thundered in his mind. Alzerion turned to him. *That fool brought me twigs and a few berries.*

*I take it that it is not something you enjoy?*

Endrus sat up as his navy eyes bore into him. *Would anything other than a nice meat dinner satisfy you?*

Alzerion smirked. *Sorry.*

He stepped toward Endrus and opened his hands enough to show what he had in them. Endrus' wings perked up, as the claw of the closest wing shot out and grabbed the animal. In a second, Endrus wrapped his wings around itself in a giant bat-like form. Only sounds of crunching filled the space. Alzerion noticed Calderon shudder. *He couldn't blame him.* Alzerion tried to keep his composure, but his lip curled as he wrinkled his nose.

Endrus' slender wings did kind of look like a bat. They slid back to his side as he moved his taloned legs and sat straight up. Alzerion smirked. He could have passed for some tamed pet. Alzerion heard the shuffling of feet. Eirini and Calderon moved nearer to them.

*I'm ready, young ruler.*

Alzerion tilted his head to the side. *Ready for what?*

*Didn't you want to leave this dreaded prison? Isn't that why you helped me—to ask a favor of me?*

Alzerion shook his head.

"What's going on?" Brentley's voice wobbled, slightly.

"He's offering Alzerion his help," Eirini whispered.

*Endrus, I offered our help because—*

*If not to gain something, then for what purpose?*

Alzerion gazed down. He despised talking about himself. He stepped closer, as he let his hand reach toward Endrus' snout.

Endrus shifted his crystal looking spikes that ran along his head. Eyes focused on Alzerion. Endrus lowered his head and Alzerion rubbed him.

*I didn't enjoy seeing what they did to you. I don't know who did it, but I felt —*

*Connected?*

Alzerion nodded.

*Well then, young ruler, you and your group may be saved after all.*

Endrus raised his head as he shifted into view of the group. "You all should sit and get comfortable," Endrus' voice was low and proud. "The tale I have to tell will show you what you're up against."

Brentley helped Calderon to the nearest stone which he sat upon. Quairken didn't move a muscle. His eyes were large as he kept his gaze fixed on Endrus. Eirini shuffled over to Alzerion and slid her arm around his until her arm curved around and held his hand. Alzerion's gaze was sharp.

*Don't forget you wanted me to stay near someone and I had the choice of who. Get used to it, Alzerion.*

He bit the side of his lip as he breathed out, already regretting his own instructions. He pushed it out of his mind. *For now, learning what Endrus had to tell them, and how it could alter their quest.* He had to start somewhere. *Knowledge was power, after all?*

Endrus sat on his two legs and raised his magnificent head. His navy eyes appeared to shine, and then Alzerion felt a wind blow. The others clung to the stones they sat on and even Quairken pressed his hand to the nearest stone wall. He glanced around, but Eirini just smiled as she clung to his arm and hand. Alzerion ignored it. *Last thing he needed was her reading his thoughts. They were in proximity.* As the wind slowed down, he heard a scraping sound. Then a large flat cracked boulder laid out in front of him. He tilted his head to the side.

"You can sit on it, young ruler."

Alzerion gazed down. He kicked the bones off to the side—Eirini paled a bit at the sight. Alzerion worked to clear the bones from her view. He held her hand as she sat down on her part of the boulder seat, and then he followed. Her hands grasped hold of his arm. When he had more time, he had to figure out why he felt such warmth at her touch.

"I'm grateful for the food and drink," Endrus' voice was like nothing Alzerion ever heard. It was this controlled calm of wisdom. Its eyes moved about, scanned them all.

"More will be required, but I had enough to do a base level of movement to free us."

Alzerion looked to his side as he saw Brentley and Quairken nod. Calderon still had a grimace plastered on his face as he pulled at his left ear. Alzerion snapped back to Endrus.

"What is this place?" Quairken's voice sounded uneven.

"I thought it was obvious, loyal one." Endrus stared at Quairken as he shifted his two muscular legs that ended in talons.

A whistling sound escaped Endrus' snout as a small cloud of steam or smoke erupted.

"No need to flinch, obedient ones." His head motioned to where Brentley and Calderon were. "No harm shall come from me. The same cannot be said for others in the DarkFlower Jungle."

Alzerion cleared his throat. "What does that mean, Endrus?"

"You will encounter different beasts above us." His spiked head tilted to the side.

"M-more l-li-like you?" Calderon's voice wobbled.

Alzerion slid Eirini and his seat more at an angle so that he could have a better view of everyone. Calderon's shoulders slumped. His eyes were wide.

Endrus shook his head. "You won't have that honor."

"Why is that?" Eirini asked. "I read that wyverns lived in close knit familial groups."

*Eirini, don't push him, please.*

She exchanged glances with Alzerion and then focused back on Endrus.

Endrus' head lowered. Eyes closed and then opened to reveal the whites of his eyes masking its color. There was a grow, and Alzerion felt his muscles tighten. He raised an eyebrow, but he didn't waver. Alzerion felt a wave, no, a rush of emotion. It came on suddenly, with such an overwhelming sensation in his mind.

Pain. Sorrow. Anger. Regret.

Alzerion blinked, only to feel a stinging deep in his eyes. He clenched his hands. Then Eirini placed a hand to his and rubbed gentle circles over the skin of his hand.

*It's okay. Try not to let it overpower you.* Her voice was sincere.

"They are gone...everyone."

"Endrus," Eirini's voice was light. "I'm sorry."

Endrus bowed his head at her words. "That means more than you know. I'll refer to you as the loved one." Endrus moved forward—wings held back, yet at the ready.

Each step sounded like a crunch until Endrus sat back down. Endrus was within Alzerion's reach and nearer the group. Calderon covered his mouth, as his eyes remained enlarged.

"Things changed here some time ago. This realm is unique, with many beings and animals. The magic weaved all around and made it quite the home." Endrus paused.

He spoke with such calm, but there was still an ache behind his words.

"What changed?" Quairken shot a glance between Endrus and Alzerion.

Alzerion had this empty stare.

"New management," Endrus shifted his sights to Alzerion. "Young ruler, it's not like it is at your home. The laws of nature and magic govern here. For many years, they co-existed in harmony. That was before the first Dark Sovereign."

"Dark Sovereign?" Alzerion tilted his head.

"Indeed. *He* came like a lithe panther—sneaky, powerful, and quick."

Alzerion's head shook, taking in his words. Each word had Alzerion on the edge of his stony seat. Such a velvety tone, like Endrus was a seasoned storyteller, spinning a tale to entertain.

Endrus continued. "Things changed. The creatures and people here were different. Since then, every so many decades, there would be a new Dark Sovereign."

"But where do they come from? How is this decided?" The weight of Quairken's words rang clear.

"We do not know, for sure, only that they come from the male in the family line—they are always twenty-five when they arrive. Time moves much slower here, because of the magic that is stored all around. Once the new Dark Sovereign arrives, then he has the power to remain young. But he is not immortal. He can be killed."

"How long has this been going on?" Alzerion bit his bottom lip.

Endrus' wings moved up as he shrugged. "A long time. The current Dark Sovereign is not the original. No. He's worse. He's the reason I've suffered imprisonment down here."

His head sagged. Alzerion reached his other hand out and grazed it against Endrus' scaley textured skin. In one continuous motion, he rubbed down Endrus's neck with the back of his hand and then grazed up with his fingers. Endrus calmed, but then he shook his head. Alzerion snapped his hand back, so that he wouldn't get poked by the pointed scales close to his head. Endrus stepped back, raising his tail as he backed himself closer to the wall.

Alzerion didn't dare rush to him, but he knelt as he held both of his hands up. "Steady, Endrus. Nobody here will harm you, I promise."

Wings flapped as the claws on the tip of the wings flexed. Alzerion swallowed as he reached out once more. This time Endrus bent his neck down until Alzerion touched his head. *Ugh*, he thought as he felt a prick, almost like a zap. Then Alzerion heard Endrus' voice like earlier, before he spoke to the whole group. *He was sure that he was the only one to hear the great wyvern, except for Eirini if she honed in on his thoughts.* Alzerion kept his guard down, so she could hear it too, if she wanted.

> Flail until you fail.
> Suffer thrice times five.
> Confined by your own magic.
> Waste and rot till you cease.
> Never to see the light of day.

Alzerion pressed his fingers to his forehead. He spoke, but then fumbled with the words. Alzerion's nostrils flared as he put some pieces together. He looked at the group and relayed the mantra from Endrus.

"He felt he couldn't speak it. He still hasn't fully recovered from the trauma."

Eirini sniffled as she stared back at Endrus. "I'm so sorry that you have been stuck down here, *alone.*"

"Thank you, dear loved one." His voice shook, but then grew in strength once more.

"They fated me to this because I wouldn't bow down." Endrus shifted his stance and looked up at the top of the cavern.

Alzerion wondered how many times he did that over the years. No sky. No wind to feel, only the stale and stagnant rock, dust, dirt, and death.

"After they slaughtered all my brethren, some of them left down here to bleed out or were eviscerated—the bones." His right winged talon gestured out.

Alzerion pressed his hands against his stomach. Eirini laid her head gently on his shoulder. Her scent saved him from upchucking everywhere.

"I'm sorry, obedient ones."

Alzerion turned to face Brentley and Calderon. Brentley stood still like the perfect soldier, but Calderon looked as if he would run away, if he could. There was no place to do that stuck in this cavern. Alzerion focused back on Endrus.

"A band of people that live in the jungle betrayed me. They are called the darkolytes—followers of the Dark Sovereign."

"They did this to you?" Alzerion raised an eyebrow. "People?"

"Something you must know is that they are not all bad. No, some are kind. There was a generous family that protected me, but when I was found, the Dark Sovereign forced me to choose."

"You chose this?" Quairken grimaced.

Endrus shook his head and let out a low growl. "Never. That low life, Dark Sovereign, wanted me to join him. Join the ranks of the very darkolytes that had betrayed me and that kind of family. I swore I would never help him—never join his ranks."

"So, this was the punishment?" Alzerion asked as he pulled at his fingers. "Death."

"No," Endrus's voice was a low rumble now. "He wanted me alive to see his reign, to claim power. More power than he already possessed. No.

It was about control and keeping those that live here in place, where he felt they should be."

Alzerion tasted this sourness in his mouth as his nose wrinkled. He shook his head as he kept listening.

"Young ruler, he wants me to live until I wither. To feel the changes he has wrought across the DarkFlower Jungle, my home."

"Why not just leave?" Calderon finally spoke. His eyes did not look at Endrus but off to his side.

"Obedient one, I was doomed here. The cage that your kind ruler plucked me out of was spelled. They made it from the ancient magic of the jungle. Magic from the deepest secret—the source of all magic in the realms — is here." Endrus stepped forward again.

Calderon's head pulled back.

"No need to fear me, obedient one. I sense you are true of intent." Calderon bowed his head at Endrus.

"The cage was not just forged from magic. They imbued it with some of the magic that was stolen—not taken when the Dark Sovereign killed my fellow wyverns. I could not use my own abilities to get free. I had to wait until either I died or someone born of magic and true of heart freed me. Therefore, young ruler, I am at your service."

Endrus raised himself to his full height, placed one foot back as he bowed low—wings fanned out.

Alzerion and Eirini rose and moved toward Endrus. *I will protect you. I promise.* Eirini reached her hand to Endrus' head, but her eyes widened as she jerked her hand back for a moment. Alzerion smirked and rubbed Endrus' neck and between his wings.

"I appreciate that," Alzerion said. "We are in search of someone. A young woman. Aironell. She was the princess of my kingdom, but sacrificed herself, thus saving my life and keeping her kingdom from falling into the wrong hands."

Endrus shot up, and Alzerion flinched. "How long has she been gone?"

"About three years. Why?" Alzerion tilted his head.

Endrus shook his head. "No. No. No."

"What?" Quairken strolled over to the other side of Alzerion. "She was the sweetest, kindest soul. You won't help us find her?"

Endrus spoke in what sounded like a growl. "Not what I meant. I vowed to serve you, young ruler. I am a wyvern of my word."

"What do you know you haven't told us yet?" Alzerion folded his arms.

"The magical faction of casters that used to live among the wyverns cursed that Dark Sovereign. It dates back many centuries. The sacred Fates decreed it in the ancient texts. It tells of a Dark Sovereign who will come to power and be the change of all, but to succeed, he needs to find a spare. The spare to tame his whims. A desire to burn amongst them—can form a union to succeed in the ultimate power. Without it, he will doom the realm and its magic to the darkness within—opening up its borders once more to outsiders. Cracks will surface, weaknesses. Darkness will spread."

Alzerion swallowed.

"You have come through one of those cracks. It used to be that you couldn't get into the DarkFlower Jungle unless you already inhabited the place or if the Dark Sovereign brought you or gave you safe passage. Did either of those happen?"

Alzerion shook his head.

"Well, then I fear your princess' essence must be here. A spare. If she was found and saved, she may have been living amongst the foulest beasts. The darkolytes or the preservers. I have been imprisoned down here, so I don't know as much about what has been happening up there." Endrus looked up. "We should seek counsel from someone that has always been trustworthy."

"Who is that?" Quairken stared at Endrus.

"Gael, he's a good man."

"The jackrabbit?" Eirini asked.

Endrus's head shook.

"We've met Gael," Alzerion spoke quickly. "He was punished, it seems, and turned into a jackrabbit."

Endrus huffed.

"Which would be better?" Brentley coughed out. "You said something about darkolytes and preservers."

"Neither are good. They are really different sides of the same evil that lurks. Darkolytes serve the current Dark Sovereign. Where the preservers are about their own agenda. They claim to want the best interest of the jungle, but they want the power for themselves. There are few of them around, not like the numbers of the darkolytes. They would love nothing more than to cause harm or unhappiness to the Dark Sovereign."

Alzerion stepped back. He felt a stabbing feeling wrench in his gut. He bit his lip, hard. "What does this all mean for the one we are looking for?" Alzerion asked. Not sure if the answer was one he wanted.

"I wouldn't waste your time, young ruler. She is dead or on one of those sides. She may not be the same woman you once knew."

"We know she can't be dead," Alzerion spoke quickly. He patted Quairken on the shoulders. "Jezzabell has seen her alive and our success in finding her."

Quairken nodded as he wiped his fist against his jaw.

"Endrus, regardless of the outcome, or what the Fates have lined up for us, I have vowed to bring her home."

"Then I will help you." Endrus bowed his head.

This time he moved behind them, ran forward, and then whipped his wings up and down. Dust and dirt swirled around. Alzerion pulled Quairken and Eirini away and they ran toward Brentley and Calderon. Endrus shot up and flew until he attached his claws and taloned feet on the stone off the side of the cavern wall. He breathed out a tantalizing smolder of red and brilliant orange as his face barreled into the top of the cavern. He looked like a giant mole burrowing into the rock. Stones and debris fell down, and Alzerion's hand flew up. A transparent glow formed. As the rock and crud fell down and hit the glowing encasement, the rocks shattered and fell off to the sides of them. Then Endrus dropped back down and landed on his legs with a thud. The swirl of the dust cloud was large as Alzerion struggled to keep his eyes open.

# CHAPTER 16
## Tree Filled Tension

The dust settled and Endrus stood like a statue of a wyvern—tail curled, wings out and ready, as the forest green and gray marbled around his body.

"Let's go, daring travelers."

Eirini moved toward Alzerion. Following him was her newest adventure. She promised to be useful. Her lips pursed almost like a pout. She hated the talk about this woman Alzerion came here for. She knew that was his quest, but it still nagged at her heart. Eirini shook her head and kept a smile on her face. Alzerion wanted to do this to keep his word. *But she wondered if that was all it was for him. That moment they shared, well, it was all she could do not to let herself take him and never let go.* She pursed her lips. *Maybe they would get another sweet moment. How exciting it would be to make out in this jungle.*

Brentley and Quairken helped Calderon over and they used their considerable muscle to lift him onto the wyvern.

"UGH!"

"Calderon, what's wrong?" Alzerion narrowed his eyes.

"The damn spikes," he swore under his breath.

"Young ruler, touch your hand near my snout."

Alzerion followed Endrus' instruction. Eirini fixed her amber eyes on

Alzerion's hand. As he placed it close, the wyvern blew out and Alzerion's hand looked ice blue, like the glassy water on a wintry day.

"Press the hand to my neck."

Eirini strolled over. Face lifted as she peered up to see what was happening. In moments, the places where Alzerion touched looked just like that shiny, glassy surface. Alzerion's hand returned to normal the instant he finished. She clapped her hands together and almost bounced as she watched Calderon's expression become more relaxed.

"Is that better, obedient one?" Endrus' head arched back to look at him.

Calderon nodded. Brentley was next, followed by Quairken.

"Now you," Alzerion pulled at her arm.

"Where will you sit if I go next? I'm smaller. I can fit in another spot, with ease."

Alzerion shook his head. "Eirini, you are sitting up there next. I'll be fine. I'll fit."

Eirini felt a thickness in her throat. She felt like a ball of jumbled up knots in her stomach. "Alzerion, I—"

Alzerion was so fast. In seconds, he was there and then somehow he was behind her as he scooped her right up and heaved her on. Next thing she knew, Quairken grabbed her arms as she straddled herself on Endrus. Her nostrils flared. *Alzerion—had to have his way. Sometimes it was cute, but other times, like now, it annoyed her. She was genuine in her concern for him.* Her lip pouted as Alzerion climbed up. True to his word, he found a spot behind her. He barely fit.

"Don't be mad," he whispered in her ear as one hand moved her hair to the side and then both hands wrapped around her waist. "Eirini, please."

His face cracked, just enough that she felt her heart melt. *No. Don't let him off the hook that easily.* She did not turn around. His grip tightened. She felt the side of his face rub against hers as he nuzzled her cheek.

"I'm sorry."

*His apologies were getting better.*

"Hang tight," Endrus' voice thundered.

As he darted up and his wings started beating, Eirini felt this dip in her stomach. She held her breath for fear of vomiting. Oh, that would be bad. It would end up on someone. *If it ended on Alzerion, that would be fine. He deserved some punishment for his demands.*

She grabbed onto Quairken's arm as Alzerion clung to her, and they soared higher. Each moment that passed, she felt uneasy in her gut. *Don't look down.* She kept her eyes up and she saw the opening that Endrus dug through. *Finally.* She felt lighter as she smelled the fresh air around them. She let out a gasp as they soared through the murky evening sky. Endrus made his descent just off of a cove of twisted trees.

"Is he going to land?" Eirini asked.

Alzerion leaned closer as he held onto her waist. "He's searching for a spot. You're not angry anymore."

Eirini's body shifted backward as Endrus flew down. She felt Alzerion's muscled arms around her as her back rested right against him, and she gulped.

Eirini craned her head as his eyes stared at her. "I wasn't mad, maybe annoyed. I got my revenge in my head."

"Oh?" Alzerion caught a laugh in his mouth.

Endrus's body landed off a thick wooded area.

Calderon and Brently got off so fast, and then Calderon literally kissed the ground.

Quairken laughed so hard that it could have shaken the jungle awake. "Well, I guess that means you weren't a fan."

Calderon shook his head as they exchanged glances. "I don't need to give that a second thought."

Eirini moved to the side. She pushed off and slid down Endrus' wing. She landed right on her feet. Alzerion jumped and landed beside her.

Eirini couldn't get over how the sky was darker here. It seemed to change depending on where they were. She heard a noise from behind them, and Eirini spun around. She felt a dizzying feeling in her head. Images of someone not with them flashed through her mind. They were close.

"Alzerion, we're not safe here." She circled back to him. "We need to go now."

"I'm not following."

She grabbed his hand and squeezed. "Trust me." Her eyes pleaded.

She leaned her head close and whispered, "I saw into someone's mind. Someone not in our group. They must be close."

Alzerion patted her hand as he turned to the rest of them. "Endrus, I need you to fly around and tell me if there are others nearby."

Endrus pumped his mighty wings and up he went while Eirini stayed close to Alzerion as he paced the wooded space.

"Follow me, over here." Alzerion motioned to Quairken and the others. She was already on his trail.

Alzerion bent down low as his hand touched the ground. There were tracks of some sort and these tiny slug-like things. Something wasn't right, she felt it. Eirini felt the wind pick up as she spotted them.

"Alzerion, look out!" She shoved him to the side as the magical blast missed him as it scorched the closest boulder.

His eyes narrowed. "What the hell. Run."

Alzerion's hands moved her forward. "Where are the others?"

"I had them run through the trees. More cover for them, plus it might deter those cloaked strangers from following them."

Eirini nodded as she ran. This was more exercise than she ever got. Her legs felt heavy, like lead weighing her down. She felt her body slowing down, and Alzerion's hand pressed against her back as he muttered something. Her speed picked up as he navigated the two of them. His grip on her waist tightened, and they veered off the path.

She turned but didn't see the cloaked figures, instead she saw the blast of magic hit right where they were. Eirini looked up, but Alzerion's face was alert. A fault of his, but she didn't mind. They stopped when they reached this pretty meadow amid the jungle. There weren't that many trees, but she didn't mind. Her muscles tensed at the sound of twigs cracking, and she turned toward the noise. Alzerion moved as he stood by her. His face was expressionless, and she sensed he was ready to grab her.

Eirini bit her lip as she allowed herself a moment longer in his mind.

*Endrus can you hear me?*

*Yes, young ruler. Are you alright? I spotted them but couldn't make it to you in time.*

*Are there more?*

*No.*

She fled his mind. *The last thing she needed was to upset him right now. At least Endrus was monitoring them.*


It had been more time than he hoped. Alzerion tried to remain calm but … where were they?

Out of the bush stumbled Calderon, Brentley, and then Quairken.

"Did it work?" Quairken asked.

"I think so," Alzerion said, "but we cannot stay here."

Calderon sighed.

"What's wrong?" Alzerion knelt beside him.

"I think it may be from lack of rest, sir." Brentley bowed his head.

"I'm sorry, but there's no good place to rest. Those figures may return."

Quairken took off the pack he was wearing and rummaged through it.

"Now's not the time," Alzerion reminded him.

"Well, we have some apples and three sets of ropes."

"What would we need with rope?" Alzerion asked.

"I have an idea." Eirini's tone was too cheerful. *Whatever it was he was sure not to like it.*

She dashed forward and held one rope. "Well, we have some trees. What if we use the rope to secure ourselves up in the trees?"

"That actually could work." Quairken pulled out the rest of the ropes.

"Wait, no," Alzerion shook his head.

"With all due respect, Your Majesty, we need some rest." Quairken stared at him.

*They're right, young ruler. I can find a spot for myself. But you all need the protection and sleeping in a tree is not so bad.*

Alzerion sighed as he turned to the trees. They were close to each other so that he could oversee everyone, but there were only three of them.

He took a breath as he faced them. "Alright, I'm okay with this. How do we make it work? We have five people and only three trees?"

"That's easy." Quairken's mouth curved into a broad smile.

Alzerion hesitated, but then moved toward him. "What do you have in mind?"

Quairken scratched the back of his neck. "We could buddy up."

"Your Majesty." Brentley bowed. "I could join Calderon. You know, keep him from hurting himself."

"Great idea." Quairken nodded as he handed a rope to him.

Alzerion watched Brentley and Calderon make their way to the farthest tree on the right.

Quairken gripped a rope and handed the other to Alzerion. He stared at it but didn't take it.

"I doubt we should let Eirini stay in a tree by herself, right?" Quairken's eyebrow rose.

A tightness in his chest started as he took the rope from Quairken. Alzerion looked to Eirini. Her smile was so wide, he was sure the enemy could see it from here.

"Eirini, who—"

She dashed toward him. "Do you even have to ask? I told you once before who my choice is. That won't change."

"Fine." Alzerion motioned forward as Eirini practically bounced forward toward the tree. Alzerion glared at Quairken, whose lips pinched in as a brightness washed over his face. *Not funny Quairken.*

Alzerion placed the rope over his shoulder as his hands grabbed the thick tree branches. *At least they would hold them.* He climbed, grasping one branch at a time. Alzerion stopped as he wrapped an arm around one branch as he looked down at Eirini. He watched as her hand kept slipping. *Must be too far a distance.*

Alzerion slid down to the branch below him as he held out an arm. "Grab on."

Her fingers almost reached. But he needed to be closer. Alzerion's grip on the tree tightened as he leaned forward as far as he could. Any more, and well, he would fall out of the tree. The tips of her fingers touched his as Alzerion tugged. Her body rose, and Eirini's face turned ashen as he pulled at her hand and then let go for a moment. Then, he grabbed at her elbow and pulled. Her body laid on the branch almost on him.

He gulped. "We should move up. A higher branch for safety."

Eirini took a few breaths as she grabbed the bough above them. Alzerion nodded and then climbed up. After he ascended, he angled down and grasped her arm to pull her up. Finally, they got as far up as they could. Alzerion looked at the tree next to him. Quairken sat already tied to the branch.

"We need to tie ourselves here."

For once, there was no disagreement. Eirini slid her body nice and slow to him. Alzerion had his back against a smooth branch. It was a nice little spot that felt like it cradled him in the tree. A warmth stirred in his chest as she laid in the spot with him. Most of her body had to touch his as they faced each other. He swallowed as he wrapped around the surrounding rope. Around it wound as he tied a knot in it. He pulled to secure the knot.

He gave her a nervous smile.

"Thank you," she whispered. "I've never climbed a tree before. Didn't realize how much strength it took."

"No problem.," he breathed out.

From their position, Alzerion felt the swell of her breathing as it pitched her chest against his. He cleared his throat. "I'm sorry about this."

"You did nothing wrong. Never apologize, Alzerion." Eirini curled into him as she angled her head in as her caramel head of hair snuggled into him. He placed a hand on the back of her head. He rubbed his fingers through. Each strand was soft as he twirled the curls around.

The tightness in his chest moved. He felt a tingling sensation in his stomach. Eirini kept her head still, but her lower body moved. She angled her hips toward him as one of her legs rested on his as she bent her knee. It relaxed against his upper thigh. Alzerion took a deep breath as one of her hands laid on his chest. He bit his bottom lip.

*Okay, relax. Your mind needs to be as clear as possible, so she isn't forced to meld into your mind.* The pep talk wasn't working. He felt the right pressure her hands held on his chest as she swirled her fingers around. They lowered in perfect circles as he pressed his hand to hers. His other hand slid down to her back as she picked her head up and her eyes gazed at him. He felt her fingers squirm under his hand.

"What was that for?" She leaned her face forward. So close that he could smell the sweetness of her breath.

"It tickled." He realized how pathetic he sounded, but it was the truth. *Well, that and her touch was making his insides do things he couldn't explain.*

She tilted her head and then moved her face even closer. "Alzerion, relax. We're safe up here."

"Are we?" His teeth cut into the flesh of his cheek. *Shit. He immediately wished he could take it back.*

"Do you see an enemy up here?"

He opened his mouth, but Eirini placed a finger to his lips. She shook her head. Again, that feeling inside increased. His mind focused on ways to get out of this. Trouble was, he had no solution. He had to endure the night in the tree, tied to her.

"Is being stuck here with me so terrible?"

Alzerion stared at her. His eyes narrowed.

"I didn't mind meld. Don't need to, as I can see the look on your face."

"It's not you. It's hard to explain." Alzerion squeezed his legs tighter together.

Her mouth twitched from side-to-side. Then her lips curled up into a smile.

"What?"

Eirini traced her fingers along his collarbone and then rested both hands on each of his cheeks. Her gaze was soft, and he felt a heat stir in his face and below. Alzerion swallowed hard.

Eirini touched her nose to his as it trailed down, and he felt all the nerves in his body, like they screamed at him. He took his hands and wrapped them around her back. Alzerion couldn't keep from shutting out the thoughts. They invaded his mind like a wave as they crashed into him. His arms pulled, as her body and his entwined on that branch.

There was no space between them. He felt her knee as she grazed it against him. Alzerion closed his eyes for a moment and took a breath. When he opened them, his lips parted as Eirini's one hand lowered to just under his chin as her lips grazed against his cheek.

Alzerion attempted to arch his back, but the bough was rigid behind him.

"Eirini," his voice was deep as he whispered.

"No talking." The thumb of her right hand rubbed his lip.

Alzerion smirked and then opened his mouth so that he caught her thumb with his teeth.

Her eyes dazzled as her lips parted.

He moved his head closer. "I'm not sure about this."

"I know, but your body says otherwise." Her eyes didn't waver as he saw what looked like a sexy confidence.

He didn't know what to say. His breathing was deep. *Maybe it would be nice for once to let loose, just a little at least.* Alzerion's hands slid from her hips as they rubbed at the sides of her ribs.

"That tickles."

Alzerion straightened his posture as he pulled her forward, and he felt her breasts rise and fall. "Now you know how it feels."

Eirini's hands rested on his shoulders as she held her breath. His hands roamed to her back as he clung to the fabric of her leather bodice.

"You really should have just let it go, Eirini."

Her eyes didn't waver as her thick lashes rose. The moisture increased in his mouth. *He wanted this. He could feel it over his body. The hunger—the ache for his lips to glide over hers once more.* His gaze was firm as he pressed his mouth closed. Eirini pushed down on his shoulders as she hoisted her height up. Her face was level with his. The softness of her candy-red lips lingered on his neck as they moved and left sweet kisses on his jawline.

"I-I think we should, maybe, just rest up."

The look on her face made him gulp, and he felt his resolve weaken. It was hard to push her away when his heart felt like a puddle in his chest. Somehow, she melted through his icy barriers. Her eyes darted down, ogling him.

She pressed her forehead into his. This time, Alzerion's hands moved like they had their own mind. They touched the skin of her arms as his lips glided over the skin of her face. His eyes closed as his mouth lowered to hers. His lips parted as he felt the need inside of him. The need to kiss her—for his mouth to have his way with her. He brought his face lower. The pull between her lips and his felt, well, unlike anything. His hands explored as they grazed against the laces of her corset bodice.

"Tsk, tsk," Eirini's voice was sweet and low.

Alzerion felt a rush. His hands quickly moved to her face as he pulled her in. His lips touched hers and it was like some sort of intense frenzy. Alzerion shivered as she deepened the kiss. He nibbled at her top lip as he slowly sucked it back into another kiss. Alzerion grabbed a hold of her shoulders and nudged her back.

He took a breath. A fervent storm brewed inside. He didn't want to stop, but he did at the same time. His hands clenched together as his gaze moved back to her.

"Alzerion, how are they going?"

Alzerion froze as his eyes glanced over at Quairken. He took another breath out.

He angled his body around so his voice projected toward the tree he was in. "Well, she hasn't killed me yet."

"The night is still ahead of us. There's time." Quairken laughed.

Alzerion watched as Eirini crossed her arms. He chatted a bit more with Quairken and even asked about Calderon and Brentley. Everyone was doing well, except maybe him. Alzerion and Quairken chatted about strategies when they left the trees. Alzerion yawned as he stared back. He knew Eirini was still there, but she fell asleep. She was so peaceful, adorable even. He carefully slid an arm under her head. She stirred but didn't wake. Then he continued as he slid her head onto his chest. His finger rubbed from her forehead to her temples and twirled her hair. *At least she would be comfortable. Better than the hard branch.* He laid his head back as he ran his hands through her hair.

## CHAPTER 17
# Entangled Path

E irini popped a bit of her apple into her mouth as she followed Alzerion and the others. A sense of exhilaration coursed through her veins. *Between sleeping in a tree and some impromptu kissing, the night was great.* Though, Alzerion kept his eyes away from her today. She couldn't help but feel that he either regretted it or was seething. *In their short time together, she knew one thing to be sure...Alzerion liked to be in control.* Her mouth swallowed the last bite of her apple. She hurried as her legs caught up with Alzerion. He barely turned to face her.

*Enough already.* Eirini jogged and maneuvered her way in front of Alzerion. Her one foot planted ahead of her with her arms curled in tight.

"Where are we going? It feels like we passed this same copse of trees before."

The others remained silent as Alzerion paced around her. She wanted to respect his wishes, but he was leaving her no choice but to mind meld.

Eirini tilted her head as she felt her talent stir within. An overwhelming pull as she felt it travel through her mind and eyes until her mark tingled and her mind felt this jumbled buzzing. She closed her eyes and there was a swirl of thoughts and emotions. *Something was wrong.* This was new. Alzerion's mind was always busy, but this felt different. Her eyes shot open, and she stared at him.

169

"What?" Alzerion asked.

She shook her head. It was a challenge to pinpoint his main thoughts, but some feelings were easy for her to detect. Alzerion was conflicted. A mixture of confusion, desire, embarrassment, and his need to maintain control. She swallowed. *More pieces to add to the puzzle, that was Alzerion.*

Alzerion wrinkled his nose. He didn't have the right words. He was sure Eirini just mind melded. *But could he blame her?* Alzerion's mouth coiled down into a grimace as he turned from her and paced around the more open area. Sure, there were trees, but most places looked the same.

*Endrus, come down, please.*

*As you wish.*

Alzerion moved away from the group as he took a slow breath to control his feelings. Then he turned. Eirini had this pained expression. His chest tightened as the heaviness grew. The idea of going to her, apologizing, and just embracing her crossed his mind. The idea of seeing her upset or hurt bothered more than he thought it could. Instead, he shoved the emotion out of his mind—for now. The sounds of whipping wind grew as Endrus came into view and descended.

Endrus's wings flapped as his taloned feet touched down on the ground.

"How did everyone fare last night?" Endrus moved his head around to each of them.

Alzerion observed his group, but nobody said anything.

"It was fine for us," Brentley said.

Quairken and Calderon nodded back.

*What about you, young ruler?* Endrus' navy eyes fixed on him.

Alzerion's brows pulled in as he stared down at the dirt on the ground. *He didn't know how he got into this mess.* His face picked up as he flashed a glance at Eirini. At that moment, she was still. Her gaze was strong, but all he could see was this questioning gaze as her face brightened up a bit.

*It was interesting, Endrus.*

*Interesting, good...or bad?*

Alzerion shifted his gaze back to him. *I'm not sure.*

*Now may not be the time to discuss it, but we will when we have more time, young ruler. I see the look you give the loved one, Eirini.*

Alzerion's eyebrow rose.

*No need to deny it. Not to me.* Endrus straightened up as his feet took a few steps back. *I won't betray her response to my question, but step with great care about your words and actions. I will say, she cares, young ruler.*

"Sir, what is the plan?" Quairken's voice broke through the silence.

"Sorry." Alzerion cleared his throat. "Endrus was speaking with me."

Eirini moved forward, but veered to Endrus. She patted his neck. "Endrus, did he mention the strange cloaked figures yet?"

"No, he did not." Endrus's spiked head stared back at him.

Alzerion took a few steps toward Endrus. His eyes locked on Eirini's, but then he shifted them to Endrus.

"They came in groups of at least two. We encountered them twice."

"Yes, but what did they look like?"

Alzerion saw Calderon shrug from the corner of his eye.

"They wore cloaks, Endrus." Eirini said quick. "We didn't get good looks at their faces."

Alzerion rubbed at his chin. "Well, the one had a wooden staff of some kind, and wielded magic from it."

"Dear, brave ones, they are preservers."

"And what does that mean for us?" Alzerion asked as his arms hung at his side.

Endrus moved around. Alzerion noticed he looked at them all.

"They are the other faction of the Realm of Magic, as you all call the DarkFlower Jungle. Let me say that we would be best to avoid them."

Alzerion felt the sense of urgency rise.

"Neither group is all good, but they would use any of us as bait against the Dark Sovereign, as I'm sure he will be curious about your quest."

"What do we do?" Eirini's tone was more hitched.

"Again, let's try to do our best to keep away. We must be in their territory or part of the jungle. Their magic can rival the best of them. Those with the magical staff are stronger than some others."

"That makes sense." Alzerion tapped a finger against his lower jaw.

"Well, it all goes back to the age-old grievance between them and the Dark Sovereigns. Now, more than ever, we need to find Gael."

Alzerion nodded.

"My imprisonment has left me at a disadvantage of knowledge. Gael will help us fill in the gaps, and he may have heard rumblings about the one you seek to find."

"That all sounds promising." Quairken shuffled his feet.

"Hold on." Calderon's fingers picked the skins around his nails. "You mean that rabbit we saw when we got here?"

"Correct, obedient one," Endrus said as his talons appeared to flex on the dirt and gravel.

Calderon's face shot up. "Oh perfect. Our fate rests on a hare?"

Brentley made an audible noise but pinched his mouth in and held up a hand to cover it. Alzerion shook his head with the faintest smile.

"It's better than nothing." Alzerion's voice was crisp.

Calderon lowered his face as Alzerion circled around them.

"It may be wise to split up," Endrus boomed. "Just be alert. Each one of you could be in danger, and this is their terrain. There could be traps and any manner of mishaps around these parts."

Alzerion sucked in as his lips pulled in. He always focused and stayed alert. His head quirked as he glanced at Calderon and Brentley. *Would they be safe?*

*Maybe send Quairken with them, young ruler?*

"Endrus, why don't you soar up and keep a watchful eye on us from above? You could send a warning message to me if you see a sign of trouble."

Endrus' body bowed low, but then he pressed off with his powerful legs as he rose higher and higher.

"Are we going to split up?" Eirini's voice had a slight crack to it.

He observed them; she straightened up as she breathed in, and he could sense a bit of her fear, but she masked it by holding her chin up.

"Endrus is right. We may do better if we split up."

Eirini and Quairken spoke, but Alzerion held up a hand. Quairken backed down, but Eirini had a look of determination about her.

"Look, we would have a better chance of moving around undetected. We would be less noticeable if we didn't travel with an entire group of us together."

"I trust you." Quairken bowed his head. "How are we going to group up?"

"I have an idea," Alzerion said.

Eirini shook her head. "I don't mean to be pushy, but I'm going with you."

She strolled over to him and wrapped her arm around his.

Alzerion felt a tightness in his throat.

"I guess that settles it." Quairken tilted his head to the side as his hand covered the smile that grew on his face.

"So we travel together?" Brentley pointed at Calderon and Quairken.

Alzerion sucked in a deep breath as he felt Eirini's soft hands on his arm. "It looks like it, Brentley. Be careful, the three of you. Remember what Endrus said."

"Don't worry about us," Quairken sounded controlled.

Alzerion nodded. "I know you have it covered. Why don't we aim to meet back here?" Alzerion pointed to Quairken and muttered, destinare.

Quairken blinked. "Whoa, that was...different."

"Endrus gave it to me just now." He looked at the others. "There is some sort of makeshift camp site with an overhang for Endrus, too."

Quairken nudged Brentley and Calderon, and then they turned and left as they pushed away a bush branch.

"They won't get lost?" Eirini's voice was sweet as her other hand pressed to his arm.

"No." Alzerion looked down at her. "What I did to Quairken was like giving him magical tracking, so to speak. As long as they stay safe, they should make it there fine."

Alzerion turned them as he saw a path riddled with weathered rocks, vines, and even some roots that stuck up on the path. Eirini let go, but he watched as she kept his pace. He intentionally walked slower for her so as not to tire her out. A silence passed for some time as they walked. Alzerion kept his focus on the path ahead, even as the grayness from the sky mixed with the shades of deep red. The path narrowed, forcing them to walk closer together, almost like they were tied back up with that rope. He was behind her but their bodies were almost touching. He felt a heat spread over his cheeks. *Relax. Not now when she's so close.*

Eirini angled her head to him. His eyes darted to her, briefly, she winked. Alzerion forced his gaze back on the path.

"Am I making you uncomfortable?"

"No, of course not." He cleared his throat.

"Mhm ...then why have you been silent?"

"Oh, well, I'm just keeping a watchful eye. I don't want us to fall prey to a trap." Alzerion leaned forward as his hand touched a low hanging frond from one tree. His chest touched her back as he did so. A jolt rippled through his well-toned body. In an instant Eirini rotated, grabbed onto both of his arms, and pushed him up against the trunk of that tree he was pushing them past. He gulped, but his heart quickened.

"What are you doing?"

Eirini held onto him as she allowed herself to press against him. Her smile reached up to her beautiful eyes.

"Alzerion, I can feel that you're being less than honest."

Eirini let one of her hands move as it trailed up his arm and across his chest until it rested over his heart.

"I'm not." Alzerion's upper lip quivered. He spoke with as much confidence as he could muster. His hands gathered around her elbows and tugged until her arms lowered. Then he shifted as he made to move away.

There wasn't much room to move other than forward, so he pulled back that frond once more. Eirini's gaze narrowed.

"What?" Alzerion bit his lip.

"Fine, I'll play it your way this once." She walked past the frond.

Alzerion let it go as he grabbed her hand. His thumb rubbed the valleys between her knuckles. "I'm just a bit distracted." His eyes met hers.

Eirini didn't move. "Why?"

Alzerion felt his jaw tense as he opened to speak.

"There is no reason to be distracted."

Alzerion tilted his head as his eyebrow rose. He pushed away the doubt in his head that nagged him to drop it. Instead, he moved the hand of hers he had up to his mouth. He let his lips press into the softness of her skin, kissed her hand, and then let go.

"You know that's not true." He angled his face down toward hers. "No matter what pretense I give and, however, you joke it off."

Eirini's hands grabbed at his shirt and tightened as he felt his shirt bunch under the fists from her grip. She pulled as her head rose higher, closer to his face. He stared down at her.

"What are you saying, Alzerion?"

His heart thudded even louder, he was sure. He wasn't often good at telling. "I'll show you instead."

Eirini's mouth hung open as his hands grasped the sides of her head. He brushed some hair behind her as he lowered his face to hers. They were close. He could smell that sweetness from her waft up to his nostrils. Alzerion smirked as Eirini licked her candy-red lips. He wanted to suck and nip at them until they puffed from their kiss. He didn't want to keep pushing away, but there it was. That voice in his head that disapproved. Alzerion hovered over her.

"Well, what are you waiting for, then?"

"I can't," he sounded exasperated. Alzerion pressed his forehead to hers instead. "I want to, but I just can't."

He felt Eirini's hands release his shirt as they laid on top of his. "It's okay. You don't have to feel obligated to kiss me, ever."

One of her hands slid down and hooked under his chin as she lifted at his chin. "Alzerion, when you're ready, I'll be here." She beamed. "I never want to be a duty, but your choice. I sense that you're not there yet."

Alzerion had no words, but felt his breath catch. He couldn't admit it to her yet, as he barely admitted it to himself. A lightness flitted inside at her proclamation. *Nobody had ever said that to him—been so honest or allowed him to put what he wanted first.* Eirini strolled forward as he watched with eyes wide. *Screw it.* Alzerion took a few quick strides, grabbed hold of her elbow, and tugged gingerly. He spun her around as he closed that space.

Eirini squealed as his hands cupped her chin and his lips pressed to hers. He blocked that voice of duty from his head. Alzerion leaned into her as he pulled at her bottom lip. He let out a gasp and then wrapped his arms around her back as he kissed her once more. Longing, gone as he felt her arms entwine around his neck. Alzerion shifted them off to the side and then they veered forward. He stumbled but held onto her. Eirini's mouth pulled in as a laugh escaped. Alzerion drew her back in and nibbled at her lip as her mouth parted. His tongue darted into the open space as it explored the openness of her mouth.

Eirini shoved him back. "Wow," she panted. "What was that for?"

"Being you," he whispered.

Her face scrunched up.

"Maybe I just wanted to kiss you. Do I need a reason?" He chuckled.

"If you keep kissing me like that, never." Eirini beamed.

"Good," he said. He pulled her back in as his mouth watered. He felt a hunger inside.

*It's okay, Alzerion. Don't worry about blocking me out.*

*Eirini.* He felt the tug at his heart once more. Eirini grasped his hair, and he felt her tug as she coaxed them around. He felt a pleasurable tingle across his skin. It surged all over as he snatched at her waist. If they could be closer, he would. Lips pressed back into hers with such firmness. He teased their mouths into a quick rhythm. Her hands grazed the back of his neck and he felt a satisfying chill.

Alzerion heard a faint voice hiss in the air. "Just a bit more."

Eirini tried to speak, but he couldn't make it out from their kissing. He felt her hand on his chest as she pushed. Alzerion stumbled back.

"What's that sound?" Eirini's voice wavered between gasps for air.

Alzerion's mind was jumbled. He tried to focus on it but he couldn't get past the fact that his body ached, no yearned to kiss her again. Alzerion took a few steps back.

"Alzerion, no!" Eirini ran toward him.

He cocked an eyebrow as he angled around. There was some sort of loosened rope that looked like a vine. He must have backed into it.

"Eirini, what's wrong?"

She stood near him. "I thought it could have been a trap that you tripped."

Alzerion examined the area. "I don't see anything or hear that voice anymore." Alzerion inched forward as his eyes scanned the space ahead.

There was a rumbling as the ground started to quake underneath them.

"Run." Eirini shouted. "Look out."

Eirini pushed him back as he saw a feathered arrow pierce through the air. Alzerion stumbled as the ground continued to splinter under him. Eirini dashed toward him as he fell down. He grappled in the air as he found a thin rock that jutted out. His hands grabbed and held onto it. Alzerion struggled to keep his grip as some other rocks, dirt, and earthen materials fell. He looked down, but it was dark. No clue where that would send him. Then finally, it was silent. *Please let her be okay.*

"Eirini? Are you alright?" He yelled. Alzerion's fingers were moist with sweat as he readjusted his grip. He clawed at the rock as he tried to pull himself up, but there wasn't enough room. He heard feet pound on the ground above and Eirini's head hung over the edge from above.

He felt a weight lift. "Thank the gods you're safe."

Eirini didn't say anything. She lowered her hands to him, but he shook his head.

"I cannot reach." He said through gritted teeth. "Find a thick branch or something."

"I don't want to leave you." He saw her face turn pallid.

"Eirini," he spat out, as his face scrunched up. "Now isn't the time. Go find the branch."

With a wrinkled brow, Eirini bounced up and disappeared. He heard the occasional rustling nearby—it soothed his concern over her well-being.

Beads of sweat collected on his forehead. He felt them slide down his face. "Hurry," he grunted.

"Is this good?"

"Hold it out over the edge." Alzerion's tone strangled as he forced the words out.

Eirini did just that.

"Extendo," Alzerion muttered. The log grew in length, as it cascaded down to the thin rock ledge that Alzerion held on to. He took a quick breath as he grabbed the log and pulled. Eirini leaned over the ledge, her body laid out as she stretched her hands down. *Foolish, but very welcome*, he thought. Alzerion wrapped his legs around the extended log as he used his arms to pull himself across it. Once he reached Eirini's hands, she tugged until she fell backward. Alzerion watched as she dug her boots into the ground and kept heaving him toward her. So close to the edge, she tugged, and he lunged off of it and collapsed onto the ground. Alzerion's breaths quickened as he laid on his back. Eirini rolled over as she gazed down at him.

"Thank you," his voice was breathy.

Eirini nodded. She also took in a few deep breaths.

His hands pushed off the ground as they propped his body up. This way, he was close to her face. "No, Eirini, really. Thank you." He wanted her to catch the sincerity in each word. "I couldn't have done it without you."

"Don't mention it."

Alzerion leaned toward her and ran his hands through her hair. He smirked as he watched the dazzle in her eyes.

He heard voices not far off.

"Are they there?"

"Was it them?"

Alzerion heard the sounds and scrambled to his feet. Then he drew his sword as his other hand helped Eirini to her feet. Alzerion stood in front with his sword held out. The figures emerged.

"What are you guys doing here?" Alzerion tilted his head.

"We heard the tremble on the ground," Quairken said as he moved closer.

Alzerion sheathed his sword as Quairken grasped him in an arm shake.

"It was touch and go for a bit." Alzerion glanced over at Eirini.

"But you're alright?" Quairken asked.

Brentley and Calderon said nothing as they paced around him. He felt their eyes on him as they returned to Quairken's side.

"Did I miss something?"

"Of course not." Quairken said. "Just wanted to be sure that you weren't injured."

"He's fine." Eirini stepped forward. She gazed up at him. "We kept each other safe from that weird fracture of the ground."

Quairken's face was solemn as his eyes darted between the two of them. Alzerion knew Quairken well. He had an inkling of what he was possibly thinking.

"Anyway, maybe we should—"

*Young ruler don't separate. Change of plans.*

*Explain.*

*I have spotted a hidden passage nearby. A spot that Gael used to enjoy. He may be there.*

"Sir, what's wrong?" Calderon asked.

Brentley nudged him.

"What? He just stopped mid thought?"

Brentley's gaze narrowed as he looked at Calderon. Calderon backed down.

"I'm sorry." Alzerion cleared his throat. "No need to be concerned, Calderon. Endrus had some information, that's all." Alzerion looked up to the dark sky as Endrus came into view.

"Anything good?" Quairken's tone was hopeful.

Alzerion nodded. He motioned up as Endrus spiraled down. Alzerion moved closer to Quairken, Brentley, and Calderon to make room. Eirini followed close behind.

Endrus landed and shifted his legs as he moved toward this cove of thick bushes.

"What's he doing?" Calderon whispered.

"Come, and you shall see."

Alzerion motioned for them to go. The whole group moved closer as Endrus lowered his snout and took a large sniff.

"This is the place. I can feel the magic and smell Gael."

Alzerion's eyes pinched in.

Endrus lowered his fierce head until his snout could touch the leaves from the bush. He breathed out, and Alzerion felt the wave of magic. The bushes shuddered under his breath until they rippled like a piece of peeled fruit and the smells of food and drink mixed with the chatter that abounded. Alzerion stepped forward. It was like a small tavern hidden in the bushes.

"He's in there young ruler. Welcome to Low Bush Tavern."

Alzerion led them in.

## CHAPTER 18
# Night in the Jungle

There was so mistaking. Magic swirled all around ... Alzerion could feel it—it oozed from every inch of the little place. From the tenders who, with a wave of a hand, made drinks and orders float toward the customers. It was a mixture of creatures. Alzerion felt his heart race. He was one step closer to getting the information he needed.

He felt a hand on his shoulder, and his face turned. Eirini smiled. They walked ahead, and Endrus followed. He didn't think he would fit, but as they entered and the bush closed behind them, the tavern seemed to grow. Alzerion blinked as he stared out.

"My old friend," Endrus spoke with a voice that could shake the whole building.

There he was at a table with another, but Gael's ears perked up as he turned. He bounded up from the table. Endrus moved toward them, and Alzerion motioned to the group until they all gathered around. Alzerion and Eirini sat while the other three stood around him.

"It has been long indeed, Endrus." Gael spoke as he laid a paw on Endrus' shoulder.

Gael stood on his haunches as his nutbrown eyes landed on Alzerion.

"We meet again, Your Majesty." Gael bowed as his long ears flopped over.

Alzerion tensed as he stared back at Gael. "Endrus speaks highly of you."

"We go way back," Gael scratched at his nose.

Endrus lowered his body as he rested his belly on the stone floor. "Gael, the young ruler is looking for someone. A young woman."

"Ah yes, I remember." Gael pawed at the tip of his ear. "I guess you haven't found her then."

"No. Your directions were a bit off," Quairken fired back.

"Off?" Gael spoke with a twist of his head. He batted the whiskers around his nose. "I believe that you all went where I thought best."

Alzerion straightened up as his index fingers hooked around each other. He tugged as he maintained his gaze. The creature next to Gael looked like the picture of a fiery bird, silent until Gael continued.

"I'm sorry for the theatrics," Gael's jovial voice lowered. He hopped once toward Alzerion. "I thought it best if you met Endrus. They had him locked up for quite some time. Well, you had what was needed to set him free."

"It was appreciated," Endrus loudly said. . "But our young ruler would like better information going forward."

"I still seek the location of the one I came for."

Gael shook his head as his whiskers swayed.

"Hehem."

The bird, which looked to be ablaze, flapped his wings as its eyes pierced into him.

"Oh, how silly of me. This is Surge. He's good company," Gael added.

"I don't mean to be rude, but Surge, are you a-a, phoenix?" Eirini's eyes went wide as she stared at the other creature.

"I am. You know about my species?" His voice was deep and had all the air of wisdom, like Endrus.

Wow, she mouthed. "I have read about them, but never met one before. I'm Eirini." She bowed her head.

"I like this one," Surge quipped. "She knows how to approach someone."

Alzerion cleared his throat as his gaze shifted from Eirini to Gael and then to Surge.

"I've heard the rumors of travelers here in the DarkFlower Jungle," Surge said. "Have you been warned?"

His reddish orange feathered head turned to him. There was an appearance of some kind of golden tint as the candlelight from the tavern reflected. The muscles in Alzerion's forehead creased as his eyebrow rose. "Warning?"

"He has been warned about the factions and a bit about the Dark Sovereign," Endrus said.

"But what about the flowers?" Gael added. "You can't trust them either." He leaned forward. "At least not the delicious smelling ones."

"Why is that?" Eirini placed a hand to Gael's ears as she rubbed the fur.

Gael did not stop her. If anything, his eyes squeezed shut, much like he was enjoying the massage.

"What he means is that they have been compromised," Surge said. "Some time back, those flowers became deadly. If you fall into their sweetness, you can die."

Alzerion recounted his experience the first time he came here. He gulped. *But the voice saved him.*

"I can see you have something on your mind, young ruler." Surge stepped closer. "What is it?"

"I came into contact with them once before, but some mysterious voice saved me. It sounded like that of the woman I am here to find."

He saw Surge straighten up, and Gael's eyes shot open as his thumping foot moved back.

"What?" Alzerion stared at them.

"It's not possible, hearing voices. Only entity with that kind of power is the Dark Sovereign. I doubt he wanted you here. Maybe he just wanted you gone."

"Wait." Surge held up a feathered wing. "What about the other entity? That sounds exactly like something it would do."

Gael's furry face drooped as a frown covered its features.

"You don't mean *that* entity?" The timbre of Endrus' voice was low but firm.

Alzerion heard the muttering of Quairken to Brentley, but he focused on the creatures before him. "What do you mean by *it*?"

They exchanged glances, but there was a moment of silence as Gael sighed. He bounced closer and then spoke in hushed tones. "The darkness. It takes on a life of its own."

"But I thought the Dark Sovereign held it at bay?" Endrus asked.

"He does, but the Fates have decreed its rise in power. I don't know the whole of the prophecy, but the Dark Sovereign has been taking measures to shield us from the darkness. It wants out, to break free and escape into neighboring realms. At least that is what we have heard."

"Only the Dark Sovereign can tell you more." Surge lowered his head. "But take care, young ruler."

"Why?"

"Surely, Endrus has spoken of the Dark Sovereign?" Surge's golden red eyes burned into Alzerion.

"He is not much better," Gael added. "He has mellowed a bit in the last few years, but there has been talk among the creatures. That he has married another brave soul—a woman to bind the darkness here to our realm, but there are cracks that have formed as of late."

Alzerion felt a grip on his shoulders. His face angled to see Quairken. "Do you think it could be her?"

Alzerion's mind moved so fast. *Could it be*? The timing seemed to fit. He felt Eirini's presence in his thoughts, so he looked over at her, but she didn't meet his gaze.

"Do you know something?" Alzerion asked, as his gaze didn't waver. "Is this what your mother kept from me? Did you both know that she has married another?"

Eirini's cheeks flushed. "I-I don't know what my mother saw." She picked at the skin on her fingers as she continued to look at him. Her nose wrinkled as her lips pressed together.

Alzerion bent his head as he gazed deeper into her eyes. He cupped a hand under her chin and lifted...a gentle touch was best. "Tell me, please."

Her fingers traced the lines of the hand on her chin, before she grabbed his hand in hers and held onto him. "It's not a vision. I had this feeling. I warned it was a waste of your time to chase after her. I'm not sure why, but that was all I was given. A feeling that this quest of yours will cost you more than you will gain."

Alzerion licked his lips as his teeth pressed into the fleshy part of them. He didn't know what to think.

"We've already come this far." Quairken patted his shoulder. "We should see it through. The only way we'll know if Aironell is his bride is if we find her."

Alzerion nodded as he stepped back. He breathed out and then focused in on Gael.

"This time, will you tell us how to find the heart of the jungle? No tricks or detours."

Gael straightened up to his full height. "As you wish, young ruler. The best we can do is give you a gift, but we should head out of the tavern first."

In one bound, Gael was halfway across the room. Alzerion motioned to his group, and they followed him out until the jungle surrounded them once more.

Gael rested his tailed bottom on a stump as his paws settled on his furry lap.

"What in the world?"

Alzerion turned. Calderon jumped as his arms flailed.

"You should step on it," Surge spoke as he came into view.

Calderon's boot rose and crushed it with a splatter of guts on the grass and dirt.

"What was that?" Quairken asked.

"A spy," Surge said.

Alzerion looked at Gael.

"He speaks the truth. They are called Whulgs."

Alzerion didn't understand. He felt Eirini's presence in his mind. Not invading, but comforting.

"They're small and they move slowly, but that slowness allows them to move undetected most times because they are silent. But do not be fooled they are spies for the Dark Sovereign and the Lady of the Jungle."

"They listen on anything they hear and report it back to the Dark Sovereign."

"Did we stop it since Calderon killed it?" Alzerion asked.

"Hopefully," Surge added.

"Wh-what does that mean?" Eirini stood beside Alzerion.

Gael bounced up and moved closer to them. "We don't know if it sent its report before it was killed. The glossy middle of it with the sharp barbed looking teeth that are also magical. It sends its reports automatically through its opening."

"So, if you hope to find this woman of yours, young ruler, then you want to do so quickly, in case the Dark Sovereign knows what you're here to do."

"Sir," Brentley spoke. "We will need to rest first. It has been a day and the grayness of the sky seems darker."

"Of course," Gael added. "You may want to get that rest. You will need it for you journey to the heart if the jungle."

Alzerion watched as Gael hopped to Surge. Surge flapped his fiery wings and Gael leaned his horns into the reddish orange fire that burned from his feathers. Then something fell to Gael's paws. Gael faced Alzerion and held it out.

"What is this?"

"It's the help you asked for. Now that Endrus is freed and you know more of your obstacle, I will indeed do as you asked."

Alzerion grabbed the warm leathery parchment, and he slowly unraveled it.

"This is a map of sorts. Forged in the flames of the phoenix. Be careful. It shows you where other creatures are. We hope that keeps you free of the Preservers."

Alzerion nodded as his eyes roamed the magical map. Bright letters glowed on it to show different parts of the DarkFlower Jungle. He even saw images and the one that stared out at him was marked; the heart. It was smack in the middle of the jungle.

"Just be careful. It is guarded by magical wards. You may now know where it is, but magic keeps it hidden. Unless you are already in it or brought there by the Dark Sovereign, it is quite difficult to enter."

"Good luck," Surge bowed his head. He flapped his wings and disappeared into a ball of fire.

Gael gave a curt nod and bounced off.

"Well, young ruler," Endrus spoke. "Will we take refuge for the night?"

Alzerion folded it up and placed it in a pocket. Then he nodded.

"Then I will fly up and find a space large enough for me to rest. I suggest you all head north, like we discussed. That spot used to be a campsite, but it is no longer used. It'll make a good place to rest." Then Endrus flew up to the sky.


They walked for what felt like hours, but they made it. Calderon, Brentley, and Quairken dropped the bags they carried to the ground.

"We will gather the wood," Brentley said as he pulled Calderon as he sighed.

Quairken rooted through the abandoned campsite. Eirini observed the worn materials of the campsite. It was much more like huts. Alzerion brushed by as he knelt placing stones in a circular pattern. *It must be for the fire.* She rummaged on the ground for twigs and anything that could be used for kindling. After she made piles on the ground near Alzerion, she focused on the shelters which looked like glorified shacks. Her hands were on her hips as her eyes went wide. *They barely would provide privacy, let alone shelter from the elements.*

"Why do you want privacy?" Alzerion's voice was low and teasing.

She felt his words tickle her ear. Eirini turned her head to see his cinnamon-red eyes staring down at her.

"You know why." Eirini winked at him.

"Do you mean to get some good rest?" Alzerion folded his arms.

She placed her hand on his folded arm. "Sure. If that makes you less uncomfortable."

Alzerion's lips cracked as they parted.

Eirini pulled herself up as her lips reached his ears. "Which one is ours?"

Alzerion cleared his throat, but before he spoke, Eirini placed a finger over his lips. Her finger glided across his lip in a quick motion. "Don't tease, Alzerion. Remember, you will always be my choice."

He grabbed her finger, and she felt the warmth of his hand flood over her skin. An overwhelming sensation that brought a smile to her face. His face lowered to mere inches from hers. "Only one of us is teasing, and well, it isn't me." Alzerion turned as he spoke. "But ours is the one on the right. I already fixed it up the best I could." Then he walked away as he continued preparing the site.

Eirini moved toward their shelter. The top was like a wooden canopy with green leaves that cascaded down with a mixture of what felt like wood, mud, and twine all molded together.

Eirini took a breath and went in. Her eyes wandered over the surroundings. There was a bed of leaves strewn across the ground. As she stepped forward, she heard a creak in the floor. She glanced down and, in that moment, an arm wrapped around her. Eirini angled her head to see Alzerion, as he turned her around and then pulled her in.

The smell of cinnamon wafted off of him. Being so close to him, why she could melt into a puddle of chocolatey goodness just from the closeness. Her senses worked on overdrive. He was content being near her, of that she was sure, but those walls of his were up as always. He hadn't fully let go. His nose rubbed against the bridge of her nose, her cheek, and then he gazed at her.

"What are you thinking?" The words flowed out of her mouth playfully.

"Don't you know?" He smirked.

"I can if you want me to mind meld." Eirini's fingers made tiny swirls over the fabric that covered his chest.

Alzerion sat up and held out a hand to her. Her eyes bounced to his fingers as she grabbed him, her palm rested with his.

"I want to show you something. It's close to the campsite, but I thought you might like it."

Eirini felt her smile grow so wide that the muscles of her face pulled.

She licked her lips, then allowed him to guide her. True to his word, it wasn't far. Alzerion brought her to this sweet little spot.

"What is this?" Her eyebrows drew closer.

Alzerion laid a finger over his inviting lips. He stopped them amid massive trees that acted like a border. In the middle, she saw a bigger bed of leaves and a small little fire that crackled. Eirini glanced up at him.

He smirked. Then he strolled over and sat on the bed of leaves.

The different shades of green popped against the crimson hue of the fire nearby. Eirini pursed her lips. She weighed the choices in her mind. *He was handsome and challenging, in a good way, but he also seemed reserved, like some controlling force still had a hold over him.* She sat down by him. He seized her waist and slid her closer—his arm bumped against hers.

Eirini looked up at the black sky. A unique twinkle swirled around.

"Do you like it?"

She felt his hot breath against her cheek. She swallowed and then looked down. Her face bumped into him.

"This is amazing, Alzerion. Did you do all this?"

"I added the little things for us to sit comfortably." He cupped her face and gently coaxed her chin up. His cinnamon-red eyes were different. This time, they didn't look so cold and exacting.

"What's going on with you tonight? You seem different, somehow."

"Nothing." Alzerion's tone was firm. His thumb grazed her jaw as he spoke. "Eirini, I...never mind." He pulled his hand back.

"You don't have to push me away. Alzerion, I wasn't criticizing you. I just, well, you seem different." She ran her hand through his hair as his eyes met hers once more.

"I don't enjoy talking, at least not about feelings."

"Are you upset about the news that Aironell could be, well, moved on?"

Eirini watched as Alzerion's back straightened. "The idea bothered me at first."

Her eyes probed him as she picked at the leather of her bodice.

"All I care about is knowing that she is indeed alright. That she isn't

189

someone's captive. I wanted to bring her back to her kingdom and her parents, but I guess we shall see about that."

"So loyal," Eirini whispered. "Bachusa is lucky to have you as its ruler."

Alzerion looked at her. "That doesn't sound much like a compliment." His eyes focused on her.

A question weighed on her, but she didn't know what his response would be. Eirini's lips pressed together, tight. Alzerion's head angled down as his hand grabbed hold of a piece of her curl. Eirini felt something wash over her as Alzerion twirled the curl around his finger again and again. *Much like how she felt about him. He grew on her, but was it mutual?*

She bit her lip. "What matters the most to you right now?"

Alzerion's arm rubbed against hers as he moved...angled toward her. "Eirini." Her name sounded sweet somehow.

She glanced at him as his eyes softened once more. Her shoulders relaxed as her heart moved so fast, as he lowered his face near hers.

"I want to enjoy this moment—the beautiful spot with you."

Her lips parted into a wistful smile. Then she straightened up as she placed her hands on the ground, about to stand.

"Where are you going?"

Eirini was on her feet as she gazed down. His eyes glued to her. The look tugged at her heart. His gaze was intense, like he yearned for her presence. It was gone as quick as she saw it, replaced by a frown.

Eirini blinked.

Alzerion reached up and grasped both of her hands and pulled. Eirini sank back down. Alzerion grabbed her before her knees hit the ground. Instead, he cradled her in his lap. Her back braced against his chest. She didn't know what to think. She had little chance, anyway.

Alzerion pressed a kiss on her forehead and then rested his cheek on the top of her head. Eirini nuzzled her face into his broad chest. She placed a hand over his abdomen, feeling the warmth of his skin through his shirt. She let her fingers graze against the fabric as she bit her lip.

"Don't...leave." The hum of his voice vibrated her to her very core.

His tone was different, strained. Like he was battling some sort of grip. She knew what he meant. A fire burned in her eyes. *If only she could take him away from here. Get him out of his head and this obligation of his. She took him at his word. It wasn't about love for him, but his duty to save Aironell.* She rubbed her head on his chest, with her nose taking in his scent. *Ahh, spice and trees.* It was intoxicating.

His tensed muscles relaxed. *There was only one way to find out what he meant. If he wanted this as much as she did.* The thrill of it all was more than she bargained for. Eirini looked up at him and rubbed her lips against his jawline. She heard the intake of air as his lips parted and thrust her shoulders back. Eirini followed his gaze as he scanned her body. His eyes trailed each place on her frame and her heart beat faster as his eyes idled on her chest before he fixed on her face.

He stared, hungry. It sent chills on her skin. Eirini touched her fingertips to his face and then outlined his jaw and chin. Her mind flooded with his barrage of thoughts.

*Kiss. Don't kiss. Just let loose. She'll be like the others and leave. He was nothing special.*

His thoughts pained her, like someone jabbed her with a dagger to the heart. Her eyes filled with the sting of it all, as if she might blink down heated tears. Alzerion was still. It was an accident—she swore she would be careful. *Could their bond have grown?* There was no denying what she felt in that touch—his desire.

Eirini shoved his chest back. He toppled backwards, hands flew out to catch him, as he propped himself with both elbows. His eyes widened. In one fluid motion, she straddled him, a leg on each side of his hips. Then she leaned forward, her body squeezed against his hard chest. Her right hand laid against his cheek as her left hand shot right to his hair. Her fingers twirled the pieces.

"Eirini," his voice was low.

She shook her head—placed her index finger from her right hand over his lips. It was her turn. Alzerion's lips parted and his mouth maneuvered her finger over as his teeth as he playfully nibbled.

Eirini giggled.

She pressed flat against him as he released his elbows. His hands clamped on her back. Eirini skimmed her nose against his jaw and then nuzzled his neck. She heard him gulp. His grip on her back tightened. Eirini licked her lips and then rubbed them up and down his neck in slow motion. Alzerion's legs shuddered. She felt the heat of his skin as a hand laid against his face.

"Mmhmm," Alzerion grumbled.

His nails dug in. Eirini pressed her hands into the bed of leaves as her hip backed up, placing her knees on the ground. Alzerion's grip tightened, and she collapsed back on him as he yanked. They rolled over until they landed before a large rock. Alzerion grasped her waist as he stood them up. A smirk crossed his lips as his other hand held the back of her neck and eased her in.

"Is this what you want?"

His words tickled her skin as he spoke in a breathy tone near her ear.

Eirini tilted her head back and nodded. "But do you want it, too?" She asked. There was no going back.

He took a deep breath, as his gaze didn't waver. Neither did hers. She asked it with such determination and the weight of her lilting words weren't lost on him.

He thrust her against the firmness of the rock behind them, and his mouth devoured her. Each kiss was firm as he nibbled her bottom lip and then thrust his tongue in. It moved in a rhythmic pattern—in and out. He felt a growing frenzy at his core. He only had a singular thought. For once, he listened.

Alzerion's hands ravaged her body. They pulled at her arms and glided over the curve of her body. He cupped his hands around her lower back side as her legs wrapped around him. His hands skimmed her limbs. She gasped, catching a breath, but then he pressed his lips back on hers. This time, Alzerion clung to her thighs as he hoisted them up. His body pressed against hers. She let out another quick breath. Alzerion's fingers twirled around the laces of her leather bodice. Her lashes rose with each movement of his fingers. Alzerion bit his lip. He wanted to.

He could feel it. A yearning, a passion that he never felt before. He stared at her.

Alzerion steadied his own heavy breathing. The coolness of the air around kissed his body. He felt his muscles tighten. His hands moved up as his hips held them in place against the rock behind them. Her eyes closed tight as she licked her lip. Then he let his hands stray to her side— feeling the goosebumps on her arm. He grumbled and then pressed his chest to hers as his mouth sucked in her tantalizing lips. Suddenly, he loosened his weight against her and then his hands grasped her hips and turned her body. Her head bent to the side as his kiss deepened. He felt a heat rising as he shuddered.

"Eirini, no." He said between kisses. He wanted to let each fantasy, each desire, play out.

*He couldn't.*

Alzerion took his hands, and he moved her away. He darted over to the bed of leaves and sat down, knees up, as his nails dug into the skin at his wrists. His arms hugged his knees in tight. Eirini folded her arms as she stared down at him.

*Damn it.*

He turned to face the trees of the jungle. His hands balled into fists. Alzerion pressed his eyes shut. She probably thought him a big tease.

"Alzerion."

All he heard was concern. He opened his eyes at her touch against his forearm. Alzerion rubbed his hand on hers as he bent his face down.

"Are you alright?" Eirini shuffled around until she was in front of him.

He nodded. "It's nothing."

Her head tilted as she pulled her hand away.

Alzerion's jaw tensed. He watched as her shoulders drooped and she took an uneven step back. "Why not just tell me? I can handle the truth, Alzerion, whatever it may be."

His chest tightened. Eirini had sat down beside him. There wasn't anger in her eyes, only concern, and he sensed something else. A question that hung between them. *Gods, no, please don't ask about it.*

Finally, she stood up and held out a hand to him. Alzerion grabbed it and hoisted himself up. She was right in front of him, within touching distance—yet he couldn't bring himself to let those walls down. He watched her with a pained expression, but he couldn't do it.

Her eyes fixed on him. They pleaded with him. Her mouth twisted into a grimace as she rested a hand on his arm. Alzerion pressed his nails into the palm of his hands. *Idiot*, he thought to himself.

"Eirini, I'm sorry." His voice was solemn.

He saw the gorgeous features of her face, like she was a magnificent painting, but her face looked firm.

Eirini's arms rested at her side as she spoke. "Why do you push me away? I've sensed your walls before."

"Then you already know the answer," Alzerion swallowed.

She shook her head as she took a half step closer. "Alzerion, I don't need to mind meld to know what I can see plainly with my own eyes." Eirini glimpsed down at her hands and then back at him. "You wanted it, maybe even more than I wanted us to share a moment."

Alzerion's chin lowered as he rubbed the back of his neck.

Eirini placed a hand on his forearm and continued. "I can feel what is unsaid between us—the growing connection. It's not all in my head, is it? I mean, you have pushed me away twice now, but who's counting?" She shrugged.

He felt a sadness in her voice, despite her attempt to brush it off.

"Eirini," his voice was low, almost inaudible.

"I guess I need to know."

He felt her eyes search his face for some answer. She deserved an answer, but he couldn't give it.

"I don't do feelings," Alzerion said.

Eirini flinched at his words as she stepped back. Alzerion moved closer to her. "Listen." Alzerion touched her chin as he gently lifted her face up. "Eirini, I think you're the most clever and gorgeous woman I have ever laid my eyes on."

He saw her cheeks blush. "Then why pull away?"

Alzerion rubbed his chin and pinched the skin under his lip as he sat down on the bed of leaves. Eirini kept a couple of paces from him, but sat down near him. Her eyes fixed on him as if he was the last man in the realm. Her eyes glistened, but she straightened up her back.

He knew she valued fun and experiences—*was that what this was all about for her*? She had said that once before, but *had her feelings grown, too*? Her head lowered as her fingers weaved in and out of the ends of her hair. His fingers fidgeted with each other as he thought about what to say. He *knew he was the broken one—Eirini was damned near perfection to him.*

He cleared his throat. "I rarely let myself feel things. The last time I did well, you know what happened. She was the only woman I ever loved."

Her amber eyes glanced back at him. "That was Aironell, I presume." Her voice didn't waver.

"Yes." He maintained his gaze as she blinked. He swore he saw tears, but Eirini was on her feet so fast, and then she ran.

*Crap.*

"Eirini, come back!" He chased after her.

## CHAPTER 19
## Matters of the Heart

E irini dashed through the jungle. She fixed her eyes on the path ahead as she pushed branches aside. The darkness that loomed around made it difficult to find the best place to run. *How could she have been such a fool?*

The back of her hand rubbed at the tears in her eyes. It made little sense. Alzerion, well, she always wondered about his motives behind this whole adventure. To hear him actually say that he loved Aironell well...it was more than she could bear. *Did he love her still?* She bit her lip as the pricking behind her eyes stung as she blinked.

She felt a tightness that pressed on her ribs and lungs. Each successive dash and jump forced the nagging pain to burn...as if her lungs would burst into tears if they could. Even her legs felt weighed down from sprinting. *Maybe she had enough distance from him?* Eirini hunched over with a hand on the cracked bark of a purple flowering tree. She gasped for air—as if each inhale overwhelmed her frame. She sniffled as she slowly straightened up, as her hand still rested against the tree.

This was her reprieve or break. A moment to clear her mind of the doubts. Was this what it felt like to burn for someone? A slight shuffle of branches blew in the breeze. Eirini's vision was brief and not quick enough.

Crack.

Her energy was still low, but the sound forced her body to turn, albeit sluggishly. She didn't see anyone, but called out anyway. "Leave me alone, Alzerion. I'm not interested in talking right at the moment."

The only sound she heard was the continued crunching of twigs on the ground and the wind as it howled. Then a figure loomed from around the bend. It was not Alzerion. *How did she not foresee this? Her vision was, well, incomplete to say the least.*

The figure wore a cloak the color of pine, and arms raised as they lowered the hood that covered a handsome face. His hair was the darkest she had ever seen, with a shade as black as ink. Eirini swallowed as she stood—frozen. Her eyes squinted between blinks. His boots crunched once more as he took a couple steps closer. The light of the moon revealed his piercing light green eyes, that spied her confused look.

"Wh-who are y-you?"

The man stepped closer. He tilted his head at an angle forward, and his dark curls frothed over his brow.

"How did you get here?" His voice was deep and commanding.

Her mouth lowered, but nothing came out.

"Do you side with the Dark Sovereign or the Preservers?"

The fog that clouded her mind shifted a bit. *Why did that sound familiar?*

*Endrus. Yes. He mentioned something about this.*

The man motioned for her to come to him. She shook her head. Her mind hadn't gone completely foolish as to bend to the whims of a stranger.

His mouth twisted into a grin. He rose his hand until she glided toward him. It was like he was pulling the strings, forcing her to move as he wanted.

As her body moved he pulled on the hood of his pine-colored cloak. It covered his features except for the faint visual of his sculpted face.

"Eirini!"

She knew Alzerion's voice.

Still, she couldn't move other than the magic that anchored her toward the stranger. In seconds she saw Endrus' wing out of the corner of her eye. He landed and Alzerion dashed toward them.

His hands shot out. "Vitis!"

She watched as the vines from the closest tree hang whacked the stranger that had her rooted to the spot. He didn't even flinch! A hearty chuckle rang out clear. He raised his other hand. It glowed a deep purple as the vines snapped and then flew to the other side. Alzerion's jaw sank.

"Young ruler, be careful."

Eirini watched Alzerion. She wanted nothing to happen to him.

"Alzerion, go." Eirini pleaded. Despite whatever was true in his heart, she knew what was in hers.

Then the cloaked stranger muttered something ancient sounding as he clasped his hands together and a ripple of magic bolted out. His right hand spun in a half-circle, masking them in a shroud of smoke. Finally, she could move. She covered her face from the smoke. When she heard the silence and no longer smelled the magic smog, she lowered her arms. Face pale. *Where was she? What happened to Alzerion and Endrus?* Eirini looked around, but all she saw was this stream and then a crystal fortress of sorts.

She rubbed her eyes, but still the image remained the same.

"Good. You're awake."

The voice was soft, gentle even.

Eirini spun around. It wasn't the man who brought her there. A woman stared down at her. Eirini took in as much as she could. Her hands clung to this delicate material — a floral bed. Soft, much like an actual bed, but composed of flowers.

"Where am I?" Eirini whispered.

The woman wore a green gown that clung to each of her curves. She knelt down next to Eirini. The pattern on the dress looked like six-pointed leaves that were gray across her forest green dress. The arms did not have sleeves, only netting with what looked like a delicate greenish gray material.

Silence passed between them.

"My friends will look for me," Eirini said.

"I know." The look in her eyes shifted. Her cerulean-blue eyes had this eerie calmness about them. "Don't worry, we want them to find you."

Eirini tilted her head. Her eyebrows furrowed.

She felt a shiver caress her skin as a warmth erupted from the mark of her talent. She swallowed as a rush of images danced across her mind. Alzerion and the group would find her, but the outcome, well, that was something the Fates clearly didn't want her to see.

Eirini scrutinized the woman before her.

The woman stood up and fixed her light-brown hair. "Come. I'm sure you must be hungry." She moved about with this air of confidence.

"Wait," Eirini called. "Are you a friend or foe?"

The lady walked up the steps of the crystal fortress, and then her head angled toward Eirini. "I guess that depends on what brings you to the DarkFlower Jungle."

She breathed out.

"Those that live here call me the Lady of the Jungle."

With that, she entered the ornate building.

Eirini took a deep breath and then followed her.

# CHAPTER 20
## To the Heart

Knocked to the ground, Alzerion fumbled for Endrus. He squinted at the mass that laid just out of reach of his hand, and the tips of his fingers grazed the scaled body.

*Endrus.*

Alzerion crawled in the dirt as he slid toward Endrus.

*I'm okay, young ruler. What about the loved one?*

*Eirini?* With one knee pressed into the ground, the other bent as his boot held firm. The shroud of mist hung in the air, but it cleared. Empty. There was nobody but them and the trees and bushes.

The stranger was gone...and Eirini.

He bolted to his feet and dashed around the perimeter, but there was nobody in sight. Alzerion stood still as he cupped his hands around his ears. Eyes closed as he focused on the sounds and his magic, but nothing.

He bit down on his lip so hard that he tasted blood while so many scenarios played out in his mind. None that were good, and each one ended with Eirini in danger or... no. He couldn't go there. It was his fault she ran from...him. A pain whacked him as clear as if she slapped him. He had to keep his opinions and, well, feelings in check. But first he had to find her.

His hands clenched into fists to keep them from trembling.

*You must center yourself, young ruler. Allow me to fly up and search.*

*Do you suspect someone in particular? Could it be the same that chased after us before?*

*I'm unsure. But I have a different suspect.*

Alzerion's gaze was sharp as Endrus' taloned feet stepped forward. His wings furled out.

"Where do you plan to search?" Alzerion made his way over to where Endrus stood, ready to take flight.

"The darkolytes. They may suspect her of being one of the preservers." Endrus' head lowered as his scaled body dipped.

Alzerion rested a hand on Endrus' snout. "You mean to tell me she is being used like some kind of pawn?"

*Possibly. The Dark Sovereign and the preservers have a long history of mutual discontent for the other.*

"We must get her back!" A fire burned in his words. No hint of panic, but a rage that rivaled any other. "I'm coming with you. Let's scour the skies."

He clasped Endrus' neck as he hopped on him and held tight, and as Endrus kicked off and soared up, he spoke once more.

*I'll be taking you to the darkolyte camp first.*

Alzerion rode in silence as he barely blinked. He focused on the surroundings, searching for her. He muttered under his breath the spell to enhance his vision so he could see almost as good as Endrus. His mind was a sea of thoughts and emotions—each crashed into the next. An insurmountable guilt clung to him as he whipped his head to the side, and he focused in at the make-shift tents below.

*That's the site?*

*Yes, young ruler. I don't see her, though.*

Alzerion felt a growing clawing feeling in his stomach. Now what?

*Well, there is one other location, but I'm not sure if we will be able to see it.*

*What is it?*

*The secluded soul or the heart of the jungle. The home of the Dark Sovereign himself.*

*Endrus please deliver us back to the others. We can't go there without them.*

*Of course.*

Alzerion felt that pitted feeling in his gut as Endrus soared down and right around. He picked up speed as Alzerion gripped onto one of the spikes.

Soon enough, Endrus landed. Alzerion jumped down right as Endrus' talons touched the ground. He dashed toward the fire pit and as Quairken caught sight of him, he stood.

"We must go," Alzerion called out.

"Go? Where?" Calderon asked.

"Alzerion, is everything alright?" Quairken's eyes moved from Endrus to him. "Where's Eirini?"

Alzerion's face paled. He felt like vomiting. "Someone took her. Endrus thinks he knows where."

Quairken stared at him for a fraction of a second. That briefest moment was enough—Quairken understood, of that he was certain. Alzerion watched as Quairken hurried the other two and they grabbed the packs. Brentley and Calderon stood at the ready, sacks on their back.

"Sir," Brentley stood at attention. "How are we going to find her?"

"We are going to ride on Endrus to get us where we need to go. It'll be quicker."

Calderon made a scrunched-up face.

"Sorry." Alzerion patted Calderon on the back. "It is the quickest method we have. No time to run into any unwanted strangers."

Calderon's cheeks puffed out with each exhale, but he nodded. "Of course, sir.

"You don't think they will harm her, do you?" Brentley asked as he took a few steps toward Endrus.

"They may if they think she is working for the wrong faction here in the DarkFlower Jungle," Endrus added. "We should move."

Calderon was silent. Brentley had no words. Instead, he flung a leg over Endrus's neck and sat at the ready.

Alzerion moved only to help Calderon up, then he sat on Endrus as Quairken climbed aboard, last.

"Let's do this," Alzerion thundered.

Endrus kicked off and his wings beat up and down. They shot

around the starry night sky of shades of red and tints of grays. He fought the ache he felt in his chest. Whether it was his fault or not, Eirini was alone, and he had to find her.

"Amplio visio," he muttered. Then he closed his eyes tight, only to open them up to that enhanced vision of his.

It was like seeing the world in shades of deeper, richer tones. Alzerion quickly looked at his men. He was also responsible for them, too. Calderon sat with his face pressed into Endrus' scales. Almost like a child hiding from something unpleasant. Then there was Brentley, who rubbed Calderon's back as he held onto him. Alzerion smirked. They were like a pair of brothers, always looking out for the other. He darted his eyes to his side toward Quairken, who sat with an air of calm.

"You alright?" Quairken said.

Alzerion nodded. Then he leaned a bit more to the side as he stared out. Out of the corner of his improved sight, he saw this glowing. He quickly glanced around to find the source, only it came from his arm. Alzerion flipped his arms over to see that mark of his, glow. Alzerion's mouth opened as he stared at it. Endrus veered to the right and, as he did, the light brightened. Alzerion looked out, but as they neared an open space below them with only a path and what looked like a stream, the glowing ceased.

"Endrus, fly to the left once more."

Endrus spiraled around as he flew full force back. The wind whipped against his face as he worked to keep his eyes open. The mark glowed once more. He heard sounds of retching as Calderon's head lowered even more. Alzerion kept his eyes peeled out. Calderon would be fine, eventually but, right now, he had to see what was below them. All he could see were tops of trees and then nothing. He blinked twice, but still it was the same.

"Can we lower here? I sense her presence."

"Are you sure?" Quairken asked. "I don't see a thing."

"It's magic," Endrus crooned. "This area is part of the heart of the jungle or the secluded soul... it is masked."

"So can we descend or not?" Alzerion spat out.

"As you wish, young ruler. Just be prepared."

"For what, Brentley called out?"

"Anything." Endrus spoke with such intensity.

Endrus spiraled like a magic ball as they zoomed down. Endrus moved with such precise movements—a vision of marbled colors made it even more magnificent. As they neared the ground, Alzerion saw the light of his mark brighten. His feet touched the ground as his wings slowed. The last wyvern of the DarkFlower Jungle, but he was incredible. Now, if only he could help him find Eirini here at the heart.

*No insults.*

Alzerion smirked.

Alzerion was the first to jump off. He touched the ground with his hand and scrambled to his feet. Alzerion stepped forward and his jaw clenched. Quairken, Brentley, and Calderon formed a semi-circle around him. Alzerion focused his eyes on the structure before them. The entire space was enchanted, and he sensed the magic all around. The large crystallized structure was nothing short of magnificent. It looked like a miniature palace. Alzerion swallowed. He moved toward the entrance, but felt Endrus' pull on his mind.

*Young ruler, I cannot follow you.*

Alzerion's neck craned to Endrus. "Why not?"

Alzerion saw his group turn to face Endrus. By now, they were well aware of Endrus' mind communication. Alzerion turned his body towards him, too.

Endrus lowered his scaled head. "I...can't. I'm sorry."

Alzerion tilted his head as he focused on Endrus. The muscles of his neck tightened. He looked at those big navy eyes—devoid of emotion except that of despair. Alzerion gulped as he saw his reflection in Endrus' eyes. A pain that could not be matched.

"I cannot willingly enter the dwelling of the Dark Sovereign." Endrus lowered until his belly rested on the ground. Endrus wouldn't change his mind.

"I understand," Alzerion said in a lower-pitch. His jaw set as he gave Endrus a reassuring nod. "We will be back."

Then he turned, waved at his group, and led them up the staircase. Once they entered, the door snapped shut behind them. Alzerion glanced around, but Eirini wasn't in sight. He didn't see anyone, really. His trio walked ahead of him.

Brentley nodded and then Quairken turned to Alzerion. "It's safe. No traps we can see."

Alzerion walked across the open space. His boots clicked against the crystal floor. He moved toward a staircase that rose higher to another level, but then he saw another room off to the left. He motioned for the others to come, but he did not wait for them. Alzerion walked on. It looked similar to the jungle that lay outside. He darted to the closest wall, but it was still smooth, crystalized. The walls were forest green with a magnificent sheen. Quairken examined the large window that took up most of one wall. Alzerion saw shelves that looked like a tree, with some shelves going up like the trunk and others angled to represent the branches.

*Did you find them yet, young ruler?*

*No, Endrus. It's strange but I don't see anyone here.*

*Don't let your guard down. They are somewhere. I can feel him.*

Alzerion gazed up at the ceiling. It had this painted mural. Alzerion twirled about as he squinted to make out the image. It seemed abstract. He bumped into something and his gaze rushed down. He steadied the little end table.

"Who may you be?"

Alzerion spun around at the sounds of the newcomer. Quairken was by his side. Brentley and Calderon stood just off to his left.

"What is this place?" Alzerion said. He took a deep breath.

The man moved closer to them and then lowered his hood. "This is the secluded soul."

Endrus had said as much. At least he knew they were in the right place.

"We are looking for someone?" Quairken added. "She is a friend of ours."

The man's light green eyes scanned them. "You suspect her to be here?"

Alzerion took a step closer. His eyes furrowed. "You knocked me down and when everything cleared, she was gone."

"I did? But are you certain?"

Alzerion stared as the man watched him carefully. Each movement caught in his eye.

"Who are you?" Alzerion uttered over the deafening silence.

"Ah, well, a better question, who are you? I've heard rumor of travelers here in the jungle, but one can never be too careful."

Alzerion's lips parted, but before he uttered a word, the door across from them opened. Two ladies emerged. His eyes found Eirini, and they lingered on her just a bit. *Fate must have smiled on them. She seemed unharmed.*

His eyes brightened as she gave him the faintest of smiles. A woman who was a vision in dark green escorted Eirini forward. Alzerion's eyes narrowed as he tried to catch a better glimpse of the woman, but Eirini ran to him. Her arms flew around his neck. Alzerion pulled her in tight.

"Thank the gods we found you," Quairken said.

Eirini pulled back as she cast a smile at Quairken. Then her eyes fell back to Alzerion. He placed a hand on her cheek. "I was worried."

Her amber eyes lit up as she gazed at him.

Alzerion held onto Eirini as he locked eyes on the other two before them. The man waved his hand and a sleek wooden table and chairs emerged.

"I believe you asked for introductions before. I'm the Dark Sovereign," Alzerion noted the dark sound of his voice. "As you can see, no harm came to your *friend*."

Alzerion heard Calderon mutter something, but he ignored it. Alzerion motioned for them to sit. "We wouldn't want to be rude guests."

As they sat in the chairs, the Dark Sovereign spoke once more. "Now, who are *you*? I have been curious as to the identity of our newest guests in the realm of magic."

"I could've given you those names." The woman to the left of the Dark Sovereign strode closer and rested a hand on his shoulder.

Alzerion's lips parted as he exchanged a quick glance with Quairken.

He observed the scowl on the Dark Sovereign's face soften, as he gently squeezed her hand.

"The travelers come from Bachusa, am I correct?"

Alzerion stared at the woman for a moment. Her voice was familiar. Harsh, maybe, but familiar nonetheless. He swallowed as he remembered what Gael and Surge told them. *Could it be? Aironell?*

"You couldn't possibly be here for me? Not after all this time, could you, Alzerion?"

His jaw tensed, and his face didn't waver as he focused on her features. It was all there: Cerulean blue eyes, light brown hair, and her fair complexion. She certainly looked a bit older but there was something different about her. He gulped. A sense of unease coursed through him.

"So, it's you? Aironell?" His eyes narrowed.

Her lips curved into a sly smile. "I may have changed, a little." Then she turned her gaze to Quairken. Alzerion saw Quairken move to his feet faster than it took him to unsheathe his sword. The chair wobbled as he stood.

"Aironell. You're not hurt." Quairken's voice was soft but shaky.

Her expression was still. Alzerion thought she would be happy to see them, or at least have fond memories, especially for Quairken. Instead, she remained unchanged and hardened. It was Aironell ... yet not. The creature before him was not the girl he remembered. He felt Eirini squeeze at his hand that lay on his lap, and his eyes gazed at her for a moment. With a slight shake of his head, he turned back to Aironell.

He watched as Quairken leaped around the table and made his way to her. Alzerion felt Eirini's eyes on him, still.

Alzerion touched his fingers to the mark on his wrist. *Eirini, don't intervene, not now.* He didn't need to look at her, to feel her scowl at him.

"I'm sorry. I lost faith that you were still alive." Quairken spoke between breaths that pitched. "Your parents—the kingdom; it is some miracle." He rushed closer with arms outstretched.

Aironell's cerulean-blue eyes were not bright. A gray tint shrouded them. She cocked her head to the side. Her curls lapped against her shoulders. Her slender hand shot up and a faint glow emanated. Quairken was halted mid hug. Aironell strolled around him. Her eyes bore into Quairken.

"You shouldn't have underestimated me, Quairken. The father of my youth." Her eyes looked hard, like the finest metals forged in fire.

Then her hand pushed forwards, and Quairken flew, until he fell against the wall.

"Aironell, enough." Alzerion's voice was deep. "I don't know what has happened to you, but this isn't you."

Aironell turned, her chin lifted as her lips twisted into a thin, sly smirk. "That's just it, isn't it?"

Alzerion's eyes narrowed.

She took small and purposeful steps around the other side of the table. Each one brought her closer to him and Eirini, who stood at his side.

"She said she had friends here." Her eyes flashed to Eirini. "I didn't realize she was such a close friend of yours." Her voice was toneless, but he heard the malice in her words.

"So, you came for her...but not me. I mean, all those years ago." She grazed her index finger against Eirini's arm, inspecting her with such coldness.

Her gaze shifted from Eirini to Alzerion. He swallowed. His hand grabbed Eirini's arm as he moved her to the side. He stood nearer to Aironell. His eyes buckled under the harshness of her stare.

"Can we talk?" Alzerion looked around at the Dark Sovereign and back at Eirini and the others.

Aironell twirled and strode away. "Is there anything left to say?" She stopped when she was beside the Dark Sovereign.

He bit his lip. *That was a good question. What was left for him to do?* His mind was spinning, but he remembered something Jezzabell said. *How did he feel about any of it? She made a good point—why did it take him so long to come after her?*

"I still think we should talk, the two of us." His eyes didn't waver as he watched her. Her mouth twisted into a smirk. He blinked, twice. It reminded him of how Ulbrick would look when he thought he was about to get the better of him.

"Don't think that's going to happen," the Dark Sovereign said.

Aironell shook her head and then gazed at him. Her eyes softened, and Alzerion's mouth parted. He took a few steps toward them.

"Dref, let me decide how to handle this." Her hand grasped his forearm as she whispered something into his ear.

He gazed at her and nodded. "Fine, my love. Anything you want, my little twit."

"So, they are a couple?"

Alzerion knew the lilt of Eirini's voice. He didn't turn as his eyes fixed on the two before him. He should have felt something, but he didn't. The sight of Aironell wrapped around the arms of another—nothing. This was political business.

"Alzerion, I will grant you your wish. I suppose I owe you that. After all, it was you who protected me, until you couldn't."

She turned to the Dark Sovereign, nuzzled against his neck, and then motioned for Alzerion to follow. He moved, not much, when he felt someone grab him.

"Please, don't go," Eirini's voice whispered, "Alzerion." Her eyes had that glassy look.

"Don't worry so much." He took her hand and squeezed lightly. "I'll be right back, you'll see." He winked and then strode forward until he went through the domed archway after Aironell.

As he entered under the arch that had colorful blooms twined around vines, he stepped into the room and a transparent film lowered, like that of a sleek curtain. Alzerion's eyes shot to Aironell, who took another couple of paces and then twirled around. With the faintest tilt of her head, she sat down in what looked like a leather-bound chair. A finger pointed to the chair next to her. Alzerion sat down. She snapped her fingers and then a metal tray with two cups and a little teakettle appeared and sat on it. "Take one if you like," Aironell said as she grabbed the mint-colored cup and took a sip.

Alzerion felt the pitted porcelain of the cup. "Aironell, what happened?"

She laughed. "Alzerion, I waited for you, but you never came. I had to adapt to the environment that I found myself in."

A lump rested at the base of his throat. He took a sip of his warm drink.

"I never gave up." He swallowed. "Aironell, I was well, it was difficult at first."

"I bet." Her words were calm. There was no anger or sadness. Almost like she rehearsed this very moment.

His eyes followed as she took another sip of her drink.

"I'm not angry, not anymore." There was a pause as she stared back at him. "As Drefan says, you did me a favor."

"A favor...how so?" Alzerion's left eyebrow arched up as he clung to the porcelain cup.

Aironell leaned forward. "I learned how to take care of myself, to stand on my own. Alzerion, so I don't need saving."

He noticed a glow emanate from her like an aura as she spoke. Then she spoke again, this time softer. "I can see that you've changed, too."

A silver mixed with pale blue shone like her eyes resembled two magical orbs. "I see you still have those walls of yours, but now, well, they are more like shields."

"I ... how?" Alzerion turned off to the side. Her powers grew since he last saw her. He shook his head as he gazed at the vines that draped around a large window that overlooked some sort of pond. *Did she honestly think he would have lowered those defenses? If anything, she was surely the reason they intensified.* He took a deep breath and returned his gaze to her.

A thin smile took hold of her. His eyes narrowed.

"Do you trust me?"

Alzerion had no words. His eyes widened as he pressed his fingers into the arm of his chair. *Was she serious?*

"I know it has been some time."

His lips parted. A light flickered in his mind, like a tiny candle ignited. "You asked me that when I thought you were dying, those years ago." Alzerion pursed his mouth.

Aironell nodded. Her expression became solemn. "I fear I must ask that once more."

Alzerion closed his mouth. *How to answer that? She didn't seem like the same woman he knew, but could she be worse at her core?*

Aironell leaned forward—within a distance to place a hand on his.

Instead, she placed her cup down on the marble table and gazed at him. The level of focus was unnerving.

"Well, do you?" The increased pitch of her voice was noticeable.

Alzerion bit the inside of his cheek. He chose his words carefully. "Much has changed between us."

"True. But that should always be the foundation. Without that, well, we cannot even be friends."

"Friends?" He tilted his head. That sounded strange given their history, but she was with another and he was, well, it was complicated.

Her eyes softened once more than she smiled. "I hope so, but I have a question. What with your guarded demeanor and such?"

He straightened up. "You can ask me anything. As far as trust, well, we shall see."

Aironell reached a hand out to him and gently squeezed. "Eirini is a lovely woman. Strong-willed and I sense that adventurous heart of hers. But I didn't realize that you were the man she spoke of when she first arrived here."

Alzerion pulled his hand back. He bit his lip and then said. "Aironell, you speak as if I own her, but I'm not sure what the question is."

Aironell tapped her fingers on her chair. "I know she is not your property, but in some ways, she is yours."

Alzerion's brow quivered.

"Maybe you haven't noticed her feelings for you. Whether you admit it, she is wholly yours, I can tell." Aironell pressed off the arm of her chair as she stood. "My question, Alzerion, is have you let yourself indulge in her, in a love that could be yours?"

Alzerion blinked back his surprise.

Aironell paced around him as she spoke. "I appreciate you coming here, but I am not that girl, and I don't need saving. I'm content here."

In that moment, his eyes furrowed as they inspected her. She wasn't a child anymore. A grown woman. No longer that naïve princess who was easy for her enemies to manipulate.

Alzerion stood up but didn't move. He felt a dryness in his mouth as he formed his words carefully. "Aironell, I vowed to your parents that I would find you." His eyes darted up. "I am determined to see this through. To bring you back to Bachusa...your home. Your kingdom."

Aironell strode around until she was in front of him. His eyes scanned her very being.

Aironell spoke with a tone sweet like honey, and yet it was jarring. "Alzerion, hear what I'm saying. I will not return to Bachusa—not to rule."

She placed a hand on his cheek. Her skin was smooth, but he felt a chill on his skin. "Fate knew what it was doing. Loving you. Saving you. Well, it brought me here to my true destiny." Her arms stretched out as she spun around.

His eyebrows drew together as he pursed his lips.

"Don't do that," Aironell said. "Alzerion I couldn't wait forever, and well, we've both moved on."

"Do you love him? The Dark Sovereign? I haven't heard great things about him, I must admit."

Aironell's face lit up. A brightness washed over her. It was as if she was lighter, devoid of something that held her back.

"I love him so much more than I could ever express. That's why I married him about a year ago."

Alzerion scratched the back of his neck as he swallowed.

"I believe I needed to love you, to know what I was capable of," she shrugged. "The Fates have said as much. You and I, well, we were never meant to end up together. You were my first love, but not my epic romance."

Alzerion nodded. "I can see that. But yet I need to be sure. Need to feel the difference. May I?" He motioned for her to come closer.

"Whatever it takes to set you free," Aironell whispered.

Her arms fell to her side. Alzerion placed his hand under her chin and pulled her face up to kiss. Her lips felt cool against his. She smelled of the jungle. He allowed his lips to part. *Sweet.* Then he backed away. He felt nothing except guilt for kissing someone who wasn't Eirini.

"Well?" Aironell smirked.

He shook his head.

"As I suspected. You, Alzerion, came for me out of your duty to

Bachusa. But don't you think it time you find what makes you happy?" She winked at him.

Aironell held out her hand. "We can part as friends. Who knows, maybe an alliance between our realms could be beneficial?"

He smirked. "Always." He patted her on the shoulder.

"Excellent." She clasped her hands together. "Now, I should get my husband in here. He heard the most unsettling news."

Alzerion quirked an eyebrow.

"There is an entity here in the DarkFlower Jungle that wants to trap you here."

Aironell smacked her hands together. The shielded film dissipated in seconds. The Dark Sovereign strolled in, followed by Eirini, Quairken, Brentley, and Calderon.

Brentley and Calderon stood at attention near the door. Quairken's eyes focused on Aironell. Eirini dashed to Alzerion. She grabbed his hand and squeezed. Alzerion let his fingers graze her hand.

The Dark Sovereign stood next to Aironell.

"Has she told you already?" His light green eyes fixed on Alzerion.

Alzerion nodded.

"Sort of. Dref, I thought you would best fill in the gaps. You learned more than I on your last outing in the jungle."

The Dark Sovereign's gaze focused on him, like a sharp knife ready to cut. "How much do you know about our realm of magic?"

"A little." Alzerion shifted his stance. "Most of it pertains to the history."

"Ah," his chin rose. "The wyvern told you."

"How did you know?" Quairken probed.

"I know many things, Quairken. That's part of being the ruler here. A great deal of power and magic runs through my veins. It allows me to sense other magics, like the wyvern."

Alzerion observed the Dark Sovereign with such keenness as he moved with a quickness.

He spoke like an artist painting a masterpiece. "I'm descended from a magical and prestigious family. I can trace my roots back to your kingdom, Alzerion."

Alzerion stood. He refused to shudder, but each time the Dark Sovereign used his name...like they were acquaintances, gave him an uneasy feeling. He may be Aironell's husband, but his voice was deep and commanding with a dash of condescension. Alzerion bared his teeth.

*He was from Bachusa?* Alzerion tilted his head as his eyes kept on him. Despite it all, he hung on each word like his life depended on it.

"I have distant relatives. I believe you know of them. He used the ancient texts about this place to make contact."

Alzerion quirked an eyebrow. "Wait, you have relations in Bachusa? Who would that be? Why would they make contact now?"

The Dark Sovereign's eyes fixed on him as he motioned to Aironell. His lips pursed together. "First, you need to know that there are bigger problems for you and your kingdom."

"The darkness," Aironell spoke so low it was almost an airy whisper.

"What did she say?" Calderon looked at Brentley.

The Dark Sovereign patted Aironell's hand, but his eyes never wavered from Alzerion. "As always, she is correct." He kissed Aironell's finger and then paced across the floor.

Alzerion followed him. He led them back into the main entryway of the manor. He heard the others behind him.

"Dref, darling, he needs to know." Aironell strolled past Alzerion and stood somewhere in the middle.

"The darkness is an ancient foe," Drefan's voice was controlled, calm, even.

Alzerion steadied his gaze on the Dark Sovereign, Drefan, but he didn't turn. Alzerion reached out a hand, but Eirini grabbed it and pulled it back. Alzerion bent his head to her, but she shook her head as she placed a finger to her lips. Then she stared after Drefan as well.

Drefan tilted his head to the side and then turned to face them. "The darkness is our punishment. Here in the DarkFlower Jungle or the Realm of Magic, the Sovereigns have not always made the wisest of choices for the land."

"What about you?" Alzerion asked. He folded his arms across his chest. Eirini's hand squeeze against his arm, but he ignored it.

"I guess that depends on who you ask?" A devilish grin formed over his lips. "I'm not claiming to be perfect." He cleared his throat.

Aironell glared back at Alzerion. He shrugged and then focused back on the Dark Sovereign.

"Look, I don't want to bore you with all the details. So what you need to know is that the darkness has been here...longer than I have been the Dark Sovereign. The darkness is why we are called *Dark* Sovereigns."

"I don't understand," Quairken said.

Alzerion raised his eyebrow and shifted his feet. His cinnamon eyes watched him.

Drefan's eyes darkened to a deep forest green color, and he rubbed at his chin and then spoke with a firmness. "It is the power. The darkness was a consequence of a sovereign's greed and misdeeds. The only benefit is that it was fated to be stuck here in the DarkFlower Jungle. Its power courses through the jungle as much as my own."

The Dark Sovereign's hands held out before him as they glowed. Images of the darkness erupted before them. Alzerion swallowed hard. "People have tried to tap into it but have failed. I've been able to hold it here—to maintain it but things have changed."

Drefan glared back at Alzerion.

"What changed?" Alzerion asked.

Drefan opened his mouth, but Aironell raised her hand and forced her fingers to her palm. Then Drefan closed his mouth.

"That doesn't matter." Aironell faced Alzerion. Her eyes roamed to each person and back to Alzerion. "Bachusa is your kingdom now. They are your people and you *must* keep them safe. This is my home now."

Drefan walked closer to them. A smug look covered his face. "Alzerion, coming here was a mistake. You don't realize the depths of that just yet."

"What do you want us to do?" Quairken stepped forward.

Alzerion glanced back at Calderon and Brentley. Both stood still like statues, except that Calderon couldn't fix his face—it revealed him. Alzerion focused back on the Dark Sovereign.

"We want you to succeed," Aironell said.

Drefan walked away toward the front door and opened it, and then angled his head around to face them. "You have little time, I fear. You must leave the DarkFlower Jungle and go home. Protect your kingdom from those who want to see you fail and from the darkness. I can feel it, Alzerion. It's drawn to you."

"Who dares plot against the King?" Quairken's voice thundered.

"Adrastus. He conjured some of the darkness here." Aironell didn't hesitate to respond.

"The noble?" Calderon's voice wavered.

"How could he do that?" Brentley said.

"It was the moment you left Bachusa," Aironell spoke softly.

Alzerion felt his disdain rise. *That meddlesome prick. He needed to deal with him as soon as he could, but this darkness sounded worse than Adrastus. How much damage could he do compared to the darkness? Either way, it was his fault. They had to return as soon as possible.*

*Alzerion, we will fight it, whatever comes. I will always have your back.* Alzerion felt his heart flutter as he looked at Eirini.

"Don't worry, we will take care of him." Quairken patted Alzerion on the back.

*They would, but it would take some planning. They couldn't just kill a noble, not without proof of his traitorous deeds.*

"Aironell, is there any help that you can give?" Alzerion asked.

Her lips pressed together. "There's not much I can do." Her uneven voice told Alzerion all he needed. If she could, well, she would help. But she could not do so.

"I, however, can send you back home," Drefan crooned. "I control portals around here, and that is something that I can do for you."

"Very well," Alzerion seethed. As they left the crystal manor, he saw Eirini watching him out of the corners of his eye. She knew what he felt. He stared out as he followed. He didn't want to be pitied.

# CHAPTER 21
## *Harsh Realities*

E irini glanced at Alzerion, but then rushed to Endrus. She patted his snout, and his scaled face bent toward her. Alzerion chuckled. She acted like she wasn't rubbing a wyvern but a common house cat. Alzerion heard his low hum.

Eirini pulled her hand back as Alzerion smirked, and the others moved closer. Endrus's wings flapped as he straightened to his full height. The fleshy parts that looked like veins pulsed. His hind legs appeared shaky.

*It's alright. Endrus, they mean no harm.*

His head whipped up and then all around—like he was a half-crazed animal.

Endrus' navy eyes locked on the Dark Sovereign and Aironell. Their dark attire contrasted against the backdrop of the crystal manor. A low fog misted around their feet and slowly rose around them. Aironell made her choice. *It hurt that he couldn't bring her back to Bachusa, but she never looked more alive.* Alzerion smirked. *Who knew that all she needed was a jungle and a condescending arse like Drefan?*

He felt Eirini in his mind—a strong presence. *Eirini, are you alright?*

*Hmph.* Her arms folded across her chest.

Her gaze was fixed on Aironell and the Dark Sovereign. *Great.* Alzerion gazed back at the group, but his mind stayed on Eirini. He listened to

217

their chatter, but he attempted to focus his mind on her. Alzerion rubbed at the mark on his wrist and then he got one burst of something. It was a strong negative feeling. *She's not even that clever or pretty.* Then he felt a sharp pain in his mind, like something scraped against his brain. Alzerion pressed a hand to his head.

"Alzerion are you alright?" Quairken's voice was sincere.

Brentley and Calderon ran over and checked on him.

When the pain subsided, Alzerion glanced up. Eirini strolled by and with her lips curved, she smirked at him. She stood off to the side, back against an oak tree. Her glare was harsh and didn't let up. Alzerion bit his lip.

Alzerion ran his hands through his hair as he straightened up.

"What was that all about?" Drefan watched him with an incredulous stare as he strode closer to Alzerion.

Endrus bucked against the ground as his legs stepped backwards.

"There, there," Aironell's voice was soft. Her hands stretched out in front of her—palms up.

Endrus didn't ease up. Aironell furrowed her eyebrows.

"Endrus!" The Dark Sovereign's voice boomed.

Endrus froze.

"I'm not here in an official capacity."

"I don't believe you," Endrus growled.

"If I wanted to punish you, then I would've done so. It's of no interest to me." His hands folded over his stomach.

Endrus steadied himself as he angled around Alzerion.

"It looks like you're the victor." The Dark Sovereign turned to Alzerion.

Alzerion's brows furrowed as he held his wide stance.

"Endrus seems content with you."

Alzerion couldn't ignore the hint of malice in his words.

"Dref, what is this all about?" Her eyes were a shroud of annoyance.

He ambled over to her and, in a swift motion, laid a hand on her waist while he pulled her closer.

"Nothing. Just some old issues—grievances would be more accurate."

He tapped his other finger to his chin. "At any rate, it was many years ago, my little twit."

Aironell slithered out of his grasp. She strode a few paces away and her eyes widened. They had that same icy coldness, like grated metal. She snapped back to him.

"Dref, you didn't."

"Aironell, it was before I met you. You know what I was like—at least have a decent idea of the man I was."

She shook her head and then focused back on the group.

Alzerion took a breath. Their interactions made him chuckle, and he felt Eirini tighten her grasp on his hand. He glanced over at her by the oak. *I'm sorry.*

She said nothing, but instead she glanced away from him, and Alzerion resumed his attention. "How do we return?"

Aironell lifted her chin as she spoke. Her words were firm, but not harsh. "Alzerion, we will create a portal for you."

The Dark Sovereign placed his hands on his hip. His stance was wide as he spoke. "Isn't that making the journey too easy?"

"Dref, don't be an ass." Her voice was sharp. Aironell forced a smile.

Alzerion pressed his lips together as his teeth dug into his top lip. She turned as her curls swayed around her.

Alzerion couldn't stop watching them. It was like watching live theatrics. The Dark Sovereign's mouth twisted into a scowl as his eyebrows pulled a crease across his forehead.

"They don't need to take the risk by traveling more of the jungle. That could take time, which they don't have." She half stared at him as her body angled at Alzerion.

"Oh, why? You think the great king of Bachusa can't handle it?" His arms crossed as he grabbed at his elbows.

Alzerion's eyes darted back and forth. It was like watching a cat toy with a mouse before putting it out of its misery. Alzerion watched as the Dark Sovereign's grin darkened.

"If we have a choice," Alzerion started. "I'd prefer it if —"

He watched Aironell stalk back to the Dark Sovereign. Her hand lashed out like a cheetah on the attack. She clutched his arm and pulled.

He could have dug in, but he moved with her. Aironell spoke with a sweeping gesture. The Dark Sovereign flexed his fingers as they spoke.

"Can we trust them to get us home safe?" Calderon asked in a hushed tone. Alzerion patted him on the back.

He bent his head down. "I think so. At least she seems to want to help."

Alzerion glanced at Quairken and then to the oak tree at Eirini. She remained silent with a pout on her face.

He felt a tap on the shoulder. Aironell stood right before him as she rested her hand on his arm. Alzerion felt a blistering heat over his mark. *Please stop.* Eirini didn't respond. He felt the heat lessen at least a little. *Thank you.*

Aironell chatted pleasantly about the arrangement. The pressure on his wrist returned. Like someone took a blazing hot poker and placed it to his skin. The Dark Sovereign didn't look put off by the interaction. *Then why was Eirini?*

*Young ruler, may I suggest you go after her?*

Aironell and the Dark Sovereign were mid-sentence when he twisted around to Endrus. Calderon pointed off by the path that veered behind that oak tree from where she stood.

"I have to go." Alzerion rushed toward the oak tree. "I'll be right back."

Alzerion sprinted. The path veered right. He pushed off the tree trunk with his palm and then used it to gain momentum. There she was, on a stone bench with ivy and vines twisted around—like the jungle grew around it.

Alzerion stepped over the rocks and roots that were so thick they penetrated above the ground. A twig cracked and Eirini's gaze rose.

"What?" her mouth thinned, like the shriveled-up skin of a prune.

He raised an eyebrow. "Eirini, what is the matter? We have to return to Bachusa, but you seem upset." Alzerion clenched his jaw.

Her gaze fixed on the ground, but he noticed the slightest tremble in her chin. Alzerion knelt down in front of her. He reached out his hand and let his fingers graze the skin around her chin. Then he pulled her chin up. Her amber eyes speckled with tears.

"Eirini," his voice cracked.

Her shoulders drooped. She attempted to turn, but Alzerion cradled her face with his hand.

"I don't understand." His voice was crisp and low.

Her lashes rose as she stared at him. His heart cracked a bit.

She sniffled. "There's nothing to discuss."

Alzerion ran his hands down her arms until he reached her delicate hands. His fingers grazed over hers. "I don't believe you. Eirini, I can see something is wrong."

She slid her hands out from under his and wiped at her eyes. "It's the feeling I get when you're around her." Eirini shifted down from the bench and stood up. "We should go."

Alzerion's lips parted as he rose to his feet. As she moved past him, he placed his hand on hers and twirled her around. She was a vision in her cream-colored blouse as she whirled around. Alzerion pulled her in as her free hand rested on his chest. His right arm pressed against her back as his right hand laid against her back. He gulped. The tightening in his chest returned. Being near her, well, it did things to him. It set his heart ablaze and his head spun.

Alzerion pressed his forehead to hers. Finally, she was still. Alzerion's left hand pressed against her chest, where her heart was. He drummed his fingers at the beat of her heart. *It beat fast, too.* He took a deep breath.

"Eirini, my actions should be enough. There's no need for jealousy. If that's what this is all about."

Alzerion felt a yearning within. *He wanted to tell her what he thought—how he felt. He just couldn't bring himself to do so. What if she didn't feel that way or worse, what if she hurt him?*

She breathed out and her sweetness tickled his nose as her eyes closed for the briefest of moments. *The way she kept him on his toes and her thirst for life. Even when she's challenging. Her long lashes on her tanned skin, to the way her hair curled. It did something to him.* He placed the gentlest of kisses on her closed eyelids before she opened them.

His left finger rested against her smooth lips. "Say nothing, please. I know we have a long discussion coming up, but we need to be sure that we get that chance." He licked his lips and then continued. "Eirini, I care. That much should be clear."

He let go of her waist and then side-stepped backwards.

"I wasn't sure. Sometimes you make me doubt."

"Doubts?" He cocked his head to the side.

Alzerion closed the meager space between them and cupped her chin in his hands. His eyes settled on her. She stood motionless. The smell of honey and jasmine filled his nose as his other hand pulled her closer. Alzerion kissed her forehead and then his nose glided down as he placed a gentle kiss on her cheeks, nose, and then stared down at her. Eirini's eyes brightened as her lips parted. Alzerion smirked and then bent his head nearer to hers. The hand that held her face up, moved, as he grazed his thumb over her lips. In a swift motion, Alzerion placed his lips on hers. It was a slow kiss. He struggled to compose himself—to settle the growing urge. Instead, he placed his hands on each side of her head as his mouth moved in a continuous pattern until each kiss deepened. He felt Eirini shudder as her body pressed into his.

Alzerion slowly pulled away as her eyes opened, and they stared at each other. "I told you, no words needed." He smirked as he curled his fingers around hers.

Eirini beamed. She squeezed his hand as she pulled their hands up to her cheek. Alzerion felt the warmth of her face in his hand.

"Eirini, I'm not the most articulate."

"I know," she whispered. "Alzerion, I don't want you to change. I want you as you are."

Alzerion felt his heart open once more. He leaned forward. "I think I'm falling—"

"Here, I thought you wanted to return home?"

Alzerion felt a heat in his ears. He glanced to the side...Aironell. Alzerion straightened up as he turned to face her. Eirini let go of his hand and darted toward Aironell.

"Was it necessary for you to come out here?" Eirini folded her arms across her chest as she maintained a wide stance.

Alzerion gulped. Eirini's eyes darkened into this raging inferno of amber. As if they would melt anyone that looked at them.

"What's that supposed to mean?" Aironell didn't back down. Her voice had the same commanding tone as the Dark Sovereign.

"Surely you saw we were in the middle of something?" Eirini's boot tapped on the ground.

"Listen, *darling*," Aironell countered. She closed the gap between them. "You've got some nerve."

Alzerion stormed over to them.

Eirini clenched her teeth. Alzerion rubbed her arm, but she didn't even look his way. Her eyes focused on Aironell. Her features were tight.

"I believe you're the one with some kind of nerve," Eirini's voice was firm. It didn't buckle under the intensity of Aironell's stare. "Can't you let him be? Don't you think you did enough damage?"

Alzerion choked back his feelings. *It felt good to know she had his back, but now wasn't the time. They needed Aironell's help.*

"Why don't we just head back?" Alzerion shifted his gaze between them.

Eirini tilted her head to him. Alzerion squeezed her hand and nodded. He watched as Eirini snapped back to Aironell. Her eyes were less than friendly.

*Eirini, enough. Don't make things worse.*

*Alzerion, I don't like how she interrupted us.*

*Eirini, please let it go. She's the only thing standing in the Dark Sovereign's way of forcing us all on some sort of absurd trek through the jungle and probably certain death.*

Eirini stepped closer to Alzerion, leaned over, and kissed his cheek. "If that is what you wish. For you...anything."

Aironell said nothing. Her eyes looked more like a storm of grey that swirled around her cerulean blue eyes. She lifted her chin up as she glared at Eirini.

Alzerion felt discomfort in the pit of his stomach.

Aironell mumbled under her breath as she moved back toward the group. As she brushed past, the sides of her outfit billowed about like a cloak.

"Alzerion, you could have told her to go away," Eirini pleaded. "It's almost like maybe you're holding out for her."

"Don't be ridiculous." Alzerion choked out. He took a step away from her.

Eirini fiddled with the ends of her hair and then spoke once more. "We both know you came here for her. I just, well, I wonder if your feelings are complicated because you still care for her."

Alzerion felt like someone took a dagger and jabbed it into him and then twisted it about. A wave of heat washed over him as he shook his head slowly. *He had no words. How could she think that?*

Eirini moved toward him. "Alzerion, I didn't mean to—"

He blinked back the dryness that pricked his eyes. "It's fine. We need to go anyway. I'm sure the portal must be ready for us."

Alzerion strolled back the way he came. His hands clenched as his nails dug into his palms. He heard Eirini's footsteps, but he blocked her out of his mind. *There wasn't time for any games.*

Nothing but silence passed as they came around that oak tree.

"You're back, finally," The Dark Sovereign crooned. "I was wondering if you were going to make it."

Aironell stood near him with a grimace on her face. Alzerion turned around—Brentley stood at the ready and Calderon was wide-eyed as he lowered his head. Quairken scratched his neck and nodded. *They were ready.*

*They have readied the* portal. Endrus' words had a low timber in his mind. *By the two trees that twined together.* Alzerion watched as Endrus' head shifted in its direction.

Eirini strolled past him...still silent as she made her way to Endrus. She grazed her hand over his scaled head.

Alzerion turned back to Aironell and Drefan. "How do we do this?" He tuned out any worry about anything. Getting home was all that mattered right now.

Drefan motioned for them to follow. Alzerion nodded and then kept a close pace behind Drefan and Aironell until the group stood before the twisted overhanging trees. Their roots wrapped up and around almost like a frame of sorts.

"You must stand near the threshold," Aironell said.

Drefan and Aironell strode forward and waved their hands around.

The light that emanated from their hands grew as they raised their arms up. Then they side-stepped, over and over, like some sort of ritual. When the warm light reached its peak, they reached their hands forward, one on each side of the entryway. The wind whirled as an opaque grayness emerged in the center.

"It's done." Drefan looked at Alzerion. "Be quick to leave. We want nothing else to creep through."

Alzerion's eyes narrowed. *What else could creep through?*

*You don't want to know,* Endrus' words hung like a stiff word of caution.

Alzerion stared back at the portal with its shining light that transmitted from the center of the two overhanging trees. *The perfect mixture of mystery and magic.*

He shoved the thoughts from his mind. They had to return. "Brentley. Calderon. You both must go through now."

Calderon's shoulders slumped as his mouth fell open. "I-I don't understand."

Brentley stared with such determination. "No, Your Majesty. We won't go until you do. Our mission was to see to your safety. That has not changed."

Alzerion's jaw tightened as he turned to Quairken. "Then you must go. Quairken, Isabella, would never forgive it if I left Audrina fatherless."

Quairken's face was somber, but he nodded. "If that is what you want." He patted Alzerion on the shoulder and then walked toward the portal.

Aironell stepped forward. Her thin mouth twisted into a smile. "Good luck, Quairken. Please tell Isabella, well, tell her I'm alright."

He bowed his head, nodded, and then held out his hand toward the portal. His hand shook as he neared it.

"You will arrive straight to Bachusa." Drefan's words were deep and controlled. He stood with his cloak that billowed around him. "There are no tricks, Quairken."

Quairken frowned and then glanced around as his eyes rested on Aironell.

Aironell moved toward him. "You must go. It's safe, I promise."

Quairken took a deep breath, closed his eyes, and walked without opening his eyes until he disappeared.

Alzerion cleared his throat. "Alright, Endrus, you and Eirini should go next."

Eirini bit her lip, but for once, she did not argue. Instead, she dashed toward him, threw her arms around, and hugged him. He smelled the mixture of honey and jasmine as she squeezed him.

"Stay safe, okay?" Eirini whispered in his ear as she pulled back. She rubbed at her nose and then strolled to the portal and waited.

Alzerion felt a sense of calm, as he knew Eirini would be fine. He tilted his head to Endrus.

"Alzerion, you need to get out of here," Drefan's voice was crisp and deep.

He stared at him. "What are you afraid will escape? You're the Dark Sovereign. Why do you seem concerned?"

The Dark Sovereign's grin had this hint of darkness. "I almost never open up portals out of here. Alzerion, you're the idiot who risked far more than you understood on a fool's journey for a woman you cannot have." Drefan glowered at him. "The darkness is more powerful than you have *yet* to realize." He moved closer to Alzerion. "You did enough by letting some of it out when you arrived. That is your burden...*your* price to pay."

Alzerion's nostrils flared. "Endrus go, now."

"I can't." He shook his scaled head.

Alzerion shifted back to the Dark Sovereign with a smug look on his face.

"I don't understand." Alzerion said through gritted teeth.

"Dref," Aironell nudged him. "They have little time. I can feel it coming closer."

The Dark Sovereign's expression pinched as he clenched his jaw. "She's right." He twirled his hands around and then aimed them at Endrus.

"What are you doing?" Alzerion moved toward Endrus, but then stopped when he heard Endrus' low growl.

Endrus took a few steps toward them and his eyes fixed on the Dark Sovereign. "You freed me."

The Dark Sovereign nodded solemnly.

"That is out of character, but I guess I shouldn't complain."

Endrus made his way to the portal. Alzerion watched as Eirini hopped on his back and they went through the portal.

The air around him felt thicker somehow.

"Endrus couldn't leave, as was his punishment from years ago. I freed him so that he can help you save your kingdom."

Alzerion's eyes narrowed. "Thank you..."

"Endrus seems to have bonded to you. Take care of him. I never wanted to kill him. He was such a powerful creature, which was why his punishment was imprisonment."

Alzerion's mouth opened a bit more. As he moved toward the portal, he felt a chill through him. He reached a hand out to the portal and then he heard this low hiss.

"What was that?" Alzerion angled his head back.

Brentley and Calderon stood behind, ready to leave.

"It's here!" Aironell shrieked.

"Alzerion, you must leave, now!" Drefan demanded.

A dark shroud took shape around them. He grabbed Brentley and Calderon and shoved them through the portal. He held his breath and followed.

## CHAPTER 22
## *Return*

Alzerion stepped forward, and he found himself in some sort of wooded area. He blinked.

"Alzerion, over here." Quairken's voice was abrupt.

It was so dark. He struggled to make sense of his surroundings.

"Lumen," Alzerion said, as he held his hands out.

A glimmer covered his hands until it coated the whole of them. He held them out to act like a light in the darkness.

"Alzerion, thank goodness." Quairken pulled him closer. "We thought they double crossed us when you didn't come through."

"No, they didn't. In fact, they tried to help me." Alzerion glanced to the side as he saw Endrus and Eirini stood between them.

"How so?" Eirini asked.

Alzerion didn't answer as he searched around them. "Where are the other two?"

Eirini shrugged.

"We only just got here and found you," Quairken added. "The portal didn't send us top the same spots here in the little forest by the palace."

A shriek reverberated through the woods.

"Don't follow," Alzerion spoke with such force.

He felt his heart race as he tore through the woods, using his hands to light his way. *It had to be them*; he thought. As he ran, he felt this ache in his wrists. He glanced down for a split second—the mark throbbed. *Eirini.* She was with Quairken and Endrus. She would be fine.

*Endrus, what's going on?* He squinted his eyes as he struggled to dodge the low hanging tree branch. He stopped to catch his breath. There, he saw what looked like the silhouette of someone.

*Alzerion, we are fine.*

*What's wrong with Eirini? Is she alright? I can sense her.*

He stepped over a fallen tree as he realized where he was. This was the wooded aread behind the palace. The same woods where he had to run after Warren those years ago.

*She won't admit it, but she's afraid. Alzerion, there's this noise taunting us. Saying such horrible things like one of us will die before we are done.*

*Keep her safe, Endrus.*

*Of course.*

There was a noise, so he twisted around. Alzerion squinted to get a better view, but heard a shriek once more. Alzerion stumbled over the body on the ground. A heaviness gripped at his chest.

*Death. Death. Your fault.* A voice hissed around him. It was the voice from the DarkFlower Jungle. Alzerion fell to his knees at the sight.

"Brentley, what happened?"

He stretched out his glowing hands. *Please no.*

Brentley didn't speak. His face glanced up for a moment to Alzerion as tears streamed down his face. He heard the faint sobs from Brentley.

"Brentley, are you hurt? There's a lot of blood. Where's Calderon?"

Brentley's sobs grew louder as he looked back down. Alzerion swallowed the lump rising in his throat. Blood pulled across the rocks and splattered across the nearby trees. His eyes lingered on Brentley, who hunched forward. His arms clung to something. *No, please no.* Alzerion finally caught them in his sights. *It was Calderon!*

Alzerion clambered over and stared down with his jaw open. Calderon looked mangled, torn with blood splattered everywhere. Alzerion placed his hand under Calderon's head, but his eyes were hollow —vacant.

"Brentley. What happened?" He felt his voice pitch. Alzerion cleared his throat.

"I-I, couldn't say." His arms went limp at his side.

Alzerion wrapped his arms around Calderon as he pulled him close. Memories of Calderon's goofy personality plagued his mind and he felt a tightness in his chest. Alzerion shook his head as his eyes flashed with anger.

*Endrus, get them out of here.* He laid Calderon down as his blood-stained hand pressed to his wrist. *Eirini, follow Endrus out, now!*

*Alzerion, what's wrong?* Her voice in his head wavered. *Don't make me meld into your mind.*

He watched as Brentley's hollow stare fixed on Calderon. Alzerion closed his eyes for a moment. *Eirini, now is not the time. Please don't push it.*

Alzerion's eyes flashed open. *Endrus, do it. Get them out. Keep them safe. Tell Quairken I said it is an order!*

A weight rested on him as he took one more look down at the carnage. *Could it have been that ominous voice?* Alzerion took a deep breath.

*As you wish, young ruler.*

He felt this anguish deep inside. The feeling that kept nagging at him until he saw the truth in front of him. The gashes across Calderon's body brought tears to his eyes.

Alzerion muttered something as he held onto Calderon. His body glowed as he laid him down on the ground. A protective casing shimmered around him.

"Wh-what's that?" Brentley mustered.

"It will keep his body safe until we can bury him."

Brentley shook his head. His face was pale. Alzerion saw the toll.

"We have to do this, Brentley. We have to do our duty. Do you remember?" Alzerion placed a hand on his shoulder.

Brentley breathed out. "Protect you, our king, and keep Bachusa from falling into the wrong hands."

"Very good. Brentley, I need to know what happened and we need to get out of here. If we are to keep from the same fate."

His head lowered, but then he stared up at him. "Your Majesty, it came out of nowhere."

"What did?"

"I don't know. It was a voice... dark and harsh." His voice quavered. "Then we tried to find you. We stepped through but didn't see anyone. Somehow we stepped into some sort of trap and then the voice materialized into this dark mass and we ran. Calderon wasn't fast enough." His voice faltered. "It had to be that injury from the DarkFlower Jungle. He couldn't outrun it. Then he stumbled and..."

"I'm sorry. I know he was your friend."

He sniffled and then wiped his face and stood up. "I couldn't keep him safe, b-but I must keep you safe, Your Majesty."

"Stay close." Alzerion maintained his control.

He led with his arms outstretched, one for the light, but also because his mark would act like some sort of compass. It would lead him to Eirini. Alzerion tried to keep his focus on getting Brentley out unharmed. They ran through the woods, dodging bushes and tree branches as they darted around larger stones. They had to be close. His mark glowed so brightly it could have lit the whole of the woods.

*Young ruler, where are you? There's a chill in the air. S thin sheet of ice freezing the trees like statues.*

*What? How?*

*Not sure. I will take care of it. I will melt it for you. Be careful.*

He didn't need Endrus to finish that answer. He saw the mixture of red and orange. A fiery tunnel headed right toward them. He grabbed Brentley by his vest and pulled.

Before he could speak, Alzerion pressed his finger to his lips and then whispered. "Endrus said something is trying to trap us in here, but Endrus has a plan."

Brentley's face went white.

"Don't do that. I need you to remain focused. Brentley, there should be an opening for us to run."

Terror filled his eyes, but Alzerion patted him on the shoulder and grabbed his hand.

"Don't let go, for anything."

Brentley hesitated, but nodded.

Alzerion stood up and ran. His grip was tight as he ushered Brentley on, to keep his pace. He would not be responsible for another death. *No.* That horrid shrieking voice played in his mind like a nightmare. He saw the glow of the flames from Endrus. *Thank the gods.*

"Brentley, go."

He blinked, but his head arched away.

"You won't get burned. Run through the hole in the flames. I'm not taking no for an answer."

Brentley's eyes were those of someone who saw the horror of death, but he ran anyway.

Alzerion took a deep breath, and then he rushed forward. That dark hissing voice spoke once more. It sounded like a tongue he couldn't make out. Then the flames ebbed down and seared the back of his hand.

Ahhh. *Damn it.* He clutched his hand. The flames licked his skin, but he didn't have time to worry about that. His eyes narrowed as he stared back at the opening. The flames didn't budge. Alzerion twisted around, but there was no other opening.

"No ssuch luck," it hissed, much like some sort of serpent.

Alzerion turned, but there was nothing except for this growing darkness.

He gazed back at the flame tunnel that looked like it was swinging back and forth and said, "Ventus." A gust of wind shot forward.

The flames held firm, but they wavered about, encircling faster. *Idiot.* He coughed as the smoke worsened.

*Endrus.*

Nothing.

He hunched over, coughing. The voice was back. "*You won't make it out alive, Your Majesty,*" it hissed.

Alzerion blinked twice as he raised his arm to cover his nose and mouth.

"You want to kill me?" Alzerion coughed out.

An audible eerie laugh echoed around him.

Alzerion blinked and then saw it. An opening formed in the flames. He did not hesitate. He ran for his life. As he lowered his body to fit under the lowering arched flame, he felt the fiery heat blazing on just above him. Like he was some meal cooking over a roaring fire.

When he came out, he stumbled to catch his bearings. The sweat dripped from his face as he looked up. A gloom hung over the kingdom. It wasn't as noticeable as it was in those woods, but it was there. His kingdom was at risk. Alzerion spelled his hands to stop the glowing light. He took a breath and felt the dryness in his mouth, but the palace was in sight. He forced himself to run toward it.

Endrus bowed his head as Alzerion approached. Eirini's amber eyes brightened as he stood before them. They had the remains of what he assumed were tears. He gave the slightest smile and then looked at his group. Alzerion bit his lip as he saw Brentley. He stood with arms clutching his elbows.

Quairken patted him on the shoulder and looked back. "I'm so sorry."

His seasoned face looked grave as he gave Alzerion a light squeeze and strode away toward the palace. Alzerion took a breath. He knew Quairken would feel the loss, too. After all the practice and time spent with Calderon, well, he would be missed.

An ache coursed through his hand as the pain still smoldered from the fiery tunnel. He sucked in a breath, clung to his hand, and strode forward until Eirini dashed toward him. Her arms flung out, but she stopped before ever hugging him. She said nothing. Her chin trembled as her elbows pressed to her sides.

"I'm fine," Alzerion whispered as he gazed down at her. "It could have been worse."

Eirini's hand trembled as she reached out and laid her delicate fingers over his charred skin. Alzerion winced.

Endrus lowered until his body laid flat. Then his snout pressed cool on the burn. Endrus breathed against his skin. Alzerion bit down on his lip to keep from whimpering.

Eirini grabbed his unburned hand and held on. "I'm here."

The breath was quick and felt like mint cooling over his skin. Then the pain subsided, as only a scar remained in its place.

"Thank you," Alzerion's voice was low.

Alzerion strolled up the stairs of the palace, aware of Eirini's grip on him.

"I'm okay now. There's no need to keep watch like I'm some child."

Eirini's lashes flitted up and down, but kept quiet. *Alzerion don't be a jerk.*

He angled away as he was speechless. She didn't waver. Instead, she slid her arms up and wrapped around him.

*Get used to it. I was worried about you.*

Alzerion swallowed as he pushed open the doors. He heard the clacking of boots behind as he entered the palace. He entered and turned around as he took it all in. The once crowded and loud palace, his home... was nothing but a shell.

"Where is everyone?" Brentley's voice was shaky.

Alzerion looked back and saw Quairken close by Brentley. He glimpsed out the door before it closed. "Where's Endrus?"

"I had him go to the barracks for now. I thought it would be the best for him."

Alzerion nodded. He repositioned himself back around and the darker light that filtered through. "It's quiet, calm, almost eerie."

Alzerion headed toward the grand staircase as Eirini followed arm-in-arm. His next concern was safety. Where was everybody and were they alright?

"Relax," Eirini's words were but a whisper. "There's no use getting yourself worked up."

Alzerion took a breath as he led them to the Family Room. He placed a hand on the metal knob and then held it for a few moments.

Alzerion turned to Eirini. "I know we have our faults, but I need you to tell them nothing."

Eirini's brows furrowed.

"I mean it. Please don't say what comes to your mind. I have grown accustomed to it, but it will only worry them."

She pursed her lips, but for once she did not argue. Alzerion felt a lightness. Eirini held her hands over his as she turned the knob.

Eirini leaned closer. The scent of jasmine smacked into him, making his mouth itch to kiss her.

"If you promise you will stop putting yourself in danger, then I will do as you wish."

Alzerion smiled as Eirini's cheek grazed against his. She leaned back and then he opened the door.

Francisco and Evalyn sat on a seat near the bay window. Francisco's arms wrapped around his wife as she leaned against him. He glanced to the fireplace, toward his mother. Melinda sat in her rocker by the roaring fire with her knitting needles on her lap. Even Isabella was there—on a small cot off from the fireplace. Audrina curled up like a little ball against Isabella.

Quairken rushed into the room and put his hand on Isabella. She hopped up with her arms in defense. Her mouth curved into a smile and then embraced Quairken. Alzerion moved farther in.

"Thank god you're back." Francisco's voice was deep, but it sounded different.

"What's going on? Why are you all here together?" Alzerion scanned the room. "Is my mother alright?"

"She's just resting." Evalyn's voice was strained, but soft. "To be honest, we have gotten little rest."

Alzerion's gaze flickered back to Evalyn.

She continued. "Oh, Alzerion." Evalyn's voice cracked like a child in need of reassurance.

Francisco rested his hand on her shoulder as he pulled her in.

"A darkness came," Isabella added. A low cadence masked her words. Her eyes hollow as she stared down at Audrina sleeping off of her side.

Alzerion felt the warmth of Eirini's hand on his arm. It felt nice to know that he had her, not that he would admit that to her.

"It was mysterious," Evalyn said. "A bizarre blackness that covered the sky like ink spilled across a sheet of paper."

"Then the reports came in," Francisco added. He kept his arm around Evalyn.

"Reports?" Brentley's voice sounded hazy, like a phantom overtook his senses.

Alzerion moved Eirini's hand down as he made his way to Brentley. He tapped his shoulder. "Why don't you sit by the fire? Rest up."

Brentley nodded.

Alzerion muttered something under his breath as he waved his hand in a circular motion. Then a medium-sized bed appeared, and Brentley sat as Alzerion returned to Evalyn and Francisco.

Alzerion cleared his throat. "Reports about what?"

Alzerion noticed Francisco's pale complexion and weary eyes.

Francisco bent his neck as he pressed his head to Evalyn. "Reports of missing people."

Missing? Alzerion mouthed.

"It is like a faceless, nameless monster." Evalyn spoke in such a low tone it was almost impossible to hear her.

Alzerion shifted his weight from one foot to the other as he focused on Evalyn's words. Then he glanced out the bay window behind Francisco and Evalyn. The sky was mostly gray, like some sort of ominous cloud shrouded them in dark mist. This had to be what Aironell and the Dark Sovereign mentioned. The darkness did, in fact, follow him here. *But the question was, could he defeat it?*

*They seem* scared. Eirini's voice rang in his mind.

He peered down at her. Eirini fiddled the ends of her hair between her fingernails. Her eyes met his, but Alzerion said nothing. He felt the weight of it already. The impact of his choices.

"Well I should check in, maybe have a meeting."

"No," Francisco said.

Alzerion's face twisted like knotted up dough.

"It threatened us, Alzerion," Evalyn added. "It forced us to stay here in the palace."

Before Alzerion could ask his question, Francisco continued. "The voice from the bleak shroud had clear instructions. Stay here. Do nothing. Let things fester or if we acted, then we would all suffer. It would end the whole kingdom."

The muscles of Alzerion's jaw tensed. He felt his pulse as his jaw hung open.

"Is that why there are no servants?" Quairken broke the silence.

Francisco took a breath as he nodded.

"Some stayed here, but most went to help their families." Evalyn clasped the fabric of the cushion she sat on. "We closed off a safe location for them in the palace just as we have for us here in the Family Room."

Alzerion let the information settle in his brain. He peered around the room. "With our little group, we need more room."

"Alzerion," Evalyn's voice was meek.

He turned to face her. "Didn't you have another soldier with you?"

Alzerion felt a chill nip at his skin. He gulped. "He didn't make it."

"I'll sleep with my family," Quairken added.

Alzerion nodded as he turned about, staring at the edges of the room. He closed his eyes tight and let his hands hover in the air.

"There is the annex that's right off this room. That should be plenty of room," Francisco spoke with certainty.

He let his mind fill with thoughts of partitions and make-shift beds off the floors. Then his eyes flung open as his hands glowed a deep red.

Alzerion lowered his hands. "It is done. Brently already has his little space and Quairken is fine with his wife, so Eirini and I will take the annex."

Evalyn forced a tired smile as she nodded. "Let's talk more tomorrow, Alzerion. We want to know all about your journey, but—"

"We don't have it in us tonight," Francisco chimed in.

Alzerion bowed his head. He motioned to Eirini, who strode toward him. He placed a hand on her shoulder and then pushed open what looked like part of the wall with his other hand. As he walked through the opening, he glimpsed Quairken as he leaned toward Isabella.

Eirini crossed the room, gazed out the window, and then faced him. "What?"

"This is a room in a palace? It's kind of, well, dusty."

Alzerion pressed his hands against his cheeks as he peered around. It was drab, but he added the partitions and the floor bed was there with blankets and pillows.

"I'll do what I can tonight."

He moved around, lighting the candles in the room. Then he knelt down by the fireplace and set to work on the fire.

"Alzerion, would you like my help?"

He craned his neck to see her standing nearby. "You know how to light a fire?"

Eirini opened her mouth.

He smirked.

"Don't assume that I have no skills." Eirini's face was rigid as her hands rested on her hips.

"I would never." Alzerion rested a sooty hand over his chest.

Eirini's eyes thinned as her arms folded across her chest.

"Sorry, I didn't mean to assume anything. I thought I'd just light a small fire for tonight so we can get some rest."

She turned on her heels. He watched her for a moment and then resumed setting the pieces of wood for the fire.

"Eirini, there should be some clothes over on the low wooden end table. I hope it fits." He didn't turn but kept working on setting the blaze.

She was silent, but he heard her boots against the floor. Alzerion muttered *ignis* and then a tiny flicker of yellow and red shot out at the pieces of wood. Little smoke wafted up as the embers grew. They lapped against the wood until there was a golden glow.

Alzerion stood and rubbed his hands together. When he turned around, he had to refrain from audible sounds. Eirini sat on the small floor bed. Her hair tumbled down as her caramel locks frothed over her olive-toned shoulders. He swallowed. He shifted his gaze to take in the room. It still needed work, but it would do. He tilted his head to the side as her arms wrapped around his waist.

"What are you doing?" Alzerion smirked. He rotated his whole body to face her.

The woman who stood before him looked like an angel, if there ever was one. His jaw hung down as he took a couple of slow breaths. The ivory nightgown shimmered in the light of the candles and firelight. It was torture—the way it hugged her curves in all the right places. Alzerion stepped toward her. A flood of warmth washed over him. *He wanted to close the space between them, but to act on his feelings—that was something else.*

Eirini reached out and laid her hands on his chest. Her fingers trailed along the edges of the traveling vest. With a twinkle in her eye, she unclasped it and tossed it off to the side. Alzerion held in a breath as her hands moved so nimbly to tug his shirt up. It laid against his thighs as her amber eyes seemed to smile at him.

His heart pounded with a desire he did not know was possible. Alzerion took a half-step back and then sat down on the little bed. Eirini lowered as she sat next to him. His eyes focused on the flames of the fire.

"I'd love to know what you're thinking."

Alzerion gazed at her. A sense of adventure clung to her eyes. "Eirini, it's late. Why don't we just get some sleep?"

He fumbled with the pillows behind them as he propped them off the dip in the floor. Eirini rested her hands on his. A slow smile hung over his mouth. She shuffled around on her knees, and Alzerion angled his head to watch as she flung her arms around and rested on his chest. She squeezed him in a tight hug. Alzerion couldn't catch her eyes, but Eirini nuzzled her nose into his cheek and then whispered. "Can I ask you a question?"

He felt goosebumps down his arms. The sweet timber of her voice and being near her ...it did something. His insides felt like pudding, and he knew it was a bad idea. Screw it. Alzerion twisted around, pressing one hand off the ground while the other gripped her soft nightgown and pulled her closer. Eirini wrapped both arms around his neck as he cradled her into his body. Then he rolled to his side as she laid against him. Her face rested on his chest, but close to his face.

Alzerion pressed his lips to her forehead. "What do you want to know?" He felt his heart beat faster in his chest. There were a thousand ways this could go wrong, but he didn't care.

"What is the deal with you and your mother?" Eirini grazed her fingers over his arm hair. It tickled, but he kept from laughing.

"Of all the things you could ask."

"Well, whether you want to admit it, we both know it's a waste to ask you about your feelings. Your mind gives you away more than you know."

A heat crept across his face as he swallowed.

"So, I want to know something I can't get from your thoughts."

Alzerion rubbed his chin against her head. "It's a long story." \

Eirini touched his chin, and he gazed down at her. Her soft hands gently tilted his chin up. "I am an excellent listener."

Her honey scented breath flooded his senses. The smile on his mouth grew as he laid back and Eirini nestled into him. Alzerion spoke of the situations of his youth. He saw the water that pooled in her eyes.

"I'm sorry." Eirini placed an arm around his neck and pulled herself up. She stared back at him, level. "Alzerion, I'm going to kiss you now, and I thought you should know."

A burst of desire coursed through him as her lips pressed to his neck. A small smile escaped his lips as he clenched his hands on the bed beneath him. Her tongue slid across his skin to the rhythm of tiny licks and sucking. His eyes closed. The urgency within grew. Every fiber of his being was on edge. He knew what he wanted. Without thinking, Alzerion laid his hands on her back and pulled her closer. Eirini straddled a leg on each side of him, like he was some sort of chair. His hands clenched on the fabric of her nightgown, and then released as he rocked forward. Her hair splayed out around her as she stared up at him.

"That wasn't a kiss." Alzerion's eyes narrowed. "That was something quite different."

Eirini's eyelashes fluttered at him. "Don't act like you didn't enjoy the attention."

"Not the point."

With that, Alzerion leaned his face closer to hers. He pressed his lips to hers. His lips moved in quick but deep movements. Each kiss ended with his teeth tugging at her bottom lip before another kiss crashed down. He felt a sense of spontaneity, which was new to him. He ignored the urge to stop. Instead, he let his hands graze over her back until his hands moved over her stomach. Then they skimmed upwards, over her breasts with a squeeze, and then both hands cupped her chin.

Nobody was around this time. No excuse to stop.

"Alzerion, don't think." She said between kisses.

He pulled his head back a bit. "Stay out of my mind."

"I'm...trying," she panted.

A sense of relaxation washed over him. "I know it may sound odd, but I swear I can kiss you all night or until our lips fall off." Her lips curved into an irresistible smile.

He laughed.

Eirini pulled him in. "Alzerion, I want more. I want you."

"Eirini, I—"

She brushed her finger against his lips. "What we are doing will be fine for now." She winked.

Alzerion breathed out. "You never cease to amaze me."

He rolled to his side and took a few quick breaths as he gazed at the ceiling. Within seconds, he felt hands rub down his chest and rest around the top of his pants. Alzerion pressed her hands into his lower stomach. He peered over at her and shook his head. She maintained eye contact as her mouth parted.

She leaned in, gripped his sleeves, and pulled him closer. Eirini kissed him, and it was not slow. There was a hunger in the deepness of each kiss. Alzerion allowed himself to let it fill him. Lips locked in a fiery embrace as his tongue explored each crevice of her mouth. Their hands scoured each other as he felt beads of sweat on his forehead from the fire that blazed.

Their lips didn't part as her hands roamed over his body. Her hands clenched and then pulled at his shirt. Alzerion took a breath as she took his shirt off and tossed it away. He smiled as he watched her. The desire in her eyes was enough. *But what did she desire?* He lowered his eyes, lost in thought.

"Alzerion?" She spoke between breaths.

He looked back at her. "I'm alright." He licked his lips. "I think we should call it a night."

Alzerion rolled onto his side, eyes focused on the stone of the wall. A few moments of silence and then he felt her touch on his forearm. Eirini's chin rested against his shoulder.

"Don't push me aside," Eirini's words were firm.

Wafts of jasmine tickled his nose as her hair brushed against his face. He angled his head to the side. "Eirini, don't make this harder than it needs to be. I don't need to read your mind to know what you want."

Eirini flinched at his words. "I guess you don't know everything."

Alzerion turned over and faced her. "Oh? You're not looking at this as another opportunity to express your freedom and have a good time?"

Eirini's jaw hung open. Then her eyes flashed with hurt. "I-I can't believe you just said that."

"Tell me I'm wrong." Alzerion laid there with his arms crossed.

She closed her eyes and then opened them with some hesitation. "I know you can't say it, but I sense you need to hear it." Eirini sat up as she took a breath.

Alzerion's eyebrow rose, but he sat up, too. "What?"

"I love you, okay?"

Alzerion felt the tension relax at her words. He reached out and held her hand.

"I know you have things you don't talk about. But, I don't care. Alzerion, I know what you're afraid of and I won't do that. I'm not going anywhere."

His eyes locked on her.

"I'm yours already, whether you take me or not." She chuckled. "I fell in love from the moment you cornered me at that ball of yours."

"Do you mean that?" He tilted his head.

Eirini's lips curled into a large grin. "I want you, but that means I want all of you. From your many, many flaws to your cocky smirk, and your controlling ways."

"Eirini, I—"

She placed a finger to his lips as she shook her head. "Alzerion, I will never leave you."

Every concern washed away at that moment. Alzerion leaned forward and whispered. "An eternity with me? Be careful what you wish for."

Then he kissed her as his tongue thrust into her mouth between the cadence of kiss and nip.

## CHAPTER 23
### *Light of Day*

Eirini rubbed her eyes. Realization of the truths she shared. She craned her neck to the side. There he was, still asleep. Her mouth curved into a thin smile. She wiggled closer to him from under the blankets.

First, she gave him a peck on the cheek and then pressed her lips to his mouth. It took more seconds than she thought it would, but Alzerion finally scrunched his nose as his eyes opened. There he laid, staring back at her. She loved the way he gazed at her, the way his hair did that flippy thing. He didn't say the words, but she was pretty confident in his feelings. She could feel it. He grasped her hand and pressed them to his lips. She slid the rest of the way over and laid her arm across his chest as she squeezed. His head laid against hers.

"Well, this is a nice way to wake-up," Alzerion chuckled.

Eirini pulled her head back to look up at him. One of his hands cradled under her chin as she felt him ease her up a bit more. He pressed his lips to hers, and her mind felt light as he kissed her. When their lips parted, Eirini burrowed her face into his chest.

"Alzerion, I can stay like this forever."

"Good. But unfortunately, I have work to do." He sat up.

"You want to leave already?" Her voice faltered.

"Never," he whispered as he let his nose graze her forehead, "but I have kingly duties to attend to and I'd rather nobody walk in on us."

He had a point.

Eirini got up and dressed. She smoothed her clothes down and then tied her hair back.

There was a shuffling of boots. Eirini turned, and Alzerion stood with his back propped against the door—arms crossed.

"What are you doing?" Eirini asked as she stepped toward him.

His eyes scanned her body. "I'm just admiring." He smirked.

She shoved his arm as she grabbed the doorknob. Her hand twisted it as her eyes gazed up at him. Alzerion placed a kiss on her mouth. It sent a dizzying feeling through her body. Eirini nibbled at his lip as she tugged. She pushed her hand into his chest and then turned the doorknob.

Alzerion bent his head low. "Morning." He winked and then eased her hand on the knob as the door opened.

He strolled out ahead of her. A fluttery sensation clung to her heart. She watched as Alzerion joined Quairken.

Alzerion noted Audrina was still asleep on her bed, but the others were gone.

He glanced over at Quairken. "Where is everyone?"

"They'll be back."

Alzerion nodded. He scanned the room once more, and his eyes met Eirini's. Her smile radiated across her face. A heat crept over his cheeks.

"Alzerion." Quairken taped on his shoulder.

"Huh? I'm sorry. What did you say?"

Quairken stared at him—eyebrows furrowed.

"How are Audrina and Isabella?"

Quairken's tall figure just stared back at him.

Alzerion shifted his gaze as the door swung open. Melinda's eyes brightened as she dashed to Alzerion.

"You're okay." She squeezed him in a tight hug. Her eyes filled with tears, and after a moment, she let go of him and then slapped his arm.

Alzerion rubbed the sting of her hand. "What was that for?"

"A note?" Her voice hitched. "What if you didn't make it back from your journey?"

Alzerion felt the tension in his face as he rubbed the back of his neck. "I'm sorry."

Melinda hugged him once more. "Just be careful."

He nodded as she sat down in her chair by the fireplace. Alzerion paced around, but his eyes lingered on Eirini. She smiled at him and he felt a warmth wash over his body. He exhaled. There was no use trying to force his thoughts away, but he made his way near Isabella. Then he felt a hand on his shoulder. Quairken exchanged glances. Then Francisco and Evalyn strolled in and sat on the ruby-red satin couch. Alzerion felt like his mind was all over the place.

"What's going on between you two?" Quairken pointed to Eirini.

Alzerion lowered his head as he looked at the pattern of the nearby table.

"I'm not blind. Between the DarkFlower Jungle and now..."

"Shush." Alzerion nudged Quairken. "Nothing alright."

Quairken's eyes narrowed.

"Fine. I might like her, but that is *all* I am admitting, too." His jaw tightened.

He caught Eirini's gaze. *What's with the whispering?*

He shook his head. Then he strolled to the middle of the room and sat down in a small chair. There, he had the best view of everyone in the room. Even Brentley, who sat shrouded in his blanket in his little corner, arms wrapped around his legs. Eirini pulled a chair and sat beside him. He felt her presence.

"How did your journey go?" Evalyn said. "Is she...gone?"

Francisco's gaze fixed on him. *How to tell the truth, when the reality was far more troubling.* If he didn't see her himself, he wouldn't believe that she was better off—but she was.

He described their arrival and some trials they encountered. He added how they found Endrus and that he returned with them. Evalyn craned her neck to Quairken and then back to Alzerion and Eirini. She remained silent. Alzerion took a brief pause and then continued. The tales of the Dark Sovereign and the jungle itself. Each detail piled on the other, as if they had been gone far longer than they had.

Francisco grasped Evalyn's hand at the mention of Aironell. Alzerion saw the glint of hope in their eyes at the reality that she was alive—but it was soon washed away with the fact that she would not or could not return. Alzerion swallowed as he looked about the room. Isabella's face was faint as her lips fell flat. Then she glanced back to Quairken. He nodded. He wondered if Quairken had already told her about the details.

"But ... she helped us," Quairken blurted out.

Evalyn blinked her water-filled eyes as she stared at them. Francisco held firm, but Alzerion could see the hurt in his face. Instead, he squeezed his wife's hand. Evalyn wiped at her eyes.

"It's true. Aironell and the Dark Sovereign helped us to leave the DarkFlower Jungle safely."

"Stop, please," Francisco held up a hand.

His words were sharp and sounded strangled. Evalyn held her fingers tight, as her eyes did not wander from him.

Alzerion sighed. "Francisco. Evalyn. She won't be coming back."

"Even after you came to rescue her?" Melinda straightened in her rocker.

"Aironell doesn't want to return," Quairken added.

Alzerion's head lowered as he studied the floor. He didn't want to see their faces. Shock. Disappointment. Two things they were inevitably going to feel, but there was nothing to do about it.

Alzerion straightened up as he focused back on them. He felt Eirini's hand squeeze into his as she placed her other hand on his shoulder. The warmth of her touch gave him strength. He took a deep breath.

"Aironell married the Dark Sovereign." His voice was low.

Francisco shifted in his seat as his eyes narrowed. Evalyn frowned.

"She what?" Isabella's voice rose among them.

Alzerion didn't get to speak.

"She's happy?" Evalyn tilted her head. "She doesn't want to come home or take her place here?"

Alzerion shook his head as his fingers clutched at the fabric of his seat. "The way I understand it...Aironell views the jungle as her home."

"They call her the Lady of the Jungle," Eirini added with a reassuring smile.

Alzerion shifted in his seat. He waited.

Francisco grabbed the back of his neck—eyes avoided them.

"Anything else we should know?" Evalyn picked at her fingers.

Alzerion's fingers rubbed his chin and then he shook his head.

"What about that guy?" Eirini said.

Francisco straightened his back as he focused back on Alzerion.

He gritted his teeth. "The Dark Sovereign mentioned Adrastus as someone to look out for."

"Adrastus," Evalyn's mouth formed the whole of his name.

"Maybe he wanted to cause a rift?" Melinda said as she laid her knitting needles on her lap.

He shook his head. "No. He was genuine in his tone. Aironell verified, too." He licked his lips.

Francisco's face paled like a wilted rose.

*They will* adapt. Eirini's words were soft and calm in his mind.

He gazed down at her. *I know. It doesn't make any of it easier.*

Alzerion paced around and gazed out at the far-left window. The darkness was a living, moving thing. It needed to be dealt with. *This was his kingdom. It may have been Aironell that was born into it, but he did the hard work. These were his townspeople.* His nails dug into his chin.

A heavy hand pressed into his shoulder. Alzerion pivoted enough to see Francisco. The concern that covered his face was clear.

"The darkness came out of nowhere." Francisco's words were solemn.

"Audrina saw it when she was playing outside and she came running and screaming." Isabella spoke loud enough to hear.

Alzerion glanced over as she checked on the little one still nestled in the make-shift bed. The thought of her witnessing the darkness invade

Bachusa-it was too much. The pressure churned in his stomach like the heat of a thousand fires burned within.

Alzerion closed his eyes and focused on the chatter he heard.

"We are at a loss for what to do." Evalyn's words sounded stifled.

Alzerion's eyes pushed open as the muscles in his neck tensed. "I will take care of it."

Francisco rested his hand on the windowpane as he turned to the side, his back propped on the window.

Alzerion strode toward the door. "I'll work on a plan." He shifted his eyes around the room.

He pulled the door open and left. Alzerion breathed out as he made his way to the grand staircase. He peered out and gripped the rail in his palms. Learn about and defeat the darkness. Check on the townspeople. Keep those he loves safe. Alzerion clenched his teeth.

"Alzerion," Eirini's voice was sweet as it lilted in his ear. A calm rushed over him as he collected his thoughts. "It's going to be alright."

Eirini rested her hand on his forearm as she nudged herself next to him.

"I hope you're right."

Her head nuzzled into him until he wrapped an arm around her. Alzerion lowered his head and placed a kiss on her forehead.

"Thank you for showing up—for using that gift of yours."

A small smile crept over her candy-red lips. "At last, you don't mind my powers on you."

He leaned his face closer to hers. "Maybe just this once." Then his lips pressed into hers. A wave of desire filled each nip and pull of her lip.

Alzerion cupped her chin and then took a step back. "I must get into town and see what the people know about this darkness."

Eirini opened her mouth, but Alzerion grazed his finger over her lips. "Please don't ask. I would much rather you stay here. There's no telling what I will find out."

Eirini stiffened as her arms folded across her chest. "Don't forget that I am more useful by your side than sitting around here."

Alzerion smirked. "How could I? You saved my life once and you seem to think I'm incapable without you."

Eirini rushed to him and both hands held onto his arm. "Don't tease. I'm not some little girl that needs protecting. Alzerion, I'm your equal and you know it."

He stroked her cheek. "That may be, but at least for this time, I'd like you to stay here with my family."

Eirini's nostrils flared—her hands clung to her arms. "Fine. I'll get Quairken for you." Then she stormed off.

# CHAPTER 24
## Suspicions

Eirini gazed out the window in the annex bedroom. Her eyes squinted as she watched Alzerion out the window. Two weeks had passed and yet Alzerion was busier than she ever thought possible. She pressed her hands to the sides of the wall as she gazed down. The darkness grew, which made it harder to see what Alzerion and his men were doing. *Stupid court politics*, she fumed.

The people were welcoming. They allowed her to have some tasks, but it felt like a slap in the face. In the jungle, she followed Alzerion and felt more like a partner. But here, well, she couldn't help but feel like a pretty flower that was expected to sit and wait for his return. Eirini scowled as she leaned closer to the window.

She sucked in a breath as her maid tightened the corset around her waist.

"I'm sorry, my lady."

"It's alright, Calistra. I'm not used to such constricting clothes."

She winced as Calistra pulled the laces of the back of her dress. With each tug at the laces of the back of the gown, Eirini had to work hard not to gasp. The fabric clung to her body. The clothes may be more modest than that of Lyricao, but somehow they felt more cramped and uncomfortable.

Eirini pressed her fingers into the thick wooden pane as she observed

Alzerion instruct with hand-to-hand combat. Her view was still dark, but magical orbs of light filtered around the training field. As his arm brandished his sword up and over his head, she noticed his muscles through the tight training shirt he wore. She swallowed. Eyes closed for a moment, her mind flooded with the memory of the last time his muscled arms wrapped around her. *Hmmmm.* He had been busier since the trip he made into town when they arrived.

"Miss?"

Calistra's voice invaded her mind. Eirini blinked a few times and her head angled to the side.

"The laces are done."

Eirini gripped the skirt of her rose-red gown as she turned. Her hands smoothed down the billowy fabric as she took slow steps toward the mirror that Alzerion hung for her. Fleur de lis covered the metal of the mirror. Eirini bit her lip as she gazed back at herself. Hands placed on her hips as her eyes scanned her appearance.

Her locks billowed down as Calistra stepped closer and started fumbling with her hair.

"Must you pull so hard?" Eirini flinched as a hand shot to the back of her head.

"I'm sorry. I'll do better. Please."

Eirini craned her neck to look at the maid, who was barely younger than her. Her bright white eyes cut sharply to her hands. Then her hands let go of some strands of hair—movements slower than before.

"Calistra, I'm not angry with you."

Calistra's gaze shifted back to the hair in her hands. Eirini's fingers moved over as she patted Calistra's hand.

"It's alright. Really."

"Thank you, miss. I've never been a personal maid for someone before." She swallowed. "Before your arrival, I was a common palace maid."

Eirini turned around and felt Calistra's hands fall to the side. "Don't say common. Never sell yourself and your talents short."

Calistra bent her head and then continued.

Eirini thought about what she wanted to say. She took one step forward as she pushed a loose strand of silver hair out of Calistra's face and pushed it to the side. Her hair hung off to the side in one long braid.

"Thank you," Calistra bowed her head, "you are too kind."

A wide smile crossed her face as Calistra stared back at her. Then Eirini picked at her chin as she spoke. "Calistra, have you always lived in Bachusa?"

"Of course," her voice was velvety.

"Have you ever traveled to other kingdoms?"

Calistra's almond-shaped eyes furrowed.

"I'm not accusing you of anything." Eirini backtracked.

She paced around Calistra. "I feel like I've met you before."

Calistra grabbed Eirini's hand and ushered her back in front of the mirror. Her hands slid through her hair with such ease. The bristles of the brush glided through her locks.

"Which do you prefer?" Calistra laid out two beautiful clips on the side table.

One was a jeweled Fleur-de-lis while the other was a detailed rose with emeralds for the leaves and what looked like rubies that made up the petals of the rose. One thing she learned since being in Bachusa was that Alzerion loved roses, more than anything. She pointed to the rose clip. Calistra grabbed it and gathered her locks as she pressed the clip into place. Eirini felt a few loose pieces of hair. Calistra moved around in front of her and used her slender fingers to twirl the pieces of hair around her fingers. They wound around and around until Eirini felt a tug at her scalp.

Calistra mouthed, "three, two, one." Then she unraveled Eirini's two loose strands of hair. The curl heightened as the strands cascaded down against her face. Calistra stepped off to the side. Eirini shifted her gaze to the mirror. Wow! Calistra handed her an ornately crafted hand mirror. Eirini held it behind her as her eyes gazed back at the mirror. The back of her looked luscious as the curls tumbled down. The clip dazzled her like nothing she had seen before.

She placed the tiny mirror down and turned. Calistra was gone. Eirini lifted her chin as she strolled over to the doorway. It was the only way out. She looked left and right, but nothing. Nobody was in the

Family Room. Eirini strolled out of the room and made her way down the hall.

Despite the darker gloom that cast over the palace, it was rather beautiful. Not at all what she was expecting. She missed the views of the sea from out her open windows, but Lyricao was missing one thing she wanted. No, needed—Alzerion. Her face gave way to a wide grin as her hands trailed along the walls. All she needed was her prince to whisk her away. Eirini descended the main stairs.

"Enchanting!"

Her eyes glistened as they shot up. *Alzerion*. There he stood in his black leather pants and knee-length boots. She blinked, twice. His long-sleeve shirt was even more captivating. She never saw him dressed like that.

"What are you doing here?" She teased.

"We finished, and I cleaned up down here."

Eirini's steps echoed with each clack against the floor—signaling her closeness. She saw the bobbing of his throat as he swallowed.

"This has your attention?" She pointed to her gown. "It's alright, I suppose. Calistra did an amazing job." She spoke very crisp and slowly.

Alzerion lunged forward. Closing that gap between them. He placed his index finger over her lips. Eirini's lips parted just enough for her teeth to show as her teeth dipped into her lip. Her heart pounded in her chest. Surely he would hear its loudness.

He was a vision in his formal wear. Her hands trembled as they grabbed his muscled forearms. She felt the hardness beneath his blood-red shirt. Her fingers rubbed into the velvety material and then trailed across the black splotches that accented his shirt. Her hands moved and laid across his chest, just under his neck. Then they slid down, slowly feeling the plain velvet and the ties that kept his shirt closed. *Too bad*, she thought. She wanted to rip it wide open. It would be exhilarating to kiss him right here. Her cheeks flushed.

He laid his hands over hers. "Don't be naughty, Eirini." He whispered.

His tone was smoky. His eyes had this sly glint as his mouth twisted into that smirk of his. Those cinnamon eyes of his locked onto her with such intensity. She wanted nothing more than to get lost in every moment with him. *He was trouble. Alzerion, the King of Bachusa, was her weakness.* Eirini rocked onto the tips of her toes. His face came closer as her calves stretched, raising her height a bit. She felt goosebumps across her flesh, and her eyes fixed on his handsome face. Alzerion's hands clung to her, and she felt this tingling where he touched. It crept through her body until she felt it deep in her stomach. She swallowed.

Each of his fingers touched the black lace that accented the deep red of her gown. Eirini bit down on her lips as her eyelashes flickered up—her eyes gazed at him. Alzerion licked his lips, nice and slow, as his gaze shifted down, scanning her body. He twirled her around and watched the bottom of her dress billow out. What caught her attention was how his cinnamon-red eyes lingered on her.

*Do you know what I want?* Her breathing increased.

Alzerion's fingers grazed against her black lace sleeves as they glided up her arm. *I can imagine.* His lips twisted into his sly smirk.

A slight blush crept across her cheeks as his jeweled hand glossed over her chest as his fingers traced the black lace that decorated the neckline of the gown over her breasts. Eirini felt a tingle inside. His hands rested on the curves of her waist and held onto her, tight.

Her body responded. Her hands trembled under his elbows as she fiddled with the fabric of his shirt. Those skilled hands of his trailed until they held onto the sides of her neck as he pressed her body against his. There was no space between them. *She loved being close to him.* She licked her lips until they were nice and moist. His head bent in toward her as his lips parted, just enough. *Heavens, he was perfection—every part of him.* Even the way he toyed with her.

Her hands laid limp at her side. At any moment, she felt like she may faint if he didn't kiss her already. His mouth finally came near her lips.

"Damn, you're gorgeous," his voice was breathy, "but a kiss will have to wait." He released his grip on her and held onto her hand as he tugged them toward the Great Hall.

"Huh?" Eirini shook her head. Her mind was focused on, well, other things that she swore she had misheard him. But he kept urging them toward the door.

"Are you going to pretend you didn't just lead me on?" She whispered as he pulled them closer to the Great Hall.

Alzerion laughed as he stopped and gazed at her. There was a playful glint on his face. "Sorry. If I kiss you now, well, we won't be on time for our morning duty." He rubbed the back of his hand down her cheek.

Eirini swallowed.

"Believe me," his voice lowered, "I want to kiss you. I love being with you, even if it is just to talk or sit in silence."

Eirini's lips parted. This was the only time he had alluded to his feelings, and her lips curved into a broad smile.

Alzerion wrapped his arm around her once more and slid her closer. "If time wasn't a factor, I'd kiss you all day. Hell, I would take you to our little annex room and never, ever let you leave until we were both satisfied." He winked.

Her voice cracked, but other than that, she had no words. A dizzying frenzy took hold of her heart. She took a large savoring breath. The touch of his hand on her cheek made her stomach do little flips. Eirini's knee buckled.

Alzerion steadied her. "Are you alright?" His eyes fixed on her, like an interrogation.

She nodded. *Words were too much right now.* Alzerion wrapped her arm around his as he led them into the Great Hall. They strolled down the carpet until they reached the thrones. Eirini took slow breaths as she worked to steady her feelings. She didn't want to embarrass Alzerion or herself in front of his people. Alzerion sat on his throne and he had her seated to his right. The *queen's* seat. Nobody challenged her position, but they watched her when they came to see Alzerion.

Every so often, he would glance over at her and she smiled or nodded back. Today was going like it had since they arrived in Bachusa. Alzerion was speaking with a merchant, but then the big wooden doors opened. She observed Alzerion's eyes dart to the latecomer. His face changed. His lips pinched together as his eyebrows drew in.

"I didn't miss today's gathering, did I?" The man walked forward with such an air of confidence. His clothes told her he was one of the nobles.

Alzerion shifted on his throne and straightened up.

"Of course not, Adrastus." Alzerion's voice was deep and confident. "I rarely see you at these gatherings." His eyes narrowed. "Not really your time to visit."

Adrastus stood with his legs apart, and his hands folded in front of him. He wore what looked like the finer silks as his eyes stared back at Alzerion. Eirini tilted her head as she just watched. He had eyes so brown that they kind of looked like milk chocolate—puddles of it placed on his face for eyes. Then those chocolate eyes refocused on her. She gulped. His gaze was menacing...intense. Something about him didn't feel right. His gaze pierced through her. Alzerion touched his fingers to her wrist.

"Adrastus, what can I help you with?" Alzerion's voice was a mix of sharp and commanding. "I am almost done for the day. Surely it can wait for another time?"

"Of course, Your Majesty," he bowed his head. The way he said that sent chills through her.

This was the man the Dark Sovereign warned about. From the short exchange, she could tell Alzerion didn't like him, either.

Alzerion stared around the room at the others still there. "Let's call it a day."

Alzerion waved his right hand, and the remaining merchants and townspeople bowed and left.

"I'm not sure what you came for, but you're no longer welcome in my court."

Adrastus' mouth curved into a tight grin. His eyes bore into Alzerion. *He suspected something.* She felt the unsaid moment between them.

"I feel introductions are in order." Adrastus strolled toward them with one arm folded behind his back and the other waved around in a circle. Eirini pressed her nails into the wood of the throne. Adrastus' grin felt ominous—more like a snarl. Then he shifted his sights to her. In his hand was a bundle of purple irises.

"For you, my lady." He held them out to her as he bowed his head low.

She could sense Alzerion seething in silence. A wrenching sensation plagued her stomach, but she stood anyway. Eirini stepped down onto the main floor and strolled to Adrastus. She didn't waver as she grabbed the flowers from his hand. His hand held onto hers, and he felt like the coolness of glass as he lowered his lips and kissed her hand.

Eirini took a half-step back as he stared at her. "I'm Adrastus Acidinus. I'm from the noble family Acidinus of the House of Sorcery."

Eirini nodded and forced a diplomatic smile as her eyes met his. He took another small step closer. Alzerion darted to his feet.

"Adrastus, did you have business with me, or did you only wish to meet my quest?" His tone was deep and firm.

Eirini could feel the tension between them. She looked around, and Quairken was the only one left in the room.

Adrastus shot him a glare that made her skin crawl. "Well, she was worth meeting." He was bold. "But why am I not welcome, Your Majesty? I'm one of your nobles."

Alzerion stood an arm's length from Adrastus. "You really want to pretend that you're not a traitor?" Alzerion paced around him. "That you did not conspire with another realm to bring about our demise?"

Adrastus' smile flattened. "My, what an accusation." He didn't flinch. "The only thing I am guilty of is reaching out to an old relation. Oh, and flattering a guest that I've heard you have been close with."

"Wait, you're the one related to the Dark Sovereign?" Eirini asked.

"I am," his chest puffed out as he spoke, "but I have done nothing."

Alzerion's eyes looked like a snake—twisted with a rage that she felt through their bonded mark. They hooded into slits. "Do you dare accuse me of something?" Alzerion stood still as stone—like a chiseled god.

"Nothing, of course." His voice had an air of condescension.

Alzerion's teeth bared as he lifted his chin up. "Rumors, I assure you, but what I said about you, well, I *know* that to be true." Alzerion stood his ground.

"Surely, I don't have to tell you how harmful rumors can be, especially to a young unmarried ruler."

Alzerion's hands contorted into fists at his side. "Adrastus, are you threatening me? Don't you see that there are bigger issues going on? Certainly, your petty issues with me can wait until we make sure the people of Bachusa are safe from this dark menace. This darkness threatens the entire kingdom."

Adrastus didn't cower. "That's more of a problem for you, now isn't it, Your Majesty?" One hand rubbed at his chin. "But if you need someone to do the job for you, well, I would have completed the job by now." Adrastus' teeth flashed in his grin.

Alzerion's nostrils flared, but Adrastus continued, "Or I could keep your guest company while you are busy overseeing things. I'd be *happy* to give her a tour."

Alzerion's hand came down over hers possessively. The line of his mouth tightened a hair more.

Eirini grabbed his hand until she held onto his forearm. "Alzerion, don't we need to go?"

Adrastus' piercing gaze locked on them. "I guess some rumors are true. Now aren't they, Your Majesty?" Adrastus's eyebrows rose inquiring and then he focused on her. He bowed his head. "Don't want to make your suitor jealous."

She felt the Alzerion's muscles tense in her hands. Eirini swallowed. "I think the mistake is with you too, Lord Adrastus."

"Oh?" His dark eyebrows slanted.

Eirini opened her mouth to speak, but Alzerion stepped a fraction ahead of them.

"Stop baiting me, Adrastus. Who cares what you think...so what if I was—courting her? It's still hands off either way." Alzerion slid an arm to her waist and pulled her close.

Eirini's heart fluttered at his declaration. A heat crept across her cheeks. If they were alone, she'd kiss him until he begged for her to stop.

Adrastus's laugh was deep and menacing. "I guess we shall see how that ends for you." He shrugged his shoulders and shifted his gaze to Eirini. "He doesn't have the best record of courting women."

Eirini's lower jaw sank at the comment.

"I mean, hell, you couldn't keep Aironell's interest." He shifted his attention back to Alzerion as he pressed a finger to his chin. "I guess she wasn't anything special after all."

"How dare you!" Alzerion shouted. He stormed over to him. "You know nothing."

Adrastus chuckled. "I know she saved you and left you the kingdom. You're not royal or their family. You are nothing—a nobody who has no right to rule this kingdom."

Alzerion's hands clenched into fists that hung at his sides. Adrastus stood tall, with no hint of retreat.

"Eirini," Adrastus' words were the charm itself, "I mean, you can do better." His eyes narrowed as he shifted his sights to Alzerion. "Better than an ineffectual king. A king that can't even protect his people...can't even keep a woman from leaving or choosing another."

Eirini didn't get a chance to say anything. It escalated so fast. Alzerion darted toward Adrastus, fists raised as he went to swing at him, and Eirini pressed a hand to her mouth as she watched. The two shoved the other and Alzerion got him in a hold before Quairken pulled them apart.

"Your Majesty...Alzerion, he isn't worth losing everything." Quairken's words thundered.

Alzerion pulled himself as he tugged at his shirt. Adrastus continued to grin as he wiped at his mouth.

"Did my words hurt? You obsessed over one thing for so many years, but look where it has gotten you." Adrastus crooned. "You know what they say about the truth?"

Adrastus took slow strides as he kept a wide distance from Alzerion as he circled around him. "Alzerion, you are a nobody of a power-hungry traitor of Bachusa. Someone that Aironell's parents took pity on." He grinned. "You won't ever fill the void you feel. Face it, you're damaged and beyond what someone could ever love."

Alzerion didn't move. His face was expressionless. Eirini strode toward him and rested a hand on his arm. But he didn't look at her—didn't budge.

Adrastus folded his arms across his chest as his eyes looked a shade darker. "I'm going to ruin you. Make you beg for a swift end."

Eirini pressed her other hand to her temple. Glimpses of images invaded her mind. It was fuzzy, but one thing was for sure—Alzerion was in some sort of danger. Raw hurt lingered in her eyes, like a burning she couldn't control.

She cleared her throat. "You need to leave." Eirini steadied her breathing as she set her earnest eyes on Adrastus.

Adrastus shook his head. "I wouldn't get too comfortable, my lady. Our king has fickle tastes, at best. Wouldn't want to see you passed over for his latest whim."

Alzerion said nothing. His eyes darted to the floor.

"He can't even deny any of it." Adrastus moved toward the door, stopped and stared back at Alzerion once more. "I am good at keeping my word, *Your Majesty*." He bowed in mock ritual. "I will use the chaos to my advantage."

Then he left the room.

Eirini didn't know what to make of him. She turned to face Alzerion. His face was expressionless. She took a breath as she tapped into their bonded mark. Anger. Frustration. Insecurity.

"Alzerion?" Her voice was soft.

He said nothing.

Quairken patted her shoulder. "Maybe you should spend some time with the others? Alzerion needs a moment."

Eirini looked back at Alzerion, but nothing. He was devoid of any emotion. She hated to leave, but Quairken was right—Alzerion needed to regain his bearings.

## CHAPTER 25
### *Setback*

E irini smoothed out the velvety gown they forced her to wear. The beaded bodice and tight fabric along her arms confined her. She wanted to make Alzerion happy, but now? Her eyes welled with tears. She wasn't sure. An ache took hold of her heart like a tight grip that squeezed. She wiped the tears from her eyes. The thought of the note he had Quairken give her—it hurt. Alzerion kept his distance in the days that followed.

Eirini sat with Audrina as they sketched.

"Look," Audrina chirped, "I made my family."

The sweet little girl showed her the portrait. It was hard not to laugh at the funny images before her.

She started pointing and naming the people in the picture. "That's mommy and daddy. There's Evalyn and Francisco, oh and the shorter one is Melinda." Her tiny fingers darted across the page.

"Who is that?"

Audrina giggled. "That's Uncle Alzerion. See, I drew his messy hair and crown."

Her cheeks flushed. That dull ache moved into a constant throb. She closed her eyes for a moment, remembering what Quairken told her ... he needs time. That Alzerion was working on his plan and that he had to keep away to lead men on trips to find more about the darkness.

It still sucked. A yearning took hold of her aching heart.

Then Audrina chatted on. "The pretty one over here is you, my new friend."

Eirini felt her heart lighten. Audrina was so pure. "That's so sweet, Audrina."

"I hope you stay with our family forever." Then her little arms wrapped around her beaded waist.

Eirini swallowed. The lump in her throat grew.

"I see you two are getting along."

"Mommy," Audrina chorused. She ran over and hugged Isabella.

"Daddy is finishing up a conversation about the nasty business with Uncle Alzerion. Why don't you go down and see them?"

Audrina's face brightened as she skipped out of the room.

"Eirini, are you alright?" Isabella's eyes honed in on her.

"Oh, I'm fine. Audrina wanted company sketching."

Isabella moved over and sat down in the closest chair. "May I?"

Her hand was outstretched as she placed her sketch in Isabella's hands.

Isabella scanned the paper. "Listen, I overheard the last bit of what my daughter said. I just wanted to see that you're okay."

Eirini grabbed one of her locks and dug her nails into the strands of hair. "I've been better."

Her other hand gestured to the sketch. Eirini drew what was in her heart. Isabella handed back the drawing of Alzerion.

"It's a nice likeness."

Eirini forced a smile, but it fell flat.

Isabella slid off the chair and sat next to her on the make-shift bed. "Look, I don't know what happened between the two of you, but don't lose hope. Alzerion, well, he's complicated."

"Complicated?" Eirini tried to mask the bitterness in her voice. "He has always been straightforward. But now." She shook her head. "I don't even know why I'm still here. He wants space from me, clearly."

"I'm sorry." Isabella's worn hands patted against hers. "Then what's keeping you here?"

Eirini sniffled, but raised her chin to Isabella. "Part of me wants to return home. I miss it. But I-I." Her lip trembled.

"You will miss *him*, too." Isabella rubbed her hand.

A war of emotions raged within her, but she nodded.

"What did he do? If you don't mind my asking." Isabella's voice was sincere.

The words scrawled on that note were like an imprint on her mind. Words in his own hand. Eirini bit her lip until it throbbed like her pulse.

"It was what he said...in a letter." She spoke in a broken whisper. "He didn't want to see me...that I was a distraction he didn't need." Her lashes drooped to hide the hurt. It didn't matter—her eyes filled with tears. She felt knotted up like the dough used to make her favorite treats.

Isabella's eyes brimmed with compassion. "I'm sorry." She rested a hand on her shoulder.

Eirini watched Isabella's face wander deep in thought. A chill washed over her as she caught some of Isabella's thoughts. Eirini hated when her magic intruded on others. She bit the fleshy part of her cheek.

"I appreciate your kindness, Isabella."

Isabella swallowed. "I wish I could do more. I think Alzerion may feel put out by Adrastus. They have something of a tense relationship."

Eirini shuddered. "He was harsh."

Isabella scrunched her nose. "I'm sure he chose his words carefully. Everyone here knows of Alzerion's past."

Eirini exhaled. "Is he as damaged as Adrastus claimed?"

Isabella furrowed her brows. "Eirini, you've spent a fair amount of time with him lately. I'm sure you know that isn't true." Isabella gave a comforting squeeze on her hand.

Eirini pursed her lips. *Truth was, Alzerion didn't like to talk about himself, but he opened up when they were in the Dark Flower Jungle.*

"Isabella, will he bounce back?" Eirini choked on her words.

Isabella shrugged. "Sounds like it was enough to send Alzerion to his dark place."

The weight of her eyelashes felt like a burden as she urged them up.

"It's not a violent dark side, but Quairken is worried about him—so I know he isn't acting himself."

Eirini took a breath. Her brain wracked with worry for him. She regretted nothing.

"You won't leave, will you?" Isabella's eyes probed her like her answer was life or death.

Eirini's mouth flattened, but she nodded but shook her head. "I won't leave him. I just wish he would speak to me."

"Good." Isabella stood. "Be patient." She gave a faint smile and left.

Alzerion swiped his hand against his sweaty brow. His pulse quickened with each breath. He worked to steady himself as he sat on the ground.

"I took care of the bodies." Quairken's voice was solemn.

He appreciated that, but he couldn't face Quairken. Another trek over the lands in search of answers ended horribly wrong. The losses. *They were on him. Each life clung to him like an executioner.* Alzerion didn't speak. He pressed his hands to his head as he stared at the gravel path near his feet.

*Don't take it personally, young ruler.* Endrus bent his head and rubbed his snout on Alzerion's arm. Alzerion patted him.

"Do you want me to stay?"

Alzerion heard the despair in Quairken's voice. He was selfless in all he did—a good friend. He slowly picked up his head and stared out at the woods with a scowl on his face.

"No. I appreciate the thought, but you should clean up and see your wife and daughter."

"Alzerion," his voice softened. "I can stay."

Alzerion craned his neck to look at him. "Don't be silly. I could use the time to think, anyway."

Quairken nodded and then left.

*Endrus, go to your nesting area.*

*As you wish, young ruler. I do like my new home. I hope you don't dwell in your sorrow for long.* Then he flew off toward the barracks.

He fixed his sight on the town off the left of the woods. A heavy darkness clouded the sky like a thick smoke. Alzerion closed his eyes and took a breath as he swallowed a painful lump. A low sigh whistled in the air. Then his eyes flew open at a touch on his upper back.

He grabbed his sword from the ground, turned, and swung at once. There was a shriek as he saw Eirini. His swing was too powerful and didn't stop in time.

"Ouch, ahh." She stepped back as she held onto her palm. Alzerion rushed to his feet and threw his sword to the ground.

"Eirini, what were you thinking? You shouldn't be here." He felt panic rise in his voice.

Alzerion closed the space between them as he grabbed her hand. He stretched out her palm and saw the gash. Her face winced.

Alzerion moved with such precision. He pulled at the fabric around his wrist until he felt the material give way and ripped it off.

"Hold out your hand," his voice was sharp.

Her hand trembled, but she did as instructed.

Alzerion wrapped the fabric around the back of her hand and then tightened it over her gash. She whimpered as he pulled. His fingers held onto the unhurt area of her hand as they grazed over the back of her hands.

The lump in his throat grew so much that he felt nauseous. *He hurt her.* Eirini's eyes glistened with tears. That tightness in his chest worsened, like someone stabbed him and twisted the blade.

"Eirini, I'm sorry." His voice strained. He took a step back and turned away toward the open field and the woods.

"Alzerion, don't push me away."

Her words stung. He shook his head.

"Don't ignore me." Eirini grabbed his arm as she spun herself around to face him. Alzerion stood still as stone. Eirini moved toward him. She rested her bandaged hand on the side of his face—her fingers pushed aside a wayward strand of his hair as her eyes loved him. The muscles in his jaw tensed as he pulled away once more.

"I-I guess I shouldn't have come." Her words wavered. He heard the quaking of her voice.

Alzerion turned to see her dash back to the palace. The ache in his chest intensified, but he knew he had to let her go. That was his punishment...after all, it was his fault that the darkness was here. A king had to focus on the kingdom. His feelings had to wait.

Then Eirini spun around. Her eyes pierced him like a pointed-edged sword. *On second thought, I'm not leaving without having this argument.* Her frustrations rang in his head. Alzerion swallowed as she stalked back toward him. Her eyes were like fiery amber as her gaze intensified.

Her hands folded in front of her. "I wanted to talk to you. I was worried about you and wondered if my being here was only a burden on you, what with all you have going on." She took a quick breath. "Now, I don't care. I'm standing here, Alzerion, and you still ignore me. Fine. I have a request, *Your Majesty.*"

He cleared his throat. "What is it?" There was no mistaking her tone.

She took one more step toward him as her hands clung to her arms. "Send me home."

Her words tore at another little piece of his heart. His mouth hung open for a moment, but then his mouth flattened.

He shook his head. "No."

The lurch in his stomach felt more like a knot that twisted inside. Alzerion shuffled back.

"Alzerion?"

He took another step away. This time, he turned on his heels and stormed away from the palace.

"You can't just walk away from me. Alzerion! I'll follow you."

He heard her feet as they shuffled behind him. He didn't care. *How could she wish to leave?* He kicked some pebbles from the path that dipped near the woods but led back to Gorgeous Garden.

*Will you top? How can you be angry? You've pushed me away with that note. So, I mean, if you don't want me here, then there's nothing to keep me.*

He slowed his gait. *Nothing keeping you here?* Her thoughts sliced deeper. His nostrils flared, but he stopped.

Eirini circled around him and then stumbled. Alzerion reached out and caught her. His arm wrapped around her waist.

"Be careful, please. I can't always be here to protect you."

She shoved her hands into his chest, pushing him back. "I didn't ask for your help. Don't forget that you're not above needing help once in a while, too, Your Majesty."

Alzerion bit his lip as his gaze softened. "Eirini, you promised me you wouldn't leave." His eyes glistened. Eirini's chin dropped. "No, don't look at me like that." He held up a hand as he stepped back.

"Like what?"

"Like you pity me. I don't need that. I thought you were someone whose word was solid."

"Alzerion, you sent that heartless letter saying that you couldn't be bothered with me." Her chin trembled as she darted toward him.

Her hand rested under his chin as she coaxed his face to look at her. "I don't want to break my word. Alzerion, I don't want to leave you. But things are dangerous here and if I'm not wanted, then I shouldn't stay. I deserve more than that letter."

*She was right—about all of it.* He licked his lips as he stared into her amber eyes. He rubbed the middle of his forehead, trying to piece together his options. *Screw it.*

His eyes scanned her and then rested on her inviting lips. A silence passed between them as Alzerion's head lowered as his mouth covered hers hungrily. His lips brushed against hers as she tried to speak.

*Not now, Eirini.* Then he pressed his lips to hers. Her mouth was still warm and moist from his kiss. He cupped his hand around her waist as his mouth devoured the softness of hers. Alzerion tugged at her bottom lip with his teeth as he let it fall.

He smiled at her. "Don't leave. Okay? Eirini, I was foolish. I hate being away from you."

Her eyes brightened as specks of water kissed the corners of her eyes.

Alzerion slid his hands to her back as he coaxed her closer. His other hand held the back of her head as he moved her face closer. His nose traced her face, and then he kissed her once more. Each kiss was more demanding than the last, and he felt the urgency. His tongue traced the softness of her lips and then explored the recesses of her mouth. Eirini pushed him back and gasped.

Alzerion smirked, and he watched as her brows narrowed.

"There's no way you can be upset after a kiss like that. Eirini. You get I was apologizing, right?"

She shook her head. *Something is off, Alzerion, I can feel it.*

He turned and then faced her again.

"Alzerion, watch out!" Eirini lunged toward him as she shoved him to the ground. Instincts kicked in and he held onto her as they plummeted to the ground.

"What was that about?"

"There," her voice trembled.

*Crap.* He bolted to his feet and grabbed her arm as he helped her up. The darkness of the sky grew more ominous. A hissing in the air swirled around, shouting threats.

"I've got your back—just like you had mine." He held out his hand, and she grabbed it. She literally saved him from a metal lance that fell from the sky, and now he would return the favor.

"You can't keep eluding me," the voice hissed.

"Watch me!" Alzerion shouted back. With her hand in his, he bolted. He could go only as fast as he she could in her impractical outfit.

"Stand on my feet." Then he pulled her in. Once she was against his chest, she rested her feet on his. Alzerion muttered a spell under his breath to improve speed. He dashed like a rabbit as Eirini wrapped her arms around him. Her nails dug into his back as he secured them into Gorgeous Garden.

Eirini did not budge from her grip. He raised his hands and shouted, "Praesidium."

A shroud the color of lilies emitted from his hands and funneled around the garden and the palace.

"Are we safe?" He heard the hesitation in her words.

"For now." He gazed down at her. "It's a spell I learned from one of Aironell's books."

The sound of singed metal was loud as things continued to fall from the sky. The magic held, as the chaos turned into puffs of smoke when it hit the protective shield.

"Let's go inside." Alzerion grabbed her hand and led the way.

# CHAPTER 26
## Change of Heart

A constant barrage followed for the week. He had to put more protective wards around the barracks to protect Endrus from the turmoil and the town itself. There was no telling how long they would hold. Alzerion shifted as he observed Isabella cradle Audrina. Melinda told laughable stories—anything to distract them. He needed that as the nobles met with him about concerns. The tone was very much the work of Adrastus. Alzerion tried to keep calm, but he had to do something about him. He had the other nobles whipped up into a frenzy, thinking that he wasn't doing anything. He shook the thoughts from his mind.

Alzerion opened the door to his annex room and closed it behind him. Eirini sat in her opal silk nightgown, reading a book. The light from the candle caught her in just the perfect light. Her clothes looked almost transparent. He swallowed. Calistra was evil for picking that for her to wear.

"I'm sorry. I didn't realize you were here." His eyes shifted to the door as he started toward it.

"Alzerion, you don't have to go. We have talked little since kissing outside."

Alzerion nodded. "Things got hectic."

His hand tapped against the door, and then he strode toward the middle of the room. He wanted to be sure that he was forgiven, and mend what he ruined with that idiotic letter he sent her. He was mentally kicking himself for that, but he thought the distance would help, and she had to believe that he didn't care. *What good that did.*

Alzerion ambled off to the side and ducked behind the partition. He pulled on his loose cream-colored shirt, which dipped to the middle of his chest. Then he slid into a pair of fitted brown trousers. Alzerion sauntered around the partition and saw Eirini glance at him, and her slight blush crept across her face. He breathed out and then sat on the makeshift bed and pulled the blankets up as he rolled to his side.

Alzerion closed his eyes but found it near impossible to sleep. He smelled jasmine and honey—he smelled her. He turned to his other side and watched how her eyes swayed over the words of her book.

She flipped the pages. "Alzerion, do you need something?"

"Oh, no, of course not," he cleared his throat.

"Only asked because you're staring." Her eyes glanced over her book she pressed into her chest.

He picked at his blanket as he spoke. "Eirini, am I forgiven?"

"For—"

"My stupidity at thinking it was wise to separate myself from you. I know it may not make sense, but I swear it did."

Her lips curved into a smile that grew with each second. "Alzerion, of course I forgive you. I just want us to be a team."

Alzerion nodded. "I will try."

Then he shifted and laid on his back, looking at the ceiling.

He heard the book close and out of the corner of his eyes; he watched as she blew out the candle near her. The only light that remained was that of the fire that glowed in the fireplace. He closed his eyes, and his mind wandered to the darkness, their safety, and, of course, what it would be like to have Eirini. A gentle squeeze on his arm forced his eyes open. He bent his head and Eirini's head was on him. His heart beat faster. He ran a hand through her hair, so soft in his fingers.

"Alzerion," she spoke tenderly.

He slid down, just enough to be eye-level.

"I never meant to upset you. You know I won't run from a challenge —even if that obstacle is you." her lips curved into a seductive smile.

"Good," His fingers traced the side of her face and rubbed at her chin, "but I only want you to stay if you want to, not because you feel obligated."

Eirinis' fingers grazed his chest as her thick lashes rose. Her eyes gazed upon him with such intensity. "I never do anything I don't want. You know that."

Alzerion chuckled.

Eirini pushed off his chest and sat up as her hair was a gorgeous shade of candy amber in the firelight. He couldn't help but watch her. *She was perfect. Smart. Sassy. Sexy.* His eyes lingered as he gazed at the openness at the top of her nightgown.

"I know there is so much we don't know, but I feel I need to be honest about something," Eirini said.

Alzerion let his hand rest on the blanket.

Her lip curved in as her soft gaze fixed on him. "When I first met you, I thought you were just a way to have an adventure." She swallowed.

He tilted his head. "Well, I thought you were foolish, but I've never been happier to be proven wrong," Alzerion smirked.

"I'm not saying I will ever settle for boring, but I've realized that you are more than all that I had been denied my whole life."

Alzerion felt a tightness in his jaw. *Where was she going with this?*

She drew a deep breath as her fingers wrapped around the others. "Alzerion, what I now know is that you're all that I need."

Alzerion's eyes widened at her declaration, and his mouth felt dry.

She leaned forward. "It's not the adventure or the title or even your attractive qualities."

Alzerion sat up as he gazed down. His heart quivered in his chest, as if it would fly right out. His mouth opened, but he couldn't say anything.

The beginning of a smile tipped the corners of her mouth as she cleared her throat. "I don't care that you're the king. That means nothing to me."

An audible chuckle followed his smirk. She continued to fiddle with the skin at her fingers.

"It doesn't bother me if you don't have it all figured out...if you were just the guy traipsing through the jungle. Fearless. Take charge. No sugar coating, anything; including your flaws. You don't need to convince me to love you. Don't need to lavish me with gifts, Alzerion, you already have my heart, my love—raw and unending. All I want is you."

Alzerion's heart thudded faster than he thought possible. He shoved the blankets off as he sat on his knees. Alzerion leaned over as he drew his lips in. The longing in her eyes radiated as he arranged his hands on her cheeks. In a quick motion, he slid her closer as he pressed his lips to hers. His eyes raked over her.

"You're stuck with me," Alzerion whispered.

His lips crushed into hers like a wave against the shore. He sucked her lower lip in, pulled and nibbled until she groaned.

She gasped and then traced her lips over his cheek and to his neck. He felt a pleasant chill run over his arms as her soft lips pressed to his neck. He let out a low hum, almost like a deep purr. Alzerion bent his head and peered down.

Eirini choked on air as she panted.

"Are you alright?" He gazed at her as his fingers twined her locks around them. Much like how his heart was bound to her.

She took a few steadying breaths. "I wasn't expecting that."

He cupped her chin. "Well, I like to keep you guessing." He winked. Then he took a breath as he bent his head closer. "Eirini, listen. I love you more than I can ever express." He pressed his mouth to her hands and kissed each of her fingers.

"Well, aren't we a pair?" She giggled.

His mouth lifted and then kissed her cheek. "A perfect match."

She returned his kiss with reckless abandon—each quicker than the last. Alzerion swept her into his chest. Gently, he rocked forward as her body lowered onto the sheets. His hands slid down and explored the hollows of her back, as he leaned over her with knees pressed into the little bed; at her sides. Her head and hands moved in unison with his, the desire burned within him. The way she followed without hesitation— giving herself freely to the passion of his kiss.

A low moan erupted from his mouth, but she nibbled down on his lip. Alzerion tugged at her nightgown as his gaze slid downward, pulling at the fabric down her arms. Eirini's legs entwined around his as he tugged at her nightgown until he was at her stomach. Alzerion bit his lip —a growing need filled him.

He looked at her, hands rested above her head...eyes bright as she licked her lips. "I'm not stopping you," she panted.

Alzerion relaxed his hands over her breasts. He felt the quiver in her body as it perked up. He laid on her and twirled his fingers in her hair. "Are you sure?"

"Yes. Never been more certain about anything." The sincerity and trust were exacting.

Alzerion felt the pull of his heartstrings as his tongue slid around the warmth of her mouth. His hands pressed at her thigh as he pulled her in.

## CHAPTER 27
### *Trek for Answers*

Eirini pressed her fingers into her temples as her eyes wandered over to the pages of the latest book. She found it hard to concentrate when images of his solid chest danced in her mind. *Focus. You want to help.* Alzerion was searching for any details about the darkness or a weakness. So far—nothing. Her mouth pursed as she flipped to the next page. Three times he took a small group out to the woods and the town, but he wouldn't let her go. Each time, she felt a crack in her heart, a lightness that burned in his presence, which she never wanted to extinguish.

"My lady, have you been through the back shelves?" Calistra asked as she strode toward her with another stack of books.

She held her head high as her eyes wandered over the tall wooden shelves. "I don't think I did."

The sound of the door opening forced her attention over to it.

Alzerion stood there, devastatingly handsome, as he strode toward her in a commanding manner. His messy hair frothed over his brow, and she swallowed as she dug her nails into the wood of the table.

"Any luck?" Alzerion stroked his jeweled hand over the crinkled page.

Eirini shook her head.

Alzerion's mouth twisted as he held out a hand. She grabbed hold of it as he coaxed her to her feet and pulled. The scent of cinnamon and mint flooded her nose as she crashed into his toned body. She wanted to melt into him.

"I was just suggesting the older tomes, your majesty." Calistra bowed.

Alzerion kept his eyes on her as he spoke. "That is an excellent idea. Calistra, we will take it from here."

She watched from the corner of her eye as Calistra left.

Eirini tilted her head. But he entwined his fingers around her as he escorted her away from the table. Her heart thumped away in her chest. Shelves towered on both sides as he whisked her down the aisles and around even more—her dress billowed after until she glimpsed a cozy little corner.

Alzerion traipsed toward the shelves that overflowed with books. His hands glided across them. His eyes narrowed with such focus, then he grabbed a book and handed it to her.

"Look for reference to mystical forces, darkness, or even magical curses."

Eirini gazed down at the thick book with its tattered cover. She flipped through while watching him between page turns. He inched toward a section where two shelves spiraled toward the other. In the middle, nestled a gray tapestry with images depicted across. Eirini placed the book down on a small wooden table and walked to the tapestry. Eirini squinted her eyes as she knelt down and touched her hand to the images. Her body shuddered as a chill filled her.

"Eirini are you alright?" She heard the quick clicking of Alzerion's boots as a whirring sounded. Then she saw the images flash in her mind.

"Eirini, answer me?" She could sense his concern rising, but all she could do was press her hands to her head as the images continued. Darkness...death...a noble crest...and then a grey washed over it all. Like the end was uncertain.

"Eirini, my love." Alzerion's hands grasped her shoulders as he spun her around. There he was on his knees before her—with a raised eyebrow. "What did you see?"

"Maybe a way to track the darkness." Her voice was hazy.

He gently pulled her chin up. "Show me."

She bit her lip as she thought about her words, but she laid her hands on his palms. "Close your eyes."

After a few moments, Alzerion pulled his hands back to his chest. His eyes locked on hers. "That crest is the symbol of our nobility." Alzerion rubbed his fingers on his chin.

"What does that mean? Alzerion, I worry about the element of death, too."

"I think we should search the lands that lead to the manors of the noble families. Maybe it is seeking refuge in that part of the kingdom."

His fingers trailed down her temple and cupped the side of her face. "We don't know what it means. But I will need to form another search. Hopefully, it will be the last one."

Eirini pulled back. "I want to come with you. You could be in danger." The pitch of her voice rose.

Alzerion smirked as he rubbed his jeweled finger against her chin. "Eirini, I can't bring you with me."

She shoved his hand away. "Why not? I'm more than capable. You saw I held my own in the DarkFlower Jungle...plus my talent can be helpful."

He leaned in and bent his head, pressing his forehead to hers. "It's not because I think you are incapable. I, well, I worry about you. I want to keep you safe—I would never forgive myself if something happened to you."

Her eyes filled with tears. "Alzerion," she whispered.

She wrapped her arms around him and pulled tight. His face fell toward her as she straddled a leg on each side—as if she were sitting on his lap. Alzerion's hands twirled her hair as she kissed him with more passion than she could muster. His hands slid over her body as they squeezed each curve. Eirini pulled at his top lip and then trailed her nose down his neck. Her tongue swirled in circles in the sensitive spot near his ear. Alzerion's moan was deep.

Then he pulled his head back. "Eirini, I am not taking you," he panted.

"We shall see." Her lips curved into a wide grin. Then her nails grazed into him, sliding down his chest.

Alzerion rolled his eyes. "Okay. You win."

Eirini bounced up, but he grabbed her before she plopped back down. "But you must promise to do what you're told out there. Eirini, I really don't think my heart can take it if you were to get hurt."

"Awww." She pressed her hand to his cheek. "That would be flattering and sweet if it weren't so condescending."

"Just don't make me regret it."

"No regrets, my love." Eirini pressed her lips back into his. Then he flipped her over against the cozy space between the shelves.

"Eirini, are you with me?" Alzerion hollered as he led the small group.

"I'm still alive, if that is what you're so darn worried about."

Alzerion mumbled under his breath as he kept the pace. He heard Quairken asking Eirini some questions to the side of him.

"How will we know when we have arrived?"

"I'm not sure," Eirini's voice got closer to him.

Alzerion glanced to the side and there she was in her traveling outfit from the jungle.

She pushed a low-hanging branch off to the side as her foot stepped onto stones. He heard the clacking of her shoes as she picked up her pace to match his. Trees and bushes covered each side, and Alzerion focused his attention ahead as the town neared.

"Quairken, we will follow the dirt path. Can you let the others know?"

"Of course."

Quairken turned to speak with the soldiers they brought on the trip. Each of them was capable and brave. Alzerion hoped they wouldn't run into trouble—he wanted to find some answers, but didn't want to risk any lives this time.

He felt the warmth of Eirini's hand in his. "Take us to the country of Bachusa near the nobles' lands."

As they crossed, the darkness loomed over the country, like an omen.

It wasn't from the tall trees and bushes that lined the area. Alzerion felt the chill in the air. Branches swayed as leaves rustled. *Could it be just the wind?* Alzerion followed the path as it inclined to the top of the hill. He saw the manors.

"It's very open. The vast fields below with the houses."

Alzerion nodded. *Endrus, come join us, please. I have a feeling I can't shake.*

*Of course.*

A solid hand touched his shoulder, and he turned. "Quairken don't scare me."

"Sorry. But what are we waiting for?"

Eirini watched him with questioning eyes.

Then he heard the flapping of wings as Endrus descended near them.

Eirini rubbed his snout. "Why did you call him? Alzerion, what aren't you telling us?"

"It's just a precaution," he said.

The soldiers he brought were used to Endrus, so they wouldn't run screaming.

"Do you feel the shift change?" Endrus boomed.

Alzerion reeled around so fast there was nothing. But Endrus was right, there was something. A feeling that filled the air—thick and deadly.

"Alzerion, look." Quairken pointed. He turned once more as Eirini stood motionless. Hands clung to her temples in fists. He dashed toward her. Alzerion gently pulled her chin up, but her eyes looked hollow. Then she screamed.

"It's no use, Your Majesty." A voice hissed.

Quairken had some soldiers move in a circle as a perimeter.

Alzerion grazed her cheek, but she pulled back, and a twisted grin shadowed her face. "Such a cool power she has. It allowed me to enter her mind."

Alzerion stumbled back a half-step. "You're the darkness."

"Yes," it hissed from her beautiful mouth.

How was he to kill it? He couldn't possibly harm the one person he loved more than anything else.

"Are you going to do it? If you strike her body, you will end my existence." It jeered.

"Never," He thundered. He motioned for the soldiers...they moved in with swords raised.

"Silly king. Unless you kill this body, you cannot beat me." A cruel laugh erupted as a swirl of gray enveloped Eirini.

Endrus growled.

Alzerion ran toward her, but a loud crack filled the air. Alzerion squinted as the wind whirled around and the darkness flowed out of Eirini like smoke floating to the sky. The darkness looked like a shroud of mist that blanketed the sky.

*How many more will we kill before you do something?* Its harsh voice loomed in his head. Alzerion cast a spell to anchor him from flailing in the gust of wind. His soldiers crouched to the ground and Quairken crawled toward Alzerion, but then a burst of light shot down and flung Quairken back.

*This is between us.*

Alzerion's mouth remained taut as he tried to move with the wind forcing him back. He glanced over to Eirini as she stood there, pale. Her mouth hung open as she looked up at the darkness, and she stepped forward but wobbled. Alzerion tried to reach her, but a bolt of magic shot down and he darted to the side. The hum of magic grew louder as Endrus Started forward and flapped his wings. The sky lit up a mix of red and black as Endrus was forced back down.

*I cannot move, young ruler. It's holding me down somehow.*

Alzerion felt a putrid fury within. "Are you okay?" He shouted amidst the whipping wind.

Some branches broke free and flung in all directions. Alzerion escaped to the side. He tripped over a branch, grappled with a vine that clung to a sturdy boulder, and pulled up as he ripped his shirt on the pointed edge. He heard Eirini shriek. Alzerion held his hands up, muttered a spell, and then a crimson color rushed out. Eirini caught his gaze, and she darted to him. Alzerion moved to her—then a bolt of magic flew down and hit Eirini, and her body soared into the sky and hit the trunk of a tree.

"Eirini!"

*Young ruler, I can see her. Her eyes are struggling to stay open.*

"Eirini?"

She said nothing. Her head moved up as he reached out and grabbed her. He slid to the ground as he laid her in his lap. Tears stained his dirty face as he bent over her. "Please don't leave me."

Alzerion's eyes filled with fury as he glared at the dark shroud that loomed above. "Please," His voice wavered, "I can't go through this...not again. I'll do anything."

Then the wind swirled around like a vortex around him. Only he and Eirini remained in the middle of the rushing dark wind.

"Anything?" The voice purred.

Alzerion felt his heart tear into a million little pieces. Eirini's eyes kept going in and out as the blood from her wounds soaked his shirt. He sniffled and said, "Yes."

"Excellent choice, Your Majesty."

An eerie silence passed as Alzerion stared around.

"Don't do it, whatever it asks," Eirini said.

His face faltered. "I have to." He kissed her forehead. "I cannot lose you—you're my other half."

A faint smile buckled over her lips. "Alz—"

"Wait," he said. "I hear it saying something." His eyes pinched in as he listened to the mocking voice. Then he felt a drain as he realized the deal he would have to make. Alzerion swallowed.

Eirini forced her eyes open. "Don't do it. Nothing is worth that."

He wanted to take her advice. But he shook his head as he kissed her forehead. "I'm sorry."

He stared back at the darkness. "I accept."

Eirini held out her hand, but then it dropped to her lap. He watched as the light of her amber eyes extinguished.

# CHAPTER 28
## Plans

A massive ache thrummed in her head. Her body felt shooting pains over her arms. She sat up and winced as she looked around. *Where was she?* Eirini stood up. She was in different clothes, a pale blue gown that accented each of her curves.

She swallowed. Eirini ambled over to the door and opened it. Calistra was there.

"What's going on?"

Calistra placed her finger over her mouth and gestured back into the room. Eirini followed and waited as Calistra closed the door and walked right up to her.

"Eirini, what is the last thing you remember? It's important."

Eirini scratched her head. *Foggy.* A dull ache remained. Eirini shook her head.

Calistra placed her hands on her forehead and closed her eyes tight. Her hands felt warm against her skin. Then pain. Eirini slumped over as Calistra kept her hands on her forehead. Her mind raced with so many images. A jumbled and bewildered mess played on a loop in her mind.

"Stop, please." She begged.

"I can't until it doesn't hurt anymore."

Eirini felt like someone took a blade and wiggled it around in her mind. The pain was excruciating. It felt like hours of torture until finally the pain dulled into nothing but just a flood of images.

"Good. Now focus on the images. It's important."

Eirini closed her eyes and did as Calistra asked.

After a few minutes, Eirini opened her eyes as Calistra's hands lowered. "Well?"

Eirini clutched at her heart. "Where is Alzerion? Is he alright?"

"Eirini focus. What happened?"

She detailed the attack and then remembered the deal.

"Lady Eirini, are you alright? You look as pale as cream."

"Alzerion made a deal with the darkness. Please, I need to know that he is okay."

"Deal?" She stumbled over her words. Calistra handed her a cup. "It's water. Drink up my lady."

She felt a throbbing in her head. It made it hard for her to focus on Alzerion. "What did you do to me?" A thirst took hold, so she guzzled down the water.

"I have magic, too, my lady. I showed you the truth of what happened."

Eirini pulled back.

"Please don't. I won't hurt you. I fear Adrastus was angry and, well, I needed to know that you were alright."

Eirini felt confusion flood her mind. She pressed her hand back to her head as she rested her back against a wooden beam in the room.

She gazed around the compact room with its nature themed colors. "Where am I?"

"Adrastus' manor."

Eirini's eyes widened.

"Don't panic. He seems fond of you, so you should be fine-ish."

"Ish?" Eirini shuddered.

"My lady, we must get you out of here. The darkness has worsened since your black out. Heavy attacks have bombarded the town."

Eirini straightened up as she inched forward. "Why are you here? Are you helping Adrastus?" Her nose wrinkled.

Calistra closed the distance between them and whispered. "At one point I was sort of his eyes and ears at the palace."

Eirini's lip curled as she flinched at the words.

"Let me explain." She laid a gentle hand on her arm. "Adrastus can be cruel at best, but he has also been the one person monitoring me most of life."

"What?" Her voice faltered.

"Adrastus, well, it's complicated. But he wanted information about the king and I had to. He threatened me if I didn't."

"Calistra, I don't know what to say."

"I swear I never told him anything truly damning. I realized our king was kind and didn't deserve Adrastus' evil agenda."

Eirini thought about it and then patted her shoulder. "I believe you."

The door swung open. Adrastus stood, arms folded across his chest, with a piercing gaze.

"Ah, you're awake."

"My lord." Eirini bowed her head.

Adrastus stepped toward her. He wrapped an arm around her waist. Eirini tried not to shiver at his touch. He led her out of the room and into what she assumed was a study. The walls were the color of straw with an irregular shape. Shelves of books lined the awkward corners of the room. A fireplace nestled in another one of the odd shaped corners. A thick fur rug laid on the floor. He moved to the sofa and sat down. Eirini followed.

"How did I end up here?"

"Let's just say that I found you." Adrastus sat with his brown eyes fixed on her.

She didn't know what to say. Would he be understanding and let her leave?

"May I call you Eirini?"

She swallowed a thick lump, but nodded.

"I'd like to be a little nice, but that'll depend on you."

Her brows furrowed. Adrastus snapped his fingers and a pair of leather cuffs rested in his hands.

"Will I need to use these, or can you stay on your own?"

"Adrastus, sir, you have a visitor." Calistra called over. She stood in the doorway.

Eirini felt a pit in her stomach. She bit her lip as her eyes shifted back to Adrastus. He had a dark gleam in his brown eyes. His mouth poked into a menacing smile.

"I have to speak with my guest, but don't move. It would be unwise to leave my home. I can keep you safe from all this chaos. As for our king, with any luck, he won't be a factor for much longer."

Then he rose and stormed out of the room. Eirini heard the faint sound of his voice, but nothing else.

Eirini turned, and Calista remained at the doorway. "Why does he want me to stay?"

She shrugged. "He keeps his plans close to himself, my lady."

"Calistra, if I may die by his hands, the least you can do is call me Eirini."

"As you wish. Eirini." She stepped closer and whispered. "But do as he says. Alzerion wants you safe."

Eirini grabbed the cuffs and placed them on the small wooden table. Then took a few quick breaths. Calistra moved to the other side of the table.

"What do you suppose he and this guest are discussing?"

Calistra opened her mouth as she heard shoes on the wooden floorboards.

"I see that you're alive."

Eirini's eyes widened.

# CHAPTER 29
## Her Return

Aironell strode across the room until she smoothed her hands against her outfit and sat on the wooden table in front of Eirini. Her hands clung together. Her eyes had that same coldness from the DarkFlower Jungle. Eirini furrowed her brow.

"I don't understand. What are you...how are you—?"

"You can thank Alzerion for that. I wouldn't be here otherwise."

Eirini shook her head. "I'm sorry, what?" She struggled with the reality of it all.

Aironell smiled. "Alzerion contacted me and Drefan with some concerns about your safety and the darkness." Aironell shifted as her hands folded on her lap. "In his letter, he mentioned how dire things were."

"Alzerion is in such a state of worry. Eirini, how did you end up here? Didn't we tell you all to beware, Adrastus?"

Words wouldn't come out, so she nodded. A dryness in her mouth felt all too much as her mind tried to piece things together. "Are you working with Adrastus, too?"

Aironell laughed heartily.

"It's a fair question." Eirini gripped the edge of the sofa. "I know I'm not your favorite person."

"True," she sighed. "But I care about Alzerion. I may not have been his soulmate, but I want to see him happy."

"I love him very much," Eirini mustered.

"I can sense that. But Adrastus, well, he wants to punish Alzerion in a most cruel way."

Eirini's eyes pinched in.

Aironell shifted a leg under her other. "Adrastus doesn't fully trust me, but enough, as he's related to my husband. He wants our help to defeat Alzerion. So I'm afraid he will not let you go back. Said there's something Alzerion must do first."

Eirini felt a rush of energy leave her body, and she gasped. "Please change his mind."

Aironell's eyes flickered. "What does he want?"

"Before I succumbed to my injuries, Alzerion made some bargain with the darkness. I-I can't."

Her head lowered into her hands. Then a pat on her shoulders forced her to gaze up. Aironell hovered over her. "Tell me."

"I can't," her voice quaked, "but I can show you."

Aironell held her hands out and Eirini's shaky hand grabbed hold of her. She took a deep breath as she let the events fill her mind.

Then Aironell tore her hands back as she straightened up. "A life for a life. Is he serious?"

"I see you've discussed the cards that dealt." Adrastus sounded grim.

Eirini angled toward the muscular man with evil in his heart. *What was he playing at? All to what, make Alzerion pay for insulting him?* Eirini bit the fleshy part of her cheek as she listened to him.

"Our king will risk everything, even his people, for the love of you. I can assure you it'll be the choice that will set the course of a kingdom." His words were laced with venom. She felt them like poison stinging her.

She felt a sinking void deep in her stomach.

He chuckled.

Aironell strolled toward him with such ease as her hands laid flat at her side. "Which life must he choose?" Her tone was emotionless.

Eirini felt goosebumps over her bare arms. Aironell didn't flinch as she sat down in the chair nearest Adrastus, leg crossed over the other.

Calistra averted her gaze. Adrastus paced around them. His eyes were hooded like an animal on the prowl.

"Any life of importance to him will do. It has to be a soul the darkness will deem worthy. Then his debt will be paid."

Aironell sat like a statue, but Eirini noticed the quickening pulse in her neck.

*No, no, no. Her vision of death hung in her mind. But whose death was it*? She felt nauseous.

"Don't you think that's a bit much," Aironell said.

"You know better than me the rules at play. It's what the darkness has demanded, and it gets what it wants." His tone sounded ominous.

Adrastus stalked back to the door. Her lip quivered as she watched him move, like some animal gearing up for a fight. He gripped the door.

"You are staying until Alzerion chooses. You may roam the grounds, but I'll know if you leave the boundary of my estate."

He left as a dark laugh rebounded against the walls.

Alzerion paced around an empty Family Room. He didn't want to startle anyone, but he knew that her return would be a surprise. He stared into the flames as they devoured the wood in the fireplace.

The darkness, Eirini. Alzerion shook his head. *Did she survive*? He closed his eyes. Relief from the burning he felt was a pleasant reprieve. It was a devil's bargain, but he made it anyway. His eyes opened. The image of Eirini's motionless body stuck in his mind, like a horrible nightmare. The lump in his throat grew. He slammed his fist into the top of the fireplace.

"That's not wise."

Alzerion twisted around. *Aironell*. He bent his neck forward—body hung in place. He rushed toward her. She strolled in with such grace and confidence.

"Aironell, where is Eirini?"

One arm pressed into her chest as her other hand reached up against her cheek. "What, no hello?"

He followed her with rapt attention as she moved into the middle of the room. Aironell pursed her lips as she turned around slow. Her eyes scanned the surroundings. When she turned back to him, he surveyed each movement.

Aironell locked eyes on him. "Alzerion, she won't be coming. Adrastus dug his heels in on that."

"She's alive?" He noticed the raise in pitch of his own voice. He didn't care. The Fates would have to save Adrastus if he harmed her.

Aironell squeezed his hand. "Try to calm, but yes, she is alive." She ushered him around as they made their way to the couch and sat.

It was a comforting feeling. "Thank you."

Alzerion cleared her throat. "Alzerion I've realized the challenge you must be facing." Her words oozed sincerity. "I'm sorry."

"You did nothing to apologize for." He scratched the skin above his brow.

"It has dawned on me what this must be like for you."

He saw her face wrinkle into a pained expression.

"Aironell it's-"

She shook her head. Her hands slunk away as they laid on her lap and pulled at her forest-green leather pants.

Her face lifted as her darker, cerulean eyes focused on him. "The similarities must cut deep."

A dull ache churned in his stomach.

"Alzerion, I never meant to leave you with such a burden." Her head turned away, and then when she faced him again, he saw her eyes glisten.

She swallowed. "You meant so much to me. I didn't know what love really meant." Aironell stood up and paced around.

He watched as her fingers picked at the skin around her nails. He felt her sincerity.

He stood. Aironell closed the gap and grasped his hand.

"I know you did. Aironell, I felt the same." He swallowed. "I meant it when I said I loved you. I always will, but it's not the love I thought."

"Alzerion, I was always your obligation. A noose forged on protection."

He nodded.

She pulled her hand back as she squeezed his hand. "Alzerion, I wouldn't change what we shared or even how we parted. It was what I needed."

His mouth formed a small smile.

"One more thing." Her tone was more serious.

He tilted his head.

"Eirini, isn't me."

He went to speak, but Aironell held up a hand. Instead, he waited.

"Night and day." She moved, so that they were in such proximity. "Don't treat her like a fragile little doll. She isn't me and she won't like you for it. Don't keep her at arm's length with all your secrets and hidden thoughts."

He gulped.

"Eirini can handle things. She's capable. She loves you. I never doubted that for a second. And she's probably more clever than you."

Aironell's eyes softened once more. Then she grabbed his chin and her hands held onto the sides of his cheeks. He couldn't move his head. Alzerion frowned.

"Now this one is the big one. Eirini, the daughter of Eros and Jezzabell, she will not leave you. I am making it my mission to ensure that she remains safe."

Alzerion felt a little less tangled inside. Where Eirini was concerned his web of trust issues had disappeared long before now.

Aironell breathed out. "But that means you must keep your end of the deal."

His eyes squished together.

Aironell's face screamed, you're such an idiot.

Alzerion stepped back. "Aironell, I had too. She was dying." He shook his head. "I couldn't let her die."

"I understand ... I do, but Eirini is worried about you."

Alzerion folded his arms across his chest. "I'm not sure why."

Aironell laughed. Alzerion pursed his lips.

"I'm sorry, Alzerion, she knows you better than you think."

He backed away as his eyes wandered. He already knew what he was going to do.

"What?"

He heard her steps draw nearer.

"Alzerion, what are you thinking?"

He angled toward her. Her eyes widened as her hand flung to her mouth. *Damned face gave him away.* Aironell stumbled back. Then the door flung open.

# CHAPTER 30
## Darkness

Alzerion glanced between Aironell as Evalyn. The silence hung like a deafening scream. Evalyn didn't move.

"I can explain." Alzerion broke the silence.

He strolled toward her. Her eyes fixed on Aironell. Alzerion placed his hand on her back and urged her forward. She moved a few steps.

"Hello, mother." Aironell said.

"Aironell?"

Aironell drifted toward them. She grabbed Evalyn's hand and pressed it to her cheek. "Alzerion needed my help. I don't want anything terrible to happen." She swallowed.

Evalyn was transfixed as confusion brimmed her eyes.

"Please say something?"

"Wh-why don't you want to come home?" Evalyn's tone was riddled with sadness.

He watched as Aironell moved closer and leaned in to hug her mother. "I'm happy in the DarkFlower Jungle. There isn't this pressure."

"What pressure?"

Alzerion took a step back as he observed them. Aironell sighed. Then she glided to the set of two chairs and sat down. Evalyn followed.

"Living here." Aironell motioned. "The expectations. I hated feeling like I had to play perfect. Like I never had the chance to figure out who I was and what I wanted. I'm sorry, but I feel more myself, more at home where I am."

Evalyn reached out and squeezed her hands. "I'm sorry if your father and I ever made you feel you weren't enough."

Alzerion couldn't help but feel a tug at his heart. He never wanted Aironell to feel trapped, like she was a doll on display. Time changed her —no longer the naïve little princess.

"I'm here because I don't want to see the kingdom suffer."

Her eyes shifted to him. He straightened up.

"Alzerion needs help to end this darkness and restore order; and in doing so, will save Eirini from Adrastus."

Evalyn stood up and rubbed Aironell's cheek. "Thank you."

Then she turned to Alzerion. "Wait, did she say Adrastus?"

Alzerion nodded. "He's far worse than I thought. He's in on this threat from the darkness, I'm sure of it."

"What threat?"

The door opened. "Evalyn, what's taking so lo-"

Francisco stopped in his tracks and took a few steps forward, followed by Melinda. Even Isabella clung to Audrina as she and Quairken folded in.

Silence.

"Mommy, why is everyone staring?"

Alzerion smirked.

Audrina pointed. "Who is that?"

Alzerion moved around.

Francisco strolled right over and hugged Aironell. "We thought you weren't coming back?" A wide grin covered his face.

"I wanted to go undetected," Aironell finally said. "I'm here to help."

Evalyn turned to her husband and grasped his hand. "I'll explain later." She whispered in his ear.

Alzerion saw Francisco's head drop just enough that made it hard to see the frown that escaped his lips.

"I'm sorry that I didn't tell anyone about her arrival, but it had to be a secret." Alzerion said. "She has insights about this evil."

Quairken said nothing, but his hand pushed Isabella and Audrina toward their spot in the room. Aironell took a breath and explained, again, some of her journey.

Francisco's hands tightened into clenched fists.

"Now that we are all on the same page, I think we should discuss strategy." Alzerion added.

Evalyn nodded.

"Does this darkness have a weakness?" Quairken asked. "Each time we have confronted it, it seemed impossible to kill it and we took losses."

Alzerion snapped his gaze to Aironell. "Is there?" His face scrunched up.

Aironell tapped her fingers to her chin—then her mouth twitched side-to-side.

"Aironell?" Francisco's voice was low.

"Yes, and no." Her lips tightened. "The darkness stems from an ancient dark magic that took root in the DarkFlower Jungle."

"You said that earlier." Alzerion leaned forward as he shifted his weight-arm rested on the back of a chair.

"Correct."

Alzerion saw some confused looks exchanged, so he chimed in. "The DarkFlower Jungle is also the source of all magic."

"So, this thing that has been wreaking havoc is from over there?" Isabella stared at Aironell.

Aironell nodded. "If I could have kept it away from you all, I would have." She swallowed. "It is a beacon of cruelty and was drawn here."

"It was the doing of a broken cow many years ago. A Dark Sovereign didn't hold up their end of their bargain. The consequence was that it could slowly consume the DarkFlower Jungle."

Francisco gasped as he held onto Evalyn.

"According to the ancient texts, a prophecy foretold the destruction of all magic, but there was a way to protect it."

"How did it end up here?" Isabella asked.

Alzerion saw her press Audrina closer to her chest.

Aironell looked to Alzerion.

· · ·

Eyes flashed to him as he moved by the fireplace. He rubbed the back of his neck.

"Alzerion, do you know why it's here?" Evalyn tilted her head.

Quairken kept his eyes down on the ground.

This was his fault in every way.

Alzerion scratched above his eye. "When I went to see Jezzabell about how to rescue Aironell, she cautioned me." Alzerion swallowed. "There would be a price to pay and I said that I would pay it ... I didn't know what it was." He cleared his throat. "When I found Aironell and the Dark Sovereign, I realized the cost—this darkness."

"Why would you send it here?" Francisco's voice rose.

"We didn't."

"This was beyond our control," Aironell added. "There were more than ancient texts and dark magic at work. Not to mention the pull was strong."

"What does that mean?" Evalyn pursed her lips as her gaze looked between Aironell and Alzerion.

Alzerion swallowed.

"Adrastus wants to see me fail. To replace me as ruler."

Francisco's eyes bulged. Melinda remained still.

"To what end?" Francisco asked.

Evalyn held onto Francisco's hand.

He fiddled with the hem of his shirt as he continued. "It has grown worse. He wants to punish me." He stepped forward.

"Is he responsible for Eirini's disappearance?" Melinda finally spoke.

Alzerion nodded. "Aironell went to him. To gain some information because she's the wife of the Dark Sovereign, which makes her related by marriage."

Melinda's head shook.

"Adrastus is keeping her until..."

"Aironell, until what?" Quairken sounded sharp.

Everyone stared at her.

"It all comes down to me." Alzerion bit his lip.

He felt a burning in his stomach as the pressure rose against the pitting in his chest.

Alzerion felt a heat in his eyes. "Alzerion." He felt the comforting warmth. It was his mother. He wiped his nose and faced them all. "Adrastus wants my decision."

He pushed Melinda's hand away as he took a few steps to the door. "I begged the darkness not to take Eirini. She laid in my arms bleeding... dying. I agreed, but I had to make a deal."

He heard the gasps.

"Alzerion, you didn't..." Evalyn's hand shot to her mouth.

He breathed in. "I did." He steadied his breath.

"What is the price?" Quairken folded his arms across his chest.

Alzerion bit his lip. "It's a basic exchange." He swallowed. "It wants a life for a life. I must decide who I'm willing to sacrifice."

"You trust this darkness?" Francisco's brows furrowed.

"I didn't." He gestured to Aironell.

"The darkness kept its word. It spared Eirini. Adrastus holds her captive until he makes his move and Alzerion reveals his choice." Aironell said.

Alzerion paced around with his back to everyone.

Each person spoke at once. He held up his hand. All voices ceased. Finally, all mouths closed. He snapped his fingers.

"I made my choice."

"And you weren't going to tell us?" Melinda's voice was sharp. "Alzerion, this is not something you should do alone."

"Listen," he cleared his throat. "I could hurt none of you. You are all my family."

"Then who did you pick?" Melinda's voice shook.

Alzerion grabbed the door and opened it. "Myself."

He stormed out before he could see their faces.

Alzerion strolled outside. Face glanced up at the dark sky. He still felt the lump in his throat. He sighed. Alzerion veered down Royal Lane. A walk —change of scenery was what he needed. He felt the gravelly stones beneath his boots. He shook his head. After everything, this was how it would end.

"Alzerion, there you are."

Alzerion shifted a bit to see Quairken dash toward him.

"What are you doing here?"

"Alzerion, you didn't think we would let you alone," he swallowed. "Especially after what you told us."

"Quairken, I, well, I—"

"I know." Quairken placed a hand on Alzerion's shoulder.

The presence of it felt warm … so much that they have been through together.

"I know you very well, Alzerion. So I will come with you to clear your head. We can walk. Talk. Travel in silence. Whatever you need—I'm here for it."

Alzerion forced a smile as he gripped Quairken's arm. "Thank you."

He turned around and walked. As he looked around, his mind flooded with memories. This place gave him so much—more than he ever thought possible as a six-year-old sent to live here. He swallowed. The lump in his throat was still there. Alzerion followed the path, but didn't go near the woods. Calderon's body still haunted him. Instead, he strolled toward the town.

"It got worse." Quairken spoke just above a whisper.

He was right. He hadn't been down, what with Eirini's disappearance and thinking she was dead. Alzerion gulped.

*Bachusa.* He blinked away the thick smoke that seemed to fill the area. Alzerion stumbled as he strolled into the main part of town. He caught his balance as he pressed his hand to the tavern. Stones crumbled as his movements were quick as Alzerion spun around. Buildings worn down, and some charred, falling apart, and others were downright pitiful. He rubbed his ash covered hands against his eyes.

"What happened?" His voice trembled.

It faltered as he stalked around buildings. The markets seemed abandoned. Where did everyone go?

"Alzerion, over here!"

Alzerion searched for Quairken. He moved toward the spot where the butcher shop used to stand. It looked nothing like the space it once was. Alzerion gulped. No longer any smells of the fresh meats being prepared, now only the scent of smoke and dirt. He swore Quairken's voice came from over there.

"Here." He found him.

Quairken's hand shot up from the ground. Alzerion ran and then stopped as he saw a crater sized circle in the ground. No butcher shop, but the remains of stones and cement angled to the ground. Alzerion swallowed. He saw Quairken in the space as he pushed some debris and pieces of roof to the side.

Alzerion squinted as his eyes narrowed at the shallow opening that shown from below the pieces that Quairken tossed aside. A low hiss filled the air around. Alzerion spun around, but nobody.

"Alzerion, come on."

He turned back and jumped—hands to the ground; he stayed crouched as he focused where Quairken pointed. The hole was tiny. Alzerion moved closer and saw wooden beams that spiraled down. *Stairs.* Without giving it another thought, Alzerion descended. The walls held steady as he took step after step. They compacted the walls - the dirt and root - until he came to a space where there was a door of sorts. It wasn't an actual door, but it covered the entrance—blended well, with its brown tanned hide that sagged. It mirrored the surrounding walls—clearly; to make someone think that they had hit a dead end.

Alzerion breathed out as he pushed the tanned hide to the side and stepped forward. It got warmer as he walked.

"Where do you think this goes?" Quairken's voice echoed.

Alzerion thrust his hand and caught it on the back of Quairken's head.

"Ouch." He rubbed the whacked spot.

"Sorry," Alzerion whispered. He leaned in toward Quairken. "We don't know what we may find. I'm thinking we should keep the noise down."

Quairken rubbed his forehead and then nodded.

As they walked, he realized little tunnels that veered left and right. He followed the one that had boulders and mild obstacles in the path. Alzerion strolled around them until he stopped. His jaw gaped open.

"Are we seeing things?" Quairken asked.

Alzerion blinked and rubbed his eyes. *Were they hallucinating? No.* The image before him remained. It looked like a whole miniature of the town. Like a town on the go. It reminded him of camping out. Alzerion walked through. People saw him and bowed. Others cheered.

Quairken grabbed his arm. "What is this?"

Alzerion didn't know what to say. Then Quairken pulled Alzerion behind him.

An elder woman stepped forward and bowed, so low. Her clothes, worn. The look in her eyes was bright as she looked up at him.

"Your Majesty, we are glad to see that this darkness hasn't taken you."

Alzerion scanned the room. Even some children stopped for a moment.

A man hobbled forward. He had burns that ran the length of his arm. Alzerion focused his eyes on his face.

"Tyrus? Is that you?" Alzerion moved closer.

"Aye, Your Majesty." His long unkempt hair swayed as he bowed his head, quick.

Alzerion frowned. "What happened to you? What is this place?"

He sighed as he shifted his weight. Alzerion noticed his one leg bandaged.

"Your Majesty, there has been slow bombardment. Which you know." He coughed into his arm.

"When did it get this bad?" Quairken's voice was crisp and to the point.

"Since you left," the elder woman said. "Mean no disrespect. The late King Francisco and queen did their best, but they were no match for this gloom that came."

"No. It was more of a shroud—a blanket of darkness." Tyrus corrected.

Tyrus hobbled as he motioned for them to follow. Alzerion bit his lip, but followed. It looked like a line led by Tyrus, then himself, followed by Quairken and the elder woman. Tyrus sat in what looked like a baked mud chair. Alzerion sat next to him. It was so low to the ground that his knees felt like they might reach his chest.

Quairken stood behind him, watching.

"Your Majesty, would you like one?" The woman held out a wooden tray with a couple of meat pies and bread.

"Sanira, we are busy right now."

"I'm good," Alzerion said.

She bowed and moved away.

"Tyrus, what happened in my absence? I know it came, but I've been back."

Tyrus pulled at the back of his neck. "We made this to protect us from that misty thing. We knew you were working so hard, but we started the underground tunnel city to be safe." He cleared his throat. "We heard rumors of an attack on you and that your guest was taken."

Alzerion winced.

"I'm sorry, Your Majesty." His tone was gruff but sincere.

"I appreciate it, Tyrus." Alzerion forced a thin smile. "How did the town get ravaged?"

Tyrus' face fell. Alzerion swore he saw pain and fear in his experienced eyes.

"The darkness appeared in its shadow form, Your Majesty. It said that you had forsaken your people. It wanted us to surrender, but many of us didn't."

Alzerion clung to the cracks from the hardened mud he sat on. "It attacked you?"

Tyrus was solemn as he nodded. "It was a slaughter. The figure set a large fire that spread, and it hissed in glee." Tyrus shuddered. "That thing wants, well, I think—"

"I know." Alzerion reached over and patted his shoulder. "I'm sorry Tyrus. I didn't know." Alzerion swallowed hard. "I would never have let you all fend for yourself. I love my people."

Alzerion stood up. "This is our home. I will defend it, even if it kills me." Alzerion turned.

"Your Majesty, let us help."

Alzerion's head faced him. "You have done so much." He gestured around him. "This is my duty. I promise I will make it right."

Tyrus' hardened face looked brighter.

"Quairken," Alzerion boomed. "Get some soldiers down here. They can help protect our people."

Quairken nodded and disappeared out of the space.

Alzerion strolled out of the tunnels as he made his way back up to the town—what it left. He kicked at the rubble as his heart sank in his chest. In his own grief, he failed to protect the town and his people.

*Endrus?*

*Yes, young ruler? Are you alright?*

*Nothing that we can't fix together. I need you to fly down here, to the center of town.*

*Of course.*

Endrus was above him as he circled around. Endrus' talons touched the ground as the rest of his powerful body landed.

*Well done.*

"You've finally come out?"

Alzerion turned around. Nobody was there.

"Where are you?" He looked up.

The sky darkened. A cloud of dark gray and black, with flecks of silver, spiraled. Alzerion clenched his fists. He stepped back a few steps closer to Endrus.

Alzerion saw Quairken and some soldiers getting closer. He squinted as he tried to make out who else was with him—crack.

Alzerion snapped his attention back to the spinning vortex. The wind picked up as it spiraled into what looked like a human form. A human shadow, just like Tyrus explained. He couldn't make out its face. A swirl of some smoky film. It raised its hands, and Alzerion felt this ripple as it tore through. The ground quaked as he flew back. He hit the rubble of one of the old market stalls. Then the wind picked up, like a raging storm. Some horrible windstorm—things whizzed around. Alzerion ducked as he ran toward the shadow.

Then a pale light whirled around. It melded with the wind as the army was before him, with Quairken. Alzerion breathed out, tilted his head. He scanned the area until he spotted Aironell. Her eyes locked on his as she hurried behind the remnants of the tavern. She kept to her word. The plan was well underway. The soldiers spread apart, swords out, and ready to fight.

"Alright, let's do this!" Alzerion motioned to them. The soldiers split into two groups—one on each side, with him in the middle of the groups. Quairken pulled out his sword as he joined the group to the right of Alzerion.

"Please tell me you left the others at the palace?"

"Of course." Quairken shifted his eyes away.

"What?"

"They agreed to stay up there, but they're not safe *inside* the palace. Everybody wanted to help, Alzerion."

He shook his head. "We can deal with that later. For now, we fight!"

Quairken honed in on the shadow. Endrus to his left. At least the men practiced with Endrus. There should be no hiccups. Alzerion gripped his sword and hollered the order. Some men to his left got there first, but their swords went right through it. Alzerion's mouth went taut. *How?* The men swung back and again it went through the shadow.

"Is that your best?" It hissed.

Alzerion bared his teeth.

A wide, shadowy hand reached out and grabbed Evert by his shirt. It lifted him up. Alzerion heard the screams. It cut through him. Some froze, and he saw their terror. Others charged at the shadow more fervently, but some doubled back, closer to Alzerion. He stopped mid-lunge. Alzerion cursed under his breath as he watched the shadow bring Evert closer to it. Evert twisted around. He screamed as the shadow's other hand moved to its mouth and its head washed over Evert. It dropped him. His body lay there. Alzerion wanted to go to him. He wanted to check on Evert, but he knew in his gut that Evert was gone. A tightness overcame him. Just like Calderon. He pushed it out of his mind. Couldn't let that sink in, not now. He had to keep as many of the men alive.

The shadow figure's laugh was sharp, like a hissing laugh that grated on him. His nose wrinkled.

*Let's do it together, young ruler.*

Alzerion nodded. Then he leaped. He felt Endrus by his side. The soldiers followed, but Alzerion took the lead. He moved his sword above his head and slashed it down. No hit. The shadow figure materialized into smoke. Alzerion turned to keep it in his sights as it reappeared off to the side.

"Congelo!" Alzerion aimed his hand at the shadow. Another loud hiss. As it stood stuck to the spot. Alzerion smirked as he lunged forward. As soon as his blade slashed, the shadow shot up and its shadowy hands glowed this blackish gray.

*Hop on!*

Alzerion dodged the bursts of fire the shadow shot out at him. Then he jumped as Endrus swooped under him. Alzerion held onto the wyvern's neck. They flew around the shadow. *Endrus, let's get a better angle. We need to end this.*

Endrus soared lower and around the shadow. *At least he was faster than the damn shadow.* Alzerion saw movement as he saw Aironell changing positions. His distraction was perfect for this. Alzerion felt them lunge toward the shadow—it loomed up.

The wave of its hand brought on the forces of nature as the soldiers tried to defend themselves.

"Now, for you." It hissed as it targeted Alzerion and Endrus.

Endrus flew up and down, avoiding the bursts of magic, but then the wind howled as tore at Alzerion. He held onto Endrus, knuckles growing white from the pressure. But it whipped Endrus around like a toy with such ease. Suddenly, fiery balls appeared in the sky.

*Endrus down!*

Too late. A fiery rain came down. Alzerion heard some men scream below, and he shook his head. Pain filled him with such guilt. Endrus dove around them, but he couldn't avoid them all. Sure enough, it hit Endrus on one of his wings.

*Ahhhh.*

He felt them falling through the air. Endrus arched his body forward as they collided in the field between the palace and the town.

*I'm sorry. Endrus, please be okay.*

*Young ruler. Go. It takes a lot to kill me, but not so much for everyone here.*

Alzerion nodded. Then he sheathed his sword as he ran. Ran up the path, weaving forward. He craned his neck back and saw the shadow materialize back into the ominous cloud as it followed him. Good. At least they would be safe. The people. The soldiers. Eyes narrowed. He needed to move faster. His muscles felt rigid as he forced his legs to keep going. He was close to the palace.

"Vitus."

A vine from the nearest tree swung down. He grabbed it, dashed and let it soar. Alzerion let go when he swung forward. He muttered something, but it didn't take fast enough. He landed on his side. The pain from the impact clung to him as he gripped his arm. He was bleeding. Quickly, he ripped a piece of his shirt and wrapped it around the cut.

The shadow was upon him as it materialized back into its human-shaped form.

Alzerion bit his lip as he forced himself back to his feet. He felt the pains and aches over his body. The shadow figure didn't look as if it took any beating. It waved its hand, its shadowy self had this swirl of darkness that wrapped around. Alzerion squinted as he tried to watch. He squeezed his eyes closed and then opened them. Still the same image of the man before him with his smug face.

# CHAPTER 31
## The Cost

Brown eyes glared back at him. Adrastus stood, mouth rigid and curved—grinning.

"How is that possible?" Alzerion spat. Rage smoldered.

"Dark magic linked us." His mouth twisted. "It follows my will."

Adrastus took a few steps toward him. "What I want is to be rid of you."

Alzerion crossed his arms as his stance stiffened. "You're out of luck."

"We shall see. Won't we?" Adrastus' face had this darkness that lingered over him. Like the darkness embodied him or was part of him. A thought struck him. Alzerion smirked.

Alzerion pulled out his sword and held it tight in his hand—never breaking his gaze. Lips pressed together as his chin rose. He wanted nothing more than to wipe that smug look off Adrastus' face.

He darted toward Adrastus, who moved each time out of the way. Alzerion snapped his fingers, and a sword appeared. Adrastus stepped back and parried his blows. Well, he wasn't a horrible swordsman. Alzerion stood, one foot before the other. He wanted to remain light on his feet as he deflected Adrastus' blow. Then he stabbed his sword forward. It caught Adrastus on the arm. His eyes blackened.

They continued like this for some time. Their swords locked onto each other until their faces neared.

"You will lose *Your Majesty*." His voice seethed. "Then maybe I can collect my prize."

Alzerion shoved Adrastus. The force of his body caused him to stumble.

"What prize? The kingdom will never be yours. You know that."

"Maybe...maybe not. But I seek an added prize."

Adrastus lunged forward. Alzerion parried and deflected his blows. Sweat streaked across his forehead as he jerked his sword forward. *Smug didn't seem to cover it. No. Arrogant. Proud. Delusional. These seemed more accurate.*

Adrastus was near once more. "My other prize will be...Eirini." He spoke with this low, careful voice.

His jaw tensed. Alzerion stabbed and slashed his blade at Adrastus. Each movement was fast and frenzied. Their swords clashed. Adrastus twisted his wrist, and the swords clanged together as they soared to the side. Alzerion's cinnamon-red eyes ran cold as he darted for Adrastus and shoved him. Each punch hit his jaw and then another on his shoulder. Adrastus crouched as he grabbed Alzerion's legs and rolled around, trying to gain the superior position. Adrastus kicked him away and bounced up, and Alzerion breathed out as he rose to his feet. Adrastus glared.

"Adrastus, I will stop you!"

A blood curdling laugh escaped his mouth, then he snapped his fingers, and Eirini appeared. Her hands shot up, but something was amiss. She couldn't move toward him... confined to the spot. A whirl-wind of emotions flooded in. Alzerion wanted to close the distance between them—wanted to feel that she was alright.

"Now, Alzerion, I believe you have a decision to make. Enough messing around and posturing. So, who is it going to be?" He crossed his arms. "Who are you willing to sacrifice just to have her?" Adrastus reached his hand toward Eirini and grazed his finger down her arm.

Alzerion's nostrils flared. "Don't touch her!"

"Oh, what will you do about it?" Adrastus strolled behind Eirini. His hands strummed each side of her arms. He stared at Alzerion.

"Adrastus, I swear I'm going to end you!"

Alzerion twisted his one hand up and then it twirled until he crushed his fingers into a fist. It knocked Adrastus to the side. Then he rushed toward him.

"I said, don't touch her. No harm must come to her." His voice was deep as he roared.

There was a twinkle in his dark eyes. He smoothed out his shirt, scrunched his face as he looked to Eirini and then back. "Do you know that we've shared ...moments?"

Alzerion swallowed. He glanced over at Eirini. She bit her lip. He glanced down at his wrist. The mark stung with bitterness. Alzerion shook his head and brought his focus back to Adrastus.

"See," his voice crooned,"I could easily have her and this kingdom." Adrastus paused as he gestured around. "Bachusa needs a firm hand to run things."

Alzerion's hands balled into fists. He felt the storm boil. Then he saw the glimmer of Aironell emerge behind Adrastus. Alzerion blinked, and his sword flew from its sheath to Adrastus. Eyes narrowed into slits as he watched. Adrastus grinned, cruelty. A wave of his hand sent the sword hurtling to the side.

Aironell ran out and drove both hands up as she muttered something.

"That's not possible," Adrastus uttered. His eyes dulled.

Aironell's words sounded old and mysterious. A bright light shot out from her hands that cupped like a half-moon. Such a force beyond what he had ever seen. Adrastus shot the magic back, but the light of hers grew brighter and stronger as it soared toward him. Finally, it hit him until he stumbled back from the blast. Alzerion dashed toward Adrastus and wrapped his arms around his chest and neck, then he pressed.

Alzerion held onto his grip around his neck as his other hand hurled to his waist and grabbed a dagger. With no hesitation, he spun Adrastus around and allowed his hands to clutch his throat like a vise grip. No remorse. Alzerion took the dagger and plunged it into his chest. Adrastus fell to his knees as Alzerion released his throat. Then he leaned in and pressed the dagger further. Aironell stood by him, her hand glowed as it waved above Adrastus' limp body.

"The link is severed."

"Thank you."

Aironell nodded. Alzerion rose from his squatted position. He sprinted to Eirini as she met him. His hands clung to her face as he smirked.

"I'm happy to see you alive and well."

"You're not upset with me?" She swallowed.

Alzerion licked his lips and pulled her in for a hug. "Not really. Later, we will discuss the details." He whispered.

"You did it!"

Alzerion kept his arm around Eirini as he turned. He saw his mother and the others move toward them.

"Nicely done, Alzerion." Francisco patted him on the back.

Francisco looked to Aironell. "Thank you."

Aironell nodded.

"Sorry. Seems like we missed the fun," Quairken panted as he and the soldiers arrived.

"Well, there is still one thing left to do." Aironell's voice was crisp.

Audrina wiggled out of Isabella's hands and ran to her father. Quairken crouched down to pick her up as he said. "Did we not defeat it?"

"Technically, no." Alzerion breathed out. "But it's weakened, correct?"

Aironell nodded. "The darkness used Adrastus as much as Adrastus was using it." She strode toward Adrastus' body.

Her hand spun, whirled around as a blackness oozed out of Adrastus. It hovered like a medium-sized cloud of ink.

"Alzerion," it hissed.

The shroud of darkness hovered by him. Alzerion let go of Eirini as he positioned himself in front of her.

"We had a deal. What is your choice?" The voice was harsh and cold.

Alzerion took a few steps closer. He stared back at the darkness. "I decided." He swallowed. The lump in his throat grew.

"Well?"

"It'll be me."

"No!" Eirini's voice cracked.

He didn't look back. He didn't want anyone trying to talk him out of it. Nobody else would decide this for him.

The shroud spread as it circled around him. It created some kind of sucking vortex. He could barely see beyond the swirling gray and black. Occasionally, he made out the forms of people, but that was it. Alzerion reached out but found it whirred around, keeping him in. Fists tightened as he was less than an arm's length away.

"You didn't think we'd let you do this alone, did you?"

Alzerion turned. Aironell moved closer. Her hand on his shoulder. "How?"

Aironell smiled. "Now, who is so curious?"

Alzerion smirked as he pulled her hand from his shoulder and just held onto her. "Thank you for that. I'm glad that we have overcome the odds stacked against us. Promise me you will always be happy—and safe."

Aironell nodded. "Alzerion, I could never forget the kindness you have always shown me." She glanced at the darkness and then continued. "My magic allows me to be here. Nobody else can. Not without either myself or the darkness willing it."

"That's for the best, honestly." He sighed.

"Are you ready, Alzerion King of Bachusa?" It hissed.

"I am." His voice didn't waver.

Alzerion moved forward and then pressed one knee to the ground similar to how they gave out titles in a ceremony.

"To be clear, what brings you to this point?"

"The pact we entered." He felt something force his head down. Like he was bowing.

"Is this of your own will? Your choice to submit to this cost—the cost of our bargain. A life for a life."

"It is." He swallowed.

Alzerion felt an unbearable pain from the mark on his wrist. *Eirini.* He closed his eyes. They burned as he felt the sting of tears prick. He took a deep breath and then stared back at the shroud. He watched as a shadowy hand emerged from the dark shroud. Then a hand on his shoulder wrenched him out of the way. He stumbled back, hands caught his fall on the ground.

"I'm sorry," Aironell said with a voice so soft. "I know you wanted this to be your choice."

She touched the dark shroud's hand, coaxing it to her mind. There was a hissing laughter.

"I accept!" Its voice thundered.

"Wait, Aironell, what's going on?" Alzerion steadied himself as he rose.

Aironell turned to him. She swallowed. "After you left, everyone was upset by your proclamation. Before I left to follow Quairken, to come to your aid, well, someone approached me."

"Approached you?" Alzerion saw a dark smoky shroud of an oval that appeared. "What is that thing doing?"

"Alzerion, it's preparing for the sacrifice." Her eyes looked softer as she spoke. "Listen, I don't feel good about doing this, but she begged me. Made many points, too. Ultimately, I agreed to the plan."

Alzerion tilted his head.

"You won't be giving your life." Aironell was firm. "Someone else will."

Then she grabbed his hand and held onto it, tight. Her index finger of her other hand hovered over his palm until her fingernail looked like the sharp point of a needle. Alzerion pulled, but they locked him in place. Aironell jabbed.

He felt the sting as she twisted around, placed the drops of his blood over the oval shroud.

"Aironell." He found it hard to say anything as he felt the air around constrict.

"It'll be fine. Alzerion, I promise."

Her arms reached up as they clasped the other in a spiral. Aironell took a deep breath and muttered in that same language as before. It must have been from the DarkFlower Jungle. He wished he knew what she was saying. *Who was going to replace him? Why would anyone volunteer for this?*

A light green hue emitted from her hands as someone materialized into view. Instant pressure gripped him when he saw her. *No.* More like a knife stabbed him in the gut and all over.

"No!"

He watched as his mother amble toward him. She kissed his forehead.

"My son," Her tone was apologetic, "please don't think of this as a sad thing."

He gasped. "What should I think, mother?" His bottom lip trembled. He felt like a little kid again. Wanting something from her with such fierceness.

Melinda ruffled his hair as she looked him right in the eye. "Alzerion, I could have been better. Done more for you. I am forever grateful that you allowed me into your life. The life you earned...one I couldn't provide you." She swallowed. "You are my special boy. I just wanted more for you."

"I had everything. I don't want to lose you, mom."

"Alzerion," she forced a thin smile. "You were going to die. I couldn't let that happen. Not when you actually were about to get everything." She sniffled. "I only ever wanted you to be happy and now that you've found that... Eirini. Alzerion, this is what I can do for you."

She kissed him once more and backed away.

Alzerion started after her. Aironell waved her hand and forced him back down. He squirmed, trying to stand again, but this time he couldn't move. Held down by a magic more powerful than his.

All he could do was sit and watch as his mother entered the shroud. The drops of his blood smeared on her hand and a green glow.

"Excellent." It hissed.

"Please," Alzerion's voice shook.

He wanted to scream—run to her - to do something. He bit his lip as the water in his eyes streamed down his face. The shroud circled around her as she choked.

"Don't do it."

Aironell knelt down by his side. "I'm sorry. Alzerion, look away. It'll be best."

He shook his head. All he could do was pay witness to the horror.

As she struggled to breathe, he watched as a shadowy claw rose. It slashed and clawed at her chest until she was torn up. Alzerion closed his eyes. When they opened, her arms hung limp at her side. Then the muttering started as her body twinkled until it disappeared. The darkness slowed the vortex.

Aironell waved her hand and held some kind of vessel with odd markings on it. She moved fast. She opened the lid, and the darkness absorbed into the container. Aironell closed the lid and faced him. The swirling dissolved, and he saw everyone, his family—minus his mother. He touched his hand to his tear-stained cheek.

Eirini dashed to him, but he walked away. He said nothing.

"Alzerion, may I come in?" Eirini's voice was soft. She felt a tightness that she tried to shove away.

Alzerion needed her now more than ever.

"Alzerion."

Still nothing as she waited outside his bedroom door. This was the third place she looked. He wasn't in the library or their annex room. Eirini breathed out as she pushed open the door. There he was, crumpled up on his side.

She walked over and sat on the edge of his bed. Then she placed a hand on his back, and his back uncoiled.

Eirini crawled around to the other side to face him. He looked at her and then turned. So, she crawled around again and, once more, he turned.

"Alzerion, please." She pleaded as she pulled him to his back and sat on his lap.

Her hands pressed on his chest. His face was vacant.

"Talk to me," her voice lilted.

"Eirini, I just can't." He sat up and propped pillows behind him. "I need some time."

She placed one hand on his cheek. "I'm afraid to give you time. Too much time can be bad as you'll stew in this pain. Alzerion, let me in."

His eyes softened as he stared at her. His pain plastered across his face. As if she needed that. Eirini could feel the hurt from their bonded mark.

She licked her lips and leaned forward. Eirini pressed her head to his forehead.

"I'm here for you."

"I know." He patted her back. "I will talk, just not right now. Give me some time. My mother is gone."

Eirini pulled back and nodded. She bit her upper lip as she slid off of him and stood by his bed.

"I love you Alzerion."

She turned. Eirini felt the warmth of his hand in hers. She faced him and he kissed her hand.

"I love you more than you will ever understand."

Eirini smiled and strolled to his door. She hoped he wouldn't be like this for too long, but then again, she knew it would be a process. Then she left his room.

# CHAPTER 32
## To Brighter Days

Alzerion observed the workers patching the last roof. *Every building and house*, fixed. Only took six months. Alzerion smirked as he walked on the cobblestones. He felt a lightness as some children played. The market was open and back up, selling their wares.

"What're you doing, handsome?"

Alzerion licked his lips as he turned. *Eirini*. He smiled so broad, that he felt it in his eyes.

"I needed to be here when the last of the construction finished."

Eirini sauntered toward him. *She was a vision*. Then she held out her hand—fingers wrapped around his like the perfect fit of a puzzle.

"How are you doing today?" Her voice soothed.

He kissed each of her fingers. "Taking it one day at a time."

"That's all that you can do." She laid her head on his arm.

He took his other arm and draped it around her. Alzerion walked with her by his side. He felt a warmth of happiness wash over him. *This was a memory to remember. Much like the one at the event tonight.* He took a breath. He didn't want to think too much about it. Didn't want Eirini to feel it through their bonded mark.

"Alzerion, I have a question."

"Oh?" He tried to keep his tone level. "What might that be, my love?"

She said nothing. He looked down and saw her amber eyes narrowed in on him.

"What? Did I do something?"

Eirini giggled. "Hmm, why don't you tell me?"

He cleared his throat. Alzerion ushered them to the new marble bench. It sat under a tree with flowering honeysuckle. She stared at him. *Gods, that look.*

"Do you know what you do to me with that look?"

"I don't know what you mean?" Eirini batted her long lashes.

He grabbed her waist as he pulled her close.

"Careful, Alzerion." She leaned in. "Any closer and I'll be on top of you."

He laughed. "Is that a problem for you?" His eyebrow raised.

She slapped his arm. "No, obviously."

He laughed again. "Then what are you afraid of?"

She swallowed. "We don't want people getting the wrong idea." Her eyes shifted around them.

He leaned back as he pursed his lips. "What idea would that be?"

"That we are close." Her hands clapped together.

Alzerion choked on his laugh. Eirini stood as Alzerion joined her. Alzerion took a breath and twinned her arms around him. They passed the buildings as they made their way onto Founder's Path.

"I wish you wouldn't laugh at me. It's an honest concern."

He cleared his throat. "I think it's cute that you believe they don't already think that."

Eirini stopped. He tilted his head. Her face looked pale.

He nuzzled his nose to the side of her face. "My love. If you don't want to be late for the festivities tonight, then we must go."

She stared.

"Eirini?"

Alzerion kissed her until she pushed back and caught her breath.

"Alzerion," she clasped her heart, "save that for later."

He smirked. "As you command."

He grabbed her hand and continued walking with her as they strolled down Royal Lane and entered the palace.

"Your Majesty," Calistra bowed.

"Are things arranged?"

"Yes, sir. The decorating is complete." She clapped her hands together. "The Great Hall looks like a winter wonderland."

"Thank you, Calistra."

"Lady Eirini, we should go to your room. It'll be the last time that you'll have your own space."

Eirini nodded.

"One last thing," Alzerion said.

He pulled her in, dipped her as he placed a kiss on her mouth. A smile crept over her lips. Alzerion whisked her back up. "By tonight, you will be mine forever."

"Good," she whispered. "I'll take forever and every hour, minute, and second after that."

He watched as she swayed away with Calistra.

He shook his head. Alzerion rubbed his chin as he entered the Great Hall. Such a breathtaking wintry scene before him.

"Do you like the special touches?"

He turned to see Aironell. "Did you do this?"

"I can't take all the credit." She tilted her head. "I did the snow. I thought if you were going for winter, then we needed actual snow. None of that fake stuff."

Alzerion pulled her in for a hug. "Thank you."

Aironell squeezed and then stepped back. "No problem. Alzerion, your wedding is going to be spectacular."

He paced around until he walked down the silver sparkled aisle. A sea of snow with tiny snowdrops speckled all around. His jaw hung open as his eyes focused on the arch placed near the thrones. Icicles and snow blue roses draped down. He felt the soundness of the arch. Its twines wound around tight with winter berries twisted about.

"Who all did this?"

"We all put our own personal touches on this."

Alzerion smirked as he saw Jezzabell, Eros, Francisco, Evalyn, Isabella, Quairken, and little Audrina enter.

"It means a lot." Alzerion felt this lightness wash over him. He beamed. He gave each one a hug.

"Shouldn't you get dressed?" Evalyn said. "The townspeople will be here as soon as you know it."

Alzerion nodded as he walked back toward the door. Before he reached it, the door flung open.

"You didn't have to greet me."

"Dref, don't be smug," Aironell's voice commanded. "It's his wedding day, and he doesn't need any startles."

"Sorry." He shook Alzerion's hand. "I have a wedding present for you. Aironell thought it best if I gave it to you before the ceremony."

Alzerion's eyes narrowed on the envelope that he held out. He took it and tore open the top. His eyes were wide as he scanned the document. "Are you sure about this?"

The Dark Sovereign nodded. "You have proven to be honorable. I trust my wife's judgement."

"What is it?" Quairken asked. "I can't be the only one curious."

Laughter chorused.

"We've made a treaty to ally our realm to the kingdom of Bachusa," Aironell said.

"There will be some stipulations, such as traveling between the two, but we will work on that."

"So we can come see you?" Evalyn stared at Aironell.

She nodded.

Alzerion felt a twinge. *Be happy, Alzerion.* His mother's words rang true. More than he ever could have imagined possible.

He laid in their bed. *Damn, that sounded nice.* They had a new room, theirs. Alzerion leaned his back against the mound of pillows, topless. Eirini stepped out of the washroom. She was a vision in the most enticing nightgown yet.

He swallowed. The bob in his throat was visible.

"What do you think?" Her chin dipped, but her amber eyes gazed up as her lashes flickered.

He sat with his legs crossed on the bed—pushed together. Alzerion licked his lips. He didn't blink as he gazed upon her.

"Well?"

Her hand rose above her head, holding the jeweled clip from the ceremony. He bit his bottom lip. Each caramel lock of hair had a life of its own as her curls frothed over her shoulders. He cleared his throat. Heat rose all over. Eirini looked as if she was glowing.

She walked closer.

*Who designed that nightgown?* She stood before him. Hands on her hips as her amber eyes sparkled. Alzerion swung forward, grabbed her waist, and pulled her into him.

Her body collapsed to his as he cuddled her. Alzerion placed a hand at her ankle and glided his fingers up her calf, thighs, and up her sides. She giggled while his hands slid around the fabric, the sheerest, most transparent material ever.

"It was a gift." Eirini's voice was soft.

Alzerion laughed. "Hehem. Sorry. Are you trying to tease?"

Eirini placed her hands on his chest. "No idea what you mean." Her hair slid on her bare shoulders as she shrugged.

Her head leaned in as her lips parted. His lips roamed over hers with such passion. He let his hands slide all over—hitting every curve of her body as she whimpered. Eirini laid by his side, and he gazed at her bright eyes.

"I love you, my husband."

His insides quivered as if everything else vanished. All he focused on was her—her warmth, her scent, and her taste. He thrust his tongue into her mouth. Such intensity as he nibbled and pulled her lip.

"Eirini. My queen...my love...my life."

She beamed.

"Making you happy is my mission." Alzerion slid her against him. Her body was tight to his. "I hated ever being apart, and now we never have to. Never have to hide our love."

"Alzerion," her voice quavered.

Her eyes glistened as she stared back at him.

"You can have anything—be and do anything, Eirini. What would you like?"

She bit her lips as she tapped her chin. Her lips curled into a broad smile. "How about you grab me and never let go? I'd like for you to ravage me." She winked.

His heart thudded, and he felt a moment of breathlessness. *She was perfect. His match in every way.*

"As you wish, my love." He smirked.

Alzerion pressed forward—no gaps remained. Each touch and nibble sent a heated need over his skin, and he lowered his face to hers as he continued. Each kiss quickened, and his hands drifted over her body. She trembled.

Alzerion whispered. "I will love you forever. You're mine, never forget it. I'll protect you, always."

She pulled his mouth back to hers. Alzerion melted into their embrace.

# Coming this Spring!

Check out a new spin-off serial of novellas as we follow Aironell in the events between Binding Fate and Enchanted Fate! Stay tuned for more about Lost and Lonely, a fast-paced Romantasy.

# Acknowledgments

To my family, thank you for your words of encouragement. The dedication and love helped me even on the days that I thought that this all wouldn't be possible.

To those whose services were much appreciated. Thank you Devon Atwood for the developmental edits on this story. I took each element and used that to really make the characters have depth and a satisfying arc. A shoutout to Nikki Landerkin for jumping in to complete my line edits. You were a life-saver! Thank you Roxanna Coumans for proof-reading this final draft of my work. Another special thank you to my talented cover designer for yet another gorgeous cover! I cannot wait to see both books together.

I want to add a special thank you to my fans! Your support has meant more than you could know. This book felt easy to write knowing that I wanted to complete the story lines with a satisfying ending for you to sink your teeth into and enjoy.

# About the Author

Alyssa Rose currently lives in West Virginia with her husband, two children, and fuzzy fur babies. A resident of fantasy worlds since she was a young girl—reading under the comfort of her book light. Now she writes fantasy books with magic, adventures, and romance.

You want more updates, news, and early access to content then subscribe at www.alyssarosebooks.com to join my newsletter and follow me on Ream.

Follow me on my socials!

facebook.com/alyssarosebooks

instagram.com/alyssaroseauthor

reamstories.com/alyssarosebooks

threads.net/alyssaroseauthor

tiktok.com/alyssarosebooks

Made in the USA
Columbia, SC
09 November 2024

6016ad4b-1c88-4e9c-b516-1798fa807f07R01